The
Maid of
Lindal Hall

Katie Hutton is Irish but now lives in northern Tuscany, with her Italian husband and two teenage sons. She writes mainly historical fiction on the themes of love and culture clash. *The Gypsy Bride* is her debut novel in this genre, with *The Gypsy's Daughter* following in 2021 and *Annie of Ainsworth's Mill* in 2022. Katie is a member of the Historical Novel Society, the Irish Writers Centre, and the Romantic Novelists' Association, and reviews for Historical Novel Review. In her spare time she volunteers with a second-hand book charity of which she is a founder member.

Also by Katie Hutton:

The Gypsy Bride
The Gypsy's Daughter
Annie of Ainsworth's Mill
The Maid of Lindal Hall

The
Maid of
Lindal Hall

Katie Hutton

ZAFFRE

First published in the UK in 2023 by
Zaffre
An imprint of Bonnier Books UK
4th Floor, Victoria House, Bloomsbury Square, London, England, WC1B 4DA
Owned by Bonnier Books
Sveavägen 56, Stockholm, Sweden

This is a work of fiction. Names, places, events and
incidents are either the products of the author's
imagination or used fictitiously. Any resemblance to
actual persons, living or dead, or actual
events is purely coincidental.

A CIP catalogue record for this book is
available from the British Library.

ISBN: 978-1-83877-584-1

Also available as an ebook and an audiobook

1 3 5 7 9 10 8 6 4 2

Typeset by IDSUK (Data Connection) Ltd
Printed and bound in Great Britain by Clays Ltd, Elcograf S.p.A.

Zaffre is an imprint of Bonnier Books UK
www.bonnierbooks.co.uk

In memory of Terry Rowlandson
of Dalton-in-Furness

We dredged him up, for killed, until he whined
'O sir, my eyes—I'm blind—I'm blind, I'm blind!'
Coaxing, I held a flame against his lids
And said if he could see the least blurred light
He was not blind; in time he'd get all right.
'I can't,' he sobbed. Eyeballs, huge-bulged like squids
Watch my dreams still . . .

From 'The Sentry', Wilfred Owen, 1917

CHAPTER ONE

Roose Road Cottage Homes, Barrow-in-Furness, 1920

'Let me have a look at your pretty hair, poppet,' said Annie. She was kneeling in front of the little girl, looking directly into the child's solemn blue eyes. She ruffled the soft brown curls, then with a quick movement of the wrist, lifted the hair above the child's right ear and sighed, even though she'd expected what she found there.

The door opened behind her and Annie recognised her husband's distinctive tread, one foot dragging slightly, the legacy of a mine accident when he was a young man that had turned him to tailoring as he could no longer work down the pit. Robert McClure's entrance though electrified the little girl. The puny body which had been passive under Annie's hands, went rigid. The blue eyes widened.

'Robert,' said Annie quietly, without turning around, 'this is Molly. She's afraid of men.'

'Poor little mite,' muttered Robert. 'Hello, Molly.' He took in the child at a glance. For the inspection she was standing on newspaper, in a dingy vest and drawers, her knees slightly turned in, her bare feet grubby. He reckoned her to be about three years old, the minimum age for entry to a cottage home, though she looked younger. As a house parent in the Roose Road Cottage Homes he had learned quickly that the children who came into the care of the Barrow Board of Guardians didn't have the brighter eyes and skin, the stronger bones of the children who lived at home with loving parents, no matter how modest their lives. They looked defeated before their existence had even begun.

'Lousy?' he murmured.

'Of course,' said Annie. Without taking her eyes off the child, she reached to the right, pulling open a drawer in the desk. Robert meanwhile stumped over to the sink and filled a tin bowl with warm water. He put it, with a towel and a bar of coal tar soap, next to his kneeling wife.

'I'll get you a glass of Sass, Molly,' he said, and limped out, unable to watch what was coming next.

By the time he came back, the little girl's head was as bald as an egg, her exposed white scalp a contrast to her dirty little face, down which ran snail trails of tears. Annie too was sniffling, as Robert had expected she would be.

'Here,' he said, kneeling with difficulty. 'This is for being a brave wee girl.'

Molly took the glass of Sass with both hands and drank it down steadily, without taking her eyes off Robert.

'You'd like another one of them, wouldn't you?'

The child hesitated, then nodded.

'I'll get you one whilst Mother Annie gives you your bath. I'll bring you a special hat, too. It's a gardener's hat, a wee floppy thing you'll like wearing. I'm not very good at the weeding, you see, with my bad leg so I need a helper – and you'll get to eat the greens yourself later.'

*

'How's the wee one?' asked Robert as he turned out the light and lay down beside Annie.

'I've put her with Ada as her house sister. She went with her happily enough, though she's never said a word yet. She didn't want to take the hat off, though. Held on to it with both hands for dear life until Ada told her the hat needed a sleep too, under her pillow. Ada'll see she won't get teased for her poor head; all of the others in that room started here bald after all.'

'She's not a deaf mute, is she now? No, she can't be, she understands what's said to her, right enough.'

'She's not, no. Apparently she mouths her prayers, according to what the superintendent saw in the record. Only . . . in Manchester they didn't realise to start with that she didn't speak. They'd never encouraged her to.'

'*Manchester?* We've never had a child sent from that far, have we?'

'We've not.'

'Orphan – or abandoned?'

'Orphan. Both parents.' Annie paused. 'The superintendent was emphatic about that. "First the father, then the mother a few weeks later. It's all in the file but we'll just leave it there, won't we? But born in wedlock, for what it's worth."'

3

'Worth quite a lot,' said Robert, who hadn't been.

'There are marks on her back,' said Annie. 'And they're more than three months old, which is the time the Guardians have had her for.'

'Marks?'

'Cigarette burns by the look of them. And the superintendent said her arm's been reset.'

'Dear God! Who'd do them things to a defenceless child?'

'A monster,' said Annie, starting to cry.

'Oh, Annie,' said Robert, turning to her. 'We'll love her, so we will.'

'If we don't, she'll never learn to love anyone herself.'

CHAPTER TWO

Roose Board School, 1927

Molly didn't think having to sit with the other Cottage Home girls on one side of the classroom was a disadvantage, though she knew some of the older girls resented it. She saw it as safety. The fact that all of their group wore the same regulation clothes as her made them look more unique, not less. It meant their faces stood out more. Molly was one of those girls who made the shifts and blouses, under Mr McClure's guidance. The Cottage Home uniform, for in effect it was one, was always neat, laundered and pressed and carefully mended when necessary. The girls did all this themselves, alongside Mrs McClure as their house mother, though since coming to school Molly had learned that the other house mothers stood over the girls as they worked, whereas Annie McClure sat alongside her and her companions, doing her own stitching.

The rules laid down by the Guardians were quite clear: if the little girls from either of the girls' houses were to encounter their little boy counterparts, those little boys had to cross to the opposite pavement. Molly had overheard Mrs McClure say something to her husband about how this was 'pure silliness', which had puzzled her. So even adults had to put up with things they didn't agree with?

No such rule applied to the other little girls, the ones that went home to parents or step-parents every afternoon, the ones who probably got out to play more because they weren't forever having to contend with paying their own way by their own childish labour. That very Thursday Molly had been aware of one of these other girls staring at her in class, a hoydenish child who looked older than the others. Vivie Nevins, she thought her name was, though she wasn't sure because Vivie wasn't very regular in her school attendance and, judging by her inability to answer the questions the teacher kept coming back to ask her, was even less regular in her studies. Molly's own hand had gone up regularly when Miss Rawlinson wearily threw yet another unanswered question back to the class: 'Can someone else tell Nevins the answer?'

Now, holding her friend Myrtle's arm as they went back home, Molly said, 'I wish we could go and help that Nevins. What's the point of Rawlie making her look daft every time? If she doesn't know the answer, she doesn't know it.'

Myrtle grunted. 'She'd not welcome it, mind – Nevins, I mean. Nobody likes a goody two shoes.'

'I'm *not* a goody two shoes!' said Molly, stung. 'I just want to help.'

'I know that,' said Myrtle, 'but Nevins'll not want it from a workhouse brat.'

*

The very next day Molly got confirmation of her friend's words. Myrtle was poorly, running a temperature and coughing, so she was removed from the main bedroom and put into the little whitewashed boxroom that served as the sickbay. Molly herself was sent down to the kitchen in her nightdress and slippers to heat up a pannikin of milk for the patient and to stir in two spoonfuls of honey from the larder. Molly looked at that honey for a whole minute wondering if she could just have one spoonful for herself before deciding, no, Mrs McClure trusted her not to steal. She was sure she'd be found out; a thread of stickiness forgotten at the corner of her mouth would be enough and even if she wiped it away, her guilty expression would tell on her.

Vivie Nevins did somehow manage two consecutive school days, but claiming a 'sore leg' said she preferred not to take part in the skipping game organised at play time but to permanently hold one end of the long rope. The big, awkward girl looked bored to Molly, which made her a little more sympathetic to her. But when it was Molly's turn though to step up and jump the rope, Vivie's motive was revealed. Molly had her back to the girl, but she was quickly aware of being forced to jump higher than usual, followed by the puzzlement and then annoyance on the face of the child holding the other end of the rope.

'What're you doing, Vivie?' someone cried. Molly heard a mirthless laugh behind her, then the rope jerked up and hit her on the side of her leg, making her stumble. Then it was dropped altogether and she turned round to see Vivie stalking off, ignoring the protests of her companions.

'Aw right, Molly?' asked one of the other girls, not one of the Cottage Home group.

'Yes, I'm fine. But why did she do that?'

'Jealousy, I'd say.'

'Jealousy? Why?'

The class monitor rang the bell for return to lessons and her question went unanswered. Later, when the girls were curled unwillingly over their jotters trying to work out an arithmetic problem Miss Rawlinson had scratched out on the blackboard, Molly sighed as, with perverse stubbornness, the teacher insisted on asking Vivie for the answer she knew the girl couldn't give.

'Forty-eight, Miss,' said the girl eventually.

'Dubber?' asked the teacher, looking at Molly.

'Forty-nine, Miss Rawlinson.'

'Correct. Dubber, change places with Hewitt and explain to Nevins where she went wrong – quietly, if you can.'

Molly opened her mouth but shut it again. *She's the teacher. And you did think you wanted to help Vivie.*

'The rest of you, write down this problem.' Miss Rawlinson squeaked her chalk across the blackboard as Molly and Maisie Hewitt crossed the room in opposite directions.

Molly noticed the quick turning away of Vivie's head as she slid into Maisie's place on the form. The smooth wood was warm from the other girl's bottom and what immediately struck Molly was that Vivie was smelly, giving off an acrid, gusting stink that seemed to coat her own skin and made her itch. She didn't dare look at Vivie's tightly curled hair, sure that there would be nits. She felt sorry for the girl, despite her nastiness with the skipping rope, and grateful to Mrs McClure's insistence on daily cleanliness and the Saturday afternoon half an hour in the claw-footed bathtub with the seamed bar of carbolic soap. She took a deep breath through her mouth and whispered, 'Let me see your workings.'

Vivie's ink-stained fist stayed firmly on top of her jotter.

'Workhouse brat!' she hissed.

'Miss Rawlinson said—'

'Your mother didn't want you, did she? You got put out with the milk bottles, didn't you? Or dumped in a field?'

'My mother *died*,' said Molly, louder than she'd intended. 'Let me see—'

'No better than she should've been. Dubber's *her* name, in't it? Can't have your da's name if you don't know who he is, can you?'

Molly gasped, then flinched. Miss Rawlinson stood rustling in front of them.

'Dubber's not helping me, Miss,' protested Vivie.

'Really? Closed your jotter for you, did she? Get up and go and stand in that corner.'

The fug of unwashed skin and clothes grew momentarily thicker as Vivie got up and scuffled her way in the direction of Miss Rawlinson's pointing finger.

'Face to the wall. That's it. You'll stay there until half an hour after the class finishes. What are you staring at, the rest of you? All got the answer, have you?' The heads went down again obediently, no one wanting to meet the teacher's eye.

'All right, Dubber,' said the teacher in a quieter voice. 'Stay where you are for today. Get on with the problem.'

Molly ducked her head, sniffing loudly and rummaging for her handkerchief. She wiped her eyes and blew her nose, hoping the others, Miss Rawlinson included, would think she had a cold. The teacher briefly squeezed her shoulder and went back to her high desk.

Oh well, at least Vivie can't follow me home, Molly thought. *Not today, anyway.* Then she remembered that today she had her own special half hour, the dedicated time that Annie McClure allocated to each of her little girls every week. *What'll I tell her?*

*

After the tea things had been put away and the little girls had hung their aprons on their designated hooks, Molly followed her house mother into the little parlour.

'You were very quiet at teatime,' said Annie.

'We're meant to be quiet at table,' said Molly.

'I know that's what it says on the wall,' said Annie, 'but every thing in moderation. What happened today, Molly?'

Looking down at her hands, Molly quietly told her story, from the sting of the skipping rope against her leg, Myrtle's prophecy that Vivie would refuse any help from a 'workhouse brat' and finally the stammered assertion that Dubber could not be her father's name, her thought that perhaps this man wasn't dead after all but simply didn't know he was a father.

'Do you remember I told you your mother and father had both died?' said Annie.

Molly nodded.

'And that you were with them until you were nearly three?'

Another nod.

'Do you remember anything about them?'

There was a pause before the child shook her head so force-fully that to Annie it looked as though she was trying to rid herself of a wasp.

'Mr McClure and I have brought you up to be truthful, haven't we?'

'Yes, but—'

'Well, that *is* the truth, Molly. It mightn't be the whole truth, but it's as much as I know and as the Guardians have told me. Your father's name was Stanley and he was your mother's husband. Your mother was Mary. As Molly is a way of saying Mary, you were probably named after her. So nobody can say they didn't want you. You're not from the workhouse, Molly, you're from this home, and I'm sure your mother must have loved you and would be with you if she could – because, Molly, a loving mother will do *anything* for her child. *I* know that.'

'But *how* do you know?' said Molly, with a child's unthinking directness. 'You've only got us.'

'Oh, Molly. I'm sure I look awful old to you, but I've got a daughter of my own too. Kathleen Teresa. She works in the chemist's on Dalton Road and she's married. Close your mouth, dear, it looks like a little tunnel.'

Molly precipitately shut her mouth. Annie had always instructed her little girls not to 'gawp'; that was what rough people did, and the house mother had always impressed on her small charges that they were not 'ill-bred', no matter what the world might say. Molly hadn't really understood what that meant at the time, though she'd seen Ada nodding sagely. Ada was now a shop assistant at The Cooperative and surely couldn't have got that job if she'd been a gawper. Molly frowned, thinking.

'Why doesn't Kathleen Teresa live here?' she asked.

'Because this is a home for little girls, not for grown-up girls who are wed.'

'So when I'm a grown-up I can't live here with you?'

Annie hesitated. 'No, my darling, you won't be able to. You'll go to work, find your own way in the world. I hope you'll come back and see me and Mr McClure though.'

'I'd never want to leave,' said Molly firmly.

'You will, when the time comes and it's my job to make sure you're able to. You'll not go to work as young as I did, anyway. Thirteen I was when I went to the mill – in Ireland, that was; well, Northern Ireland as they have it now.'

'How did you come to be a house mother, then?'

'It was Mr McClure's idea. He had a little workshop – tailoring, same as he teaches the boys now – and one of the Board of Guardians was a customer. I was at the jute works by then, alongside of my stepmother – Mammy Elsie, I called her, Mr Fagan's mother – and they'd made me a doffing mistress, in charge of a whole hall of girls. The gentleman from the Guardians said we'd make an ideal couple. Mr McClure didn't have the easiest time of it when he was a little boy, even if he wasn't quite an orphan, but a nice woman had taught him the tailoring and he said if he could teach it to others he'd feel he'd given something back and helped them as hadn't had the best start in life. I'm glad he persuaded me, for if we hadn't come here, we wouldn't have met you.'

'And Mr Fagan wouldn't be training the piano tuners.'

'Perhaps not, though I think he got the job because he's good at it more'n because he's near enough my brother.'

'Poor Mr Fagan. I used to be frightened of him, you know. The way his eyes look all foggy, and how he stares at the air above my head though I'm down here and moves his eyes from side to side as if he can see me.'

'He was only a boy when it happened, poor soul. He told fibs about his age so's he could join up. But you brighten up his life, Molly. He says he always looks forward to the evenings when you read to us in the parlour. You're a great wee reader, so you are.'

'Well, I like reading to him and I like the books he brings. He's a nice face, and when I see him sitting there, thinking and listening, he doesn't look as if he's blind. I wish I'd a brother like him. And I wish my mam and dad were like you and Mr McClure.'

Annie was silent for a moment, remembering the marks on Molly's back, marks the child had never seen, and the medical officer's report of that fractured arm.

'I'm sure they love you still, up there in heaven where they must be,' said Annie slowly, not at all sure of either fact. 'What I'm not sure about, Molly, is whether Vivie Nevins' parents love her. She must be very unhappy, that wee girl, to be taking it out on you. Now you're not to worry about her. I'll have a word with Miss Rawlinson and I'm sure everything will be fine. Oh . . . we'd better get prayers organised. Do you feel a bit better about today, Molly?'

Molly nodded solemnly, then remembered. 'How is Myrtle?'

'Mending. But perhaps after prayers you'd help again with the warm milk and honey. You can make a glass for yourself as well.'

CHAPTER THREE

Tailoring Workshop, Roose Road Cottage Homes, 1931

Robert looked round as the door opened, thinking it must be a latecomer, and wondering how he could get away with not punishing the boy. The row of lads bent obediently over their machines, whirring down the seams of the pinned and tailor-chalked trouser seams. Not all of them would make tailors, he could see. The job wanted patience, an attentive eye, a feel for the warp and weft of the cloth – and a sense of responsibility. When Robert had run his own workshop, he'd been very conscious of the fact that many of his customers would come to him for the first and only suit of their lives. They'd be married in that suit, and later buried in it. Therefore they deserved the best he could give them.

'Annie?' he said. Some of the cropped heads swivelled to see the pale woman standing in the doorway, but turned as quickly back to what they were doing. Robert had taught them that sewing an even seam needed one swift, unbroken movement. 'Almost as if you forget to breathe,' he'd said.

He grasped his stick and crossed the room as quickly as he was able.

'Which one is it?' he said, taking her arm and leading her back into the corridor, the glass-panelled door a barrier between them and the boys.

'They're fine. They're all fine, poor little mites. I've been to the library.'

'The *library*?' For a moment he thought she was talking about the little Carnegie Library back in Cleator Moor where they had met, but brushed the thought from his mind. He'd seen Annie only two hours before, at dinner time in the house, an impossibly short time to have made the journey up to Cumberland and back. Everything had been fine then, so why was she pale and shaking now?

'It was for Molly,' she said. 'Because she's going out to service soon, she begged me again to find out if there was anything else I could tell her about her mother and father. She's worried in case they give out to her in her new place about being a nobody.'

'You know they're both dead. The superintendent said so, back when she was sent to us.'

Annie nodded. 'I know.'

'And?'

'I don't know what to tell her, Robert. It's *how* they died. The librarian was very helpful – said he liked a bit of a detective story and he was a Manchester man himself. And when I showed him her birth certificate, with her real name on it, he said it rang a bell. Look – I copied this out of the newspaper he found for me.'

Leaning on his stick, Robert read slowly as Annie watched his face grow pale. His eyes scanned her neat handwriting a second time. In silence he folded the paper and handed it back to her. With his free hand he squeezed her shoulder.

'You mustn't tell Molly,' he whispered. 'Let her believe anything – it was the Spanish flu, or consumption, or he was lost at sea and her mother couldn't cope and died of a broken heart – all the things she's been imagining all of this time. But never tell her this.'

'It wasn't that difficult to uncover. What if she finds out herself?'

Robert sighed. 'She'll be going into service as Molly Dubber. It's the only name she's ever known and she'll not need her birth certificate in a house in Croslands Park Road. She'll have that much to deal with that's new she'll perhaps not think about it for a bit. Only we have to be prepared for the day she does – maybe when she wants to wed.'

Annie was crying now. Robert glanced over his shoulder, but the whirr of the treadles reassured him. He was more bothered about one of the other instructors appearing and seeing Annie's distress than about the little boys, whom he was sure needed to see more human emotion than they were generally allowed. He didn't want a tale about a 'scene' getting back to the superintendent. He and Annie had the running of their house as a model married couple, but he was aware an exception had been made because of his trade. The Cottage Homes usually employed house mothers, not houseparents, as if orphan children ought to be grateful for just having one person looking after them.

As if reading his mind, Annie dug out a handkerchief and dried her eyes.

'Molly doesn't know about the marks on her back,' she whispered. 'She's never seen them and I've never told. *He* musta made them.'

'So that's why Molly was sent to us. I remember we thought it odd they'd send one wee girl that far. We'll have a little party for her leaving, so we will. Just the home, Kathleen and her husband – Mark Fagan, of course.'

'Mark'll miss her,' said Annie pensively, thinking of her stepmother's son. 'He says there's no one else reads to him as well as she does.'

CHAPTER FOUR

Leaving, July 1931

There were scenes – of course there were.

'You said I was good at the school, Mother Annie,' wailed Molly.

'You are – you were, I mean.' Annie sought to comfort the girl but there was no justification she could make. It was true. Molly had been the star pupil in all her classes.

'What was the point of all this, then?' demanded Molly, pulling from the shelf six or seven cloth-bound books, opening one and holding it up to Annie. 'Roose Board School, Reading prize, 1929.'

'You will always have that – no one will ever be able to take what you did away from you.'

'So why've I got to be a housemaid? I wanted to be a teacher!'

Annie couldn't find the words. Why crush a fourteen-year-old's spirit even further, by telling her that the Guardians, as Annie continued to call the men at the Borough Council who were now their overlords, would not be moved, in spite of her own pleadings as house mother and the support of Molly's teachers. Of the children brought up 'on the parish', the boys would get an apprenticeship in the shipyard or the wireworks and the most able of Robert McClure's pupils might have their own tailoring workshops one day. Girls were destined for service, that or the jute works. There was a shortage of servants and had been for some time because so many of those who had left service in wartime hadn't come back, many of the men because they were no longer alive.

'You won't be a servant forever, Molly,' said Annie, hoping it was true. 'And it's just one poor old lady, living on her own but for a companion and her cook. You might even like it.'

'I won't!' scowled Molly, fighting tears.

*

The final day came, with Molly's grip waiting at the door. She and Annie were expected at Miss Cavendish's after tea.

'I'll miss everybody,' she said, sniffing tears. 'That little party was lovely.'

'We don't need to go just yet,' said Annie. 'Mark said he wanted to come round to say goodbye.'

'He said goodbye at the party, though.'

'Yes ... well, you know what he's like. He's always been a bit private, has Mark,' said Annie, suppressing a sigh. 'Saying goodbye to you with all the girls there wouldn't feel like a proper leave-taking to him. He'll be round for his tea and he asked if it'd be all right to speak to you for a moment then.'

Molly shrugged. 'I won't mind.' Then, in a burst of sudden enthusiasm Annie recognised, she said, 'But there'll be a piano in the new house, surely? Don't all posh places have one?'

'I expect so. That doesn't mean you'll be let to play it, though. I've never heard of a servant doing so.'

'Mark could come and tune it, though. He always says it's not good for pianos not to be played.'

'*Molly.*'

'I know, I know. I'm there to work and represent the Cottage Homes.' She looked Mrs McClure straight in the eye. 'I'll be good, I promise. For your sake, Mother Annie, and for Mr McClure's too.'

*

Molly stood up from her chair in the little parlour when Annie opened the door to usher in Mark Fagan. The occasion felt like an odd inversion of roles, and Molly reminded herself that where she was going, she would be the one introducing visitors to the parlour and then going out closing the door quietly, just as Mother Annie was doing now. Her lip wobbled as she looked at the young man facing her, his sightless eyes scouring the air just above the top of her head. She wondered if he realised how handsome he was, a 'black Irishman', as Robert McClure called him, hinting at shipwrecked Spanish sailors washed ashore by the Giant's Causeway long ago. She bit down, not wanting him to know that leaving him upset her. Mark might be blind, but Molly had already noticed that there was not a lot that escaped him. *Except what I feel about him, I hope.*

Mark held out his hand. Molly took it. He put his other hand on top, enfolding hers.

'I'll miss you, our kid,' he said.

21

'You said that. At the party.' She could have kicked herself for being so clumsy, seeing the look of disappointment that crossed his face.

'I mean, I'll miss you too,' she added, relieved to see him smile.

'I remember the first time I met you,' he said. 'In the kitchen back there. Ada was with you and the other little mites, talking away nineteen to the dozen. But I heard someone sniffling and said "Who's new?" You'd the tiniest whisper of a voice, you did. All you said was, "I'm Molly Dubber," but the others all stopped yakking because it was the first time any of 'em had heard you say owt. Annie congratulated me afterwards.'

'I've not a whisper of a voice now, have I?' said Molly, laughing.

'You've the loveliest voice I've ever heard,' said Mark, suddenly serious.

Silence descended on the room, like a muffling blanket, as Molly looked away, her hand slipping from his. The sounds of voices in the back kitchen made themselves heard, followed by footsteps along the passage. Hearing a catch in his breath, Molly looked up. Mark looked stricken.

'All I meant was – well, your voice has changed over the years. I never got to see you, Molly. And everybody I knew before I went to be a soldier will always look to me the same – in my head, I mean. Annie, for instance. Such a pretty lady. And Robert's brown curly hair – I suppose it's grey by now. All the people I knew before will always be young to me. But hearing you speak was like watching you grow up, in a way. I can't see you, dear Molly, but I'm sure you are the most beautiful girl I have ever had the misfortune to meet.'

There was a soft tap at the door and Annie put her head in.

'There's tea in the kitchen if yous are wanting a cup,' she said.

'Thank you, Annie,' said Mark. 'I was just going.' He turned back to Molly. 'You have a good life now, our kid.' His hand fluttered out, found her shoulder, and lay there for a moment.

And then he was gone.

CHAPTER FIVE

Croslands Park Road, 1931

The first lesson of going into service was the tradesmen's entrance. The house in Croslands Park Road stood proud and confident on raised ground, looking down on its neighbours.

'All this grass,' said Molly. 'It's like Barrow Park, near enough. Think of all the vegetables you could grow here.'

'If there's a kitchen garden it'll be around the back where it can't be seen by visitors,' said Annie as they walked up the winding drive. 'But probably Miss Cavendish gets everything delivered. The cook will deal with all of that, I should think. Round this way, maybe,' she added, skirting the front porch with its coloured glass panels and gleaming brassware, to take a path around the back. 'As it's a big house it'll mebbe have a servants' stair too. Six bedrooms the place has, I was told.'

'So there are other people – not just Miss Cavendish and her companion?'

'No, just them.'

'What's the use of a big house if you don't put people in it? There's eighteen of us in the Cottage Home and we haven't six bedrooms.'

'Miss Cavendish's family live elsewhere, I believe,' said Annie, sidestepping the question.

*

It was the cook who opened the door. To Molly she looked as she imagined a cook should, floury and big-armed.

'New girl from the Cottage Home, is it?' said the woman and a little flame of hope flickered in Molly at the sound of the woman's voice. Her accent was as close to Annie McClure's as the girl could detect. Yet the similarity made her realise that she was going to be homesick, even if Roose Road was less than two miles away.

'I'm Molly Dubber,' she said as confidently as she dared.

'You'll be Dubber here, so you will,' said the woman, not unkindly. Then she looked at Annie more closely.

'I seen you before.'

'Mass,' said Annie.

'Right enough. You go to the vigil Saturday evening. I knew I seen you somewhere.'

'I have to go then. I've to take the little girls to St Mark's Sunday morning. Borough Council rules.'

'And I've to get them upstairs Sunday dinner, while *she's* out being holy with her best hat and gloves on. Still, gets it over with for me. I don't know whether yourself having to go to the Protestants as well gets you more time in Purgatory or less, so I don't.'

Both the smile that accompanied this and the woman's generous girth made Molly feel a bit happier, that and the fact that she and Annie had made a connection.

'Come away in,' said the cook. 'I'm Mrs McGovern. No, there's never been a Mr McGovern – but you knew that, Dubber, didn't you now? Cooks are always Mrs. A mark of respect.'

Molly nodded, confused. She hadn't known.

'I'll see can we not get us a cup of tay and a bit of a blether before her ladyship realises you're here,' said Mrs McGovern, leading the way down a tiled corridor that smelled of cabbage. 'She knows she's not to come into the kitchen, mind. That's my place. The parlour is hers.'

Molly glanced at Annie in alarm. What kind of house was it where the owner, who presumably paid the wages, wasn't allowed the run of the place?

'Sit yourselves down, so,' said the woman, waving at a deal table. Molly obeyed, but couldn't stop her eyes straying over the vastness of the kitchen. The range bulked against one wall, far bigger than the one in the Cottage Home that had to feed many more mouths. Above the doorway into the main part of the house she saw a row of bells, each helpfully labelled below with the room it corresponded to. Molly hadn't had time to count how many there were when she realised Mrs McGovern was addressing her. Her heart sank.

'She'll not like ye, so she won't,' the woman was saying. 'You're far too pretty, even with that short haircut you have.' Then her eyes flickered sideways and the cook put a finger to her lips. 'Best stand up and get them tea things into that their sink, Dubber,' she said, indicating the way into the scullery. 'She's on her way.'

Molly obeyed, gathering up the tray, alert to the urgency in the woman's voice though in truth all she thought she heard was what might have been a door closing somewhere deep in the house. Sure enough, though, brisk footsteps thudded on the runner leading down the passage into the kitchen, translating into the hard clack of heels on quarry tiles. Standing at the Belfast sink in the scullery, Molly forced herself not to look round into the kitchen, concentrating instead on unloading the dirty crockery into the sink in one piece, despite the trembling of her hands.

'I'll thank you to come no further, Miss Tweed,' she heard the cook say.

'Here, is she?' Molly shivered at the hard tone. *Miss Tweed, though? This must be the companion.*

'Molly Dubber is one of our best girls,' she heard Mother Annie say.

Molly wiped her hands on a linen towel and, taking a deep breath, stepped back into the kitchen.

Miss Tweed looked her up and down without speaking; Molly saw resentment in every crease of the woman's skin. She guessed Miss Tweed must have been about the same age as Mother Annie, but there the similarity ended. She saw the woman's glance slide away to Annie and realised she had refused to meet her own eyes.

'We would have preferred someone more mature, but such are not to be had. What is this girl's history?'

'An orphan, since she was three—' began Annie.

'"Ye shall know them by their fruits ... a corrupt tree bringeth forth evil fruit." Father unknown, I suppose?'

Molly saw shock on Annie's face and mutiny on the cook's but before anyone else could respond, she heard her own voice saying "'A good tree cannot bring forth evil fruit, neither can a corrupt tree bring forth good fruit.'"

Miss Tweed looked straight at her then. 'I do not tolerate being answered back.'

'Miss Dubber's parents were married, Miss Tweed,' said Annie coolly.

'Hmmph. Profligate, no doubt, or she would not have been turned over to the Board of Guardians. No provision made for their offspring, as usual. But I compliment you, Mrs . . .'

'McClure.'

'I compliment you on ensuring she received proper instruction. St Paul tells us that slaves are to obey their masters in everything, with reverence for the Lord.'

'My understanding was that Molly would be working for Miss Cavendish,' said Annie.

'Miss Cavendish is bedridden, and is not entirely in charge of her own mind,' said Miss Tweed. 'As her companion, I am obliged to interpret her wishes as best I can. Miss Cavendish is served by myself and a nurse who calls in morning and evening. Dubber will bring Miss Cavendish's meals. Her other duties will be to keep Miss Cavendish's home as clean as my employer would wish it to be were she still able to enjoy full use of it, and to assist Mrs McGovern.'

'You have no scullery maid, then?' asked Annie.

'Certainly not! An unnecessary expense when only two people live here, I am sure you'd agree. Fires must be laid by six in every room still in use; that means Miss Cavendish's chamber and mine. The rooms currently mothballed must be aired every three days, the carpets beaten and every uncovered surface kept free of dust. I inspect, Mrs McClure. No followers are permitted, of course.'

Molly wondered if Annie could see the sense in employing someone to clean closed-up rooms and not have someone where they were needed in the kitchen, as she was sure she couldn't. She also knew the hierarchy of servitude; the Roose Road girls were taught it. There were parlourmaids, then housemaids, or house-parlourmaids in smaller establishments. Then there were scullery maids. But she was to be a maid-of-all-work. It would be a job just to keep herself clean, to rid herself of the grease of the scullery every time this Tweed woman expected her to pretend to be a parlourmaid and serve her guests tea and cakes. Then it occurred to her, looking at Miss Tweed, that guests probably never called from one end of the year to the next. *How long can I last here? And from the look of that one, the character she'd give me would be for a scullery maid. Is that what I've to be all my life?*

'Well, I can't stand around here all day gossiping,' Miss Tweed said. Looking hard at Molly, she said, 'I leave this house only to give praise to the Lord on the Sabbath and for meetings of the Dorcas Society; in fact, I am expected there for an extraordinary general meeting. *You* will have one Sunday free in four, and your afternoon off will be Wednesday. You would do well to use that time in sewing or reading scripture.'

'My husband and myself will look forward to seeing Molly when she's free,' said Annie, coming to the rescue.

Miss Tweed shrugged. 'As you wish. As I am sure you have other charges to see to, Mrs McClure, I will bid you good day. McGovern, show the girl her duties.'

And without another word, the woman turned and stalked back into the main house. Dismayed, Molly looked from Annie's troubled face to the cook's, who to her surprise was trying to stifle a laugh.

'Sure, you'll be fine' said Mrs McGovern. 'You'll have noticed thon woman stopped at the door, didn't ye? This kitchen is where *I* am in charge, and herself knows it. You'll be safe with me, so you will. I threaten to give notice whenever she tries to get one over me and that keeps her where I want her – as far from me as can be. Take off your coat, Dubber, and as soon she's out the door we'll have our wee tour, so we will.'

'What about Miss Cavendish?'

The cook's face softened. 'She's a dacent aul' skin, right enough. But she's not right in the head and being shut up in this place, not seeing anyone but thon hag and her nurse, isn't going to put it right either. You'll see more of her'n I will, seeing as you'll be bringing up her meals.'

*

After their goodbyes, with both Molly and Annie in tears, the new maid-of-all-work followed McGovern up the oak staircase. Molly couldn't tell if it was the treads beneath it or the deep, silencing carpet itself that creaked.

'You'll not be let go up here when Tweed's in, mind,' said Mrs McGovern. 'I'll show you your staircase after.'

Engravings of country scenes familiar to Molly only from occasional outings from the Cottage Homes lined the staircase: Wastwater, Troutbeck, Coniston Old Man, Windermere. She glimpsed figures of gentlemanly walkers pointing a stick up at the landscape, whilst picturesque farmworkers rested beneath trees or leaned on gates. Molly was pretty sure that nobody in real life ever got to do this. Annie had told her about growing up on a farm in Ireland, a story of relentless hard work – and yet Annie's eyes had filled with love in the telling.

A lifesize portrait of a mid-Victorian gentleman looked down his nose at them from the landing. 'That's her father,' whispered the cook.

'There's a Cavendish Street in Hindpool but it looks nothing like Croslands Park,' whispered Molly back.

'One of that family, that'll be.'

'Has she family herself now?'

The cook pulled a face. 'I reckon ye'll see 'em if you're still here when the aul' soul passes on. They'll come with lawyers for to take the house. I never seen any of 'em, that's for sure.'

They passed through sad, shuttered rooms, furniture draped in white sheets like snowy mountain ranges.

'There's a big spring clean once a year when all of the sheets are to be got down and sent to the laundry and everything cleaned inside and out. The rest of the time you've to come in and out and make sure the parquet is kept waxed and there's no dust on the mantelpiece. Your woman – Tweed, I mean – has a thing about dust. She's read somewhere it's dried human skin and so she's a horror of it. I think she has a horror of anything human, to be honest.'

Molly looked at the height of the ceilings, where cobwebs would surely lurk if she didn't prevent them, and felt very small and helpless.

'What happened to the last maid?' she asked.

'Got caught talking to the butcher's boy more than Tweed thought was needful. I believe the pair of them went to Preston. Fair play to the girl is all I can say.'

Mrs McGovern showed her a bathroom, with a claw-footed tub that looked to Molly as though it was preparing to devour her, and a toilet decorated with a blue flower pattern that reminded her of Willow Pattern dinner plates.

'Tweed'll want you to get to work on this first, I should think. Them dark green tiles should be so shiny you can see the outline of your face in them. Same with them taps. Get them that gleaming that she could see to pluck out the hairs on her upper lip and she'll be satisfied – not otherwise. I'll show you where the vinegar and lemons are kept when we go back downstairs.'

Molly gazed wide-eyed at the bathroom, astonished at its spaciousness.

'Wasted on old Tweed, isn't it? The nurse washes Miss Cavendish where she lies, I believe. You and me have the privy out the back and the hip bath when we want it, but I take myself to the bathhouse on my afternoon off – get a bit of chat through the partitions that way and I like water better that I've not had to heat myself. I'd advise you to do the same.'

Miss Tweed's room was next. It was decently furnished with what looked to Molly to be a comfortable mattress with a warm counterpane, yet the room was unwelcoming all the same. Above the bed hung a dark-framed Bible quote, illustrated with a sprig of broom: 'Thou art my Help and my Deliverer' it read. Molly unexpectedly felt a twinge of pity for Miss Tweed, instinctively understanding that there was no fellow human the woman could call upon for either help or deliverance. There was a washstand, a narrow wardrobe, a low chest of drawers and a small bookcase containing a Bible and some tracts. Unlike the furniture in the larger rooms that Molly had glimpsed by lifting corners of the dust sheets, nothing here matched.

They were about to go up the last flight of stairs when Molly stopped her companion.

'We've not been in there,' she said, pointing.

'That's Miss Cavendish's room. You'll meet her when you bring her the breakfast.'

Molly was struck by the fact the cook spoke in a normal voice. It didn't matter, then, if whoever was behind that closed door heard or not.

The rooms under the eaves were mean, low-ceilinged and floored with lino. 'I'm in here,' said Mrs McGovern. 'You're next to me so don't worry if you have nightmares. Some girls do, first few weeks away from home. The other rooms are all lumber.'

Molly was heartened by the cook's kindness and it went some way to alleviating her dismay at the sight of her own room, the first she was ever to have to herself, with its uneven, dun-coloured walls, the dusty rag rug beside the bed, the tin ewer and basin on the rickety table. The iron-framed bed, though, looked so like the one she'd had in the Cottage Home, though this one's paint was dull and peeling, that she felt a tremor of homesickness.

'You could dress it up if you wanted,' said Mrs McGovern, 'only you mightn't bother if you don't want to stay long.'

Molly didn't know what to say to this, as it was too close to what she'd been thinking. *I knew I'd have to leave the Cottage Home some time. But I'm in this place with no idea of how long it'll be for. If it wasn't that the mistress is an old lady, it might have been forever.*

'When I came here first I was under-cook. Cook told me there'd been a manservant, but there never has been in any of the time I've been here. There's just old Fred comes to do the garden, but I don't let him in as he smells, so I give him his tea at the door. What I mean is there's a key in your door, see, but you don't have to lock it. Come on, then, I'll show the way down the backstairs. Them's the ones you'll use unless told otherwise. And then I'll show you the outhouses. You and me do our own laundry. Everything else gets sent out.'

CHAPTER SIX

Miss Cavendish

Molly spread her arms wide, for the tray was a big one and finely balanced. Under its muslin square, one of the plates carried buttered toast, the other the same offering but cut into nursery-sized pieces under Mrs McGovern's supervision. Molly was reminded of chopping up food for the youngest children in the Cottage Home. It was a milestone when a little girl managed her own knife and fork. But now she was about to meet Miss Cavendish at last, who in the descent down the far side of her arc of life once more needed to be fed like a child.

She reached the door and paused for a moment, straining her ears. It wasn't the first time she had been in the room, for she had gone in at six to sweep up the dead cinders and lay the new fire. There had been no sign of life in the room then, for the curtains around the old-fashioned tester bed had been closed and Molly could hear nothing from within. Then Miss Tweed had come in, wearing a dressing-gown, urging Molly in a fierce whisper to hurry up, for her own room was arctic.

Standing outside the door now, Molly could still not hear anything, yet was pretty sure she was being listened to. With an elbow, Molly managed two muffled knocks.

'Come in,' she heard Miss Tweed intone. Molly waited a moment, holding her breath, to see if the companion would come to the door, but there was no movement, so sighing, she put the tray down, the plates, glasses of lemonade and cups of tea clinking gently against each other, and turned the handle. The door swung open. Molly could see Miss Tweed sitting by the side of the bed, watching her, unsmiling. She bent down to retrieve the tray, thinking, *What would it have cost her to have come over to the door? She knew I was coming with the tray.*

Molly took a deep breath and advanced into the room, concentrating on not dropping the tray to distract her from what, or who, lay in the bed.

'Here!' barked Miss Tweed, indicating a small foldable table to her right. Molly settled her burden, aware out of the corner of her eye that something small and frail had shifted beneath the bedcovers and the over-tray hooked over the top of them. She could hear laboured breathing, then a thin querulous voice disconcertingly like a child's asked, 'Who is the pretty lady?'

Molly straightened up and met with a pair of glittering dark eyes, set in a pale criss-cross of wrinkles, surrounded by a woolly blur of white hair. She was sure she had never encountered anyone that old.

'Dubber, Miss Cavendish,' she said, and bobbed an approximate curtsey as she'd been taught, the first real one of her life. She heard Miss Tweed make a strangulated sound, as though clearing her throat.

'Miss Cavendish asked *me* who you were. Do not be pert, girl.'

Her employer went on as though Miss Tweed hadn't spoken.

'Dubber's not a girl's name, is it? What does your mother call you?'

Miss Tweed gave this a derisive snort, but Molly didn't look at her. She sensed that the old lady, frail though she might be, was determined to get the upper hand.

'My mother? Well, I am called Molly. Her name was Mary, you see.'

Miss Tweed cut in again. 'Miss Cavendish is not to be told by the likes of you what she may or may not see. You've brought the breakfast. Retire now so that we may eat it in peace. I'll ring when we've finished with the tray. Go on, then. What are you gawping at?'

Molly bobbed another curtsey and turned away. She reached the doorway when she heard Miss Tweed say, in a voice deliberately made to carry, 'Dubber is from the workhouse, Miss Cavendish. An orphan. Won't know who her father was, of course.'

It was all Molly could do not to slam the door. She fought hot tears all the way down the backstairs to the sanctuary of the kitchen.

'Take no notice,' said Mrs McGovern, the moment she saw Molly's face. 'Aul' bitch is only jealous.'

There it is again, thought Molly. *Jealousy. Just like Vivie Nevins. But why be jealous of a workhouse girl? Though I'm not. I come from the Cottage Homes. That's different.* Then she realised it wasn't different, not really. Wasn't it the Borough Councillors who had decided she was to go into service?

But when the bell rang from Miss Cavendish's room she had to steel herself to go back up for the tray. Her knock brought a tetchy 'yes?' from Miss Tweed but Molly didn't hesitate to go in. Hadn't the woman rung for her after all?

Miss Tweed didn't even lift her head when Molly crossed the room. The companion held the book she was reading ostentatiously high, so that the title – it was a collection of sermons – was clearly visible. Molly's eyes slid sideways to the bed. Miss Cavendish was fast asleep, her mouth open. She was snoring softly. Then lifting the tray, Molly saw it wasn't the only thing on the table. There was a small medicine bottle, a spoon lying beside it, but the label was turned away from her.

You'd think a nurse would be giving out medicine, not her, thought Molly. *Probably it's just something for the constipation. Poor lady, lying down the whole time like that.*

Shortly after she'd got back to the kitchen and had been handed a version of what they had eaten upstairs, Molly heard the front door open and close. She looked up at Mrs McGovern enquiringly.

'Just the nurse, Dubber. She's her own key.'

An hour later, setting the kitchen to rights for the next day, Molly heard a murmur of voices coming down the stairwell, the clack of heels on the tiles of the porch, and the front door closing again. She straightened up, a hand in the small of her back. This was only the first morning, in this strange house of women. How many mornings stretched ahead?

*

It was hard to be up so much earlier than she had been in the Cottage Home, even though all the girls there had their part to play in the housework. The difference, of course, was that Annie McClure worked alongside them, as a mother would; Molly knew from children in the other houses that not all the house mothers did this. The dirty part of the day in Croslands Park Road was dealt with first; getting the fires to light. Afterwards, she'd have to make sure she looked spick and span to take up the breakfast tray, by scrubbing her fingers in cold water at the scullery sink, peeling off her apron and buttoning on clean cuffs. The rest of the day Molly worked either as assistant cook, or slogged through her pointless task of cleaning rooms that were never used, but she never skimped on the work, for more than once she'd hear the door open behind her and would turn to see Miss Tweed standing on the threshold, wordlessly watching her.

The part of the day that she both dreaded and looked forward to was taking up the tray to Miss Cavendish's room, looked forward to because she hoped that the bright-eyed old lady who had been interested in who she was might ask her more questions. That hope was soon dashed, though, as every time she went in Miss Cavendish either had a glassy stare, lying still in the bed, or was fidgeting and muttering, scratching at her shoulders and arms through her nightdress. And she was never alone, of course.

Then came the day when Molly was putting away her cleaning tools and realised she'd left her feather duster in the upstairs drawing room. Her first thought was that it could stay there until the morning, but her second was that it would be just her luck that Miss Tweed would go in to inspect and find it and give her a talk about standards. But she'd heard the companion go out to her Dorcas meeting. Now would be a good time to fetch the duster, without having to give some tiresome explanation of what she was doing upstairs again.

As she passed Miss Cavendish's door Molly was quite sure she heard something. She paused, edging her way closer to the wooden panels.

There it was, quite distinctly this time. 'Molly!'

Molly knocked twice before turning the doorknob. To her astonishment, the door was locked.

'Molly? Is that you?' came the high, quavering voice.

'You're locked in, Miss Cavendish.'

She heard some muttering, then, 'Please, Molly. I want to talk to you.' The plaintiveness of the old woman's voice wrung Molly's heart.

'I'll see if Mrs McGovern has another key,' Molly said and ran down the main staircase. It was quicker, and there was no one to see her.

'Aul' bitch, that Tweed,' said Mrs McGovern when told about the locked door. 'What if we caught fire?'

To Molly's relief, the cook opened a drawer of the dresser and held up an iron ring, from which jangled a dozen or so keys of different sizes.

'Try them wee ones first. Thon big ones'll be spares for the outhouses.'

'Thank you!' said Molly breathlessly, and sped back upstairs. She'd lost count of how long Miss Tweed had been out, but the chance to speak to Miss Cavendish, even if only for a minute, overcame her fear.

She was nearly hopping with impatience trying the keys. *It's always the last one you try,* she told herself. *But then it would be – that's logic!*

Her heart thumped as the door swung open.

'Molly!' croaked the old lady.

'I don't know when Miss Tweed will be back in,' said Molly, coming over to the side of the bed. 'If she catches me, I'm for it. Are you all right, Miss Cavendish?'

'I've got to talk to you. You mind which key it is. Then whenever Tweed is out next doing her good works for those poor souls who've never done her any harm, you come in straightaway.'

'It's this one,' said Molly, holding up the clutch of keys. 'I'll mark it.'

At that moment, Molly heard the front door open. Eyes wide, she rushed to the door, closed it as quickly as she could, grateful that the noise was muffled by the opening of the inner door below. For an awful moment she thought she had the wrong key, but at last it slid into place and the door was relocked. Molly just had time to scamper along the landing and through the door that led to the servants' stair. She took three steps down the narrow treads, and waited. At first all she could hear was the thumping of blood in her own head but as she forced herself to master her breathing, she could just make out the thud of Miss Tweed's brogues on the landing. Then there was the rattle of a key in the lock and finally the closing of the door. Molly sat down on the stairs, panting with relief. Her armpits were wet with cold sweat. But she nearly cried aloud when she put her hand to her head and couldn't immediately find the starched frilly cap Miss Tweed insisted she wear. What if it lay on the landing, or worse, in Miss Cavendish's room? An 'oh!' of relief escaped her when putting her other hand to the back of her head, she found the cap hanging, precariously held on by one last valiant kirby grip. Molly gave silent thanks to the unknown architect who had designed the house with a servants' stair.

To Molly it felt like a long week before the next Dorcas Society meeting. There were no chances to speak to Miss Cavendish in the meantime, though Molly tried her best to get a good look at her employer every time she came up with the tray or came back to fetch it when summoned by the bell. Every time Miss Cavendish was either asleep, or staring vacantly into space, animated only by that horrible scratching.

'She always eats everything, mind,' she said to Mrs McGovern.

'Don't mean anything,' said the cook. 'Your one is capable of cleaning the plate herself. There'll be something in scripture that tells her she's to do it, so there will.'

When at last Thursday had come around again, there was one delay after the other in Miss Tweed going out. Firstly, she accused Molly of hiding her gloves, forgetting she had put them out for cleaning and that they were on pegs in the outhouse until the scent of vinegar faded. Then it looked as though it might rain, and Miss Tweed hesitated about going out 'with my weak chest.' It took Molly saying 'Won't the Society be relying on you, Miss Tweed?' to prompt her to button up her jacket with a martyred air, though she did shoot a quick, suspicious glance at the girl, who was still fishing screwed-up newspaper from inside the gloves and was careful not to meet her eyes.

At last she was gone, but Molly made sure by scuttling upstairs to the drawing room, where she watched the woman through a crack between the shutters. Miss Tweed marched down the curve of the drive with a determination that was almost military as Molly's fingers curled around the single key in her pocket. She'd cleaned and polished it in expectation of this moment.

Outside Miss Cavendish's room, Molly listened before knocking. She sensed more than heard a rustling within, followed by a quavering 'That you, Tweed?'

Molly put her face close to the door panels. 'It's Dubber.'

'At last!' said Miss Cavendish, with a bit more vigour. Molly opened the door.

'Help me sit up a bit,' said the old lady. 'I've something important to ask you. No, not like that. You'll need to come closer and hook your elbows under my armpits. That's the way the nurse does it, anyway. I don't think I'm very heavy. Then lift . . . that's it. Now plump the pillows a bit. Afterwards you'll have to lie me down again as Tweed knows I can't get myself upright on my own.'

Already Molly thought Miss Cavendish looked a bit more alert, but she didn't like the way her eyes glittered.

'What was it you wanted to ask me, Miss Cavendish?'

'I want you to get rid of my medicine, Molly. It makes me feel older and stupider and sleepier than I really am.'

'But doesn't the doctor want you to take it? Or shouldn't we ask the nurse?'

43

'I don't believe she knows about it, Molly. And I can't remember when old Dr Sambrook last called.'

'Where is it, then?' asked Molly, remembering the little bottle she'd seen the very first time she had entered that bedroom. She was thinking she'd take it to Annie McClure. She'd surely know what to do.

'Tweed must keep it in her room,' said Miss Cavendish. 'She never leaves it here for others to see.'

'Oh,' said Molly, trying to keep the fear out of her voice. It was one thing to have found the key to her employer's bedroom. If the worst came to the absolute worst she could always say that she'd heard Miss Cavendish crying out and that she and Mrs McGovern had been worried ... It was quite another to go rummaging where she could not possibly have any reason to be. To begin with, Miss Tweed had been present when she came in to clean; Molly was relieved when she stopped, as she'd thought she would never get over that creepy-crawly feeling of the woman's eyes on her back. If she'd locked Miss Cavendish's door, Miss Tweed was almost certain to have locked that room too. *But it doesn't need to be now, does it?*

'I lay the fire in there every day, and clean every other day, same as I do in here,' said Molly. 'But if I do find the medicine, surely she'll miss it?'

She would have to think of a way round that.

CHAPTER SEVEN

Laudanum

It took a few days, because Molly couldn't search Miss Tweed's entire room all at once. Each time she went into it, she would choose one drawer, or one row of books to look behind. Finally, moving an old-fashioned picture hat on the top shelf of the wardrobe, a hat that Molly had never seen Miss Tweed wear and couldn't imagine her doing so, she heard the unmistakable chink of glass. Her ears cocked to listen for Miss Tweed's approach, Molly carefully lifted out the hat, doing her best not to touch the scraggy black feathers that reminded her of cat-kill, and grasped one of the bottles, slipping it into her pocket. She carefully replaced the hat and clicked the wardrobe closed.

There were plenty of bottles, but Molly bet the companion had counted them. She'd have to think quick about what to do with this one.

In the quiet of her own room, Molly read the label. *Laudanum.* The word took her right back to the parlour in Roose Road, Mark sitting on the opposite side of the fireplace as she read aloud the novel Charles Dickens had been working on when he died. They'd had a lively conversation about how the book might have finished, with Mark teasing her to have a go herself. There'd been a lurid description of an opium den and the poor souls who drugged themselves into oblivion. In the comfort of the little parlour, with the babble of small children in the background, for Roose Road was never truly quiet even at night, Molly couldn't imagine human beings going into such an abyss.

'What's opium?' she'd asked Mark.

'Comes from the poppy plant, I believe. I was given some of it myself, I think.' He talked on into Molly's shocked silence. 'I mean under medical supervision. It's a sedative.'

Molly knew what was coming then, and could have kicked herself for asking that question.

'It deadens pain. I was given it when I was wounded. Laudanum's its hospital name. You still know you're suffering, but somehow the laudanum helps you bear it. It distances you from what you feel. I remember it tasted vile, though that might be because they put something in it to stop people swigging it, or a child giving it a try. The Victorians even gave it to babies to make them sleep, though I wouldn't say you get a proper sleep from it. More a stupor, really. But these days I'd be very surprised if you didn't need a prescription for it. It's strong stuff.'

Remembering Mark's words, Molly unstoppered the bottle carefully, sniffed, and wrinkled her nose. She pushed the stopper back in and held the bottle up to the light, swirling the tawny liquid, thinking, *If I didn't know better, I'd think that was sarsaparilla.*

*

It took some time to mix the contents of the bottles. To begin with, Molly tipped half of the laudanum away and filled the space with the Marsh's Sass she'd bought on her free Wednesday afternoon. Gradually, she had decided, she would replace the contents altogether. Molly's greatest fear was that Miss Tweed used the stuff herself, in addition to dosing Miss Cavendish with it. She watched the companion as carefully as she could without being obvious about it. She tried to reassure herself that if Miss Tweed *was* using, and encountered the sarsaparilla substitute, it was quite possible she would think the manufacturer was merely trying a more palatable compound, unless of course the woman was partial to a glass of Sass herself. Molly thought not, as there was none in the pantry, though it was the kind of harmless soft drink that she could imagine being served at the devout gatherings Miss Tweed would go to.

To her relief, Molly saw no change in Miss Tweed's behaviour. *Imagine if she* had *been taking a sedative and was still as crabby and suspicious as ever?* Miss Cavendish, on the other hand, grew visibly more alert, though, as she told Molly on the Dorcas afternoons, she still played dopey to put Miss Tweed off the scent.

But then things began to go wrong. The first sign was that Miss Cavendish would unexpectedly dissolve into tears, clutching at Molly's arm and crying out that she was falling down into a well, that it was dark there, that she would never get out again. This happened not only when they were alone, but also, to Molly's terror, when she came in with Miss Cavendish's meals.

Miss Tweed took alarm as well. Molly and Mrs McGovern would stand at the foot of the stairs and hear Miss Cavendish wailing and Miss Tweed's exasperated raised voice: 'What have *you* ever had to be unhappy about?'

'What's going on, Molly?' whispered the cook. 'You've not been yourself the last three weeks, so you haven't. You're hiding something, aren't ye?'

'I can't say,' she faltered. 'Miss Cavendish told me not to.'

*

Then the crisis came on an otherwise quiet evening.

'Dubber! Come up here now!' screamed Miss Tweed over the banisters.

Molly ran up the main staircase, not stopping to remove her apron or roll down her sleeves and fasten on clean cuffs – all of them rules laid down by Miss Tweed for her appearance above stairs.

The woman was standing in Miss Cavendish's doorway, shaking, though Molly couldn't tell if from fear or anger. Miss Tweed seized her shoulder and pushed her into the room so roughly she nearly stumbled.

'What have you done to her, you little witch? Miss Cavendish was fine until you came here, you with your simpering and curtseying. You've been putting something in her food, haven't you?'

Molly couldn't get out the words to refute this obvious calumny, though she thought them. *How could I have done? Mrs McGovern says you eat hers as well.* She was transfixed by what she saw in the bed. Miss Cavendish was moaning softly. Even from some feet away Molly could see she was drenched in sweat.

Her forehead gleamed, her normally fluffy white hair was lank and dark against her skull and there was an acrid tang to the air which was nothing to do with the contents of the commode. Sluicing that bucket was one of Molly's duties. Worst of all, the old woman was tearing at her eyelids – ineffectually, for there was no strength in those arthritis-crippled hands, and her nails were always kept short. The nurse trimmed them regularly, for Molly would be told to bring up a bowl of warm water to soften those old ridged claws.

Molly was white-lipped with fear. 'What did the nurse say?'

'Been and gone an hour ago. Thought she'd a slight fever but nothing out of the ordinary – not then. Don't gawp, girl. If you've no sensible suggestions then go and get Dr Sambrook.'

'Has she had her medicine?'

'Of course she has! But what do you know about that?'

'Nothing, I just thought—'

'Well, don't. He's in Infield Gardens. I'll write it down for you. You can read, can't you?'

'Of course.'

'Don't talk back, Dubber.' Miss Tweed rummaged in her bag and produced a notebook with a pencil attached. She scribbled in this then tore out the page.

'And hurry.'

Molly did. The address was only a short distance away, but she ran all the same, certain she was going to be sick from fear. *I stopped her taking her medicine, and now she's ill. I'll have to tell the doctor or she won't get better. Perhaps she'll die and it'll be all my fault. I'll go to prison.*

By the time Molly found the address and pulled the bell, she was crying uncontrollably. Through the stained-glass panels in the door she could see a faint glow of light. Eventually a dark blur appeared and moved towards her, but with agonising slowness.

'Yes?' said the parlourmaid, then peered at Molly under the porch light. 'Molly Dubber, in't it? From the Cottage Homes? Whatever's up wi' you?' The girl frowned, then said, 'If you're in trouble, you'll get no help here. Dr Sambrook don't do that work.'

Molly at last found her tongue. 'I'm not in trouble. It's my mistress. She's very ill.'

The girl's eyes swept down to her caller's feet and back again. Molly remembered her now. She'd lived in one of the other houses and was two or three years older than her. Jane, she thought she was called.

'Talk right proper for a scullery maid, don't you?' said Jane, reminding Molly that she'd rushed out in her apron. Cleaning the stove now seemed hours ago.

'Doctor is indisposed,' Jane went on. 'It'll have to be Dr Keating. You'd better come this way.'

'Where is he? He's not here, is he?'

Jane gave her a withering glance and pointed at something black and shiny crouched on the hall table. It looked to Molly like a kitchen weighing scales, incongruously topped off with something like a matador's hat, known to her only thanks to Mr Mee's *Children's Encyclopaedia*, back in the parlour at Roose Road.

'I shall speak to Dr Keating and then pass him to you.'

Molly watched open-mouthed as Jane lifted the matador's hat and twirled her finger in the machine below it. There was a scratchy sound then that Molly realised was distant human speech. Jane spoke a number. There was a pause, some clicks, then Molly heard Jane ask for Dr Keating. A pause, then more scratching sounds, and Jane said, 'I believe it is urgent, yes. The patient's servant is here . . . Yes, directly.' Then to Molly's astonishment Jane held the matador's hat out to her.

'Go on then,' said Jane, impatient. 'Doctors are busy men, you know.'

Thus Molly made the first telephone call of her life, relieved that the disembodied voice, though refined, sounded kind.

'I'll be straight over,' the doctor said, after listening to Molly's confused account of Miss Cavendish's symptoms. 'Wait for me at Sambrook's.'

*

Sitting beside the doctor in the leather upholstery of Dr Keating's Austin Seven, Molly longed to hold onto something, for she had never been in a car before and it felt as though they were travelling at the speed of wind. She was astonished that the doctor could talk and drive at the same time. Looking at his profile, she wondered how much she could tell him. Surely an intelligent man like that would read the guilt in her face? Instead, he asked her to tell him when it was that Miss Cavendish's behaviour had changed, and how. Molly found herself, like him, raising her voice against the rumble of the car.

*

'You aren't Dr Sambrook,' said Miss Tweed, the moment the doctor appeared in the doorway. 'I told that stupid girl to get Dr Sambrook. You look a bit young.'

'My colleague is indisposed,' said Keating, advancing towards the bed, not even turning his eyes, Molly saw, to Miss Tweed. 'And Miss Dubber appears to me to be anything but stupid. But I am thankful for the fact you consider forty to be young.'

Miss Tweed turned her rage on Molly. 'Don't stand there gawping. Get back downstairs.'

Molly backed out of the doorway.

'Wait, Miss Dubber, if you will,' said the doctor. He was bending over Miss Cavendish, his fingers on her wrist. Molly was relieved that the old lady was less agitated than she had been when Miss Tweed had called her – how long ago? It felt like ages, but when Molly looked at the kitchen clock later, she realised she could only have been out forty minutes at most.

'In fact, come over here.'

Molly obeyed, standing waiting at the far side of the bed. Miss Cavendish turned her head slowly and met her eyes, giving her a timid smile that wrenched Molly's heart.

'I'm sorry,' Molly heard herself say, and started to cry.

'Leave us, would you?' said the doctor.

'You've only just asked her to come back,' snapped Miss Tweed.

'Precisely. Would *you* leave, madam?'

Miss Tweed's mouth opened in a perfect circle. 'Well, I never.' But she obediently gathered up her bag and stalked out of the room, her nose in the air.

The moment the door closed, Dr Keating looked at Molly and said, 'Right, out with it. You gave me a pretty accurate description of laudanum withdrawal symptoms, and everything I see in my patient confirms that.'

Molly thought she had never talked so much in her life. The whole story tumbled out willy-nilly, the doctor occasionally interjecting for clarification. The calmness of his expression eventually had its effect, making her slow her pace. When she said 'Marsh's Sass', she saw Keating's face go into a kind of spasm. His eyebrows went up and the corner of his mouth twitched, but he immediately mastered himself.

Her tale told, she took a deep breath and rushed out, 'Will I go to prison, sir?'

The doctor smiled at last. 'Not if I have anything to do with it. If anyone should, it's your Miss Tweed. I'm pretty sure what she's done contravenes the Dangerous Drugs Act. I wish you'd come to me earlier, though, Miss Dubber. Laudanum withdrawal is a serious business. And I can't imagine what Sambrook was doing prescribing it in the first place.'

'Perhaps he never did, sir. Or not for Miss Cavendish. For Miss Tweed.'

A reedy voice spoke up then. 'Molly's a good girl. A clever one. And a truthful one, doctor.'

'And a friend to you, Miss Cavendish. I tell you what we'll do now. I'll be prescribing laudanum officially this time, but in very small quantities, to wean you off it. Marsh's Sass is a healthful drink, but as you've seen, it can't deal with the symptoms you've been experiencing. I shall acquaint my colleague with what I'm doing, but I wonder if you would be willing to let me care for you from now on?'

Miss Cavendish nodded emphatically.

'I think I should give you a thorough examination, if you feel able. I may need Molly's help, if you and she are agreeable.'

'Yes, doctor.'

What happened next was something that Molly was never able to forget. The doctor turned down the covers, exposing Miss Cavendish's pale, stork-like legs. He lifted a foot gently, turned it from side to side. Molly glimpsed a reddening at the back of the heel, a smear of blood on the undersheet.

'I feared as much,' he said. 'Miss Cavendish, I'm going to move you onto your side now and look at your rear view.'

'My backside, you mean?'

'Well, yes, that and your legs and back. It may pain you a bit, so I want Molly to hold your hand while I do so. Are you ready?'

Molly's heart was wrenched as the old woman was rolled, grimacing, onto her side. But beyond a small gasp, accompanied by tears of pain leaking from her eyes, she made no sound. The doctor eased up the nightdress. Molly heard him exhale, but all he said was, 'I would advise you, Miss Cavendish, to dispense with the services of the nurse.'

'Gladly,' said Miss Cavendish. 'Tweed found the creature.'

'I'll get you someone reliable, if you'll permit me. In the meantime, if you're both willing, I'd like to show Molly how to dress these sores. Would you come round this side, Molly?'

*

Three weeks later Molly breathlessly recounted the whole episode to a sympathetic Annie McClure.

'I've not had a day off until now. There was so much to do. But the new nurse is in place and she seems very capable. It wasn't very dignified for poor Miss Cavendish to have me and Cook getting her on and off the commode.'

'And Miss Tweed?'

'I was right. She had got Dr Sambrook to prescribe the laudanum for her. For women's problems, though Dr Keating was a bit rude about that and said she must be a good way beyond them by now. The laudanum was to keep Miss Cavendish quiet and probably it did ease the pain of the sores. Poor old lady – she's so frail and undefended, Mother Annie. Only the doctor says that it was the drugs made her weaker. She was so sedated all she could manage to do was lie in that bed. She gets up now, into an invalid chair, and I push her along the landing into the front drawing room. It's a pretty room, with all the dust sheets gone and we look out of the bay window and she tells me about all the people who used to come to the house, right from the parties she had when she was a little girl, but she only had brothers, so sometimes she was lonely. They were sent away to school, but she had a governess. I don't know why she never married. There were photographs of her when she was younger, under the dust sheets. She was really lovely, with a wistful look, though I'm sure I don't know how she managed to breathe, with corsets that tight. But perhaps she never met anyone, cooped up in that big house the way she was. Oh, and I nearly forgot. I've to ask you if there's anyone could come to be the new maid of all work.'

'You're *leaving* after all that?'

'No. Miss Cavendish has asked me to be her companion. Even though she will keep saying it won't be for long.'

'Well, that's an honour, surely?'

'She said why go to the bother of putting an advertisement in *The Lady* or putting up with whatever moth-eaten specimen the Distressed Gentlefolk people would send her next – that's the way she said it, Mother Annie – when she knew me and trusted me?'

'So what happened to Miss Tweed in the end? Did they arrest her?'

'She's gone on the Missions.'

'What, like that gospel wagon we saw the time we all went to Morecambe?'

'No, China.'

'*China?*'

'Dr Keating thought it was the best thing. She swore blind she'd never meant any harm to Miss Cavendish. Only Miss Tweed *did* have some laudanum left over from when she'd had problems with her monthlies. She could see the old lady was in pain from the arthritis and thought she'd try her with a small dose. That worked so well – or made Miss Cavendish so easy to deal with because she was dopey with it – that she went back and got more, until she'd got quite a stockpile. Her religious friends thought her the cat's whiskers, you see.'

'Perhaps she did good things with them. She was bitter and twisted with you, maybe, because she saw a girl full of gifts starting out on life, when she'd not made of it what she thought she could.'

'Mother Annie, why is it you're always so *kind*?' said Mollie affectionately. 'Anyway, Miss Tweed might be on that boat already.'

'Poor thing,' said Annie. 'Such a long journey. I've only crossed the Irish Sea.'

'And I've not been anywhere.'

'Yet.'

'Miss Tweed is going to teach and help out in a mission hospital. Dr Keating had some ideas about that – meaning, do the Chinese really want people coming from the other side of the world to tell them what to think? Only they have this horrible custom of folding up little girls' feet and bandaging them tightly so they only grow to half their size and it's one of the mission's aims to stop that. He said that, as a doctor, he couldn't object to anyone trying to prevent that.'

CHAPTER EIGHT

Isandlwana

'There was a piano here once,' said Miss Cavendish. 'It was in that corner, near the window.'

'What happened to it? I loved playing the piano in Roose Road.'

Miss Cavendish sighed. 'Miss Tweed must've stolen it.'

'How could Miss Tweed steal a piano? Where would she put it?'

'She dealt with all the tradesmen. The last girl wouldn't have questioned anything she did, and if Cook saw it go she wouldn't have thought it her place to object. And Tweed wouldn't have seen it as stealing. She'd have seen it as doing the Lord's work. It'll be in a church hall somewhere, with someone bashing out "Onward Christian Soldiers" for the Sunday School children. I don't mind that, not really. I haven't been able to play myself for a while.' Miss Cavendish stretched out her hands, the fingers knotted by arthritis. 'At least it's getting used. But it was the way Miss Tweed preached about it: "And do not forget to do good and to share with others, for with such sacrifices God is pleased." Easy for her to say that, because she wasn't sharing anything of her own. I never knew her to do that.'

'How did she come to be your companion?'

'The Distressed Gentlefolks people contacted me. She'd been a governess out in India, but the family had fallen on hard times because the father gambled. So there was nothing to pay her with, and she had no one to defend her; I believe she'd been a curate's daughter, but had no family left and the Association paid to get her home. I was less able to get about and thought a former governess would be an appropriate companion, and that, because she'd had those reverses in life, she might be a kinder person for it, not the embittered person she turned out to be. But I felt sorry for her and thought she might change in time.'

'Perhaps if you were born in India the idea of a long journey to China isn't so strange,' said Molly.

'I hoped her religious friends would have done something for her, and they did,' said Miss Cavendish. 'She lived for them, after all.'

Molly glanced at her employer, but there was no sarcasm in either her voice or her expression.

'You see, Molly, as a woman it's hard to make your way but because of an accident of birth, harder for you than for me, except in ways that teach you to be strong. You see, I wasn't allowed to do anything for myself, whereas you'll have to do everything. I've never wanted for anything, moneywise, I mean, and I've never had to earn my living; I'll be asking you to look at the accountant's letters for me, so you'll see I live off property and investments. But there are two bits of advice I would give you: get some education, or a skill, if you can. And never expect others to put food in your mouth.'

'I was good at school. I wanted to stay on,' said Molly in a small voice. 'Mrs McClure wanted it too, only the Borough Councillors said I was to go into service.'

'But you're not in service now. A lady's companion is different.'

'True. And I am grateful . . .'

'But? No, don't answer that,' said Miss Cavendish. 'I know this is no life for a young woman, shut up in this mausoleum of a house with just an old woman and a cook for company. But you won't live it for long.'

'You're sending me away?' said Molly in confusion.

'No. *I'll* be sent away,' said Miss Cavendish, smiling. 'Once I'm boxed up the house will be emptied and sold. Perhaps a family will come here and the nursery will be a nursery again.' Miss Cavendish tailed off, looking out at the trees. 'What I dreamed of,' she said, but Molly wasn't sure if she was talking to her or to herself.

'Miss Cavendish?' she said softly.

'Isandlwana.'

'Pardon?'

'A battle during the Zulu War in what is now South Africa,' said Miss Cavendish. 'My life died with him.'

'I'm sorry,' said Molly, reaching for Miss Cavendish's cool, gnarled hand. 'What was his name?'

'I haven't spoken it for years. My Lionel. He wasn't brought home, of course. I've got a photograph of the cemetery somewhere, but not of his grave. There are trees, and a little wall around it. It gives me some comfort, though, because until I was sent that card I thought he was lying out on some hill, with the birds picking his bones clean.' Miss Cavendish shivered.

Molly pressed the hand she held, but only enough for the old lady to know that she was listening.

'But what about you, Molly? You're fifteen, aren't you?'

'Not quite.'

Have you a sweetheart?'

'No . . .'

'No, *but,* that sounds like.'

Molly found herself talking about Mark as she had never spoken to anyone, not even to herself.

'I mean, he's really the only lad I've ever got to know at all, apart from Mr McClure, who's like my father. No, he *is* my father. He brought me up.'

Molly saw Miss Cavendish nod her approval.

'So I can't say if Mark is the one for me or if it's just because he's there. I daresay you'd tell me there are others out there who would do just as well, only I don't know them. And what if I made myself not think about him only to find when it was too late that he was the only one I really wanted?'

'You talk like a much older girl, Molly. Aren't you a bit young to talk that way?'

'It's the way we talk in the Cottage Home. I wanted to stay at the school, but as I couldn't, then it's service or the jute works or getting married, in't it?'

'Not necessarily, not that I'm any model for you to follow. But your Mark – do you think you can "not think about him"?'

'No. But it's no use anyway.'

'Why's it no use?'

'He's never said anything. Never let on that he might be sweet on me. He maybe thinks I'm just a silly little girl because he's that bit older than me. I think he must be about twenty-eight. He was in the war – well, I told you that. Lied about his age to get there, he said, and sent back blind.'

'Hmm. That's quite an age difference now. I can see that. But over the course of a lifetime it shrinks. Does that mean that you've always known him?'

'Almost. I came to Barrow when I was three. He wasn't always there. Mother Annie said he was in a hospital somewhere, when they were trying to repair him. Then he was in a place where they trained him. First it was baskets and things, then someone tried him at the piano tuning and he turned out to be good at that. Only, from what Mother Annie says, the work is never secure. Now that the talking films are coming in, the cinema pianists are losing their jobs, and if a piano isn't getting pounded every night and at the matinees then they're not going to be tuned so often, are they? And now finding work is difficult for everybody. When I was back in Roose Road on Sunday they were talking about the men who go back and forth across the Irish Sea, in the hope of work in Belfast when the hours are short in Vickers. It's so hard on them and their poor families, with all that uncertainty.'

'You've a mature way of looking at the world, Molly, but you've the impatience of the young. You *are* only not quite fifteen. Even if you were to marry at sixteen you'd need your father's consent so I imagine that would be Mr McClure or whoever the authority would be at the Borough Council. There's one thing I must ask you, though, Molly. About Mark being blind. Pity is a kind of cousin to love, I think and you're a kind person; it's not that you feel sorry for him, is it?'

Molly opened her eyes wide, thinking. 'No,' she said eventually. 'I don't think so.'

'Because, in my narrow experience, men don't like to be pitied, even from the best of intentions.'

'I've never known him when he wasn't blind. I don't mean that I forget that he is. I mean, I got to know him by reading to him. I can't imagine doing that for a sighted man. I saw every expression cross his face while he was listening to me, more than I'd see in the normal way of things. Sometimes I saw a tenderness in his look, but I never knew if it was because of what I was reading or if it was the sound of my voice.'

'It could be both.'

'Maybe. But I know that he would hate it – just hate it – if he thought I pitied him. It would go against everything he believes in – he does all this work for the National League of the Blind. Jobs not charity. Dignity, not coins in a hat.'

'Do you know if women like him, other than you, I mean?'

'Mother Annie says they do. She said that when he was learning the piano tuning that there were ladies – I mean ladies, not working women. The kind as have time to do good works. Only he wouldn't have anything much to do with them. Said he didn't want to be anybody's pet cause. So he lives alone, in the rooms he was brought up in. That's what he told me, anyway. I've never been to his home. I've a feeling, though, that

KATIE HUTTON

he's always been a bit lonely. Mother Annie showed me a photograph of him, when he was a little lad, in school up in Cleator
Moor. He's looking straight at the camera and he looks so sad.
His brother Joe is in the group as well, only he's older and looks
more confident. Mother Annie said the other children in the
class made Mark's life a misery, because his father had gone off
and left the family. Joe, on the other hand, would knock anybody down who gave him any lip about it. *He* didn't care if the
teachers thrashed him for it.'

'Has Mark ever given you any indication that he might
return your feelings?'

Molly sighed. 'He said something odd to me the day I left.
About being sure that I was the most beautiful girl he'd ever
had the misfortune to meet. I've puzzled about that many times
since,' she said eventually. 'He's a very correct person – upstand-
ing you might say. Mother Annie and the Borough Councillors
are very strict in investigating any of the positions girls are sent
out to. She told me they have to be. There are some men would
take advantage, she said. There's a lady from the Association
for Friendless Girls who works with her sometimes on finding
the places. She's always made out she had some dark stories to
tell but I was never let to hear them. But I *did* hear things, from
the girls I was at school with. Mark was never like them men,
never; you'd think they were wolves done up in collar and tie
and watch chain, to hear what was said about them. Only I did
wonder sometimes if Mark was afraid he'd be thought he was
like them, being that bit older, I mean.'

'Have you seen him on your Sundays off?'

'Sometimes. But he's like Mrs McClure's little brother, in a way, seeing as her father married his mother and brought him up. So I have no idea if he comes around because he knows I'll be there or because he was calling on them anyway. He looks pleased though when I am there.'

'I wish I still had my little piano. You could bring him here to tune it and I'd tell you what I thought.'

'What would you do if you were me, Miss Cavendish?'

'What I *would* do if I were you and what I *ought* to do if I were you might be two different things, Molly. My advice for the moment would be to do nothing. You can hardly take a run at him, after all. If you still care for him two years from now – and I know two years must seem an eternity when you're only pushing fifteen of them – then I would confide in Mrs McClure. She, of all people, would want what was best for you both.'

'Two years,' said Molly, crestfallen.

'It's not long, really, though a lot can happen. I doubt you'll be here in two years' time, but I hope you'll see me out, Molly.'

CHAPTER NINE

Thorncliffe Cemetery

Eighteen months later Molly had her second ride in a motor car. This one proceeded with dignified slowness. Looking out of the window she saw men briefly pull off their caps as the hearse passed. Some people crossed themselves. She looked down at the blacks Robert McClure had found for her ('that used to be what I made most, before we got the post at the Cottage Home'). A tear dripped onto her folded hands. Beside her, Dr Keating murmured, 'You were her friend when she thought she had none.'

The hearse glided under the central arch of the imposing gateway on Devonshire Road. Molly looked out at the weeping Victorian angels and Gothic pinnacles of the richer graves and thought, *people build fine tombstones the same way they build fine houses, but we all go in the same earth. I knew your name was Maud from dealing with your letters. But until the vicar said it, maybe nobody called you that since Lionel. You were always Miss Cavendish to all of us.*

The huddle at the graveside was a small one. Besides Mrs McGovern and the doctor, there was a visibly impatient middle-aged man who stood some distance apart, with another man

Molly didn't know. As the little group moved away and the grave-diggers stepped forward to replace the earth, this man caught up with Dr Keating to ask if he knew where he might get hold of 'the deceased's companion, a Miss Dubber.'

'This is Miss Dubber.'

'Oh!' said the man, unable to conceal his surprise. 'I'm David Somers, the deceased's man of business. I thought you'd be older. Your letters . . .'

'They were mainly dictated by Miss Cavendish, sir.'

'But the arrangements for today . . . you must have had to make them yourself.'

'Myself and Dr Keating, sir. I informed her nephew too but perhaps the letter didn't arrive in time.'

'It did, it did. That is George Cavendish,' said Mr Somers, indicating the impatient man, hurriedly getting into the car that had brought him. 'Quite overcome with grief, don't you know? I'd best follow him. I'll be in touch, Miss Dubber.' He touched his hat and hurried off.

Overcome with grief but he never wrote, never came to see her.

*

'What'll you do next, Molly?' asked Mrs McGovern, pouring the tea for both of them.

Molly looked around the kitchen that had been sanctuary to her in her early days in Croslands Park Road.

'We've our wages to the end of the quarter, you and me. Mr Somers said so. But we'll both have to be out long before then. The nephew wants to sell. Mother Annie is looking for a new position for me. She doesn't think I'll do as a lady's companion again, or at least not straightaway. I'm too young – and though she didn't say it in so many words, she knows I don't sound posh enough. I can pass as a parlourmaid, though,' she added, thinking of Dr Sambrook's Jane. 'What about you?'

'I'm going home. Back to Belcoo. I wonder will I recognise the place after all this time. I wonder if it'll recognise me?'

*

Annie McClure held both Molly's hands and looked at her intently, her head on one side.

'Molly Dubber, you've grown. I don't mean you've got bigger – though you are a bit taller, right enough. It's true what they say, isn't it? Experience teaches. Only most girls don't expect to deal with laudanum poisoning, piano stealing and bed sores in their first position.'

'Poor lady. I'll miss her. She had such a lonely life, but she was so kind to me.'

'Because you were kind to *her*, Molly. *And* you're sharp as a tack. You knew something wasn't right there.'

'She wanted to leave me some money, Mother Annie. Mr Somers said so. Only she didn't get her will changed in time. He showed me her letter. She'd written it herself, though it must have been painful for her. I remember her giving me a letter, all folded up, and asking me to address the envelope as her handwriting was so wobbly, and not to look at the letter. I didn't, of course. I wrote the envelope and sealed it up and put the stamp on in front of her. Mr Somers said he'd try to see if he could get the money for me anyway, as Miss Cavendish's intentions were so clear. It's not as if her nephew would miss it, he said.'

'How much is it?'

'It's a hundred pounds.'

'Oh!'

*

'I thought maybe the branch in Rawlinson Street,' said Robert McClure. 'It looks more like a corner shop than a bank. They'll maybe treat us more personally there. That's a lot of money you've come into, you know.'

'I do. Mr Somers wasn't sure I'd be given it, only he said he appealed to Mr Cavendish's better nature – to respect his aunt's wishes, I mean. I was only to have it, Mr Cavendish told him, when I was of age. It was to be put by for me until then.'

'That's fair enough. Put it in Martins Bank and it'll be worth more when you take it out again.'

Mollie thought the bank looked more like an undertaker's than a corner shop, though it was indeed on a corner. It was the curtains that hung from halfway up the plate glass windows, and in the panel of the door that gave that impression, as though whatever went on inside was discreet and private. But Martins Bank it said, in gilt lettering across the windows, and painted on the wooden strip above.

At the oak counter inside, the manager was all courtesy, though after nodding to Molly and shaking her hand, he addressed all his questions to Robert, referring to her as 'our young lady customer' *as though I haven't a tongue in my head.* Then, as the forms were being completed, she realised that none of this would have been possible without Robert. Neither a 'young lady' nor an older one would get to open an account without her father, husband or guardian's say so.

'Do you have proof of our young lady's age, Mr McClure?'

Robert took an envelope out of his inside pocket and produced a folded-up piece of paper.

'That'll do nicely,' said the manager, and smoothing out the paper, started to copy some details from it. Looking at it upside down, Molly saw a coat of arms, a crouched lion and rearing unicorn and the words 'Certificate of Birth'. There it was, all that was known about the little girl from Manchester, reduced to an official document.

Once they were outside, Robert said, patting his jacket, 'I have to keep the certificate, until you're of age, but this is yours.' He handed over the bank book in its smooth green cover. Molly thought coats of arms were funny things. The birth certificate had had animals on it too. This one had a grasshopper and a pelican. She opened it and gave a cry of dismay.

'But this is someone else's. My name's not Ashworth.'

'That's your name, Molly. Your real name.'

She stared at him, speechless. 'So why have I always been Dubber?'

Robert looked away. Molly hated his awkwardness, his evident embarrassment.

'The Guardians decided that. They'll have had their reasons.'

'Let me see it – the certificate.'

Robert unfolded it. Her eyes scanned the copperplate. Her father – a foundry worker, name of Stanley – and her mother, Mary. This was as Annie McClure had told her – only Stanley Ashworth's occupation was new to her, and of course his surname. There was her date of birth and it was the same day her birthday had always been celebrated in Roose Road. There was a Manchester address but it stirred no memory.

'Ashworth? I don't know what to call myself, Mr McClure.'

'Who do you feel you are, Molly?'

'Dubber – I think. I've always been Dubber to you and Mother Annie. So I'll go on being Dubber. I'll just have to remember I'm Ashworth when I'm in there,' she said, tilting her head towards the bank. 'I mean, I won't need it otherwise, will I?'

'Only when you wed, maybe.'

'When I give it up to be called something else again.'

'Right enough.'

'Yes. I'll go on being Dubber. I don't know what reasons the Guardians had, but until I do know, then whatever they were is nobody's business but mine, is it?'

'That's wise. Will you come back to Roose Road for a bit? Annie was expecting news this morning.'

*

'You'd be a servant again – housemaid-cum-parlourmaid. You'd be given a character for whichever one you wanted, after,' said Annie. 'I'm told the work is quite light – your employer is away quite a lot of the time. But not everyone would take to the place, or to him. He's known to be a bit eccentric. He said on the form he wants an "intelligent girl more than one who knows how to black a grate". And I'm a bit worried you'll feel a bit out of the way. You wouldn't be able to walk home from there.'

'Where is it, then?'

'It's still Barrow, I suppose. You get the train to Furness Abbey Station and they'd collect you from there. It'd just be you, the cook and another girl who comes in and a man who does the garden.'

'So, like Croslands Park Road without Miss Cavendish?'

'Mr Gascarth has a library, and a piano.'

'He'll not want his servants reading his books or playing waltzes, though.'

Annie hesitated. 'He might just. I think that's why he sent away the last girl. Because she didn't appreciate books and music.'

Molly stared. 'Whatever's he expecting of a servant?'

'Do you want to go and find out?'

'I'll have to, I suppose. Cook and me have to be out of Croslands Park in a week. Even if I had been able to draw on what Miss Cavendish left me I wouldn't have. She was always so clear about how I should earn my own crust. I've an idea she wished she'd been let to get her own money herself. Mr Somers told me he found receipts for donations she'd made to Mrs Pankhurst.'

'I've not seen the place myself but Mrs Studholme from the Friendless Girls has inspected.'

'I'm not friendless, am I?'

'I know you're not. But if the cook didn't live in, you'd not be going there, Molly. No Barrow Union girl woulda been sent under a single man's roof. I'm just afraid you'll be lonely.'

'There's the other girl, in't there?' said Molly. 'I could make friends with her,' though in truth that was the bit that worried her most. What if this other girl lorded it over her, or made it weigh on her that she was a workhouse brat? Or made out she was giving herself airs because she'd been a lady's companion, even if only briefly? When Molly had been at school anyone who had a mother and father to go home to seemed to think that put them one above her, though she had brazened that out, getting prizes for reading aloud and sums just to show them. And there'd been Myrtle, always steadfast.

'I hope you do,' said Annie. 'It's not as if you'll have other girls to go to if you fall out. But you'll manage. You outwitted Miss Tweed.'

'I don't mind quietness. But tell me more about the master, the one who wants me to be clever. He'll be some old josser, won't he?'

'Molly! I didn't bring you up to be disrespectful, did I?'

'No, you didn't,' the girl admitted. 'I'd never say that to his face, mind.'

'Nor to anyone else's, Molly. Anyway, he's not an old josser. Anthony Gascarth can't be much above thirty.'

'Old, then. Older than Mark, even,' said Molly. 'What's wrong with him that he hasn't a wife?'

'Nothing, so far as I know, only that he had a bad time in the war, they say. He could only have been young – maybe no more than eighteen when he joined up. He keeps himself to himself, that's all. More interested in books than people, said Mrs Studholme. He specifically asked for a girl who knows her alphabet and won't put books back in the wrong order after she's dusted them.' Annie decided to keep to herself what Mrs Studholme had also reported Mr Gascarth had said: 'Don't send me some halfwit, like the last one.' The 'halfwit' had come back to Barrow in tears, but now apparently gave great satisfaction to a demanding mistress in a rambling house in Fairfield Lane.

CHAPTER TEN

Lindal Hall, May 1933

It was only a short run to the station at the abbey, a route Molly had gone a number of times, but today it felt quicker than ever. Her bravado had left her as the train chugged away from all she had ever known: past the hulking ship under construction at Vickers, past the teeming, crouching streets surrounding the yard, past the little boys in caps too large for them, waving up at the carriage. Now, standing at the halt with her small suitcase at her feet, she was a world away, not a mere fistful of miles, in the quiet green hollow where the red sandstone ruins of the abbey nestled. Her eyes pricking, she remembered going to picnics there with the other children from the Cottage Homes, table-cloths spread out on the grass at the foot of the natural amphitheatre, and afterwards, when everything had been cleared away – both the McClures insistent that no rubbish should be left behind – the chance to roll down the embankment, grass stains looked upon indulgently. It was one of those few days when Molly felt she'd been allowed the freedom a boy had as his right.

'You the lass for the Hall?' said the man on the trap. Even his accent sounded different to Molly. Barrow's voices had that unique mixture of Ulster Irish, Cornish, Scots – all those men and women who had washed into the town that had submerged the village it had been. Working in the shipyard, the wireworks, the paper mills, the jute mill – these milling crowds left their imprint on the new generation, born far from the towns and villages and fields their fathers and mothers had had to abandon.

'That's me. Miss Molly Dubber.'

'Don't take it amiss, Miss Molly Dubber, if I don't learn your name. You'll likely not be staying long. You girls don't as a rule.'

All the excitement Molly had felt at the sight of a cart sent exclusively for herself and the suitcase Mrs McClure had lent her, seeped out of her like the air from a pierced rubber ball.

'Your bag first, then you,' said the carter. Molly handed it up. Then the man's great paw of a hand reached down, hauling her up to sit alongside him.

'I intend to give complete satisfaction,' she said primly to the pony's ears, not wanting to see the carter's reaction.

'Mebbe,' he said after whistling to the animal. 'There's some'd call the Master a queer mak of a chap, but he's never been awkert with me.' The remainder of the short journey was passed in silence.

*

'Is this it?' said Molly, in disbelief.

'That's the place,' said the driver. 'What were you expectin'? Barrow Town Hall?'

Molly started. She had indeed been expecting a grander and more formal place. Instead, Lindal Hall was a big but irregular farmhouse, with stumpy chimney pots that looked too heavy for the slate roof.

'Coom on, then,' he said, jumping down. The cart rocked gently; Molly clutched onto the seat. 'I've to get yem.'

'Yem?'

'*Home,*' he said, lifting down her case and then reaching his hand up for her.

'Oh ... yes, of course.' She tipped forward, but the man caught her and stood her down beside the cart.

'Don't weigh much, do you?' he said, not unkindly. 'How old ista?'

'Sixteen.'

'Sixteen, eh? My daughter's age. She's in service at Ambleside.' He looked away from her, fiddling with the horse's bridle.

Molly picked up her suitcase and blinked back tears. *Home,* she thought.

A rattle of harness behind her brought her back to the present. The driver was back up on his seat.

'I'll wish you luck, then,' he said, touching his cap. Molly felt a tiny surge of hopefulness. Nobody had ever touched his cap to her before.

'Thank you, sir,' she said, remembering her manners.

The driver murmured something unintelligible and the cart rumbled away.

Molly stared at the house, trying to read it from the outside. The house stared back from diamond-paned windows. It was like nowhere she had ever seen. In Barrow buildings had sharp edges; even the simplest terraced houses had angles, the bricks laid straight, windows a symmetrical distance from each other. This one looked as though it had grown out of the earth, its walls uneven, its windows haphazardly placed.

In Roose Road there'd been a garden but it had had to work for its living. Mr McClure, standing between the rows of runner beans and potatoes, had taught her all she needed to know about which vegetables to grow, whilst leaning on his stick; that old pit injury prevented him bending and weeding. 'My wee trowel,' he'd called her, a name she had treasured. Croslands Park Road had had a dull swathe of lawn, edged by dank bushes she didn't know the names of. Instead, Lindal Hall was surrounded by a riot of colour, flowers she knew more from the bright illlustrations in *The Children's Encyclopædia* than from real life: hollyhocks, Canterbury bells, foxgloves. Some of the plants were nearly as tall as she was. In Roose Road paths had been as straight as the Roman roads she'd read about in school; here, a cinder track wound its way into all that abundance. *I might like this place,* she thought. *Only what about the people?* She looked along the track for the carter, though the thud, thud of the pony's hooves and the creak of the harness had already died away. He'd said little, but Molly clung to that softening in his voice when he'd mentioned his own daughter. *Wouldn't it have been better for her to come here instead of me?* Then she remembered what she'd been told about Mr Gascarth being more bothered about books than blacked grates. Yet she couldn't repress entirely a little flash of jealousy at the thought of the carter's girl growing up in the midst of this lush green-ery, with a mother and father to love her. *Stop it Molly,* she told herself. *Mr and Mrs McClure love you like a mam and dad, even though they don't have to.*

'Are you going to grace us with your presence, or do you intend to go on admiring the view?' said a voice.

CHAPTER ELEVEN

Anthony Gascarth

Molly jumped. How long had that man been leaning against the door frame watching her? She felt foolish. *All this time, probably. He must've known when the train arrived and he'll have heard the cart.* She had an impression of floppy brown hair, lankiness, and clothes that looked as though they had adapted to the man who wore them: no collar to his shirt, a tweed jacket grown soft with use, corduroy trousers above mud-splashed boots. Molly remembered she wasn't supposed to stare and dropped her gaze.

'Sorry, sir,' she said, and bobbed a curtsey, remembering Annie McClure's advice: 'Always be polite and deferential, Molly, even if you don't feel like it. The way we have to be when the Board of Guardians come on an inspection.'

She saw the man straighten up; he was taller than the lintel of the door. *Does he have to bend to live in his own house?* She picked up her bag and wound her way through the bee-buzzing flowers, coming to a halt on flagstones in front of the house. Anthony Gascarth might have been watching her since she got down from the cart, but now he looked everywhere but at her.

For a moment he reminded her of Mark and the way his sightless brown eyes would flicker over her face but be unable to meet her gaze. This man *could* see, but didn't want to, she thought.

'Dubber, isn't it?'

She remembered just in time not to say, 'Me name's Molly.'

'Yes, sir.'

'I expect you're thirsty,' he said, turning and ducking into the house.

'Yes, sir. Thank you, sir.' She followed him into a cool, dark space, suppressing a gasp at the oddities she saw: dark, varnished furniture as irregular as the house itself, a riot of carved panelling around the walls. Every chair back seemed to be made of knotted wood, sculpted into tendrils of ivy through which mysterious faces peered. The space she stood in was not quite an entrance hall nor quite a dining room. It was both. Although there was a deep fireplace, Molly thought it must be very hard to keep such a room warm in winter, the way the front door opened straight onto it. But the most astonishing thing was the massive table dominating the room.

'You get company, sir?' she asked, counting the number of places. Twenty.

'Not really – well, not for years, anyway. That table can't be taken out without taking an axe to it. They built it in here, so here it stays. No need to gawp like that,' he added, turning his back to her. 'You'll get to know it all well enough with the beeswax. Kitchen's this way.'

Molly followed him through a low doorway, her boots sounding louder as the uneven boards of the entrance hall gave way to flagstones. An old-fashioned range reared up in front of her, blacked to perfection. A plate rack snaked its way round the room, just above the level of her head. Molly wondered if the meat dishes up there were ever fetched down and used, though they did look clean. *I'd be afraid of dropping them. That stone floor won't take prisoners.* A deal table occupied the centre of the room, bleached almost white. She smelled the vinegar used to clean it, and the waft of dried herbs hanging from a pulley. Copper saucepans gleamed on hooks; *it's baking soda does that,* thought Molly, as she calculated quickly how much work the kitchen would take, just to keep it clean. She thought regretfully of the flowers she'd just walked through. There'd be no time for her to tend the garden with everything that awaited her attention indoors. *Someone else must do the planting and that.* Then she remembered going with Annie McClure to Miss Cavendish's that first time. Where was the servants' entrance here? There had to be some other way in. She might never be allowed to walk that cinder path through the flowers again. *But where is everybody?*

'Jepson's gone to see her cousin in Dalton,' said the man as if she had spoken. 'And the other girl is on her half-holiday. I arranged it that way.'

Molly gaped at him, but he didn't see it. Anthony Gascarth continued not to look at her but to stare out the window at the blur of foliage and sunshine.

'You'll want to see your room, I suppose. It's up here next to Jepson's – that's the cook, by the way.'

'Yes, sir, thank you, sir.'

'Bring your case, then.' He took hold of a handle in the wainscot, simple dark panelling in contrast to the riot of carved

82

tendrils and faces she had glimpsed in the hallway. It opened onto a narrow spiral staircase that looked to Molly to be embedded in the wall. It certainly wasn't designed for a man of Gascarth's height, and indeed she saw him duck. This Jepson couldn't be very big then – not as big as Mrs McGovern. Someone like her would get stuck on this stair. She followed Gascarth's disappearing feet up into a bedroom on the landing. This was furnished spartanly, in complete contrast to what she'd seen of the rest of the house.

'Jepson sleeps here,' said Gascarth, waving an arm at a neatly made iron-framed bed and a plain deal chest of drawers. The only adornment on the whitewashed walls was a faded child's sampler. Molly wondered if the cook had embroidered it herself, or if it had been her mother's. There was no chance to peer at it for the date, for Gascarth had opened another door, onto a smaller, similarly austere chamber.

'You're in here,' he said.

Molly stood on the threshold. In the window embrasure, as deep as her forearm, stood a greenish-tinged bottle from Hartley's Brewery into which someone – the cook no doubt – had pushed a bundle of dried lavender. It was the silence of the little room that struck Molly most. There hadn't been anything like that absolute stillness in Croslands Park Road, much less in the room she had slept in at Roose Road, with its rows of little white-painted cast-iron beds and cabinets, all of them the same though their small occupants were as varied as they could be, even if their pinafores, stockings and shoes were identical.

'I've to sleep on my own?' Molly blurted. She jumped then at the loudness of Gascarth's laugh.

'Expecting me to come and bother you, were you?'

Molly felt the heat rise to her face despite the cool of the room, remembering what Annie McClure had said about how no girl would have gone to Lindal Hall had there not been the live-in cook. Yet this man had arranged things so that on that first day he and she would be alone. And now she'd practically invited him into her room. She wished herself far away from the hollyhocks, the polished saucepans, the weird carved faces.

But Gascarth took no notice. He'd retreated into the doorway.

'I'd asked you if you were thirsty and then never gave you anything. Unpack and come down to the kitchen when you're ready.'

Molly did so, barely taking notice of the contents of the suitcase as she put them away. She'd unwrap the brown paper package with the framed photograph of the McClures taken at Sankey's in Duke Street later, knowing the effect it would have on her if she were to look at their kind faces now. That same photograph had gone with her to Miss Cavendish's, but from Miss Cavendish's she could walk home. Molly couldn't hold her breath, though, and her linen smelled of the Cottage Homes laundry, where she and Annie McClure had washed everything brought back from Croslands Park Road. As a child, working in the laundry had been the favourite of her tasks. There'd been a lot of laughter over the dolly tubs, labour that ended each time with Mrs McClure giving her almond oil for her chapped hands. Molly sniffed back tears and pushed in the drawer of the chest, hiding the few things she had brought with her. Amongst them was the photograph of the Zulu Land cemetery. She'd found it when she and Mr Somers were going through Miss Cavendish's papers. He'd told her to keep it. 'George Cavendish will only throw it away. Take this too. I saw how you looked at it,' he said, giving her also a photograph of the dead woman, as a young and hopeful girl.

*

The kitchen was empty when she came down, but a full glass of water sat on the scrubbed table. Molly lifted it with both hands and drank down the best thing she had ever tasted, clear and cold and as refreshing to her insides as the flowers blooming before the house had been to her eyes.

She looked round, holding the empty glass. *Where've I to put this, then?*

'Leave it on the table,' said Gascarth from the doorway. *Watching me again, is he?*

'Jepson will be back soon. She'll show you everything to do with the kitchen. But there's something more important I'll be expecting of you.'

Molly followed her master through the entrance hall. What meals would she and the cook prepare if nobody came to eat at that enormous trestle? Did Gascarth eat at it alone? If there had been guests once, she wondered how far they'd have had to come. From Barrow, like herself? Or had they put up at the hotel by the abbey and been brought by the taciturn carter when he was a younger man?

Gascarth ducked under a lintel and turned to the right. Trailing behind him, Molly gasped at the sight of a vast banistered dog-leg staircase disappearing up into the gloom.

'That can wait until later,' said Gascarth. 'That staircase goes further than the house itself.'

Molly could make neither head nor tail of this comment, but hoped that Jepson, whenever she came back from Dalton, would be able to explain everything. She followed Gascarth into another chamber, and stopped dead.

'My *sanctum sanctorum,*' he said. For the first time since they'd entered the house, he was looking at her directly.

'Pardon?'

'My holy of holies.'

Molly gazed around the room. It was luminous, although cream linen curtains were closed against the sunlight. The remaining three walls were completely covered in bookcases which she could see were built solidly into the masonry, making them a part of the house itself. On their shelves Molly could not see a single gap; the books slotted against each other as closely as bricks.

'The pages are worth more to me than the bindings, but they too deserve protection,' said Gascarth. 'So the curtains are only to be opened in winter, or on cloudy days.'

'I've never seen so many books,' said Molly, thinking about the little bookcase in the McClures' parlour with Annie McClure's beloved cloth-covered editions of Jane Austen and the Brontë sisters. 'Except in Ramsden Square, of course.'

'You frequent the public library, then?'

'Mrs McClure encouraged it,' said Molly. 'My house mother. Not all the girls like to go there but I like reading to Mark, you see.'

'Can't this Mark read for himself, then?' The scorn in his voice was unmistakable.

'He could once, sir. Only he was blinded.'

Gascarth flinched.

'Dare I ask where?' he muttered, looking away again.

'The Somme.'

'So who reads to him now?'

'Mrs McClure when she can. One of the other girls will, I suppose.'

'And what do you think about that, Dubber?'

Molly paused. 'I'll be glad someone will . . . only he said he liked the sound of my voice . . . so, I suppose I'm sorry I won't be there for him.'

'What did you read him, then?' He was looking at her again.

'Thackeray. Thomas Hardy. Them was his favourites.'

'"*Those were* if you please. Not Dickens, then?'

'No, sir. He'd read them before . . . only he thought them untidy. Though he liked the one with Pip and the convict. I do too, though it scared me a bit. That old lady and the girl alone in that house.' Molly stopped short, reminded of herself and Miss Cavendish.

'I think you've passed the test, despite your grammatical stumbles. I will not, though, require you to read to me. I *will* require you to treat my books with care and save them from every creeping insect that would eat them. When you dust them, you must put them back exactly where you took them from. Believe me, I know each volume's position in this room. I shall know immediately if any are out of place.'

'Yes, sir.' Molly was wondering if this was also permission to read them, provided she made sure they were replaced correctly, but she didn't dare ask.

'Perhaps you should go and acquaint yourself with the kitchen now. Jepson should be back in an hour.'

Molly recognised a dismissal. She bobbed a curtsey and began to back out of the room as she had been trained.

'No need for that,' said Gascarth. 'I'm not the Lord Mayor and it is indifferent to me whether I see your face or the back of your head. Only, stop cutting your hair like that. It makes you look like a workhouse brat.'

Molly was stung. She knew that Annie McClure had cut the hair of all the girls that way only because it was in the rules.

'It's only because of the nits,' she blurted, tears in her eyes.

'Do not speak to me of nits,' he said, flapping a hand at her. 'You have a decent brain and you appear to be clean. Jepson will explain everything you need to know.' He turned away.

Molly made her way back to the kitchen. As she passed the trestle in the hall, she heard a door close firmly behind her.

*

Molly passed the next half hour acquainting herself with the contents of the kitchen and the pantry, glad of the time on her own to get used to things. She thought back to another rite of passage, her first day at school, and how she'd frozen, unable to take in the instructions, the lists of things she was supposed to remember, the rules. In the end she'd followed the other little girls, hoping they knew what they were doing. *So I'd better look at where everything is now, so that when Mrs Jepson explains it all to me, I won't look so stupid.*

What she really wanted to do was explore the house, but she'd have to walk past the closed door of the library in order to set foot on the stairs, which were bound to creak. *There'll be time for that.* Instead, she opened the door in the panelling as Gascarth had done, and went up to her room. This time, she unwrapped the photograph of the McClures from its brown paper and stood it on the chest.

'I'll write to you tomorrow, I promise,' she said aloud. 'I'll be back to see you the first Sunday they give me off.' She wished she had a photograph of Mark too. *Perhaps Mother Annie has one she could lend me,* though it occurred to Molly that she'd never seen any image of him other than the one taken when he was a little boy in the school in Cleator Moor. *Perhaps if you're blind, you don't like it if there are photographs of you and you'll never know what they show.*

Then, since she didn't know what to do next, nor even what time it was, she decided to lie down for a moment. In the silence of the house she was sure she'd hear Gascarth if he moved about or called, or Mrs Jepson if she came in.

Within a minute of her head touching the starched pillow, Molly was asleep.

CHAPTER TWELVE

Jepson

Molly's eyes flickered open and closed. *Still dreaming, then. But who is that?* She sat up, her hand over her mouth. Someone was watching her, a silhouette against the pale late-afternoon light. The figure shifted; the cane seating of the chair creaked gently.

'Aw right, lass, it's only Jepson.'

'I'm sorry . . . h-how long have I . . . have you . . . ?'

'You'll not be packed off to Barrow, if that's what you're thinking. Might be it's what you want, seeing as we're not lively enough for most young 'uns here. How long have you been sleeping, you say? Couldn't tell you. Jepson's only been back these five minutes. But now you've waked, you'd best look alive.'

Molly followed Jepson down to the kitchen. *I was right, then. She's only a little dot, for a cook. Probably means we're on short commons here.*

The cook rummaged in a press, handing Molly a clean but elderly apron. 'This is probably tougher than the ones you'll have brought from the Cottage Home.'

'Thank you.'

'Know how to paunch a rabbit, do you?'

'Yes,' said Molly, her heart sinking. She knew all right, but it was one of her least favourite tasks, especially if she had to scrape and cure the pathetic little skin afterwards.

'Well, whilst you're here, you can forget it, if you want. Master's a vegetarian. Says there's been enough blood, from man and beast, to do us a lifetime. He won't have another drop of it in his house, he won't. But if you've a mind for tearing something with your teeth that isn't carrots, Fallowfield is handy with his shotgun when nobody's there to say nay, and the Master's away often enough.'

'Fallowfield?'

'You came on his cart, din't yer?'

'I wouldn't want to eat meat if the Master didn't like it, though.'

Mrs Jepson fixed her intently with shiny boot-button eyes. 'That's a good answer, that is. Jepson likes that.'

'Was it a test?'

'It was too. That and the books. He'll be letting you read 'em before long, Jepson thinks. Don't presume, mind. Wait until you're told. Jepson doesn't know how long he'll be gone this time. She never does. We've to keep the place shiny and waxed anyroad, all year round. "My house shall never be covered in dust sheets," he says. Never says when he's coming back. Jepson'll be getting on with her business as usual and she'll hear a noise in his study, and there he'll be, his nose in a book as if he's never been away. He doesn't do like that to surprise us, mind. It's because it's the house that counts. We've to keep it spick and span for its sake, not his.'

'You mean he's gone already?'

'When you were up there being the Sleeping Beauty.'

'Oh.'

'He was only here this time to see would you suit. Most of 'em as come complain it's too quiet. You'll have every other Sunday off if you want to go on the razzle-dazzle as you'll not get to do it here. There's to be no gentlemen callers; if it's trousers you're after all we see here is Mr Fallowfield – he comes for to do the gardening – and the tradesmen. There's farms hereabout, but as you're a city child Jepson'll have to tell you men as works on farms are too busy for parlourmaids. Wednesday afternoons is free after dinner time up to supper, so you'd have time to wander down to the abbey if you were so minded and wanted to see a bit o' life with the visitors and that. There's waiter lads at the hotel if you want one of them.'

'I'm not after trousers, Mrs Jepson,' said Molly, flushing.

'Good lass. What you've to love here is the house, see. If you can do that, Jepson thinks you might do. For a quiet one, it's a good position. I've seen service in the big places – Conishead Priory when it was a hotel for the gentry was the worst. Well, we'd best get on. Jepson'll show you the kitchen and the pantries and that. You know how to blacklead a grate, do you?'

'Yes.'

'Lay a fire?'

'That too.'

'Clean brass?'

'With rottenstone.'

'Copper saucepans?'

'Silver sand, salt, vinegar and flour.'

'I can see from your face that's not your favourite job. Just make sure on the days you're looking after the Master's books you're clean as a whistle after them dirty jobs. Nails as well. I've to inspect, he says. Now, what about laundry?'

'I was in charge of the other girls for that at the Cottage Home.'

'Mending?'

'Mrs McClure taught me.'

'There's only you so you'll have the table linen as well as the bed linen to do. You'll get a character after as a parlourmaid or a housemaid for it, whichever one you need. There's Agnes comes Mondays, Wednesdays and Fridays for a couple of hours. She's in charge of the carvings, she is. Mr Gascarth is particular about them, nearly as much as he is about his library, but Agnes'll teach you. She's all right, is Agnes, though the Master thinks she's no more brain than her feather dusters and was all for sending her packing in the early days if I hadn't stopped him. You're the one as'll be dealing with the books. Oh, and there's no bells here, apart from his handbell and that's loud enough. Only, more often than not if he's up and roaming about he'll come down and call if he wants anything.'

'How long have you been here, then?'

'Oh, let me think how long it's been. He come back from Edinburgh – he was in the hospital there – the one for officers, I mean – and that would have been about a year after the war ended. It was on doctor's advice that I came then. The Master wanted someone he knew. But I was glad to be that person.

I remember he were such a nice little boy, Master Anthony. Sunny, he was.'

'You've known him always, then?'

'I should say so. I'm his aunt, in a manner of speaking.'

*

'So you're the new one,' said Agnes, hands on hip, surveying the younger girl. 'I wonder how long *you'll* last?'

Molly tried to think of some response but Agnes added, 'All depends if the Master likes you, even if he's not here most of the time. An' you look like a bit of class. Not like the other noggin who was here. First thing she said when she saw Mr Gascarth's library was "what would anybody be wanting wi' all them books?" Jepson thinks you'll do, anyroad.'

'I hope to give satisfaction,' said Molly.

Agnes put her head on one side. 'You *are* class, in't you? You sound like a Barrow girl but you don't talk like them. That's like something out of the pictures, that is. Do you go to the pictures much? We could go to the Empire in Dalton if you can get Jepson to give you time off. Oh, I did love that Rudolph Valentino. I've seen all his films. Wept buckets when he died – as if he'd really been mine. Them eyes he had would bore into your soul, I swear.'

'Perhaps he was just short-sighted.'

Agnes gaped at Molly, who was equally astonished, mainly because she'd managed to get a word in edgeways. She wondered if Agnes was one of those people who wouldn't stop talking even at the pictures, a running commentary to compete with the title cards and the cinema pianist, though with the talkies coming in fast she was up against some competition.

'Ooh, you're a caution, you are! P'raps you're right. That would do me, wouldn't it?'

'What would?'

'A man as couldn't see me properly. He'd overlook my big round lugs and my flyaway hair and me ankles swelling when I've been on me feet too long. He'd appreciate my inner qualities instead, that's what he'd do.'

'I think you look very nice,' said Molly, wondering what Mark would make of Agnes. She meant it. Agnes had a kind face and lively eyes.

Agnes's smile grew wider still. 'Well, *are* you class, then? I bet you are. I bet you're the long-lost child of a duke or something. He'll come and track you down and tell you to cast aside your apron for ever and there'll be a maiden aunt or a lady cousin or somebody who'll launch you into your rightful place in high society and tell you how much the duke loved your poor mother and all.'

This was so close to some of the fantasies Molly had heard the girls in Roose Road come out with that she was startled.

'No. My mam and dad both died, when I was too little to remember them. In Manchester.'

'Well, I daresay they've high society in Manchester as well—'

'Dubber in't posh, though, is it? But you could write stories, Agnes, you've such an imagination.'

Agnes hooted with laughter. 'Not that the Master'd want any of them in *his* library.'

'Tell me about him,' said Molly, grasping the chance to change the subject.

'*Agnes!*' came a voice from the direction of the kitchen. 'Get on wi' it, will you?'

'S'pose we'd better,' whispered Agnes. 'Let's start upstairs where Cook can't hear us.'

*

Molly stared up in astonishment at the ancient varnished steps. 'So that's what he meant when he said the staircase went further than the house.'

'His grandfather did that. Brought the staircase from a place they was pulling down and wouldn't have it cut. So it just goes up until it meets the ceiling.'

Molly suppressed a shiver. The sight of the steps running headlong into the whitewashed plaster ceiling made her feel claustrophobic, as though she'd been shut in a cellar – or a tomb – and her escape plastered over.

'It's him what did all the carvings, the grandfather I mean, and got that girt big table built. Trying to make the place look older than it is, though it's old enough in my opinion. I've to keep it dusted up there, right up to the last step though nobody but a mouse could set foot on it. If it was mine – not that it ever would be – I'd put a row of plates up there, make something of it. But no, nothing is to be touched. Same as his blessed books.'

'You were going to tell me about the Master,' prompted Molly, though she felt she was learning most about him through this strange house, the one he spent so little time in.

'Disappointed in love is the story. Like something in one of Miss Corelli's lovely books, really. You read her?'

'No.'

'Oh, you should. The Master hasn't got any of them, though.'

'Had he a broken engagement, then?' Molly prompted.

'Oh, yes, I was going to tell you. Here, take that duster. I'll start over here and you do that bit. I've to learn you, Jepson says, for the days I'm not here. A house like this, you've to start up here but by the time you've the whole house done two days later you've only to do it all over again, haven't you?'

Molly suppressed a sigh as the irrepressible Agnes, instead of telling her what she wanted to know, took off into a melodramatic story of a baby girl abandoned at a remote farm in a storm – 'one of Miss Corelli's best, that one!' – and maintained by a mysterious benefactor. 'Have *you* a mysterious benefactor, Molly?'

'Not if I'm doing this, no,' said Molly, waving the feather duster, but unable to be really annoyed with Agnes. *She might be a chatterer but she lights up this house all right.* What nagged at her more was *why* she wanted to know more about her eccentric employer. *I'm not about to ask Mrs Jepson either. Not with her being his aunt.*

CHAPTER THIRTEEN

The Library

Dear Mother Annie,

I am sorry I did not write earlier. So much has happened here. The Master — Mr Gascarth — is not here often, so it is just me and the cook, Mrs Jepson, and another girl, Agnes, but she does not live in. I have my own room, though I have to cross Mrs Jepson's to get downstairs. The work is not hard. I really only have to keep the place as it is. I don't know where to start with describing this house, I'm sure I don't. It's like something in a book, dark and mysterious with lots of panels and carvings. That makes it sound a bit like Barrow Town Hall that time we went for the Mayor's reception, only this house doesn't show off like that. The rooms aren't big and draughty and there's no coloured glass. I will tell you better when I see you next.

I've to look after Mr Gascarth's books, to keep them clean and not let the light fade their bindings. They're in bookcases like miniature cages, behind mesh and glass. I would dearly like to read them but I know you brought me up to wait to be offered, not to ask. Mr Gascarth was interested in me reading for Mark and thinks I have a brain which is strange because he is not a teacher so I am not sure how he knows.

Agnes says he came back from the war very poorly, though you would not think it to look at him. He was in a hospital for officers in Scotland and though she was not sure thinks it must have been his nerves. He cannot stand the sight of blood, so there is no meat eaten in this house. Mrs Jepson says as I am probably still growing that I should take Dr Williams Pink Pills to keep my strength up, though if I am honest, with all the fresh air and the chance of a walk down to the abbey when I have my afternoon off, I feel good and healthy here. Reading what I have just written I think I have made Mr Gascarth out to be a milksop or a coward but he isn't that. He just has very determined ideas. Agnes said he was engaged to be married but it ended when he came back from fighting and she does not know as much as she would like and can't say who broke it off. Anyway, I am told I will not see much of him.

I miss you and Mr McClure an awful lot and am looking forward to my first Sunday off. It's quite different being this distance away. There are trains to and from the abbey, seeing as otherwise how would the sightseers get there? Perhaps when I know I am coming Mark could be invited so I can read to him again?

Your loving daughter,
Molly Dubber

*

'Is this piano ever played, Agnes?' asked Molly. They were working through a little sitting-room Molly thought nobody ever sat in. A baby grand stood forlornly in one corner, its fall lid firmly down.

'Well, I've never heard anyone. I don't think the Master likes the pianner very much but it stays here because it was in the house when it became his and he won't change a thing.'

'Poor piano,' said Molly, running her duster over the shiny mahogany. 'Why doesn't he like it?'

'Cook says because it was made in a factory. You can see your face in it, just about, can't you? Not like those rough old carved things this place is full of.'

'Can I?' Molly's fingers hooked the edge of the fall.

'Go on, then.'

Molly stroked the silent keys, then resting her hands in the home position, tried a few bars of 'Three Blind Mice' before crying out in frustration and closing the lid.

'I know someone who could sort that,' she said. 'It sounds as if it's not been tuned since it was made.'

'Bring him here, then,' said a voice.

Both girls jumped. 'Sorry, Mr Gascarth,' they muttered, almost simultaneously, looking down at their shoes. Molly felt her face flame.

'Do you play, Miss Dubber? Other than nursery rhymes, I mean?'

'A little. Mother McClure encouraged me. Her stepbrother – the man I used to read to – he learned me. Only I'd to work out how to read music myself.'

'He *taught* you, Molly. You *learned* from him.'

'Yes, sir.'

'Do look up when you speak . . . that's better. Mark, I think you said he was called. He is, I take it, the piano tuner?'

'That's right, Mr Gascarth.'

'As I said, bring him here. It's an ugly little piano but it might as well make itself useful.' Gascarth left the room then as silently as he'd arrived, leaving Molly and Agnes looking at each other in astonishment.

'I never knew he was here. Does he always turn up like that, without warning?' whispered Molly.

'Always has done. Though usually he's away a lot longer. Only a few days this time. He'll go off again without saying anything too.'

*

Mr Fallowfield was dispatched to the station at the abbey to fetch Mark. Molly had tried to convince herself that she was pleased she'd got him some work, more than that she was simply pleased to see him. She remembered his complaints that there was less and less work for piano tuners: 'Folk like going to the pictures instead of an evening and a lot of the new films have sound.'

Mark had asked to be left alone to do the work, but twenty minutes later Molly tiptoed to the little parlour, straining from the far side of the closed door to hear the delicate tapping of the levers and mutes. There was a sudden silence.

'Haven't you work to do, Molly Dubber?'

Molly jumped, though she'd heard laughter in the voice. 'Sorry!' she squeaked, and pattered off, almost colliding with Gascarth.

'Steady on,' he said, holding her by the elbows.

'Mr Fagan doesn't want to be disturbed,' she said breathlessly.

'We'll not disturb him then. You could prepare some tea for us. Serve it in the library, if you wouldn't mind.'

*

'First time he's done that, as long as I can remember,' said Mrs Jepson. 'Not sure what the point is of showing a blind man books, myself.'

'Mark always liked to be read to,' said Molly, more defensively than she'd wished.

'It's a good thing, mind. The Master doesn't have enough friends these days.'

'Did he once?'

'Before the war, he did. Other lads used to come and see him here. They'd go for long walks, or take easels and paints and all go down to the abbey and do pictures. There'll be some here the Master did, maybe, though I can't say where he's put them. He might have burned them, right enough, same as he burned all that woman's letters. Maybe didn't want to be reminded, Jepson thinks.'

'Did his intended ever come here?'

'Intended? Whatever it was *he* intended, I'm not convinced her ladyship was of the same mind.'

Molly couldn't make out from the way the cook said 'ladyship' whether the woman had a title or whether Mrs Jepson thought her a snob. *Might be both, right enough.*

'Yes, she came here. Though the way she went on, you could see a town life was more to her taste. Anyroad, Jepson's said more than she should already.'

'The friends, though . . .?' said Molly, switching to what she hoped was safer ground.

'Them? I daresay they're dead, a lot of 'em. Or hidden away in nursing homes. They'll not be selling matches on the street, but even if you're in a nice warm room with a blanket over what remains of your legs I expect you can be lonely.'

*

Steadying the tea tray against the door jamb, Molly paused a moment before she knocked. The murmur of conversation ceased and Gascarth called out, 'Come in, Molly. We won't bite.'

She found Mark and Anthony sitting either side of the little fireplace, looking as relaxed as if they'd been friends for years. Molly settled the tray on a small table, mentally cursing herself for making the cups rattle.

'Mark has just complimented me on what he calls "a nice little Broadwood", Molly. Knew what make it was just from the sound. I shall stop being sniffy about it, too, as he informs me Beethoven owned one and prized it above others. He'll be back in six months, he says, but tells me that to keep it in good condition it needs to be played. Only I don't play, so it will have to be you.'

Molly glanced at Mark, who was smiling encouragingly.

'Practise an hour a day, if you can. I shall square it with Jepson,' said Gascarth.

Molly stared at him, open-mouthed.

'Please don't gape, Molly.'

She shut her mouth so quickly that her teeth clicked.

'Mr Fagan says he misses you reading to him. I wonder would you be so kind as to read to us both? Perhaps you could pour the tea and then go and fetch another cup for yourself while we choose something. And perhaps you'd leave your apron on its hook in the scullery.'

When Molly came back Gascarth had arranged a third chair for her, to sit facing them.

'Not our county, of course,' he said, 'but our old enemy Yorkshire. I think you'll agree, though, that this novel is peculiarly suitable for reading in this peculiar old house.' He handed her a book bound in tree calf, open at the first page. Molly glanced down, recognising Emily Brontë's masterpiece immediately. She took a sip of her tea, glanced up at the expectant faces, and began to read.

I have just returned from a visit to my landlord—the solitary neighbour that I shall be troubled with. This is certainly a beautiful country! In all England, I do not believe that I could have fixed on a situation so completely removed from the stir of society.

Molly couldn't suppress a smile. Lindal Hall wasn't Wuthering Heights. It wasn't exposed on a bleak moor but nestled in a valley only a few miles from shipyard gantries and Mr Gascarth was hardly the taciturn, dark-eyed Heathcliff, a figure who'd haunted Molly's daydreams ever since Mother Annie had handed the thirteen-year-old girl her own modest cloth-bound copy and urged her to read it. If anything, the Master was Mr Rochester – another object of romantic longing – though without, as far as she knew, a mad wife concealed in the attics. But Lindal Hall nevertheless was 'completely removed from the stir of society'. Mrs Jepson had said as much. They weren't troubled with visitors, though Molly was sure that had they known the Hall was there, the many visitors to the abbey would have been as enchanted with the picturesque chimney pots, the cottage garden and the Master's grandfather's eccentric wood-carvings as they were with the Norman arches and the monks' night stair. The house was hidden from view; you had to know it was there, beyond the sheltering trees.

*

Molly led Mark along the winding path through the flowers, walking in front of him so he could put his hand on her shoulder. Emerging onto the lane, she stopped, and his fingers slipped away. They turned to face each other.

'Mr Fallowfield comes from that direction,' said Molly, waving an arm.

'That's all right,' said Mark, smiling. 'I'll hear him coming.'

Her face heated. 'I'm sorry, I didn't mean . . .'

'Molly, I like that you forget I can't see. Anyway, I owe you thanks. That Broadwood was a delight. I don't get to work on many as good as that one. I like your Mr Gascarth too.'

'He's not my Mr Gascarth, Mark. He's the Master.'

'Well, I'd say you're lucky with him. I go to some of the grand houses in Barrow, you know. I've even been to Abbots Wood for old Mr Ramsden,' he said, mentioning Lindal Hall's closest neighbour, on the slope overlooking the railway line. 'That place echoes so much it must be huge, with just one old man in it. Not like we live in Barrow. *His* servants must have their work cut out for them, keeping a place that size running.'

'I know I'm fortunate. More so now you've been here. I'm being let to practise the piano. Like a lady!'

'Well, you are one. And I think he'll ask you to read to him again,' said Mark.

'No, that was only today, surely, because you were there? He can read himself. He has his nose in a book every time he comes here.'

'I still think he'll be asking you, Molly.' A tinge of something like regret in Mark's voice made her look up at him, searching his expression, but his head was turned away as he listened to an approaching rumble of wheels and rattle of harness.

'Molly, I said you'd to go and live your life, didn't I? Only be careful, won't you?'

Molly was spared looking for an answer to this, for Fallowfield was abreast of them.

'Bye, our kid!' said Mark once he was settled up in his place.

'Tell them I miss them,' said Molly. She waved at the cart until it disappeared round a bend in the lane, even though she knew Mark couldn't know she still stood there.

When she went in to gather up the tea things there was no sign of Mr Gascarth. She took them out to the scullery to wash, her ears straining to hear the distant hoot of the train that would tell her that Mark was safely on his way home.

*

A month had gone by since Mark had tuned the piano. Molly religiously kept to her promise of an hour's practise every day. *It's like silk instead of jute,* she said to herself, in awe of the quality of the sound the Broadwood made. To begin with, she'd been afraid to play again, embarrassed at the memory of the mistakes she had made when performing for the two men, though both had complimented her. But gradually, her confidence had grown.

She thought often of that afternoon, a window into another world. Molly wondered if Gascarth realised how fortunate he was to be able to pass his time with books and music, or whether he had any idea of how other men toiled. Mr McClure limped because of an accident in an iron-ore mine he'd been lucky to survive. Joe and Mark had both worked in the shipyard before call-up and Joe was back there now. Mark's work was precarious. *You're forgetting Mr Gascarth was in the war too,* she reminded herself. *Only to look at him you'd think he'd got through without a scratch.*

Then she remembered something Mrs Jepson had said, lost in the blur of all things new when she had first arrived at the Hall. The cook had been standing in the doorway of the little room that was to be Molly's alone.

'Up here, we can't hear him when he shouts at night. But if you happen to be downstairs when he does, you've to pretend you heard nothing. He prefers it that way.'

I wonder if he shouts at night when he's not here. I wonder if there's anyone, wherever he is, who hears him?

CHAPTER FOURTEEN

Lindal Hall, November 1933

As Mrs Jepson said he would, Anthony Gascarth disappeared from the house for weeks at a time, reappearing without notice. The year turned, the seasons making themselves felt in the flowers that bloomed and drooped and faded before the front door, in the birdsong heard through the open casements of summer giving way to the longer shadows of autumn. Draughts were stopped by long sausages of jute stuffed with old stockings and rags. Molly and Mrs Jepson shivered before the fires were got going in the mornings. Weeks turned into months, a routine establishing itself. Molly went regularly back to see them at the Cottage Home on her Sundays off. If she came back at dusk or later, Mr Fallowfield and his cart was always at the abbey station waiting for her. He called her Molly now, and for a while had taken to remarking every time he saw her that, 'there's no lass stopped on as long as you have. You'll be there as long as Jepson if you don't look out. You've a good country bloom on you too. Nobody'd think you were a town girl.'

Yet, fond as Molly had become of the cook who claimed to be her Master's aunt, she was pretty sure she didn't want to be in service always.

'I'd like a family one day,' she told Agnes.

'So where are you going to find the man you'll have one with, hidden away here with just the Master's books?' asked the practical Agnes, who by now was walking out with a farmhand called Daniel. Then she pressed into Molly's hands the latest edition of *Peg's Paper,* stuffed with stories in which girls from very humdrum walks of life but with elegantly shingled hair somehow managed to snare men with titles who were called names like Julian or Eustace, who whisked them off to settings seen only in the pictures. Given that Daniel was neither of noble blood nor had one of those rather silly names, as Molly thought them, she wasn't quite sure why Agnes thought these stories were suitable reading matter. And besides, Molly didn't dream of being like a demure Rose or a plucky Jennifer, typical heroines of the *Peg's Paper* plots. She'd prefer to see herself as a cross between the passionate Catherine Earnshaw and the principled Jane Eyre. *But I'd've settled for a nice little house with Mark.* Then came the morning when she woke up realising that she had dreamed of a man, but he hadn't been Mark.

Molly thought of those windswept Yorkshire heroines every time she entered the library, armed with a clean feather duster. The beautiful edition of *Wuthering Heights* she'd read to the Master and Mark that enchanted afternoon had not been lifted from the shelf since. To be sure of it, she'd pushed the volume a fraction of an inch further in than its companions and that's where it had stayed. Mark himself had been back since, on a day when the Master had been away on one of his unexplained absences. He'd been friendly, calling her 'our kid' the way he had when she was younger, but as before he'd shut her out of the room once he'd laid out his tools and bent his head to listen to the heartstrings of the piano. Afterwards, he'd called her in though, asking her to play something so that he could check his work. She'd played a Strauss waltz, hoping that Mark might follow her onto the piano stool with a duet, but he'd merely said, 'You've been practising, I see. Keep it up. I'll be back in six months or so,' and then he'd packed up his toolbag. She'd led him out to meet Fallowfield's cart, but he'd seemed distracted. All he'd said before he left was, 'Look after the piano for me, won't you?' Molly had gone back to the Broadwood afterwards in a room that felt empty, but when she'd tried to play again she'd not been able to read the notes, for the page shimmered before her eyes. She blinked back the tears, blew her nose and told herself to 'get on!'

Some weeks after Mark's last visit, Molly had been doing her best to 'get on' with the library. She had a system worked out: once a week the books would get a general dust, but each day she would open up one of the mesh-fronted cases and give the volumes inside it a thorough clean, moving them out to check there weren't spiders lurking at the back, or worse. Two kitchen cats, ferocious mousers, kept most of the rodent population around Lindal Hall at bay, but Molly was always alert to the creaks and murmurs of an old house. A skitter-ing behind the wainscotting could easily be mistaken for the frond of a tree scratching a windowpane, but she always made sure that's all it was. She thought of herself as tuning Lindal Hall, just as Mark tuned the little Broadwood. It made her feel closer to him. Today she was standing in front of the shelf marked with the gilt letter H. The red and gold-tooled spines of Thomas Hardy's complete novels and stories looked uniform, but the Master had told her they were all arranged in order of publication and so she had to be careful to put them back in the same way. Molly sighed. She'd read some of those novels to Mark and, in the process, had half fallen in love with Sergeant Troy and Damon Wildeve, while knowing that the men who were less obviously exciting were the reliable ones – a Gabriel Oak or a Diggory Venn. She traced a loving finger down one of the volumes, feeling the smooth bumps of the raised bands of the spine.

'I hope you're reading them too, Molly.'

The girl jumped. 'Mr Gascarth!' she cried, turning around. 'I wouldn't've come in if I'd known you were back.'

Gascarth moved out of the shadows in the far corner.

'Even if I said I'd come back to see how you did?'

Molly didn't know how to reply to this. Afterwards she even wondered if she'd heard it at all, trying to convince herself that she'd had her head full of Thomas Hardy heroes and had somehow projected this onto the Master.

He walked over, silent as a cat on the Turkey rugs, but when he stood at her shoulder it was to look at the books, not at her.

'Some would say he is an unsuitable writer for an impressionable young woman. A bishop threw this one on the fire, the

Philistine,' he said. Molly made a mental note that she would read that book next, wondering if Mother Annie had known about the bishop and that was the reason there wasn't a copy of *Jude the Obscure* in Roose Road.

'You're an intelligent person. Read it, and tell me what you think.'

'What, *this* copy?' she faltered.

'Of course,' he said as though he thought her question extraordinary. 'You mean, you've not looked at any of my books?' She thought he sounded disappointed.

'It weren't my place. Mrs Jepson mightn't like it.'

Anthony Gascarth laughed. It occurred to Molly that she'd never heard him do so.

'There are a lot of things Mrs Jepson hasn't liked about my life, Molly Dubber. You coming to work here isn't one of them.'

*

That Sunday, Molly walked arm in arm with Mrs McClure around the restrained grey cenotaph in Barrow Park.

'Poor young men,' whispered the older woman. 'There are two names there I knew. Robert made their suits for them. One for his wedding, the other for an interview for the Town Clerk's department. The only thing I'm glad of is that Mark and Joe's names aren't there.'

'Will Mark be in for tea later?' asked Molly.

Annie pulled the girl's arm a little closer. 'He won't be. He's away on Blind League business – in Manchester.'

'Oh,' said Molly, unable to disguise her disappointment.

'I'll tell him you were asking after him, shall I?'

'Yes – please.'

'Molly?'

'Yes?'

'You've been very quiet ever since you got here. You're usually brimming over with news about the Hall: what Mrs Jepson said, what Mr Fallowfield did, what other things you've discovered about that strange old house.'

'It's the Master,' blurted Molly.

'I wondered if that's what the matter was.'

'I'm happy there, honest I am. I know the work could be a lot harder anywhere else – Mrs Jepson and Agnes both say so. And the place – well, I've told you what it's like. The abbey to walk in nearby on my afternoon off. The people coming in on the train to have a look at the ruins, when I get to live near them the whole time. It's a bit like being in a fairy tale, only I'm afraid midnight will strike and I'll not be prepared. None of it will be there anymore and I'll be standing in the road in the dark on bare feet, wearing rags wondering did I dream it all.'

'The Master, you said.'

'Well, he's not the handsome prince, that's for sure. I don't mean he in't good-looking. He is, or rather, he could be, only he looks so remote and cold so much of the time. He's tidy about his person, right enough, but he's not a man you could imagine looking at himself in a mirror, though he must do, I suppose, if he's to shave. It's more as if he's looking *in* on himself instead of looking *at* himself. I'm sure he prefers the people he reads about in books to real ones.'

'You were like that too. Apart from with me and Mr McClure. And Mark, of course.'

'Was I? Well, the people in books weren't calling me names.'

'I meant to tell you. That Vivie was up in front of the juvenile court for fighting. It wasn't her first offence so she got put away.'

Molly shivered. 'That'd be the worst thing for me. To not be free to walk about outside when my work is done.'

'You were going to tell me about the Master, Molly,' prompted Annie. 'What's he done?'

'It's nothing much, but I don't feel easy about it, that's all.' Molly proceeded to tell Annie about the incident in the library. 'I can't say he's done anything *wrong*,' she said. 'It's just the way he made me feel.'

'Does he always turn up unexpectedly?'

'Oh yes. Only from what Mrs Jepson said, he's home more often than he ever used to be.'

'That could be a coincidence,' said Annie slowly. 'Did she say why she thought that was?'

'Only that he seemed to be happier in himself. The best she's seen him since he came back from Scotland.'

'They say time heals, right enough. Mark liked him, you know.'

'He said so? Well, when he was there the Master was different. I mean, I've never seen him with anyone else, apart from Mrs Jepson and Mr Fallowfield and Agnes. He's a bit stiff with them, even though Mrs Jepson talks back to him a bit, more'n Agnes or me would dare. He won't look at Agnes, really, and you can see he'd rather not be in the same room as her.'

'And Agnes doesn't get to read his books.'

'She'd not want to anyway. *I* feel I've got to, in a way, even though I want to. In case he turns up again and asks me about them.'

'You always were a clever girl, Molly. I'd've wanted you to stay on at school only the Borough Councillors told me off for it. They said you'd get ideas above yourself and it'd do you no good. "Honest toil" was good enough for any child from the Cottage Homes, they said.'

'I don't want anybody to think I'm ungrateful, most of all you and Mr McClure,' said Molly. 'Only I wouldn't want to be a servant always, even somewhere like Lindal Hall.'

Annie paused, scuffing at something on the path with the toe of her boot. 'There would be nothing wrong with being a servant who reads in her spare time. I was a mill girl who spent all her free time in the Carnegie Library – until I met Mr McClure, anyway. He wasn't a bit like anyone I'd read about in a book, but I never liked anyone so much as I liked him. I wanted a big family with him, but I never got one in the normal way. I've my Kathleen. Our other babies died before they were born, Molly, and the last time it happened the doctor told me there shouldn't be any more. He said he couldn't explain why Kathleen had lived when the other poor mites didn't.'

'I'm sorry. I never knew.'

'It's not something you talk about, is it? Anyway, I'm not a mill girl now, and I do have a big family, only in a different way.

I love all the children that have come under my roof, Molly, because they need to be loved. Otherwise they won't know how to love in their turn. I try hard not to have favourites, Molly, but you were always a bit special.'

'Why?' said Molly, a break in her voice.

Annie hesitated. 'You just looked – when you came to us – as if you'd had to climb a bigger hill than perhaps the others had. But you blossomed, Molly. You'd a face like a little pansy – and you're still as pretty as a flower. It means everything to me that you're somewhere where you're appreciated. Most of the time with the girls going into service I hear complaints.'

'So you think I should count myself lucky?'

'I do. Which doesn't mean you will be a servant all your life anyway. But do your job with a conscience and read the books you're looking after. Let the Master teach you – as that's what I think he wants to do. I'd a friend when I was your age – Teresa – and what I remember most about her was how impatient she was. You've some of that. Always wanting to try out new things, was Teresa, do them before she was ready. I'm sure she thought I was a bit slow – feart, really.'

'Feart?'

'Frightened.'

'Where's Teresa now?'

'She died,' said Annie, looking away. 'She was killed in a weaving shed – part of a loom spun off and hit her. She'd not been long on that job and was determined she was going to master it more quickly than anyone else. She wanted to be earning more – Teresa was going to be married, you see.'

'Poor girl.'

'She was. Teresa had everything to live for. All I am saying is be patient. Make the most of what you have.'

'A piano to play and books to read. I know. I'm lucky.'

*

When Molly got back to Lindal Hall it was to find that Anthony Gascarth had disappeared again.

CHAPTER FIFTEEN

Herbert Lowther

Annie liked the abbey ruins most in the winter, for she had them more or less to herself. There was something reassuring about sheltering beneath their sturdy arches when it came on to rain, though it did mean heading back early on the half-hour walk back to the hall as the days were short.

It was a bright day at the end of February when Molly met Herbert. She was sitting on the stump of a column in what had been the nave of the abbey, turning her face up to a sun which was bright though not warming. Anyone watching her might have thought she was daydreaming, but in fact she was alternating between running through in her head a particularly difficult piece she'd been practising and wondering when the Master was going to reappear. She'd read the book he'd urged her to and knew why it had gone on the bishop's fire. What on earth would she say if he asked her what she thought? The book had both thrilled her and made her weep, but she thought it might be safer just to mention the weeping.

'Aw right, are yer?'

Molly's eyes snapped open. Dazzled by the bright sunlight, all she could make out was an outline.

'Room on there for me, is there?'

'Oh . . . yes, if you like.' She gathered her skirts to one side and placed her feet, which had been stretched out before her, her heels dug into the grass, on the plinth of the column. She raised her knees slightly and folding her hands in her lap, aiming for primness to cover her annoyance at the interruption. The young man rummaged in a waistcoat pocket for a tin of tobacco and sat down beside her, not touching her. The first thing Molly noticed was that he was wearing some kind of scent, but that it wasn't unpleasant, and secondly, that he was exceptionally clean, his collar dazzling and his dark suit brushed.

'Roll one for yer, will I?'

'No. I mean, no thank you. I don't smoke.'

'Good. Lasses shouldn't,' he said, lighting up. 'Mr Slaney doesn't like it if we do either – though the guests make more smoke than a train, they do.'

'Mr Slaney?'

'Proprietor, Furness Abbey Hotel,' he said, tilting his head in the direction of that establishment. He moved the cigarette to his left hand and offered her his right.

'Herbert Lowther, waiter.'

'Molly, parlourmaid,' she said, remembering that Mrs Jepson had said that was better than being a kitchen maid, even if at Lindal Hall she did a bit of everything.

'You at Abbots Wood, then?'

'No. Lindal Hall.'

'I didn't think you looked like an Abbots Wood girl, if I'm honest. And they say old Mr Ramsden up there prefers men looking after him, anyroad. Wouldn't get me working there. Lindal Hall, though. Heard of the place, but never met anyone worked there.'

'There aren't many of us. We're really just caretakers. The Master's hardly ever there.'

'Dull, in't it?'

'No, not really. There's a library and I can play the piano.'

'Get away!'

'I can, honest. The piano tuner said it needed to be played or it'd go off quicker, so the Master told me to practise an hour a day.'

Herbert whistled. 'That's jam, is that. Good, are you?'

'I couldn't say. It's not as if I give concerts. Cook says she likes to hear me from the kitchen – makes the place less lonely, she says. Agnes – that's the other girl, only she don't live in like me – was a bit jealous at first but now she says it's like a story in a book.'

Herbert stood up abruptly. 'Fancy a cuppa tea?'

Disappointed he seemed to have lost interest in her piano playing, Molly stammered, 'W-what . . . where?'

'Tea room at the station.'

'Oh, I'm not sure I should.'

'Strictly business, Miss Dubber. To do with your pianner.'

*

Molly noticed a touch of swagger in the way Herbert behaved with the staff of the tea room, as a servant knowing just how he wanted to be served.

121

'Your usual table, Mr Lowther?' said the man, with a sideways glance at Molly. They followed him up to the far end of the row of tables, to the one closest to the roaring fire.

'Well, this is very nice,' said Molly, her fingers on the spotless heavy linen of the tablecloth. Herbert ordered scones and a pot of tea for them both; they were what she would have wanted but nevertheless she was narked at not having been asked. She was also wondering who else Herbert had brought to his 'usual table'.

'You said you had business to discuss with me. About the piano.'

'You'd be helping me out, in a manner of speaking. We had someone at the hotel, only he's got himself a permanent job at the Electric in Barrow, though how permanent it'll be with almost all the new films being talkies I don't know. Mr Slaney was going to give him his cards anyway. Asking the guests to stand him drinks, he was.'

'You want me to play in the hotel?'

'Mr Slaney would be impressed if I found him a replacement. He says I'm up and coming, you see. Says I'll go far. We've never had a lady pianist, but you'd bring tone – being ladylike, I mean. I'd have took you for a lady's maid, more than a parlourmaid, is what I mean.'

'So that's what you meant by me not looking like an Abbots Wood girl?'

'Well, Mr Ramsden don't notice what girls look like as he don't care.'

'I'm not sure that's a compliment, then.'

'You're well-brought-up and I pride myself on being a good judge of character.'

'I was brought up in Roose Road Cottage Homes.'

Herbert gaped at her. 'I'd never've said!'

Molly's hand itched with the urge to slap him. Impervious, Herbert blundered on.

'You've got what I'd call nobility, Miss Dubber.'

'I doubt it. I don't think Mother was a servant the Master had his wicked way with and I wasn't born in the Union. My parents were regularly married, they told me. Only they died when I was little. Probably it was the Spanish flu or something, because they went one after the other.'

What Herbert said next made Molly sorry she'd spoken so sharply.

'I lost Mother to the flu as well. And Father weren't right when they shipped him back home from the war so he couldn't look after me properly. His lungs were all shot with the gas. I wasn't a kiddie but I'd no one. I'd've been in the workhouse too if my Auntie Flo hadn't taken me in.'

'I'm sorry, Mr Lowther. I can see your Auntie Flo did a grand job of you.'

Herbert recovered a bit of his swagger. 'Service is a good career for me. The right place and some of the gentry's style rubs off on you, is what I think. So, would you have time to meet Mr Slaney?'

'Now?'

'Just to meet him. If he takes to you, he'd tell you a time to come and play so's he'll see if you'll suit. You could bring your favourites, that way.'

123

'I'd have to ask – back at the Hall, I mean. The hours would have to be right for them too. And the Borough Councillors would need to give their permission, I'm sure. I'm not of age.'

'You'd not have problems with them, I can tell you. There's one of them is a regular, comes on the excursion train on the odd Saturday. I'm pretty sure the little lady he brings with him isn't his lawful wedded. Very thick with Mr Slaney, he is.'

'All right. I'll meet him.'

'I'll get the bill, then.'

Some of Herbert's self-assurance deserted him once they'd stepped out of the tea room.

'We've to go this way,' he said. 'Servants' entrance. I'm not allowed to use the main door even if it is my half-holiday. Mr Slaney will receive you in his sitting room.'

*

'You'd have to ask the Master,' said Mrs Jepson doubtfully. 'I can't see what difference it'd make to him personally, seeing as he's hardly here. And if they're wanting you mainly for the summer, it'll be light until late.'

'Mr Slaney said someone from the hotel would see me home on the dog cart.'

'Thought of everything, han't you?'

'Well, Mr Slaney has. I don't know myself what to make of it – if I want it, I mean.'

'I can see from your face that you do. Well, I hope the Master says yes. It'd be a bit of life for you.'

'Their piano's not as good as his. And I'd not be let to mix with the guests, Mr Slaney said. They've the piano in a corner near the window and I'd be sitting with my back to them, in a sort of whatdyecallit, an alcove. I played a waltz I could remember without the music but it was a bit over-lively for Mr Slaney. "The notes need to sound as if you're dropping a pebble into a pond," he says, "Not so much bang crash, Miss Dubber. You've to be the background to their conversations, not the main billing at the Regal."'

*

Three weeks later Anthony Gascarth reappeared, as silently as he had left. But his presence wasn't a complete surprise. On the threshold of the library, her hand on the doorknob, Molly realised she recognised his scent, a mixture of Carter's Botanic Shaving Soap and Bay Rum, mysterious substances she had seen on his otherwise austere washstand. He'd been away so long that she was surprised she even remembered that about him, yet that scent brought everything back, from Gascarth standing watching her from the doorway when she got down from the trap, to seeing him either side of the fireplace from Mark – the only time she'd seen him talking to another man.

Her next thought was that if he'd come in during the night, the water in his ewer must have been cold that morning. It was changed once a week all through his absence, a cloth laid over the top, just as a warming pan was put between the clean sheets of his bed.

'I know you're there, Molly. Come in, will you? I don't bite.'

She opened the door. Gascarth was standing with his back to the fireplace, his hands in his pockets, looking directly at her. Her first thought was that he'd been waiting for her. *Don't be daft. He's always rung the bell if he wanted anything. Masters don't wait for servants.* Molly paused on the threshold, bobbing a small curtsey.

'Oh, do stop that,' he said. 'I'm not the King of England. Come.'

To her astonishment, he stretched out a hand. Molly advanced across the room, wondering what she was supposed to do with the hand. Shake it? It came to her then that she had never touched Anthony Gascarth. She washed his clothes, helped prepare his simple meals and brought them to him on a tray, either at his desk in this room or occasionally at the vast table in the entrance hall. She'd prepared his bath, taken in a little room beyond the scullery, a lengthy process involving heating water in the copper and walking it through in jugs, whilst he waited silently behind a screen. When she'd grumbled to Mrs Jepson about how much a toil this was, the cook had told her to 'remember how lucky you are. Another gentleman would make you lug everything up to his bedroom, never mind getting the whole lot down again. That's if he didn't expect you to ladle water over his head and scrub his back for him.' Molly's face had heated up at the thought.

Now he was holding her hand and looking down at her. He looked thinner than she remembered him, but his skin against hers was warm and dry.

'Thank you for looking after my books, Molly.'

She nodded, not knowing what to say.

'Did you read the one the bishop burned?'

'I did. It made me cry.'

'That, Molly, is a good answer. You're a better judge than that clergyman. He was offended; you saw the tragedy. But he'd probably accuse me of corrupting my servants.'

'Is there anything in particular you'd like done, sir?'

'How long have you been here, Molly?'

'Almost two years, sir.'

'Yes, that's what I thought. But you've gone back to being as stiff and awkward with me as when you arrived. Aren't you going to ask me where I've been?'

'I . . . that wouldn't be my place. I mean, even Mrs Jepson never knows.'

'Ah yes, the good aunt Jepson. But she doesn't read my books, does she? You do, so our lives cross in a way hers and mine never could. We have a shared experience, let's say. I shall tell you anyway. France – Paris, to be exact, and then Nice.' He let go her hand and leaned his left shoulder against the mantel-piece. His eyes stared out at the garden, though Molly had the distinct impression he didn't register the riot of daffodils and hyacinths trembling in the spring breeze the other side of the thick panes. Her next thought was that she would be in trouble for leaving the curtains open, though she was quite sure she hadn't. He must have opened them.

'I'm sure that must've been very nice,' she said helplessly.

'Nice? That's an old joke, Molly.'

'Pardon?'

'The more important question is why, not where.'

Molly took her cue.

'Why, sir?'

'You lamb. A woman, of course.'

'I'm sure I'm very happy for you, sir.'

'Sweet girl. That's not it at all. I went away to forget her.' He glanced at her then.

'How old are you now, Molly?'

'I'll be eighteen soon, sir.'

'You know, the way I feel now I don't think I can ever have been that young. I can't remember what it was like. It's everything that has happened since that I wish I could forget.'

'I'm sorry, sir. If there's anything I can do.'

'Stop calling me sir for a start. Sorry. I shouldn't have snapped. When I'm maudlin there's not much anyone can do for me, I'm afraid. Perhaps later. You've been practising on the Broadwood, I take it?'

'Yes s—' She managed to bite off the 'sir' just in time.

'Has Mr Fagan called?'

'For the tuning, yes. Just the once when you were away.'

'And other than for the tuning?'

Molly realised he was suddenly tense, watching her intently.

'No, not at all.'

'So you haven't seen him?'

'No . . . I mean, just once when I went to see them in Roose Road. He's away a lot, with his League work. The National League of the Blind.'

'He's sweet on you – I believe that's what the expression is.'

Molly cried out as if she'd been struck.

'And you on him.'

'*No!* I mean— Oh, I'm sorry I spoke out of turn.'

'Quite all right. I didn't think you did.'

'Mr Fagan is the next best thing to Mother Annie's little brother.'

'Explain.'

'His mother is Mother Annie's father's second wife – she had him and his brother with her first husband. So in a way he's my uncle. He's older than me too. About twelve years older.'

'Positively ancient then,' said Gascarth, with a wry smile. 'Almost as old as I am.'

'And anyway,' she said, finally confining her dreams of Mark to a deep recess of her memory, 'he said I was to live my own life.'

'Which at the moment isn't much of a life, I should think. Serving a master who is barely at home.'

'I like it here.'

'Yes, I believe you do. You care for the place. Perhaps this morning, though, I will prevail on you to care for its master. If you would change the water upstairs? And I should like a bath before luncheon too. But before you do any of that, would you pull the curtains closed? I opened them at first light to see the garden and now it's too bright for the books.'

As Molly crossed to the windows, she wondered if she'd imagined half the things he'd said before issuing those instructions. *Did he really mean that about a woman? Must've been the one that broke his heart. Poor man, to be missing her even now.*

She walked to the door as quietly as she could, not to disturb Gascarth where he now sat at his desk, reading letters. But just as she put her hand on the doorknob, she heard him say, 'Perhaps this evening you could play for me? I shall leave the choice of music up to yourself.'

CHAPTER SIXTEEN

Grasshoppers

On the journey to Roose Road that Sunday, Molly went over and over the events of that day, determined to recount Anthony Gascarth's words as accurately as she could to Annie McClure.

'I don't know what to make of him, Mother Annie,' she said. It was too wet to go for their customary walk, so the two women sat with tea and fruit bread in the little parlour, as the rain pattered against the windows. The house hummed with the sounds of confined children; puzzles and dolls were no substitute for the open air.

'Did you play for him?'

'Oh yes. I thought I should make a mull of it. I'm sure I'd find it easier to play for a group of people rather than just one, as I think they'd blur into each other. So I just concentrated on the music and pretended he wasn't there. I managed it so well that when he said "bravo" afterwards I almost got a fright.

'Anyway, I asked about going to work for the hotel some evenings. He was a bit taken aback to start with, though eventually he said he'd go and see Mr Slaney himself. He was more bothered about Herbert Lowther – he wanted to know all about what I was doing in the abbey that made him come up to me, what he said, what I said back to him. I told him I knew I should be grateful to Herbert for taking me to meet Mr Slaney but that I didn't like people trying to manage me. He laughed and was a bit easier with me after that. And he went to the hotel the very next day and when he came back he said he'd got Slaney to agree that there's always to be someone to walk me back home if the dog cart was in use and that I was to have Mr Fallowfield to take me down whenever I wanted and that he'd take care of the fee. Said it made him feel like an impressionario.'

'Impresario?'

'That was it. Well, you should have seen Mr Slaney when I went back to let him hear what I'd prepared. He was pretty brisk when Herbert Lowther introduced me but the next time he was bowing and scraping and mentioning Mr Gascarth every three words. As the "new lady pianist" I wasn't to come through the servants' entrance and traipse all the way through to the entrance hall where I'm to play. I was to come in the front door as if I was a guest. He had poor Herbert scurrying about too, bringing cups of tea, though in a funny way I could see Herbert was pleased – seeing as he'd introduced me to Mr Slaney. Now I know where Herbert got his manner from, poor lad.'

'Is that rain easing off, do you think?'

'Oh ... mebbe,' said Molly, looking out of the window. *Mother Annie thinks I'm boasting. I suppose I am.*

'I was thinking I'd go and see if Robert could mind the girls while you and I get a walk into town. You'll need some new clothes if you're to work in that hotel.'

'I've not got much money on me.'

'You've not to buy them. We can just look in the windows in Dalton Road and see what you like. Then I'll tell Robert and he can make you up a couple of dark skirts and nice blouses – neat but professional.'

*

Gascarth had left the library door ajar, a signal that he could be disturbed. Nevertheless, Molly hesitated on the threshold, as she could see he was busy writing.

'Come in. I'm sure you weren't brought up to stand and stare.'

She jumped. He hadn't even turned round.

'If it's not a good moment . . .'

'I told you to come in, didn't I?' The hardness of his words was belied by the fact he'd turned to face her, and smiled.

She obediently advanced across the room to stand by the desk, feeling as though she was back at school.

'I just need to finish this sentence, or I'll forget what I wanted to say. No, stay there,' he added as she took a step backwards.

In order not to look at what he wrote, Molly concentrated her gaze on the way his hair lay on the nape of his neck. She had noticed that the Master was particular about his appearance. His clothes did not appear to be new, but they were good ones. *A bit like his house, then.* She had repaired those garments: tightening a button, restitching a hem. In doing his laundry she had even found shirts where the tails had been sacrificed and new clean ovals stitched into the underarms, frayed cuffs that had been turned. She had never seen Anthony Gascarth anything but clean-shaven, but he was clearly not one of those men who went to the barber regularly to reduce his neck to stubble. *Mebbe because he doesn't have a manservant, or at least not here.* She thought his hair looked soft, and for a mad moment wanted to touch it.

Gascarth put the top back on his fountain pen.

'What can I help you with, Molly?'

'Mr Slaney has given me the scores, sir. I wanted to see would it be all right if I was to practise them – that's if you're still here to hear them. I don't want to disturb you so . . .' *Stop babbling!*

'Well, let's see them.'

She held out the sheaf of papers. He riffled through them.

'Hmm. What one would expect. Classic Palm Court stuff arranged for solo piano. Not all of it, though. I'll be interested to see what you make of the Boccherini. I've only ever heard it on the fiddle. Bucalossi's "The Grasshopper's Dance"? Don't know that one.'

She watched his eyes scan the score.

'Ah yes, I have heard it. In Nice.'

'I didn't know you could read music, sir.' Molly immediately put her hand to her mouth. 'I beg your pardon, Mr Gascarth.'

'No need,' he said. 'There are a lot of things you don't know about me, Molly, in common with the vast majority of people who have made my acquaintance. Indeed, there is plenty I would not want you to know.'

Still feeling awkward, Molly said, 'Mr Slaney explained I've to play them at different times. The grasshopper one when the place looks lively. The serenade when he wants them to take themselves off to bed; he thinks it's restful. I've to "judge the mood" he says.'

'Whilst keeping your back to them in that inglenook and not fraternising with them. Well, I expect you'll pull that off.'

Molly looked away, not sure she wasn't being made fun of. She was startled when Gascarth took hold of her hand and put the scores in it.

'Practise you must. You were wondering if I would be around to hear them. Well, I have every intention of being so.'

*

As suggested by Mr Slaney, Molly turned up early for her first evening at the hotel, 'so's you can get used to it.' She'd made the mistake of calling her work hours her 'shift' until Slaney had firmly corrected her.

'Your *engagement,* Miss Dubber. I am running an hotel, not a factory.' She felt better when he'd gone on to compliment her on the tucked blouse and worsted skirt Robert McClure had made for her. 'Discreet and professional,' he'd said approvingly.

She walked in that afternoon to see that most of the chairs in the entrance hall were unoccupied. There was one old lady in a pince-nez and old-fashioned bombazine reading *The Illustrated London News* and a couple of moustached men with waistcoats and watch chains whom she took for businessmen, for no better reason than that they looked as if they could be on the Borough Council. They had that air about them of men who thought that getting value for money was a pious virtue. No one looked up when she skirted the chairs ('don't cross the room directly. Go around the edge so as not to draw attention to yourself,' had been Slaney's instructions).

Molly began with the Boccherini Minuet, feeling particularly confident in it because it was her playing of that piece that had drawn the most praise from Anthony Gascarth. Losing herself in the music, she saw herself back at the Hall, seated at the Broadwood, no longer agitated by her audience of one man. When the last notes died away beneath her fingers, Molly took a deep breath and replaced the score. Although she had been told not to, she couldn't resist glancing over her shoulder. The old lady had nodded off. The pince-nez was still in place, but the magazine had dropped into her lap, her head was tipped back on the headrest and her mouth was open. The two men with the watch chains were deep in conversation in a cloud of cigar smoke. Someone in walking gear had come in and was sprawled in one of the chairs. His long legs, encased in tweed plus fours, ended in a pair of conker-brown brogues while his upper body was completely obscured by the *Northern Daily Telegraph*.

They're taking no more notice of me than of that fancy wall-paper. Feeling more relief than annoyance, Molly placed her hands in home position and began the next piece.

An hour later she flexed her fingers and reflected on what warm work it was to play the piano. Herbert appeared, carrying a plain glass of water on a doily on a tray, which he presented to her with all the aplomb of the trained waiter, a white tea towel over his forearm.

'You're right good, you are,' he whispered as she drained the glass and handed it back. She was aware now of a murmur of voices behind her.

'What time is it?' she whispered back.

'Nearly dinner time. Play summat lively now and after that I'll bang the gong.

Molly selected her music and the grasshoppers began their dance. As she played, she thought of Anthony Gascarth in a place she had never seen, in a country she had never been, listening to the same piece played by a small orchestra of glossy-haired men in evening dress, and wondered about that woman he had gone away to forget.

*

When she got down from the dog cart that evening the Hall was in near darkness. The tiny light wavering behind one of the panes turned out to be a solitary oil lamp left waiting for her on that vast table. Carrying it, she tiptoed up the backstairs and, carrying her shoes in her other hand, went in stockinged feet across Mrs Jepson's room to her own door. In sleep, the cook was as immobile as a bolster.

As Molly crept into bed that night she thought that the Hall had never been so silent. She lay awake for some time, thinking about her evening, feeling like Cinderella coming home from the ball and unable to tell anyone about what it had been like.

There was just one flat note in the whole evening. She'd been offered tea and bread and butter in the servants' hall, where

Herbert had complimented her again before disappearing off to the dining hall with the turbot.

'Mr Slaney got the piano tuner in special last week, in honour of you coming.'

'Who was that?' said Molly before she could stop herself. *If he doesn't give satisfaction I could tell them about Mark.*

'It's a lad from Barrow who's blinder'n a mole. Mr Slaney likes to find work for ex-servicemen. He lost two sons, you see.'

'I'm sorry,' she said, but reproached herself again because she knew that she was thinking more about Mark getting the train out to the abbey and not coming to see her, than about Mr Slaney's two dead sons.

CHAPTER SEVENTEEN

Technical School, Abbey Road

The following morning Molly took Mr Gascarth his coffee at his usual time of eleven o'clock.

'Good morning, Molly. And how is Lindal Hall's answer to Fanny Davies?'

'Who would that be, sir?'

'Perhaps I should take you to hear her play some time, though I'm sure her grasshoppers won't dance as well as yours.'

Molly pinked. Gascarth had turned round in his chair as he spoke and she saw now what he was wearing: tweed plus fours.

'So you were there, sir,' she said quietly.

'And I'm quite sure you weren't supposed to turn and look. I had to be quick with my newspaper.'

Molly almost said, 'You'd have had to be watching me to manage it.' Instead she asked, 'Can I bring you some breakfast? You never came down for it this morning.'

'Had it already. I went down to the hotel early and got some there. You were splendid last night, by the way. You also have an admirably straight back.'

All she could manage was to stutter 'Thank you, sir.'

Gascarth took a sip of his coffee.

'I think it's time you stopped being my servant, Miss Dubber.'

Molly couldn't suppress a gasp. 'Oh no, sir, please . . . I'll give up the piano playing. I'm so sor—'

Gascarth got to his feet, laying long fingers warmed by the coffee cup fleetingly against her mouth.

'I meant you to continue as my employee. Only without that pinny and the tins of beeswax . . . although perhaps you might continue with the cleaning in here, just in the library, I mean.'

Heart thumping, Molly said, 'I don't know *what* you mean, Mr Gascarth. Though I'm sure I should be honoured.' *Catch yourself on, Molly,* she told herself, using that odd phrase she'd heard Mr McClure using to Mother Annie sometimes. *But wait till I tell Agnes. He sounds just like a man in one of them stories she tells me about – the* Peg's Paper *ones.*

'I was told before you came that you write a good hand.'

'They said so in the school, yes.'

'And you are numerate?'

Molly hesitated. 'Adding and subtracting? Yes, though I didn't like them so well.'

'It's to my shame I have never made use of either. I think I was just so pleased to have someone who knew how to treat my books. I must say too that no one has ever made such a good job of pressing my shirts and mending my things.'

Molly's face grew warmer, but her heart gave a little leap. *He noticed.*

'Do you type?'

Her face fell.

'Never mind, you can learn. It's all the rage, I'm told. You'd have to go to Barrow for classes. To the Technical School.'

'I know it,' said Molly, in a dream. 'In Hindpool. It's where the apprentices from the shipyard go.'

'And all the maidens who'll staff the solicitors' offices, the payroll departments and the Council, unless won over by the strapping lads who work for Vickers-Armstrongs. You'd better not fall for one of them, Molly, as it would rather ruin my plans.'

'Your *plans*?'

His brisk air evaporated.

'Forgive me. I have no right to interfere with your life.'

'No! Please, I mean. It's only that I don't know what you meant by plans. I don't know why you want me to learn typing.'

'I want you to be my secretary.'

'*Me?*'

'I see no one else here, Molly.'

'B-but why?'

'I'm sure you think of me as an idle fellow. You never see me do any work – not when I'm here, anyway. You mightn't think that what I do elsewhere is honest work either. I have what they call a private income, you see. A trust fund, administered by lawyers, for the most part. So I can please myself. Travel. Buy books. Write letters. Occasionally, in a small way, write articles on the things I'm privileged to have the chance to study because I'm a man of leisure. Before the war, I thought that's what I'd always do and when I lost my parents early there was nobody to stop me. As a boy, I'd convinced myself that provided I wasn't doing anyone any harm, I could pretty much rumble on as I wanted – an expensively educated layabout. There was nobody amongst my friends who suggested I should do otherwise. I only mixed with people like myself, you see. That equation most of the world grapples with – work or you will not eat – I understood only in the abstract.'

'But Mrs Jepson. She works. And she's your aunt.'

'She doesn't tell many people that, Molly. She decided to trust you.'

'The McClures brought me up not to be nosy, so that's all I know. And Mrs Jepson – well, she doesn't talk the way you do.'

'I daresay Jepson will tell you herself in her own time, if she wishes.'

'So, you said "before the war" . . .'

Gascarth laughed. 'I did, didn't I? You think nothing has changed. Well, it has and it hasn't. I would like to tell you that war is a great leveller, but it isn't really. Some of those who made decisions about what the poor wretches in the trenches were going to do next – whether they'd live or die – didn't get so much as a splash of mud on their toecaps. I joined up, Molly, because I thought the war would make something of me. My expensive boarding school qualified me, apparently, to command men older and of much greater substance than I. With an officer class like that, it's a wonder even a foot of Flanders was won. We'd probably be there still, if the Americans hadn't decided to join us. And as for the making of me, well, the war just about unravelled me, body and soul. Wounds heal, eventually, but not the memory of them.'

'So what is different now, sir? The war is years over.'

'*I* am. *I'm* different. That's the difficulty.' A silence followed, as Molly waited for his explanation. When he spoke at last it was in quite different tones.

'You see what an impractical fellow I am? My coffee is getting cold.'

He drank off the cup in one go. 'I can say this, though. I mixed with men I had never mixed with before, or if I had, I'd not noticed they were there. Before the war, other people had simply been there to do things for me. But what the war also did is left me completely ill-equipped for holding down a job a normal fellow wouldn't think twice about. Do you see the irony of that? I at last realised I wanted to do something, anything, that might have some value, and at the same time was deprived of the means. My health isn't good, Molly. Those riveters, welders, shipwrights in the yard in Barrow are capable of things my lungs will not permit me. I had rheumatic fever as a child, which weakened my heart. And that's to say nothing of what goes on here,' he said, tapping his forehead.

'I'm sorry, Mr Gascarth.'

'You are, aren't you, dear girl? I can see from your face you mean it. Would you give me your hand, Molly?'

Silently she offered it. Gascarth's long fingers slipped under hers. His thumb traced her palm.

'It's working for me put those calluses there, but here, in the centre, your skin is soft . . .'

Molly swallowed, wondering how it was possible that such a small gesture felt so good. Looking at his bent head, as he now examined her fingernails, cut short and nail-brushed, she wondered if he knew it. Then, to her dismay, he squeezed her hand once and released it.

'Why did they take you, sir, if you wasn't in the best of health?'

'There were men who lied about their age, mostly claiming to be older than they were.'

'Mark . . .'

'There were many like him. And men who claimed to be under forty when they were over fifty. Well, I lied too, though not by many months. Got a doctor to lie for me, which is worse. They were prepared to look the other way because they thought me officer material for no better reason than my education and what they thought of as "tone". By the end they were wishing they'd never taken me. I testified twice in favour of two men who were tried for desertion – that really tested their patience.'

'Did you save them?'

'No. They were shot.'

'Oh!'

'I heard later that the people in the village one of them came from wanted his name included on their war memorial. The powers that be refused them, of course – so the villagers said they wanted no monument. I believe they have none to this day. I sent the widow something for her children and told her that her husband died bravely.'

'That was kind of you.'

'Not really, Molly. I could afford it. With your help, though, I might still achieve something,' he went on. 'I know it's more the thing for a gentleman's private secretary to be another gentleman.

Those girls who work in typing bureaux in London aren't the same thing; they're little more than medieval copyists with the advantage of typewriting machines, though I daresay any one of them is capable of more. I would need someone to travel with me, too.'

'How could I do that?' Molly heard herself say. 'It wouldn't be right.'

'I thought you might say that. No doubt the Borough Councillors would say the same – and your Mr and Mrs McClure with them. But perhaps we might find a way. Look – I will support you at the Technical School if you're willing. If, at the end of it, you want a post in the wages department at the wireworks, or to work for a circuit judge, then so be it. I will have done something worthwhile with my life – something to benefit a person other than myself. You could live in Barrow during the week – perhaps some arrangement with Mrs McClure – and sleep here on the nights you work in the hotel.'

'I don't know what to say . . .' said Molly.

'I can see from your face you want to say yes. In the meantime,' he added, turning back to the desk to rummage through some papers, 'have a look at this.' He gave her a handbill. Molly studied the drawing of a gleaming machine bearing the words 'Imperial . . . British Right Through'.

'It looks like the cash registers in the Co-op. All them little buttons front and behind.' The typewriter was framed in a black case, the fan shape of the keys reminding her of the quills of some exotic bird, seen in the illustrations in *The Children's Encyclopaedia* in the parlour in Roose Road.

'We must decide where it would be best to have it sent. To Mrs McClure's, perhaps, if she is agreeable.'

Molly held the glossy paper in both hands. She wanted that typewriter very much. *If I learn that, the world's my oyster.* She looked up into Anthony Gascarth's expectant face.

'I do want to say yes. Of course I do. But why do you want to do this for me?'

'That's easy. Because I love you, Molly.'

*

'Whatever's happened to you, our Molly?' said Mrs Jepson. 'You look as pale as if you've seen a boggart. But it's not like the headless monk to be doing his haunting that far from the abbey.'

'It's Mr Gascarth.'

The cook put down her potato peeler.

'Give me that cup and saucer before you drop them. Having one of his turns, is he? They usually come at night.'

'I don't know if it's a turn. He's said all manner of strange things, and then as quick as he said them, it was as if he hadn't. He just handed me his empty cup and said he was looking forward to his dinner.'

'Luncheon, more like. That's what he usually calls it.'

'Oh . . . yes. I'd forgot.'

'What strange things did he say, Molly?' asked Mrs Jepson, her head on one side.

Molly recounted his plan for her to go to the Technical School, the idea that she should be his secretary, the prospectus for the typewriter. As she spoke, her words sounded like babbled nonsense; it was all so preposterous, unbelievable. The very last revelation she held back. *I mustn't have heard him right – surely?*

'You must think I'm making it all up.'

'No, lass. It's the best thing has happened to him in a long while, is Jepson's way of seeing it. Frame him a bit. Give him a bit o' purpose. Is there owt you've not said, Molly?' she added, her eyes narrowing, but the girl read the look as concern more than suspicion.

'N-no,' said Molly, her face on fire.

'Not much of a liar, are you?' said Mrs Jepson kindly. 'That's all right, you don't need to tell Jepson everything. I've eyes and ears and I've known Anthony Gascarth all his life. Makes sense now, din't it? How he stayed here more often than he ever did, and then went off all of a sudden for longer than I can remember him doing. Trying to decide what to do, or trying to shake you out of his head, or both of 'em. Only that bit about travellin' wi' 'im. That's not proper, that in't. That's not fair on a good girl's name. Jepson can see you're disappointed all the same. You liked that, din't you, the chance to go somewhere a bit further than Millom? He should've thought a bit before saying that to you, getting your hopes up. Men never has to pay. Jepson knows that.' The cook told hold of Molly's shoulders. The girl braced herself, thinking she was in for a shaking.

'Don't get yourself all worried up. If he's said you can go to the Technical School then go you can if you want and not feel you've got to come back and work for him if you don't want. He said that, din't he?'

*

Molly looked down at her fingers, held up at an angle higher than her wrists, ready to tackle what she was told was 'the eight-finger method.' Each girl sat at her own desk on one side of the class while young men training to be clerks sat on the other. Everyone was dressed as though they were already at work, in demure blouses and skirts or suits and ties and cellulose collars. The men were all freshly barbered and the girls smelled of cheap scent, fighting with the reek of mothballs. Glancing round before the lesson began, Molly hoped she might recognise someone, but most of the girls were younger than her. *I'm not going to tell anyone I come from the Cottage Home. But I don't want to tell them about Mr Gascarth either.*

A middle-aged woman with shingled grey hair addressed the students from a raised podium at the end of the room. She had a strident voice which she used as if she was shouting orders in a barrack square. It was not long before Molly realised why such a voice was necessary; she had to make herself heard over the cacophony of forty young Barrovians in chorus, attacking the little round keys on stalks.

The woman began by explaining the home position and how in keeping the hands there 'means you would be able to type accurately even were you to lose your sight.'

Oh, Mark, thought Molly.

'You will shortly find the reason why you have been provided with little fingers.'

To play the piano.

'However, they, and their immediate neighbours, will not be required to work as hard as your index and long fingers, for what seems a random arrangement of letters before you has been scientifically worked out to give the lion's share of work to the stronger digits. Those smaller muscles may tire to start with, but they are there to be used. You may find that hand strength as a whole will improve. You learned to write with only one hand. Here both will be pressed into service, making you twice as productive.'

There then followed a brief lecture on the importance, amongst other things, of good posture and hygiene. 'Remember, you will represent your employer at all times and of course you must also uphold the reputation of this school, as the young professionals it is our intention you become. Your appearance should match the discipline of the layout of your page and respect your tools: keep your machine in good order, just as you would polish your shoes or hang up your clothes at night to keep their shape . . . We will start by lining up your paper and winding it between the rollers of your machine.'

By 10 a.m. keys were pressed in a ragged chorus, louder and louder, as the students filled a first page and a second with *gfhj* repeated in regular columns, percussion provided by the bass note of the space bar and the cymbals crash of the carriage return. What had started as a hesitant, sporadic gunfire had turned into a constant fusillade, drowning out the other strange banging and whirring that came from other parts of the school, where boys who were just starting to shave were learning the skills that would one day build ocean liners, aircraft carriers, submarines.

I'll never get used to this.

Yet she did. By the end of the following day she saw, inked onto the page at some speed, little phrases like 'and as there has been . . . and at the same time . . . all this may have been . . . all that you have done.'

All that I've done? Well, it's been a while since I played 'Three Blind Mice' on the piano. But that's where I started. And then she remembered that she was due to play at the hotel for the after-supper loungers, and to sleep that night at Lindal Hall.

I hope Mr Gascarth is there. I want to tell him how well I'm doing. Because I'm grateful, really I am.

CHAPTER EIGHTEEN

Roose Road

'Has Mr Gascarth spoken to you in that way again?' asked Annie.

'You mean, said "I love you"?' Just saying those words felt fantastical, absurd. 'He has not. I must have imagined it after all.'

Annie waited.

'Maybe he didn't mean it that way,' Molly went on. 'Maybe he meant "I love you" same as I'd say "I love the little boat that goes to Piel Island in summer" or "I'd love a Guselli's ice on a day like this." It's his books he loves. Perhaps he just likes me because I take care of them.'

'Your Mrs Jepson thinks he does mean it that way, though. But what's more important, Molly, is what you think about him.'

The girl was silent for a moment, aware of Annie's eyes on her.

'I don't know,' she began. 'I'm a bit frightened of him, I think. I don't mean he's done anything to scare me, though he has this habit of popping up where you don't expect him. He's as quiet as a cat, and then you look round and he's there. I don't know anything about him, not really, not more than a servant should know – apart from his troubles in the war, and not all of that. He likes his things to be taken care of, even if they're old and mended. He's not what you'd call flashy, though he must have the money for it. I mean, he doesn't work. Not what you and me and Mr McClure would say was work. And now he's paying *me* not to work; he's got in another girl to help Agnes and Mrs Jepson, but she don't live in. Says my room has to be free for whenever I want it. I don't know where he goes to when he goes off for weeks on end. He said Nice. Other times he's said London, but he could be in Timbuctoo for all I know.'

'Mrs Jepson is right, though, about you gadding about with him on his travels, staying in hotels and signing your name as if you were his wife. Your reputation would never get over that, Molly. It's all a girl has got apart from the work of her hands, and it's easily lost. I've never stayed in a hotel in my life. The nearest I've got was taking tea in the Commercial in Cleator Moor with Mr McClure when we were courting. I didn't even know how to use the sugar tongs, though Mr McClure made it all right.' Molly saw a quiet smile steal over Annie's gentle face.

'Mr Lowther – him at the hotel at the abbey – *he's* told me stories about the guests. The men that turn up with a younger lady and sign their names in the register as Mr and Mrs. Then over the breakfast toast he asks her if she takes sugar. Or sometimes, he said, he's seen them go away in the morning and the man is all distant with the girl, when they've been like newlyweds the night before, and you can see the poor soul is trying not to cry. Because Herbert's been there long enough, he's even seen the same man come back but with a different lass. He says the servant sees all and hears all but says nothing, like them monkeys. He jokes that one day he'd tell me it all and I could type it up and send it to the *News of the World*. Only they'd need to pay him a lot of money for it as he'd never work in service again after. Since he said that I've thought many times of what must be going on in those comfy chairs behind me when I'm sitting there playing the piano. Maybe that's what Mr Slaney meant when he said I had to think of myself as background. No, I don't want to be one of them – *those* girls.'

Annie patted her hand. 'You're a good wee girl, so you are.'

Molly's eyes dampened. Mother Annie might have been many years in England, but the girl knew that it was when the older woman was most moved that her Ulster origins came to the fore.

'What do you tell them at the Technical School?'

Molly hesitated. 'I tell them the truth. That's how you brought me up. Only I don't tell them very much of it. There's one girl I'm friendly with – Ethel. She works on the toy counter at the Co-op but wants to get into the office. I'd say I've got that in common with most of them that's on the typing course – wanting to be something different from what they are. So I've told her I'm a servant and about the piano-playing. She thought that pretty natty and said that I must meet lots of people, only I told her I don't meet any unless you count Herbert and Mr Slaney. If I've not got the lid up then sometimes a drink will appear up there. It's always a man's hand that puts it there. I just nod but don't look at him and go on playing. Then when Herbert passes through he'll take the drink away. There are plenty others that ask him to bring me something: "A little appreciation for the lady pianist and perhaps she'd like to come and sit with me when she has her break?" He's invented all sorts for me, has Herbert. A sheep farmer husband with meaty fists. A fiancé who is a crack shot in the Westmorland Regiment.'

'I've never heard of them.'

'Well, no, they don't exist. He's a bit of a card, is Herbert. When the man persists and says he can't see a ring Herbert tells them that pianists don't wear them so as not to click on the keys. But then I know they've looked.'

'Do you like this Herbert?'

'I do. But only as a friend. And I'm sure that's all he sees me as. I'm his little sister, if anything. Mr Gascarth asked me much the same question.' Molly paused. 'He always has asked questions like that, come to think of it. He asked about Mark.'

'And what did you say?'

'Much the same, really. That he's like a favourite uncle.'

Annie lifted her hand and delicately stroked her finger upwards from the bridge of Molly's nose.

'Don't frown, dear. One day you'll carve a groove there.'

'Mark comes to the hotel, you know.'

'I did. I know why he doesn't come to see you.'

'He's talked to you about it?'

'Yes.' Annie took her hand. 'Listen to me, Molly. I've had it out with him I don't know how many times, but he's mulish when he wants to be, only he calls it having principles. Mark will never court you. He wants you to lead your own life.'

Molly started to cry quietly. 'I might as well go with Mr Gascarth, then, mightn't I?'

'Ah, child, you don't mean that. That'd not be fair to any of you, least of all Mr Gascarth. He'd think he'd bought you.

I don't think he wants that from what you've said about him. Can you keep a secret?'

'Yes,' said Molly, startled.

'I've never told anyone about this, and I'm relying on you to keep it to yourself. When I was much younger, up in Cleator Moor, I spent a few weeks in a home for fallen girls – run by nuns.'

Molly gasped. '*You?*'

'Ssh! They'll hear you out the back. I wasn't fallen, though there were some made out that I was. Robert was courting me, then there was this silly misunderstanding – or a trick played on us is maybe a better way to put it. I went to the nuns in tears, thinking Robert loved someone else, but believing my reputation was already stained, though we'd done nothing. There was girls there who'd been abandoned when they'd told their young men they were expecting. There was another – poor wee soul – who'd been in service until the master laid hands on her. When the mistress found out what was going on she put her out without a character, for "corrupting a God-fearing husband" or some such rubbish. The man had forced himself on the girl, but it was the girl that paid. How many chances has your Mr Gascarth had to do the same thing?'

Molly sat in silence, avoiding Annie's gaze, remembering her first meeting with Anthony Gascarth. *What was it he'd said? 'Jepson's gone to see her cousin in Dalton . . . the other girl is on her half-holiday. I arranged it that way.'*

'Lots, I suppose.'

'But he hasn't taken them. He's sent you to learn a trade instead, even though he's said he knows it might take you away from him. He had to get the permission of the Borough Council to do it, too. I was asked my opinion.'

'And what did you say?'

'I didn't oppose it. I said I'd wished at the time there'd been some means of letting you continue your education and that this wasn't a bad way. I don't suppose he said anything to the Borough about taking you to places in London or France. Go on with the school, and the piano-playing and don't agree to anything you don't feel right about.'

Molly brightened. 'He says I'm very good at the piano. He said it was a pity the films are all talking ones, or my next stop would've been the Coliseum on Rawlinson Road. Imagine that, playing to a thousand people!'

'Talking films? I've not been for ages. The pictures will be like the Royalty then, with the real actors.'

'Might do them out of a job,' said Molly.

'I can't imagine it though, can you? Charlie Chaplin with a voice.'

'It'd be like Buster Keaton with a smile.'

Annie laughed, just as a little girl put her head around the door. 'Mrs-McClure-Mother-Annie,' she said in a rush, 'tea's up.'

CHAPTER NINETEEN

Indexing, Lindal Hall

'I think the first thing we need, Molly, is a catalogue.'

'For all of them?' she asked, casting her eye around the library.

'Indeed.'

'But why, sir? You know where they all are, what they are. And they're never out of place.'

'*I* do, and you do, Molly. Whoever comes after me won't. My books do not exist uniquely. They exist as a whole. A family isn't a random collection of people, is it? Each person in it stands in relation to everyone else in it in a different way. That's how I think of my books. I hope they won't be broken up after I've gone, as if they were children packed off to separate orphanages—Oh my God, Molly, I am sorry. I'm a clumsy oaf.'

Molly turned a pale face up to him. 'It's all right, Mr Gascarth. It's the best possible way to explain it.'

'You dear girl. I'm sorry all the same.'

Molly dipped her head to her notepad. *So I'm his dear girl. Or is that just his way of speaking?* 'Is that what that funny little cabinet is for?'

'Exactly.' He pulled out one of the drawers and ran a finger across the cards stacked inside. They flowed forward in a wave.

'They're held in place on a spike. You unscrew it at the back here. I thought something quite simple to start with. Catalogue by author, then by title. There are dividers, see? Perhaps also by subject matter.'

'Won't the noise of the typewriter disturb you?'

'I thought you could work on the big table and I would bring the books out to you.'

It was a laborious task and proceeded slowly but Molly found it utterly absorbing. After a while she barely registered the hands that appeared just at the edge of her field of vision, replenishing the pile of books she was working through and taking away those already catalogued. Opening each volume carefully at its title page she read the author's name, that of the book, the date and place of publication as if that page was a human face, providing clues to the personality that lay within. Some of the older books had elaborate designs on their title pages, like picture frames. Their thick pages crackled to her touch. Gascarth would deliver to her right hand, and walk behind her chair to collect from her left. From the kitchen drifted snippets of conversation as Agnes and Mrs Jepson prepared the broth and warmed the bread that was to be their midday meal. Molly was pleased they were close by and could hear the staccato clack of the typewriter keys. She wanted them to know that she worked too, that she didn't stand idly chatting to the Master in the library.

But when it was time to eat she was startled to hear Gascarth ask for two places to be laid at the far end of the table.

'But I've always eaten in the kitchen, sir,' she said, loudly enough that Mrs Jepson would hear.

'And you shall continue to do so, only not today.'

Their meal, though, passed off largely in silence. Gascarth broke it only towards the end, as he passed a fragment of bread around his bowl to mop up the last of the broth. He spoke quietly, glancing as he did so in the direction of the kitchen where the cook and Agnes had started washing up.

'If you have forgiven my gaffe this morning, perhaps I might ask you something?'

Not knowing what a gaffe was, Molly nodded uncertainly.

'I mean what I said about my books being broken up as if they were children going to separate orphanages . . . was there just you, Molly? Or did you have brothers and sisters?'

'They have never told me that I did,' she said slowly. 'I've wondered about it sometimes. I know this sounds strange, but I have always felt I was alone.'

'But you have – if I may – wondered about your mother and father, I expect.'

'Yes,' said Molly immediately. 'I think about them every waking day. I can't remember when I didn't. Mr McClure showed me my birth certificate but I won't get it until I am of age. My name isn't Dubber on it, it says Ashworth. But he made out that was something the Guardians did, changing names.'

'I suppose it matters for the bureaucrats only if you marry.'

'*Marry?* Whoever would I be thinking of marrying?'

At that point Agnes appeared from the kitchen with the speed of a jack-in-the-box and shot Molly a conspiratorial look as she took away her empty bowl.

'Oh dear,' she muttered as the girl disappeared into the kitchen.

'A hypothetical question,' said Gascarth, 'and as usual I'm being too presumptuous.'

'Will I mash the tea?' said Molly, getting to her feet.

'Oh . . . not for me. I shall be in the library when you're ready to start work again.'

Molly drank hers down at the scrubbed kitchen table, in the company of her old friends. It wasn't quite as before, though. She was wearing a blouse and skirt made for her by Robert McClure for her stints at the hotel, clothes which had enabled her to blend in at the Technical School, whereas Mrs Jepson and Agnes were in servants' garb. Agnes could barely contain herself.

'You *see*,' she said in a breathy stage whisper. 'I knew it! It's just like one of them Marie Corelli books.'

'Agnes, *no*! It's just his way of talking.'

'Molly Dubber, the modern Cinderella!'

'You need ugly sisters for that,' cut in Mrs Jepson, 'and you can't get pumpkins round here either. Besides, our Molly's working, not going to balls.'

*

The shadows were lengthening when Molly realised that the pile of books had not been replenished. She looked round as Gascarth came through from the library empty-handed.

'I think that's enough for today. I don't want to bring lamps in case oil spills on the books and I certainly don't want you ruining your eyesight working through dusk. Come through when you've typed the last card.'

But after she'd pulled the canvas cover over the typewriter Molly sat for a moment, flexing her fingers. *What I did today means something. Something permanent. Not like cleaning, where you've to go back and do it again two days later, or getting the dinner ready which you eat and then it's gone. Them little cards will be in that drawer for years for other people to use.*

She picked up the last three books and their cards. Gascarth wasn't in the library but Molly saw the gap on the shelf for the volumes and replaced them. Then she slotted the cards into their proper places and tightened the skewer at the back of the cabinet. She was straightening up as Gascarth walked in and came right up to her.

'Happy, Molly?'

'Oh yes.'

'So am I.' Then he cupped her face in his hands before she could answer, and bent his head to kiss her. In the minutes that followed, Molly learned that what she had imagined as a simple touching of lip to lip was something much greater, something that absorbed body and soul. It was the smell of him, the feel of his arms, one around her shoulder, the other around her waist, the gathering in to another human being, the rasp of his evening stubble on her cheek, the hardness of his torso and the galloping of his heart and her own.

At last the kiss ended, but not the embrace. He moved his hand up to ease her head against his shoulder, holding her there.

'Dear Molly,' she heard him say. 'I have wanted to do that for so long. I fought it for so long – and then I thought, why not try to be happy for as long as I am able?' He stroked her hair. 'Can you bear to look at me, dearest girl?'

161

Molly lifted her head to meet his eyes. 'Bear to? Oh yes. I wondered would you ever . . . that is, I thought I must've made up them – *those* things you said.'

'Did you want them to be real?' he said, smiling.

'Yes . . . only . . . only I didn't dare think on them, really.'

'You have only to tell me, and I won't do it again.'

Her eyes slid away then. She thought of Mark, the way when he spoke to her his eyes fixed on a point above her head, Mark who had said he loved her voice. Mark who had come to the hotel but had not let her know. Mark who had steadfastly refused to acknowledge that he was the first man she'd loved, who'd kept her at arm's length, saying that she had to live her own life.

'Molly?'

She looked up into Anthony Gascarth's flushed face, into his troubled eyes.

'I shan't. I shan't tell you not to do it again.' She saw relief flood his face.

'May I?'

Mute, Molly nodded. This time, the hands that had been pressed against his chest stole upwards and around his neck to touch his hair. *It's even softer than I thought it would be.*

Later, he said, 'I want to show you the rest of my life, Molly. Come to London with me.'

CHAPTER TWENTY

London Midland Scottish

There were so many things about that day on the train that were novel. It wasn't only being somewhere with Anthony Gascarth that wasn't the Hall. Molly realised she had never seen him outside that setting, for glimpsing a man in plus fours hiding behind a newspaper in the entrance hall of the hotel didn't really count. Standing there on the platform at Barrow while the porter managed their luggage into the first-class carriage was more than the beginning of a journey. *I'm going to find out who he is, what he does, all that part of him I know nothing about.* To begin with, the Master was wearing a hat. In fact, everything he wore was different. He was sleek, from his hatband, down the length of the dark, well-cut coat, to the tips of his black polished shoes. The look in his eyes when they rested on her, the feel of his hand on her elbow, the scent of him — all these things were the same. He had stood out in the ticket office amongst the flat-capped shipwrights and labourers. The other men who got into their carriage, however, were dressed more or less as he was, even if, Molly felt, they did not carry themselves with the style of the man who was now pushing aside the door of the compartment and ushering her inside. *It's a uniform, that's what it is. That's what you've to do when you go out into the world. You've to try to look the way other people do.* In that moment she felt a pang of longing for the Hall, for its creaking quietness, the smell of books and beeswax, the glossy smoothness of the Broadwood's keys beneath the pads of her fingers – and realised she was homesick.

'It's a bit grand for me, in't it?' she said, looking at the upholstered seats, their headrests protected with starched cloth.

'Are you worried about how you look, Molly?'

She nodded. *How was it he knew?*

'When we're in London we can get you other clothes if you want. Though if I'm honest I like you as you are now,' he said, 'in that demure blouse and dark skirt. As far as the world is concerned, you're travelling with me as my assistant – as that is what you are. I have no intention that they should think you are my mistress.'

Molly stared at him, not knowing whether he meant to reassure or offend her. In answer, he took her hand and brought her knuckles to his lips.

'Much as I might wish that you were, dearest girl.'

*

'No great rush,' said Gascarth, standing up and pulling his coat and hers down from the rack. 'The train can't go any further. Everything ends in London, or it begins. I'll be back with a porter.'

Before Molly could stand up, he had slid open the compartment door and disappeared into the corridor. Through the opening rushed a cacophony of squealing brakes, hooting, men shouting something that was like English but not English as Molly had ever heard it. She glanced out of the window opposite only to see another train pulling in, inches away it seemed, erupting with people who were buttoning coats, adjusting hats, reaching down suitcases, grasping umbrellas, talking and laughing but in dumbshow, like the actors in the old silent pictures. And so many of them.

'I'll never get used to this,' Molly murmured. The silence of the Hall seemed a mirage, something dreamed of or an image glimpsed in an old book. None of the people turned round to see her standing staring at them. They were all too occupied with their own rushing lives.

'Ready, Molly?'

'Oh!' She turned round, mortified he had caught her gawping. Behind him, a porter waited. Molly wondered if she was supposed to say hello, but the man was taking no notice of her. Gascarth steered her out of the compartment and followed her down the corridor. She had hoped for fresher air, after the heavy fug of dusty upholstery and lingering tobacco, but though it was colder out on the platform, what she breathed was no cleaner: steam, oil and hot metal. That was no different from Barrow, she reminded herself, except in scale. The shock was the number of people – a river of them, and all, it seemed, in a hurry. The women walked differently from at home and their ankles looked neater, their stockings shinier, their heels more delicate.

Already she was thinking about how she might adjust her hat in the first mirror she saw herself in, to set it at an angle the way these London girls did. Then she felt Gascarth's guiding hand at her elbow and turned into the solidity of him. He bent his head.

'Take my arm, Molly.'

Gratefully she did so, and joined the throng, thinking, as she looked out from beneath the brim of her hat, that elegant though these city women were, the men they walked and talked with so freely were nowhere near as dashing as the one she leaned gently into.

Minutes later, she was sitting back in the scuffed leather upholstery of a cab. The door slammed shut, Gascarth leaned forward to give directions; the man nodded without looking round. Molly watched her employer slide back the glass and thought how marvellous it was to get into a car like this one and know just what to do. Seconds later, however, she clung to the man sitting next to her in fright.

'Molly?'

'It came so close!' she cried.

'What, the omnibus?'

'It was right up against us. I thought it were going to topple over, I did.'

'Molly, our driver knows what he's doing,' said Gascarth, his voice tinged with laughter. 'He dodges omnibuses for a living.'

Gradually, curiosity took over. Somehow nobody did crash into each other. The cars, carts yoked to lugubriously plodding horses, bicycles, those top-heavy buses with people leaping on and off as though they were on fairground rides, wove around each other like fish in a stream.

'Where can they all be going?' she said.

'About their business. Much as we are.'

Molly wondered when she was to find out what that business was. But more than that, she wondered where they were going and what door would close behind them when they got there.

Fifteen minutes later the taxi puttered to a halt in a quiet street of terraced brown-brick houses. Gascarth paid the driver and took hold of their two suitcases.

'We're on the second floor,' he said. 'You didn't think I had the whole building, did you?'

'N-no,' said Molly, who'd thought precisely that.

'I own it, of course, and a few of the other houses. But I just keep the one flat for my use.' At the top of the steps he put down the cases and fumbled in a pocket. Molly glanced down the area steps. She caught a glimpse of crockery on a table by a window, and heard the crackle of a radio playing band music. *Perhaps them people see more of him than me and Mrs Jepson do.*

In a gracious but almost unfurnished hallway Gascarth paused by a small table, picking up some of the envelopes laid out there. 'Could you deal with these, Mollie?' he said, holding them out to her. 'No, not tonight,' he said, catching the flicker of disappointment on her face. 'When we've unpacked, I thought I would take you to dinner.'

The flat he led her up to was spacious but austere. Molly looked about her. The contrast with Lindal Hall was total. Here the furniture was new and functional, clean-lined pale oak. A few framed etchings hung from a picture rail; Molly recognised one as Furness Abbey. There was one little utilitarian book-case, holding not volumes but box files. Rugs lay on the floors, framed by varnished floorboards, but in place of the bright jewel colours of the old Turkey carpets at the Hall, these had abstract designs in toning colours of brown, russet and beige. The entrance hall at the hotel swam into her mind, with its inglenook with the piano, potted plants and upholstered chairs with the curved legs, and for the first time she thought of it as fussy and old-fashioned.

'It's not how I thought it would be,' was all she could find to say.

'It's an office one can live in,' said Gascarth shrugging. He walked to the desk under the window, where he took the lid off a typewriter. Molly saw it was an identical model to the one at the Hall.

'I had this delivered,' he said. 'I won't need to use those typing bureaux if you're here.'

'I shall start on the letters in the morning,' said Molly, trying to keep the disappointment out of her voice.

He strode over to her then and took hold of her shoulders.

'Look at me, Molly, would you?'

'Sir?'

'You must think me a dashed cold fish. I've been trying to be one, I'll admit, but it's no use. May I kiss you again, dear girl?'

'Yes please,' Molly heard herself say.

'Best if you took off that hat, I think.'

Afterwards, Gascarth tucked her head beneath his chin and spoke over her tousled hair.

'I thought you had possibilities, you know, the first time I saw you.'

'You make me sound like that flower girl in the play,' came Molly's muffled answer.

Gascarth laughed, a little uneasily.

'Eliza Doolittle? Professor Higgins was a fool. Eliza understood far more than he did: "The difference between a lady and a flower girl is not how she behaves, but how she's treated." He should have appreciated her for what she was, not as a means for him to show off. Appreciated her, and married her.'

Molly felt him grow still, as the silence between them lengthened. Then, as she knew he would, he let her go, clapping his hands on her upper arms.

'*I'm* a fool too. I expect you're hungry. Let me show you where everything is and then we shall go out.'

*

Looking in, Molly marvelled at the green-tiled bathroom, the soap holder inset into the wall, the chrome fittings, the white bath towels on the cork-seated chair, but above all the depth of the bath itself on its curled feet, all of it a smaller version of the palatial space at Croslands Park Road.

'Must take a bit of cleaning,' she said without thinking.

'*You're* not to do it. Mrs Bonelli comes in three times a week when I'm here. Once a week otherwise. I'm in here.' His hand brushed the panels of the next door along but he left it closed. Then, 'This one is yours.'

The room was long and narrow, but the sash window was deep. Molly could make out the uppermost branches of a birch tree.

'There was a bit of a fight about that,' he said. 'Some of the tenants wanted it taken down. Complained about birds singing in its branches, if you please, and leaves brushing the glass. I daresay it does block out the light a bit on the floor below, though most of the time the people are out at work anyway. I put my foot down.'

'I'm glad you did.'

She cast her eye over the narrow, iron-framed bed. It looked no different from those she had slept in at Roose Road, except that this one had a fatter pillow and was covered with an army blanket, tucked in tight. There was a small gentleman's wardrobe and, wonder of wonders, a washbasin. The room smelled of camphor.

'Not what you'd call feminine, I know. Make it your own, Molly. Flowers, if you like. Some pictures.'

Something in his voice made her turn around.

'Whose room was this, sir?'

Gascarth lifted his eyebrows. 'I expect when the conversion was done, it was intended for a manservant. I don't know that anyone in this building has one now. They've Mrs Bonelli too, most of them, and they get chaps in if they're entertaining. This was Munday's room, since you ask. He was my batman.' Molly saw his lips compress, his eyes slide away.

'I'm sorry, sir,' she said instinctively.

'They consult the family, you know, for each of those white grave markers – in Flanders, I mean. The man's first name isn't allowed, just his initials. But he can have some words from a poem, or a hymn. All has to be approved, of course. You're not permitted "a great lie" or anything they'd think of as unpatriotic.

His mother wrote to me. She wanted something but couldn't think what to put. He had a twin, did poor Munday, but he bought it too, before my lad did. I gave her "Greater love hath no man than this, that a man lay down his life for his friends". I couldn't think of anything more apt. Not that I deserved it.'

Molly wanted to ask Gascarth about his own wounds, about what had put him in that hospital in Scotland. But she didn't dare. Mother Annie had warned all the little girls not to be nosy. She could hear her voice still: "If anyone wants you to know a thing, they'll tell you in their own time." Instead, she said, 'Have you been to the grave, Mr Gascarth?'

He breathed in audibly. 'No. Never. But I owe him that too.' Then he turned away abruptly. 'Come and find me when you're ready,' he said over his shoulder. 'It's not far but it's starting to rain.'

*

'You'd probably prefer the Criterion Roof Garden,' he said as he helped her into her coat, 'but I doubt you'd want to traipse down to Piccadilly this evening. There's a little place round the corner I go to.'

'In't it a bit cold for a roof garden anyway?' said Molly.

Gascarth paused, then laughed. 'It's inside, believe it or not. It's all make-believe.'

'Oh.'

'Like so much in life.'

*

171

Molly was impressed that the waiters greeted Gascarth by name. With her, they were polite but distant. They were shown to a wood-pannelled booth. Inadvertently nudging his foot under the table, Molly drew back her own and tried to hide her embarrassment in the leather-bound menu. Only that made it worse.'

'Mr Gascarth,' she whispered, 'I don't understand any of it.'

'Ah yes . . . they're Germans.'

'*Germans?*' Aware that one of the waiters was looking across at her, Molly went fumbling for a handkerchief in her bag, her face flaming. She wondered if she'd manage to eat anything at all.

'I never did have any beef with restaurateurs, Dachshund dogs or people called Faber,' said Gascarth. 'They weren't the ones who took us to war. Germans who'd been here for years had a hard time of it. Got their windows broken and were told to go home. So I do what I can to help them recoup their losses. Do you like sausages and cabbage?'

'I'll say so,' said Molly, relieved.

Gascarth turned and summoned the waiter. Molly stared at the tablecloth, unable to understand anything of what he'd said to the man. But as she told him later, the sausages and cabbage were 'the best thing I've ever eaten,' for indeed they tasted like nothing she had ever encountered. It was only afterwards that she remembered to apologise for eating meat in front of him.

'That's all right. I know that Jepson has rabbit sometimes when I'm not there, even if she pretends she hasn't, though she told me you won't.'

THE MAID OF LINDAL HALL

'That makes me feel worse. Not eating meat when you're not there and then wolfing it down in front of you.'

'It shouldn't. I'm afraid I just translated the simplest thing on the menu for you.'

'That rice you had looked nice.'

'Liar. Actually it was, though. It's supposed to have beef in it, but they're used to my foibles here.'

'Is this where you usually sit?' said Molly.

'Do you mean have other women sat where you are sitting now? Yes, one or two. But most times I dine here alone.'

*

Gascarth offered her his arm on the short walk home. Molly didn't know if this was simply good manners or if it meant anything more. It was like his kisses, which puzzled her; they always took her by surprise, even if each time she longed for the next. *He always says he wanted to, then when he does, behaves as if it hasn't happened.* Nevertheless, she wished that the people they passed on the rain-glossy pavements would turn and notice them. She wanted them to think them a 'handsome couple' – one of Agnes's favourite expressions, gleaned from her *Peg's Paper* reading. With a little flicker of delight and terrified longing, she wanted them to think that he and she were going back to a home they shared, to sit at opposite ends of that enormous bathtub, to afterwards tumble rosily-heated and slightly damp into white sheets, from which a warming pan had just been thoughtfully withdrawn.

Only of course the Bloomsbury flat had the marvel of electric lighting but none of the familiar comfort of a warming pan. And it was Munday's old bed that awaited her, its sheets and blanket tucked in with such military precision that it would be like sliding into an envelope.

'Penny for them, Molly?'

'Oh ... I was just wondering what all them people were thinking. They all seem to be in such a rush.'

'That's London for you. Whether you're in a rush or not you'd best look as though you are. Each of them in their own world, Molly. If you want to be anonymous, this is the place to come. If you want privacy, also.'

Molly felt an unexpected stab of homesickness, thinking of the shops on Dalton Road, the women stopping Mrs McClure and herself: 'Aw right, Annie?'

'I hope though that you come to love it,' Gascarth went on, 'for I should like you to come here regularly.'

Again that little flicker of hope and desire.

'Sanderson is coming after breakfast – my agent. Perhaps you would take notes of our meeting. They did teach you short-hand in Barrow?'

Molly nodded, mute. She felt suddenly as though her shoes were letting in water, though her feet were bone dry.

*

'I'll say goodnight now, Molly. I insist that you try the bath. You're a fastidious person, and London is a dirty old place.' He leaned forward in the hallway and kissed her forehead, much as Mrs McClure had done when she'd lived in Roose Road. Molly didn't know whether to be grateful to him for reminding her of the woman she loved as a mother, or angry for treating her as a child.

'I shall not trouble you further,' he said. 'I'll know when you've gone to bed as I know the sound every door makes here.' Then he turned away and went into the sitting room.

Molly lay awake for an hour. The room had seemed quiet when she first lay down, but the noise of London rose up to meet her in the darkness, even though the window looked over the backs of other houses, not the road. She wondered if she'd ever get used to it, the clang of the omnibuses, the puttering of cars, the crack of horseshoe on asphalt. Gascarth had been right about the dirt, too. Though she'd changed her travel-stained blouse to go out to dinner, the one she'd worn only to the restaurant had a rim of grime around the inside of the cuffs. She'd seen no laundering equipment in the flat; this didn't surprise her, as somehow a dolly tub would look as incongruous here as a warming pan. Agnes had read about marvels like washing machines with built-in mangles, so she had looked around for such a thing, without knowing exactly what it was she was seeking. Perhaps Mrs Bonelli took in laundry . . .

The noise did lessen, a little. The kind of people who got omnibuses would have to go to work in the morning, she reflected. The horses had been stabled and those motor cars she could intermittently hear had to belong to those rich enough that they could stay out as long as they liked. *They'll have people like Agnes*

175

and me to bring them breakfast on a tray in the morning. Another presence now made itself felt in the not quite quiet. The faintest memory of tobacco and shaving soap. Her hands flat on the rough army blanket, Molly thought for a moment she could hear someone breathing, until she held her own breath and realised there was no one there but herself.

CHAPTER TWENTY-ONE

Marshall and Snelgrove

The first surprise when she awoke was to hear Gascarth moving about the flat. She could remember no occasion back at the Hall when he had been up before herself or Mrs Jepson. There was no reproach in his voice, though, when she found him in the kitchen.

'Ah, Molly! I trust you slept well. Do you think you could make us some toast? I can't be trusted not to set fire to the place. Bring it into the sitting room, would you? And some coffee.'

When she carried the breakfast through ten minutes later, it was to find that he had opened the gateleg table and set two places. As she hesitated, he looked at the tray and said, 'Bring yours too. I wasn't expecting you to eat it standing up in the kitchen.'

*

As Molly's previous experience of London had come out of books, Mr Sanderson turned out to be a bit of a surprise. Instead of a hand-wringing Uriah Heep, she opened the door to a suave, thin man who smelled of cologne and who looked past her as he handed her his coat, hat and umbrella with a muttered, 'Thank you, so kind.'

However, when she left her sanctuary of the kitchen for the sitting room in response to Gascarth's call 'Will you join us, Miss Dubber?' it was to face the man's frank gaze. His eyes slid to Gascarth's face, his eyebrows raised in a question.

'Miss Dubber is my private secretary. She'll take notes and type them up for the files.'

'From the secretarial bureau?'

'No. From Lindal Hall.'

'Very good.'

From then on Sanderson took no notice of Molly sitting in the corner, her pencil scampering over the pages of her pad. She took down details of rents, of defaults, of new tenancies, repairs. She didn't dare interrupt the flow to ask for the spelling of some of the names. *I'll mebbe find them in the files after.* Then, just as business appeared to be finished and Sanderson was screwing the top on his own fountain pen, Gascarth said, 'I should like to increase my philanthropic giving.'

'You'd like me to look at the funds you send to LESMA?'

'No – leave them as they are for the moment. I may increase them later. I was thinking about blinded servicemen.'

'Hmm. I saw those marchers back in 'twenty. A raggle-taggle lot by all accounts. Socialists, I should think.'

Molly suppressed a gasp. She wanted to throw her pencil at the man.

'If you mean the League of the Blind, I wasn't thinking of them,' said Gascarth coldly. 'They want rights, not my charity, so I shan't insult them by forcing my munificence on them.'

'There are the St Dunstan's chaps, in Regent's Park,' said Sanderson, unperturbed. 'They do good things. Training the men as leather workers, poultry farmers, tray-making.'

'Piano tuners?'

Sanderson shrugged. 'That too, doubtless. I can find out more if you wish.'

'I do wish. Thank you, Sanderson.'

'Your Miss Dubber will show me out?'

'No, old man. My Miss Dubber has some typing to do.'

*

Molly's hands were trembling as she pulled the cover off the typewriter. *If I get on and do this straightaway it'll be easier. And it'll help me to calm down.* She heard the murmur of the men in the hallway and a short laugh that wasn't Gascarth's. Then the front door banged shut and she heard the thud of his returning feet.

'I don't care for him much either, Molly. But he's good at his job.'

'Raggle-taggle lot! Easy for him to say!'

'His father worked for my father, and they were friends. That's really why I have kept him. And he's loyal.'

'I'm sorry. I've no right to comment on what you do.'

'On the contrary. I'd welcome your opinion on many things. For instance, a play I'd like to take you to see on Saturday.'

'A play?'

'Rather old-fashioned stuff, I should think. At the risk of boring you. *Love in a Village* at the Lyric.'

'I'm sure I shouldn't be bored,' said Molly. 'I've been with Mrs McClure a few times in Barrow and loved going.'

'Ah yes, I remember you told me. This might be a bit different.'

Molly coloured. She'd been enthralled by the Tod Slaughter melodramas she had seen at Her Majesty's, loving the collective thrill of horror as Maria Marten brought down her axe or Sweeney Todd wielded his razor. Hearing his dismissive tone, she wished she'd not said anything.

'I'd best get this lot typed up then,' she said, pulling a sheaf of paper out of the drawer.

'Good idea. Then we'll go and find luncheon somewhere and do some shopping.'

'I could do that, if you let me know what you need,' said Molly, remembering a shuttered greengrocer's they had passed the evening before.

'I meant something a little different. Don't deny me the pleasure of helping dress you, Miss Dubber. No – there's no need to look so startled. What you're wearing just now is perfect as my employee but if I'm to take you to the theatre then I wish you to appear as my companion.'

*

'Modom is slender,' said the assistant in Marshall and Snelgrove's. 'Perfect for the current styles.'

Molly was at first puzzled at the way the woman wouldn't address her directly, even though she was standing next to her in the changing room, adjusting the pleats of a shimmering crêpe-de-Chine shift that on the hanger had looked to her like a limp rag. Then she realised that of course those words weren't directed at her but at the man sitting outside the curtain, the man who would unfold the necessary banknotes, the man the woman referred to consistently as 'the gentleman'. Molly hadn't missed the flickering of the woman's eyes to her left hand the moment she had eased off her gloves.

But even the assistant allowed a genuine smile to break through her professional haughtiness when, standing at Molly's shoulder, she gently nudged the girl round to see her reflection in the mirror.

'Oh, it's lovely!' breathed Molly. She felt tears prick her eyes at just how beautifully the dress draped. It was completely unadorned but was made sophisticated by the little pleated bands on the short sleeves, and the shirred apron, as the assistant called it, that hung from the dropped waist, though anything less like an apron as she knew it, Molly couldn't imagine. Then her eyes dropped to her shoes and her heart sank. They might have been regularly resoled and polished once a week within an inch of their lives, but they looked clumpy and dull and ugly, their black killing the soft coffee and tobacco panels of the dress. The assistant saw her cue and took it.

'If Modom would let me know her shoe size then I'll ask my colleagues to bring a suitable choice – chestnut, I would suggest.'

Molly hesitated. Then a voice reached them from beyond the curtain. 'Yes, we will require shoes. Silk stockings, too. And a suitable coat. Oh, and a couple of chemises. Those I do not need to see.'

*

Molly was aware of Gascarth's eyes on her as the purchases were folded into tissue-paper. Even the scarf collar of the soft dark-brown wool coat was packaged with care.

'Tell me, Molly,' he said as the doors of the lift clanged shut on them and their purchases, 'did you choose that coat over the one with the fur trim because you liked it best or because you wanted to please me?'

'I did like it best. But even if I hadn't, I wouldn't have taken the other. Because I know you wouldn't have wanted me to.'

'Dear girl.' His head tilted towards her, but even though the liveried lift-attendant kept his back scrupulously turned to them, Gascarth didn't kiss her.

'Oh, I nearly forgot,' he said in a louder voice. 'Would you be so kind as to take us to the perfumery?'

'Very good, sir.'

*

That night, Molly sat up in a darkness that wasn't darkness, for this was London, where beyond the curtains there was always a shimmering dirty-yellow light, even in fog. Her ears strained for whatever that sound was that had woken her. A fox, somewhere amongst the dustbins in the mews lane?

There it was again. The tiny hairs on the back of her neck stiffened. Not a fox but a human cry – a sound of pure suffering, terror and loneliness. And it was coming from within the flat. Molly fumbled under the shade of the bedside light for the switch. Lit, the room was just as it had been, with her towel on the hook near the washbasin, her wrap hanging from the hook on the back of the door – another present acquired that afternoon in the West End. Her feet landed on the bedside rug, which shifted on the parquet. She waved a hand under the bed, pulling out her slippers. The cry was repeated, though this time it was more like a sob.

Tying the belt of the wrap, Molly scurried to Gascarth's door. On the threshold she paused, not knowing if she should knock or just go straight in. No light was visible around the door frame, which alarmed her. Wouldn't turning on the light not be the first thing a frightened person would do to banish the terrors of the night? That piteous cry came again and Molly turned the doorknob.

In the shadows all she could make out was the chaos of the bed, blankets and pillows tossed anyhow, as though it had been the scene of a struggle. In the gloom loomed a solid military desk, a small bookcase, a washbasin. She could hear laboured breathing, but the bedclothes were as still as death.

'Sir?' she whispered.

That chilling cry again.

Molly crossed to the far side of the bed. Gascarth was crouched on the floor, trembling. In the smudgy light from the gap in the curtains she could see his hands clutching his hair, his shoulders heaving, the nubs of his spine. Dressed, he had always given Molly an impression of leanness, not this tense thinness. There was something else though – dents and hollows in his lower back, as if he was made of soft clay out of which rough fingers had scooped lumps. Her eyes travelling over the scarred terrain of his body, Molly realised with a shock that her employer must be completely naked.

Of course, she thought, remembering. *There never was pyjamas to wash back at the Hall. I'd never thought anything of it. I just thought he must've slept in a shirt.*

He shifted then, his knees coming up as he folded in on himself like a jackknife.

'Sir?' she said softly.

A tremor ran through the man, as though he'd received an electric shock. But when he spoke, though without lifting his head, the words were clear.

'Leave me here and get back, man. I'm done for.'

'Sir?'

'That's an order, Munday!'

Molly remembered a little girl in Roose Road who'd been prone to sleep-walking, a child who had lost both parents, and though she had stood at their graveside, in her walking dreams hopelessly searched for them. Mother Annie had given Molly the responsibility of keeping an eye on the child, leading her back to bed and talking gently to her, but on no account waking her up.

'I won't leave you, sir, whatever you tell me,' she said softly, realising that although she was playing the part of the long-dead Munday, it was true.

'You're lucky I'm dying then,' murmured Gascarth, 'otherwise I'd court martial you myself.'

'Come, sir.' She put her hands on his shoulders, feeling the tension vibrating through his skin. 'We can't stay here.'

'Munday . . .'

But his voice sounded more distant now, as though the nightmare was receding, and he was falling back into a normal sleep.

How to get him onto the bed? Then inspiration struck.

'Can you stand, sir? There's a stretcher here.'

'Could try . . . Corporal Loveridge with you?'

'Right behind me.'

Gascarth raised an arm, at which Molly crouched alongside him, feeling the sweaty heat of him radiate through the thin material of her wrap and nightdress. His arm flailed at her shoulder, until she reached her right hand back and pulled his into hers. He came up with the weight of a sleeper and Molly gasped as he staggered against her, but somehow she managed to tumble him onto the bed, where he curled up again. She disentangled sheets from blankets as best she could and covered him up to the neck, realising that her heart was thumping from tension as much from effort. She stood by the bed looking down on him, trying to master her breathing. He lay still, but his eyes were open, glassy and unseeing. She remembered another trick from Roose Road, and gently ran her finger tip from his hairline down his nose. It had often worked in getting young children to close their eyes and think about sleeping, and to her relief it worked now. Anthony Gascarth's lids came down and his face relaxed; he looked to Molly as though he had been sleeping soundly for hours.

But I daren't leave him.

She glanced around the room, spotting a wicker armchair. It was light to carry to the side of the bed, but creaky to settle into.

I'll just watch him until dawn. Then I'll sneak off before he wakes up.

*

Molly woke to the sound of her name and hands holding her shoulders. Gascarth's concerned face was close to hers; she was relieved to see he was wearing a shirt and trousers, though it looked as though he'd put them on in a hurry, as one of his braces was twisted.

'Oh, I'm sorry, sir. I didn't mean—'

'How long have you been there?'

'I don't know. One o'clock, maybe.'

He straightened up but his eyes remained on her face.

'Having one of my episodes, was I?'

'You were crying out, sir, that's all. A bad dream.'

'Hmm. I wish that's what it had been. A bad dream, I mean.'

'I only meant to stay until dawn. In case you got up again.'

'Got up? Where was I?'

'Down there,' said Molly, pointing.

'You mean you had to put me back in bed?'

Molly lowered her eyes. 'There were sleepwalkers in the home sometimes. I knew what to do.'

There was a short silence before he said, 'You admirable girl! I should beg your pardon for the state you found me in.'

'It was nearly dark. And you were all huddled up.'

'One day, perhaps, I shall tell you why you've had to deal with a naked man who is not your husband, Miss Dubber. I don't have an excuse so much as a reason – I tore up too many pairs of inoffensive pyjamas, you see. Anyway, less of my maunderings. You can't have had much of a night of it in that chair.'

Then, to her complete surprise, he scooped her out of it and carried her over to the door.

'Sir?' she said, too startled to think about struggling.

'I'm taking you back to your own bed,' he said, nudging open the door with his foot. 'I'll bring you your breakfast later, but try to sleep for an hour or so first.'

Her cheek against his chest, and looking up at him, Molly said, 'I've never lain in bed of a morning in my life.'

He glanced down, smiling. 'It has a lot to recommend it, Molly. If the circumstances are right.'

*

She woke to the chink of china close at hand and sat up straight.

'What time is it?'

'I haven't the faintest idea, and nor should you. We do not have work today. It's a Saturday. And I have those tickets for the Lyric later. Eat your toast before it gets cold. I've managed not to set the kitchen on fire.'

CHAPTER TWENTY-TWO

The Lyric, Hammersmith

'This is our door, I believe,' said Gascarth, at the end of the curved corridor. He opened it and stood back for Molly to pass. What she'd heard earlier as the muffled sounds of instruments tuning up against a hum of voices redoubled in volume. Despite the whispering of the layers of her new dress, the clip-clip of the heels of her side-buttoned shoes, the effortless drape of the coat with the scarf collar, the hiss of silk stocking on silk stocking as she settled into her seat in the taxi to Hammersmith, Molly felt her confidence evaporate.

'But everyone can see us,' she said.

'Yes, but that doesn't mean they'll take notice, though they damn well should, a girl as fine as you.' He eased her coat off her shoulders, putting it on the hanger on the back of the door, then gently lifted her cloche.

'May I?' he said, a hand hovering over her hair.

'Pardon?'

'Just this,' he said, softly fluffing her curls.

*

'Well?' said Gascarth as the applause at last died away, after the cast had held hands and bowed and left and come back out three times; after the little orchestra had lifted their bows again and the harpsichordist had placed his hands delicately on the keys once more; after two encore arias had been sung to cheers.

'I didn't want it to end,' said Molly. She rested a hand on the red velvet of the balustrade, wanting to remember what it felt like under her palm. She wanted never to forget the gilt pillars, the fine ladies in flashing sequins and boas, accompanied by their suave companions, the collective laughter. All London life had been there, from those with money in the boxes opposite, the elegant wives and suited men down in the stalls, up to the caps and frowsty straw hats in the cheap seats in the gods. She wanted to remember always the expectant hush as the lights turned down, extinguishing her view of those hundreds of people and they of her, all faces were turned to the glow of the stage as the little eighteenth-century musical farce unfolded.

'A silly story,' Gascarth had said. 'A rich girl runs away to be a chambermaid to avoid marriage with a stranger, falls in love with another servant and then finds out he was the man she was supposed to marry anyway. If it weren't for all the songs, it'd fit on the back of a postcard.'

A silly story, yes, thought Molly, *because who'd run away to be a servant?* But she'd been charmed.

'The play won't end,' said Gascarth. 'Not if you remember it.'

Molly turned her face up to his. 'I have never been so happy.'

'That is the best and the only thanks you owe me. Anything else I must humbly earn from you.'

'Earn?'

'Ah, Molly. Let me take you home. Before they throw us out.'

The girl took one more look at the auditorium, but it was already losing its magic. Most of the audience had left, and cleaners were working their way through the rows of the stalls, turning up the seats, lifting forgotten programmes and abandoned cigarette packets.

Outside, reality imposed itself again. The streets were wet and Molly worried for her beautiful shoes, but somehow in the midst of carts and plodding horses and omnibuses, Gascarth managed to summon a taxi. Molly heard him give the address of the German restaurant. The door slammed and the street flowed past the windows like a film as Molly sank into the cab's scent of stale cigar and worn leather upholstery. *Everything is easier when you've money. But what do you have to do to pay for it?* She thought of the warning Mother Annie had given her when she'd told her she had agreed to accompany her employer to London. 'I'd not stand in the way of advancement for you, Molly. But remember Mr Gascarth wants to employ you in a professional capacity, so be the good girl I know you to be.'

Molly thought of a moment during the second act when she had glanced at the man sitting close by her in the shadows, only to see from the sheen of his eyes that he was looking at her. Now, sitting in the taxi, she turned from the window to find him smiling. In that moment she knew that everything in the last few months had been a sort of subterfuge – the typing and shorthand classes, the fiction about this job as his assistant. With an orphan's instinct for survival, she thought, *I'll always be able to work. He's made sure of that. But he wants me for his mistress. So how long are we both going to pretend he's after anything else?*

The smile came closer, as with gloved fingers, he lifted her chin and dipped his mouth to hers.

*

The meal was an awkward one, though Gascarth's manners were impeccable and the waiters discreet. Molly ate everything, though more slowly than usual, obedient to the Roose Road training that food should never be wasted. The moment their plates were cleared Gascarth muttered, 'This is absurd,' and screwed up his napkin.

'Sir?'

'God, Molly, would you sleep with me? Or if you won't, would you at least stop calling me sir?'

'You mean – keep you company? Because of the nightmares?'

'You dear, wide-eyed innocent. But even *you* know that's not what I mean. Hell, Molly, if there is anyone who could keep my night-time frights away it would be you.' He went on as though a dam had burst. 'I wanted you from the moment I saw you. But I'm an honourable man and you were a young girl. I watched you getting down from Fallowfield's cart and saw you look up at my house and then the wonder in your face at the flowers in my garden. I saw you were beautiful and I guessed you were intelligent. Nothing more than the look in your eyes and the tilt of your head. Not logical, I know. I've seen horrors, Molly. I still do. A walk in the country and I see a mound of corpses, when all that's there are stones and tussocky grass. I see not twisted tree roots but the bones of hastily buried men, picked clean by burrowing rats. When women laugh and draw back their lips from their teeth, all I think of are skulls. I know that in Edinburgh they tried to teach me to behave properly; that's really all you can do with the mad. I can only *manage* what I remember, and that not very well sometimes. I can't forget it. Not even twenty and an officer in charge of braver men; apparently the playing-fields of Sedbergh qualified me to lead them! A far better one than I sacrificed himself for me, Molly.'

'Munday?' she whispered.

'Yes, poor Munday. He left a letter behind for a girl in an Oxfordshire village. I found it in his things and got it posted. A man of courage would have taken it to her, but that wasn't me. What would I have said to her? "Your sweetheart died in my place. Want me instead?"' He gave a short and bitter laugh. 'Munday was denied his future. So I thought I didn't deserve one either.'

He looked away, then said in a changed voice. 'Forgive me, Molly. Forget I said anything. Try to forget my impertinence, if you can.' He was panting, his face pallid. 'Do excuse me . . . my lungs . . . I've been warned not to work myself up.'

'You're not impertinent,' said Molly, watching herself reach for his hand. 'But one day you ought to go to see Munday's girl, if you can remember her name.'

'I can. Her name and her address. Because it was his handwriting and I looked at it often enough before I gave it to the orderly.'

'Well, perhaps she deserved to know that he died saving a friend.'

'Would you come with me?'

Molly hesitated. 'Won't you be sending me back now?'

'Sending you *back*? Why, because you're a sensible young woman who quite rightly doesn't want me to have my wicked way with her? Certainly not. I told you before that I loved you. I still do. I'm a poor bargain for any woman. I'm thirty-three, with crumpled lungs and a dicky heart, and I've never done a proper day's work in my life. And that's before we even get up to my head – seeing things and night frights, Molly. If you want me to send you back, I'll do so. I'll write you a character the Barrow Town Hall couldn't complain of. But I'd beg you not to go. To know you're close by – that's a kind of happiness in itself.'

'Then don't send me back, Mr Gascarth. I don't want to go.'

*

Back home, Anthony Gascarth quietly bid her goodnight, apologising again with the words, 'I should accept I am not much good for any woman now.'

'I'm sure that's not true,' said Molly stoutly, looking up into his troubled eyes, while saying to herself *what would you know about it?*

Then she went to her bedroom – or Munday's bedroom as she couldn't help thinking of it – remembering Mark's resolution that she should get on with her life, that she should not have hopes of him being a part of it. And now Anthony Gascarth was saying much the same thing.

She sat down and began a letter to the person she trusted most in the entire world – Annie McClure.

. . . it looks to me as if every man who has come back from the war has been damaged beyond repair when it comes to living a normal life. Mark has made the best job of it, getting himself a trade and doing his work with the League of the Blind so as the men who've lost their sight can at least have some dignity and rights, not relying on getting money given to them by folk who feel sorry for them. Maybe when I come back to Lindal Hall there could be a way for me to help him sometimes, now that I can type and do the shorthand and everything. I wish he'd see that it's not because I feel sorry for him but because I've always thought him my friend and only want to be able to do something useful for him, as a friend would. Only he seems dead set against it in every way. Mr Gascarth has got me taking a record whenever he has a meeting with his agent, and he says he's never seen anyone do such a good job as me. So I wonder, would Mark accept my services as a professional, if he won't have it other ways?

To see Mr Gascarth you'd think him the picture of health, even if living a bit on his nerves. He's taller than most people I know, and quite broad in the shoulder, but not a pick of fat on him though he has an appetite. Perhaps it's because he doesn't eat meat. Maybe you do get to look like what you eat. He'd maybe be a leek then, long and straight but lots of layers to him! Other folk look like pork fat and boiled pota-toes. I'm being silly, I know. It's because I'm a bit tired and a bit mithered, if I'm honest. I've been to the theatre with him

for he wanted the company. I know you told me to mind that
I was always to behave like a professional and not cross the
lines you told me about, but he didn't want to go on his own
and I loved the play. I can't wait to come and see you to tell
you about it properly. Mr Gascarth is a gentleman.

Molly put down her pen and held a piece of her silk dress
between finger and thumb. She hadn't mentioned the visit to
Marshall and Snelgrove's to Annie and knew that if she did,
the account of her visit to the theatre would read as something
quite different from simply keeping someone company. For
the first time in her life she realised she didn't want the older
woman's counsel, because Annie would plead the caution
Molly didn't want. She wanted to go and comfort Mr Gascarth
and couldn't understand how mortified he was at the suggestion she sleep with him. Isn't that what children did, to keep
night frights at bay? It was only one remove from that night
she'd slept in the wicker chair, wasn't it? And if it would help
the poor man not to have nightmares . . . Only he'd have to find
something to wear. Molly read over what she'd just written and
picked up her pen again.

I mean he opens doors for me and that.

Another pause, in which she decided that she wouldn't mention
the breakfast on a tray.

Only it's not just his nerves that he got taken up to the hospi-
tal in Scotland for. I think he was also quite badly wounded,

though he hasn't said anything to me about that. At supper today he told me again that his lungs are not right, nor his heart. I heard him screaming one night, a noise that'd wrench the heart out of you. Mrs Jepson at the Hall said he's had funny turns ever since he came back from the Front, only up there with my room being so far away, down a staircase and across the house and then up another staircase, I never heard a squeak. Here he's right next door. His batman used to live in this room and so he'd be expected to be within earshot. But folk deal with their problems in so many different ways, don't they? You remember me telling you about Herbert who works at the hotel at the abbey, that got me the job as the pianist? He lost his mam and dad with the influenza, but most of the time you'd never know he'd been anywhere near grief, he's that cheerful. I know I couldn't be like that if I was to lose you and Mr McClure (God forbid). But maybe that's just Herbert's way. Perhaps if you always act happy you can convince yourself that you really are happy. Either that, or he just told himself he'd to get on with it because there was nobody there to get on with it for him. That might be Mr Gascarth's problem; he hasn't really got enough to get on with. You'd think that would be something to envy, wouldn't you? I'm not so sure. I love reading books – well, you know me – but I've to read them when my work is done. Mr Gascarth hasn't got work. He lives on what other people pay him in rent and even then he doesn't deal with the money himself. It's Mr Sanderson who manages things for him and I write up the notes from their meetings. It really is how the other half lives.

Well, I've gone on a bit – sorry. I'll come and see you as soon as I'm back at the Hall. I miss it, but it'll depend on how much Mr Gascarth misses it that'll decide when we leave London.

Give my love to everyone, especially Mr McClure, and Mark when you see him.

Your affectionate daughter,
Molly Dubber

*

Molly put down her pen. She was about to put the letter into an envelope, but heard muffled sounds from next door, so made her decision.

A moment later Molly stood outside Gascarth's door. Inside she could hear quiet splashing noises, followed by the hurried friction of a toothbrush, then the soft footfall of slippers on parquet. She knocked so gently she was afraid she was going to have to find the courage to repeat it. Instead, the footsteps came straight to the door.

'Molly?' He was shirtless, but in his trousers and braces, though barefoot. One brace hung off his left shoulder. 'Forgive me. As you see, I am somewhat *déshabillé*. What's the matter?'

'You asked me if I would sleep with you,' she said, forcing herself to hold his gaze.

'I also asked you to forget I ever said it. I had no business insulting you like that. It was a caddish thing to do.'

Molly lowered her eyes, as she had been taught at Roose Road that a good servant should. 'I don't want to forget it, Mr Gascarth. I'd be glad to help you in any way I can. The way you said. To have me close by.'

A horribly long silence followed, in which Molly wished she could disappear.

'Oh, Molly, my Molly,' he whispered at last. 'Don't stand out there catching cold.'

He closed the door behind them. The small lamp was on above the washbasin, and another on the bedside cabinet, bathing the room in weak orange light, giving it the appearance of an old photograph. Her face hot with embarrassment and astonishment at what she'd just done, Molly longed for these to be turned off.

'If you change your mind, Molly, just say so – now, or at any time.' He took hold of her shoulders. 'You can go back to your room and tomorrow will be as if nothing happened, nothing was said.'

'Yes, sir.'

'Molly, if I am to be your lover, you will have to stop calling me sir.'

'My *lover*?'

She felt a tremor in the fingers holding her through the starched cotton.

'Oh, you poor innocent,' he murmured. 'And how inadequately mealy-mouthed English is when it comes to our emotions. You thought I meant just that, didn't you? To sleep alongside me in case the frights came back?'

Molly nodded. Mortified, she couldn't meet his eyes.

'Then that is what we shall do. It's all we'll do. I will be grateful for your presence, believe me. Here – you get in this side. I'd better find something to wear.'

*

The bed was as warm as a nest. Molly had no idea what time it was, though there was a glimmer of grey light around the edges of the curtains. Anthony Gascarth lay on his side next to her, wearing the underwear he had left the room to put on. His breathing was soft and regular in the near dark. Molly still couldn't quite believe what she had done, going and knocking on his door. She stifled a groan as the remembrance of her mistake washed over her again.

Lover. What a grown-up word. Not sweetheart, or young man, or intended. It's a darker word. A word from a book. I could never tell Mother McClure I'd a lover.

She heard her name whispered.

'Oh! I didn't mean to wake you!'

He kissed her then, a kiss that went on, a kiss that engulfed her entire body, leaving her hungry for more, though he held her by the shoulders, keeping his own body wide of hers. Yet it was a shock when he abruptly drew away, to lie on his back and stare at the ceiling, panting as though he had been running.

Eventually he said, 'I love you, Molly. But I don't want you to tell me you love me, if you don't mind. If you don't, I don't want to know it. If you tell me you do, I'll worry it's because you feel beholden to me.'

'I like you a great deal—' began Molly, until he rolled towards her and cut her off with a finger against her lips.

'Don't. I don't want to hear you say "but".'

Then he turned away, rolled out of bed, and left the room. Molly felt adrift, just as she had when Gascarth had first told her he loved her, and then behaved as if nothing had been said. Hearing sounds from the bathroom, she slid her feet to the floor, grabbed the dressing gown she had left on the chair and pattered off to her own room before he came back.

Her unsealed letter to Annie McClure lay on the dressing table. She picked it up and reread it, feeling her own words of a few hours earlier reproach her.

I really need your advice, Mother Annie, she thought. *Only I just don't know how to put any of this into words.*

She heard the click that meant the bathroom was free. By the time she came out, a smell of coffee was coming from the kitchen, and there was Mr Gascarth with the grill pan in his hand.

'There you are, Molly. I trust you slept well. One slice or two?'

He talks as if nothing has happened.

CHAPTER TWENTY-THREE

Specials

Molly was glad that she'd not added anything to the letter, for since the night she had nestled next to her employer, nothing indeed had happened. He'd not even alluded to it. In fact, she'd seen even less of him. She'd gone to sleep ever since in Munday's narrow bed, ears straining to hear the quiet noises from the adjoining room. There had been nothing untoward. There had been no repeat of that horrible screaming and in the mornings he had gone out alone after breakfast, each time saying something like, 'You can amuse yourself today, can't you?'

Molly had, after a fashion. She'd gone to the British Museum one day, to the Soane Museum the next, liking its cluttered idiosyncrasies better. The guide book hinted at poor Sir John Soane's tribulations with his ungrateful sons. *I'd never want Mother Annie and kind Mr McClure to suffer on account of me.* She wondered, walking away from the museum, about looking for another position, something that could take her away from temptation – because she knew, as she lay in the warmth of Gascarth's bed, his mouth on hers, that if he had not drawn away from her when he had, she'd have given herself up to him to do whatever he wanted, whatever he shouldn't.

But going away would be ingratitude after all he's done for me. I think he needs me. It's only because of him I'd be able to get a job in an office now.

At lunchtime she went into a coffee shop on Holborn Kingsway to get something to drink and a sandwich. Other girls came in, chattering and laughing and teasing the young waiter. Molly watched them for as long as she could without being accused of staring, envying them. They evidently worked together, for they settled at a table nearby, and she heard them talking about businessmen who came in to get their typing done. But as Molly stared into the dregs of her coffee, unable to believe her ears, it emerged that this wasn't any ordinary typing bureau. One of the girls, prettier and louder than the others, was getting ribbed about her 'specials', but from her companions' tone, it was evident they were both admiring and envious.

'The last hotel was in Brighton. The poor fellow was quite the gentleman, but ever so nervous. Never laid a finger on me; some of 'em you've to remind that it's only pretend, but not him. I had to tell him what he'd to do when the servant knocked on the door, or his wife wouldn't get her evidence.'

The waiter came over then, asking if she wanted another coffee. Molly murmured, 'Yes, please,' although she didn't really, but didn't have any other excuse for staying and eavesdropping on a conversation that made the tips of her ears burn. The waiter came back after the group had left in a clatter of heels and a cloud of cheap perfume, to pretend to dust crumbs from her table.

'You're from up the country, ain't yer?' the man said.

'Y-yes,' stuttered Molly. 'How did you know?'

'The look on your pretty face listening to them starlings,' he said. 'You'd eyes like saucers, you did.'

'I did? Oh . . . I couldn't understand what they were talking about.'

'That Gladys is quite the thing, ain't she? I 'spect you want to know what them specials is, doantcher?'

Startled, Molly nodded.

'It's when a chap wants a divorce from 'is lady, or 'er from 'im, and they're agreeable about it. Only they've to find the hevidence, 'aven't they? Hadultery, you know. So the gent does the honourable thing and takes isself off to an hotel with a young lady, so's they can be taken *in flagrante delicto*.' The man flourished the Latin words. 'Then the butler or the chambermaid or whoever's taken 'em their breakfast in bed can be called to give evidence, and bob's yer uncle. Decree nisi and everyone's 'appy. Until the next time.'

Molly stared at him in horror.

'Oh, they don't *do* nothing. They've only to pretend. Gladys is walking out with my best friend and won't look at no other fellow. The way she's going with her specials they'll 'ave the deposit put by for a nice new semi up the line in no time at all.'

'Oh. I see,' said Molly, feeling like a country mouse. Her colossal misunderstanding of Gascarth's request across the table in the German restaurant washed over her again. She fumbled for her purse.

'You can 'ave that on the 'ouse if you'll come to the 'olborn Hempire with me Saturday.'

'Oh, I couldn't. I'm really sorry.'

'Prior engagement? Don't surprise me, lovely girl like you. That'll be one and thruppence, then.'

*

When Molly got back to the house, there was a letter from Annie McClure on the hall table. She took it upstairs to the empty flat but decided to open it later. Somehow she felt that her house mother wouldn't so much disapprove of what she had just heard from the waiter, but be saddened by it. And having wanted so much to know what Gladys had been talking about, made her feel guilty when she thought of the McClures. So, she thought, *there are ways of earning money that aren't really respectable at all, but people here don't turn a hair at them.* Molly wondered about the bright and noisy Gladys and how she'd settle down into her semi with her young man. *Will she miss the trips to hotels on the south coast with jumpy strangers? Surely she wouldn't go on with the 'specials' once she was married? She'll be bound to miss her friends from the typing bureau, but married women don't work, do they? Their job is to look after their husbands.* Molly pushed the thought of being married to the back of her mind, leaving it there with her buried love for Mark. Some of the girls in the Technical School, she remembered, had wanted to wed, but they wanted some money put by first. There were no guarantees in life, after all. Molly remembered all those poor men who'd come back from the Front expecting a hero's welcome, only to find that meant a park bench or the

Spike – the casual ward for the homeless wanderer with its thin blankets and even thinner food. *Oh Mark. That could have been you. Thank goodness there will always be pianos to tune.* Then she remembered that Mark would never have been destitute. He had a loving family and the McClures were part of that family.

But you haven't a family, Molly. Not really. You've to shift for yourself. Then thinking about Gladys in her semi, waiting for her husband to come off the train home, she wondered about her own parents, dead within weeks of each other. *Were they in love? When do you know you are, anyway?*

She went to hang up her coat and hat, the ones she had worn to come down on the train. That was only ten days ago, yet it felt as though months had passed and a kind of innocence had died. Going along to the kitchen, she passed Gascarth's door and paused. What would it mean to her to open it, to look at the bed she'd lain in with him, to touch his things? To smell them . . . *No, I daren't. What if he came in and wanted to know what I was doing?* A little voice told her she could get away with it. It wasn't like the Hall, where he was able to pad around silently. She'd hear the street door and there'd be time to get out and pretend to be doing something else. *But it wouldn't be honest. My face would give me away too.*

Putting aside the temptation, she went into her room and, sitting on the bed, opened Annie's letter.

. . . we always thought, me and Robert, that there were bet-ter things in store for you. Only be careful what you do with them, Molly. I didn't think you'd fall in with a man like

Mr Gascarth in quite the way you have, so I'm not sure I prepared you enough. Molly read on, convinced she was about to be told off, though in the gentlest possible way. The problem with him wasn't that he liked any of the girls from the Cottage Homes too much; it was that he didn't like them enough. He thought the poor wee souls stupid. He couldn't think that about a girl as clever as you, I thought. I'd have wanted you to stay on at the school instead, same as you did, and said so to the Guardians. So did Mr McClure. Anyway, you know this. It's old ground. Only when he gave you that chance to learn the typing I thought it would make up a bit for what you'd had to miss.

I trust you, Molly. You've an older head on your shoulders. But I'm still going to warn you to be careful. I remember what you were like as a little thing, when we saw the poor soldier with no legs selling matches in Dalton Road. We never ran out of them in Roose Road as you'd always insist we stopped to buy some. I think that, for all Mr Gascarth's money and taking you to the theatre and everything, you feel sorry for him. I don't mean you shouldn't but I'd be wrong if I didn't warn you that pity can be the next thing to love for a kind-hearted girl like you. Molly started at this. It was so close to Miss Cavendish's advice. You can find yourself doing things for people you feel sorry for that you'd not do for others. You haven't said what you did when you heard him screaming. But I know you, dearest Molly. You wanted to help him, didn't you? Molly winced. This was too close for comfort.

I have happier news, or at least I hope you'll find it so. Our Mark was always adamant that you should make your *own way, and you're well on the path to it. I did say to him, and not for the first time, that you'd be glad to use your new skills to help him in his work with the League. He asked me to thank you for your kind thought, but again said you needed to work for yourself. Besides, he has someone helping him now. Joan is a kind lady, a war widow who's had to bring up her little girl on her own. Her and Mark have turned into right good friends — they were at school together when he first came to Barrow. You've to say nothing as he's not said anything yet, but he's going to ask her to marry him.*

*

Molly sat a long time with the letter in her hand, trying to feel happy for Mark but only feeling sorry for herself. *I was a silly girl. I misread all the signs, didn't I? Shows you how much I know. This Joan had a husband. She'd probably laugh if I told her what I thought 'sleeping with' meant.* She held her head up so the tears wouldn't fall. *I've no business being upset. I've let Mr Gascarth kiss me and have wanted him to do it again. Well, Mark always said he wanted me to lead my own life. I'll do just that, then.*

As if on cue, she heard the street door bang shut and footsteps she recognised coming up the stairs.

*

That night, the screaming started again. Without stopping to wrap herself in her dressing gown, Molly sped out of her room and into the next without knocking. In the shadows, an almighty struggle was taking place on the bed, her shrieking employer tearing away the bedding as though it burned him.

'I'm hit!' he howled.

Molly put one knee on the bed and leaned forward, reaching for Gascarth's flailing arm.

'It's all right, Mr Gascarth—'

'*Leave me here!*' he shouted, shaking off her hand. His head and arm joined the rest of him beneath the quaking bedclothes. Molly pulled herself onto the bed and sat with a hand on the heaving, moaning heap.

'It's Molly,' she said softly. She went on repeating it as the muffled groans and cries subsided. At last the sounds died away and all she could hear were furtive rustlings, like an animal settling in a nest.

'It's Molly,' she said again into the near silence.

The rustling stopped dead. She could tell he was listening, pretty sure he was even holding his breath.

'Molly,' she said, a little louder this time. His head popped out above the blanket, his eyes glossy in the silver light that edged around the curtains, but focused.

'Good God,' he said, in his normal voice. 'What are *you* doing here?'

'You woke me.'

He groaned. 'Making a bloody fool of myself again, I suppose. Who'd want to be married to a funk like me, Molly?'

Molly hesitated, then: 'I'm sure any woman would.'

'No she wouldn't, dear girl. Believe me.' He pushed down the tangle of bedclothes and sat up. The gloom made dark cavities above his clavicles, in the hollows of his neck and the crook of his arm. Molly forced herself to look above his naked chest, but his face had a gauntness less evident when he was clothed, his eye sockets so pronounced that she felt his skull pushed against his skin. It was nearly a surprise to see that face turn to her.

'I'm all right now, I think. But please don't go.'

'I won't, sir.'

'Not sir, Molly, please. You make me sound like your client.'

'Client?'

'Forgive me. That was offensive. Even if you don't under-stand what I meant I should still not have said it. Turn away, would you, a moment, so that I can make myself decent?'

Molly slipped off the bed, her bare feet deep in the pile of the rug. She heard him get down on the other side and open a drawer.

'Will I do like this?' he said presently.

Molly looked round. *He could be one of the bathers at Walney.* Gascarth was tying the string of the waistband of his underwear. She couldn't take her eyes off his leanness, the long, strong legs.

'Yes, but let me make the bed. It looks like a battlefield.' She regretted the words as soon as she'd said them.

'That, Molly, is exactly what it is.'

'I'm sorry.'

'I'm sorry for having woken you. Allow me at least to help you.'

Between them, they pulled the sheets taut. Molly's corners were folded and tucked before his, but nevertheless she saw he knew what he was doing.

'A nurse in Craiglockhart showed me how to do that,' he said. 'I'll confess I'd never made my own bed in my life until the war.'

'I can't remember when I didn't. One of the rules in the Cottage Homes. There were inspections.'

'Anyone would think we looked like suburban young marrieds,' he said.

Molly said nothing, for his words bruised, reminding her of the news about Mark.

'You get in first, then.'

Molly did so, furtively tugging down her stiff poplin nightgown, for the bed was tightly made; she was worrying it would ride up in her sleep.

The bed shifted as Gascarth got in beside her.

'May I kiss you goodnight, Molly?'

'Yes, Mr Gascarth.'

'I cannot if you are so formal with me,' he said, laughing.

'Yes . . . A-Anthony.'

He raised himself on an elbow and loomed over her. She felt his breath warm on her face and then the tentative touch of his lips to hers.

'Ah, Molly,' he said, and kissed her again. This time the kiss went on and on as their bodies turned instinctively to face each other and his arm came over pulling her into him through the heavy cotton. His night-time stubble grazed her cheeks and chin yet didn't hurt. Then his mouth moved to beneath her ear, round to her throat.

'Could you love me, Molly?' he murmured.

'Yes . . . yes I could.' She felt his long fingers at the neck of her nightgown, fumbling a moment with the cloth-covered buttons, and his kisses landed just above her heart. His hair was soft against her neck; she put a hand up and stroked the back of his head. The other tentatively curled over his spine, her fingers splaying over his vertebrae. He felt to her as tense as a greyhound.

'Oh, Molly, your skin.'

'Oh!' she cried in surprised delight. His mouth was on her breast now, gently tugging . . . then he stopped, raising his head, and she was unable to suppress a sigh of disappointment.

'My darling girl,' he said, 'would you mind taking this off?' She caught a tinge of anxiety in his voice, as if he feared refusal. Her heartbeat thrummed in her ears, knowing that this was the cross-roads. She saw herself for a moment poised at the entrance to a typing bureau, rows of girls' heads bent over machines, the sound of the keys rattling like gunfire. Then with a wrench she saw Mark, holding a little girl's hand, talking animatedly but in words she couldn't hear, but she could see it was the child who led the man.

'Help me,' she said. He did, but it was a slow process, for in the grey London dawn she discovered that there were many places it felt marvellous to be kissed and a nightgown could be rolled around the neck for a long time before it was finally pulled off. By contrast, his undergarment was wriggled out of in haste and much movement of bedclothes. Beneath his weight her legs parted instinctively. Only then, on the brink, did fear trump desire. Her hands flat on his chest, she whispered, 'What if I had a baby?'

He paused. 'It wouldn't just be any old baby, Molly. It'd be *my* baby.'

She slipped her hands around him.

'Oh, Molly, yes, hold me, hold me.'

'*Ow!*'

'Sorry.'

'It's all right . . .'

'I'm sorry . . . oh . . . Molly . . . oh . . .'

CHAPTER TWENTY-FOUR

Afterwards

When she woke, it was broad daylight, but Anthony Gascarth's shape came between her and the sunlight. He was smiling. Molly blinked once, as the events of the night came back at her with a roar.

'Oh,' she said, remembering she was naked, and pulled the covers up to her chin.

'A bit late for that, my darling.' His face came down then and he kissed her.

'Would you mind awfully if we . . .' Another kiss. 'If we did that again?'

'We can?'

'*I* can, I promise you. I will try not to maul you so much this time. Oh, don't frown, Molly. I know I hurt you.' He nuzzled her neck. 'You poor girl. You must have thought I was doing you an injury. It was the last thing I intended.'

'I knew it would hurt,' said Molly, going a bit pink. 'My friend Myrtle told me. She was wed three months ago and couldn't wait to tell me about it – though there's not that much you can put in a letter. But she did say it got better.' She fell silent, picturing the companion of her girlhood and her husband. Fred, who worked in the wireworks, and was young enough that he must have come to his marriage bed as innocent as his new wife. She felt she'd betrayed a confidence and decided to say nothing about that tinge of disappointment that she had sensed between the lines of Myrtle's school copperplate.

'But . . . aren't you supposed to only do this in the dark?'

'You can do it any time you wish, provided you're not causing a public nuisance or alarming the horses. But if you really mean you'd rather not . . .'

Molly wriggled, trying to hide her face in the pillow.

'I don't mean that,' she said.

'Say that again, but look at me. You're all muffled.' His hand stroked her breast and her breath caught. She turned her head. *Yes, I could love you. I'd better do.*

'I don't mean that, Mr Gas— Anthony.'

*

Afterwards, he lay with his head on her breast as she stroked his hair.

'Would you like to go home now, Molly?'

'To the Hall?' For a horrible moment she thought he was going to deposit her on Roose Road.

'Where else? But not in the same capacity as before. I take it you'll allow me to make an honest woman of you?'

'What do you mean?' she said, though she was pretty sure what he did mean. It was a phrase the hack writers in Agnes's *Peg's Paper* were rather fond of.

'Marry me, Molly. I'm not much of a catch, I know. Night-time screams and a dicky heart. I don't want to add heartless corrupter of virgins to my long list of faults.'

'So I wouldn't go back to my old room next to Mrs Jepson?'

'I should say not. Did you want me to tiptoe past my aunt in my stockinged feet in order to have my wicked way with you?'

'No.'

'No you won't have me or no you won't sleep in your old room?'

'No I will have you. Yes, I mean. Yes.'

'Ah, Molly. You might regret it but I certainly won't. I'd like to make love to you again to celebrate but I expect you're hungry. But to have you for the rest of my life, Molly, however long that is, that is the most marvellous thing. Stay there. I'll bring you breakfast.'

He bounded out of bed, unconcerned at his nakedness. Molly drew up the covers again and peeked at him over the top, at the soft gouges and puckers in his lower back as he bent to pick up his discarded underpants. He turned round and smiled at her as he pulled them on. She could see he was still partly aroused, or partly relaxing, she was unable to say which. She also caught sight of a smear of blood on his upper thigh as he pulled on the rest of his clothes. When he'd gone from the room she gingerly investigated the state of the bed and of herself.

Cold soak with plenty of salt, she said to herself, once more the child on laundry duty in Roose Road. Then she remembered Mrs Bonelli was in charge of the washing here. *Maybe nothing people do in a place like London is ever really private.*

215

She was sitting up on his side of the bed, feeling the warmth in the hollow left by his body, when he came back in unexpectedly.

'My cufflinks—'

But instead of looking for them, he came over and sat beside her.

'Let me see your back,' he said, 'there wasn't much light when I turned you over that time.' There was something Molly couldn't place in his tone. She felt his fingers wander over her skin, heard his intent breathing.

'Is something the matter?'

'Oh, no, no . . . You have elegant shoulders, Molly, and an admirably straight spine. Your back is much more pleasing to look at than mine, as I'm sure you've noticed.'

'It must have been a terrible wound,' she said quietly.

'It was. I shall tell you about it some time. The last person to see it reacted with disgust.'

Molly stiffened.

'Sorry, dearest girl,' he said, his lips on her shoulder.

'Did they give you a medal for it?'

'I didn't want their bloody medals,' he said, between kisses. 'They're at the bottom of Wastwater. How many fingers, Molly?' he asked, his fingers moving again over her back.

'Oh . . . I don't know. Three?'

'Two. Now shut your eyes.'

He moved his fingers to her cheek.

'Two,' she said confidently.

'Correct. You may open your eyes. More nerve endings in the face, I suppose. I'm damn glad I wasn't shot *there*. You'd not have looked at me if I had been. You've seen those Lon Chaney melodramas I take it?'

'I saw *The Phantom of the Opera,* yes.'

'A grinning skull, and good in its way if all you need do is frighten the people in the cheap seats. But there is no artifice can come near the horrors of what weaponry can do to an undefended human face. No more than any artistry could come near the beauty of yours, Molly. Oh, bother the cufflinks,' he said, his hand straying to her breast. 'Would you let me love you again?'

'You mean, now?'

'If you wouldn't mind,' he said, unbuttoning his shirt.

*

'Oh, aren't you quite the lady!' exclaimed Mrs Jepson. 'Fine togs – but you have to be fine to wear them, and you are that. And good afternoon, sir. Did you have a good journey?'

'Thank you, Mrs Jepson,' said Molly, embarrassed. 'We did have a good journey. Everything on time. But I'd best go and get changed so's I can give you a hand.'

'You'll do nothing of the sort,' said Mrs Jepson, fists planted on her hips. 'I can see things are all different now, and not just your clothes. Nothing but what I didn't expect, of course. It was just a question of when.'

'Straight to the point, Aunt, as always,' said Gascarth, 'but don't write me off as a complete cad just yet. I've convinced Molly to marry me.'

For once, Mrs Jepson was lost for words, looking from one face to the other.

'She said yes, fortunately,' he added.

'Cup of tea!' exclaimed Mrs Jepson, suddenly galvanised, and ran off to the kitchen. Anthony Gascarth pulled Molly to him, kissing her.

'Do you mind not observing the proprieties, Molly? You will sleep upstairs, with me?' he murmured.

She was about to reply when a loud throat-clearing indicated Mrs Jepson had come back.

'I almost forgot, Miss Molly. Your brother came looking for you yesterday.'

'My *brother?*'

'Half-brother, then. He were very exact about that. But I expect you knew that.' Mrs Jepson disappeared back into the kitchen.

'Molly?'

'I don't have a brother,' she said faintly.

'Sit down, will you? You've gone pale. A long journey and then a shock. We'll see what else Aunt Jepson can tell us.'

CHAPTER TWENTY-FIVE

Norman Ashworth

In due course restorative tea and scones were put in front of them.

'Bring yourself a cup, will you, Aunt?' said Gascarth. 'Tell us more about this visitor.'

'If you're sure.'

Gascarth's hand pressed Molly's trembling one.

'He were from Manchester,' Mrs Jepson said, coming in with her cup.

'I don't remember him,' said Molly. 'I never knew I had a brother.' She tried to pour the tea, but her hand shook and the tan liquid splashed into the saucer.

'Let me do that, love,' said Mrs Jepson. 'You're not the tweeny here now. You're the mistress, in't you?' Nobody spoke as the cook filled the cups.

'They'd've put him in a different orphanage from you, mebbe. Cruel thing to do. Like separating families going into the Union. Only he was older'n you. He could've been out in the world already on his own account.'

'Did . . . does he look like me?'

Mrs Jepson paused. 'No. Not to my way of thinking. He wasn't what I'd call fine-natured either. Not like yourself.'

'Did he tell you his name?'

'Ashworth. Norman Ashworth. You've different mothers, according to him. He was very particular on that point. He wasn't what you'd call friendly in what he said about your mother, I must say. But that's often the lot of stepmothers, in't it? Even if they're nice kind souls a kid can feel the poor woman's taking a place she's no right to, can't he? I did tell him it did no good to speak ill of the dead but he laughed in my face.'

'You didn't like him, did you, Aunt?' said Gascarth.

'Jepson certainly did not. She din't like being with him alone, either. Mr Fallowfield came with a rabbit for me – sorry, nevvy – but I'm glad he did. I made with my eyes that I wanted him to stay so he made pretend to be fixing a doorknob. I know I shouldn't say that, him being Molly's brother and soon to be your brother-in-law, Master Anthony, but I couldn't wait for Mr Ashworth to be gone.'

'What could he have wanted with me after all this time?' said Molly.

'Muck, probably.'

Molly and Gascarth exchanged glances.

'Said he'd gone to the newspapers – well, the *Daily Sketch*, if you can call that a paper. Wanting to tell his story. When he'd said about having a little sister, well, he said the reporter's eyes lit up. It would add – what was the word he used? – peeky something, they told him.'

'Piquancy?' supplied Gascarth.

'That was it. A family reunion always went down well with the readership, they said. They'd told him they'd help him find you and that's what they've done. I call it a cheek, myself, and told the man so. I said "Who said Miss Molly wanted to be found?" I was feeling a bit surer of myself then, what with Mr Fallowfield making a row with the toolbox in the background, only not such a row as he couldn't hear what was going on. Mr Ashworth said he didn't like my tone much, but said to tell you there'd be something in it for you and you being a skivvy from the Union no doubt you'd be interested to know more.'

'Oh God,' said Molly, swaying in her chair.

'I'll get the brandy,' said Mrs Jepson.

'It's all right, Molly,' said Gascarth, holding her. 'We'll see him off, whoever this adventurer is. Probably just some confidence trickster, though they usually have a bit more tone than what Aunt Jepson saw.'

Molly sipped the brandy that Mrs Jepson held down to her. It burned, but managed to pull her into focus. 'What story did he have to tell?'

'I asked him that. He said as it was an ex-cul-sieve that he wasn't going to ruin his chances and blab it to me, especially as I hadn't even offered him a cup of tea, him having come all the way up from Manchester. If I'd had a cup of tea I'd've tipped it over 'is 'ed by then. But he said he'd be back. Then he took himself off, swearing. Mr Fallowfield and me watched him go in the direction of the train.'

*

Later, as they lay in each other's arms in Gascarth's great carved tester bed, he asked Molly if she remembered anything of her life in Manchester, anything at all.

'No,' she said. 'If you'd told me I was born in Roose Road, I would have believed it. There's no other place has been home to me. I used to try to imagine life with a mother and father – we all did. Only after a while there was no point to it. Mr and Mrs McClure were our mam and dad.'

'I think the McClures are where we go next,' said Gascarth.

'But I'm sure they've told me all they know. Why wouldn't they? My mam and dad died within weeks of each other, the poor things. Someone from the Guardians must have brought me to Barrow. But I was three. There's nothing left.'

'There'll be death certificates for them, the same as there is a birth certificate for you. The odd thing is sending you to Barrow. One would have thought there would be places you could have been sent to in Manchester, surely?'

'Maybe there weren't any spaces,' said Molly, but her reasoning sounded lame to her own ears.

'Molly, do you dream of orange blossom and lace and people throwing rice?'

'Oh!' she said, startled by the change of subject. 'I – I don't know that I've had time to, even.'

'Bear with me. We don't know when this unsavoury character – this Ashworth, as he calls himself – is going to come back, but I rather think he will. Him or the newshounds he's been talking to. I think you would be better protected, when he does so, as my wife. That is, I should like to protect you, if you will let me. I think we should be married straightaway. There is a solicitor's firm in Barrow which acts as registrar. I can see if we can get a special licence or whatever is necessary; the man acts for me anyway. You'll probably need the consent of the Borough Councillors, though I can't see them objecting. Question is, do you?'

'Object?' she said, stroking his face. 'No, not at all.'

'You'd like the McClures to be there?'

'Of course.'

'As our witnesses?'

She kissed him then.

Later, he said, 'You deserve a wedding breakfast at least. Shall we go to the hotel?'

'Why not? I could play you "The Grasshopper's Dance".'

CHAPTER TWENTY-SIX

Roose Road

Annie forced herself to stop twisting her hands. She'd done so almost constantly during her waking hours since receiving Gascarth's letter requesting an appointment, until Robert had asked her what the matter was. Her husband's response to the news that Molly's employer wanted to see one or other or both of them with 'questions about Miss Dubber's background' was, 'Find out what he wants, Annie. You don't have to give anything away you don't want to. Just tell him you'd need to consult the Guardians.'

'I don't know why he's come to us and not them. He went to them about sending her to the Technical School instead of writing to us first.'

'You weren't best pleased about that, if I remember rightly.'

'I wudna ha' said no, so I wudna.'

'I can always tell when you're agitated, Annie.'

'How so?'

'You get more Ulster, so you do.'

'Well, I am so – agitated, I mean. I never knew she was going to London with him either until she wrote and telt me herself.

I think she knows I'd 'a' spoken against that – never against her bettering herself in the Technical School.'

'I'd look on it in a good way, then. Whatever he wants, he's not gone behind our backs this time. And he's not dumped her back on our doorstep. If he'd taken her down there with him to . . .' He stumbled about for the right words. '. . . for to treat her wrong, he'd not be making appointments now, would he?'

So Annie wrote back, suggesting a time when the greater number of the inhabitants of the house would be at school. And now she stood behind the door, trying to calm the beating of her heart and answer that confident knock.

To her surprise, when she opened the door it was to find her visitor wasn't looking at her. He was standing back, gazing up at the gables and windows of the house, absorbed enough that he didn't appear to notice she was watching him. So Annie had time to take a measure of him. With the practised eye of a woman married to a tailor to working people, she took in a greatcoat that looked as though it had seen wartime service, garments that were sturdily made more for country than town, what she thought of as 'good' clothes even if they weren't new, and well-worn shoes polished to a conker shine.

'Mr Gascarth?'

'Ah, forgive me. Mrs McClure?'

'At your service.' She stood back to let him in.

'So this is where Molly grew up?'

'Since she came to us, yes. Never left until she went into service. Come into the parlour, Mr Gascarth. I shall organise some tea.' Annie felt more confident now. She was on her own ground and the man was courteous.

'I was expecting a place that looked more like the Union, if I'm honest. This is more like a home.'

'That's what we've always aimed to provide, sir.'

'Molly certainly thinks of it as such.'

Annie smiled, but what Gascarth said next made her sit down in surprise.

'And she loves you as a mother.'

'Oh! I . . . well, we've always loved her too. Ever since she came. Not quite three, she was. Does Molly – does Molly give satisfaction?'

'As my servant? You might do better to ask my cook-housekeeper that, perhaps. I noticed most that Molly looked after my books. She still does, but I now employ her as my assistant, not my servant. I think you knew that.'

'I did. It was very kind of you to pay her way through the Technical College.'

'I felt it the least I could do. Something that would set her up for life. She is also a perceptive musician and I think she has you to thank for that.'

Annie felt herself relax. 'That's where she learned – over there on our little parlour piano.'

The visitor glanced round.

'My own piano is also regularly tuned to my satisfaction. The young man who comes is a connection of yours, I think?'

'Mark is my father's stepson. So yes, I think of him as my younger brother.'

'Molly seems very attached to him.'

Annie noticed then that Gascarth was watching her intently.

'They weren't what you'd call playmates,' said Annie. 'Mark is too old for that. He's always seemed a bit older than his years in a way. I suppose that's how he got away with it – enlisting before he should have done. For what good it did him.'

'He bears his blindness well, I think. A dignified man.'

'Dignified . . . yes, that is the right word, Mr Gascarth,' said Annie. 'He's very active in the League – the National League of the Blind, that is. And he's going to be married soon.'

'Ah! Molly never said he was engaged. I wonder why she didn't remark on it. She knows, does she?'

'Oh yes. It's all quite recent. Joan, the lady's name is. A war widow. I wrote to tell Molly when she was in London.'

'Of course,' Gascarth said absently. From his frown, Annie worried she'd said something to offend him.

'Joan is active in the League,' said Annie into the silence. 'That's how they met. Her husband was blinded, you see, though it was his other wounds killed him.'

'I saw them march . . . when was it? I hadn't been long out of hospital. 1920 or thereabouts. The ones that set off from Manchester.'

'Oh yes, Manchester,' said Annie, on the alert again. 'Let me get that tea. Will you excuse me a minute?'

In her absence, Anthony took in the details of the little parlour, with its embroidered chair backs, worked, he guessed, by the little girls themselves. From force of habit he got up to examine the books on the small bookcase, cloth-bound editions of Dickens, Thackeray, the Brontës. He remembered his first meeting with Molly, how she'd told him she read to Mark. He wondered if that had happened in this little room. He lifted the fall of the cottage piano, noting the cellulose keys, the manufacturer in Camden Town.

'It was Mark taught her, not me,' said Annie, coming back into the room.

'She played a very pretty duet with him the first time he came to my house. That's how I knew she could. And Mr Fagan taught me to appreciate my piano more than I had.'

'Oh ... I think you must be a very kind employer, Mr Gascarth.'

'I doubt it. The girl before Molly didn't think so.'

'It's a difficult thing, I think, to know who will suit and who won't.'

'Oh, Molly suits me, Mrs McClure. In fact, that's what I came about—' He stopped abruptly, for there was a scuffling the other side of the door. Annie got up, admitting a large-boned, awkward girl. Gascarth could see straightaway that the child was what others called feeble-minded. He was struck though by the kindness with which Mrs McClure treated her.

'That was quick, Freda. You've done a lovely job of that tray. Over here ... on the little table. Just let it down slowly, that's it. Don't worry, I'll pour. And I'll make sure we leave you some of the biscuits. In fact, take one now. But don't eat it until you get back to the kitchen, off a plate. So's you don't drop crumbs.'

After Freda had shuffled out and the door was closed, Annie said, 'So you'll be wanting to keep Molly, Mr Gascarth?' and reached for the milk jug.

'I wish to marry her, Mrs McClure.'

The milk jug clattered on the tray, drops soaking into the lace doily. Annie looked up. 'Did I hear you right?'

'You did, or you wouldn't be looking at me like that.'

'You've asked her?'

'Yes, and she accepted me.'

'Congratulations, Mr Gascarth. I am very pleased for you both.'

'Thank you – though do I detect some hesitancy in your tone?'

'It's the surprise, sir, nothing more.'

'I wondered, you see, if Molly had a prior attachment.'

'With who – with whom, I mean?' said Annie, her mouth dry.

'With Mr Fagan, of course. Although he seems to have got over it.'

'Oh, poor Mark,' said Annie, wondering if she was about to cry in front of her extraordinary visitor. 'He's never spoken up. He won't. Mark has always seen his affliction as something he has to bear himself. I'll be honest with you, Mr Gascarth, as you deal plainly with myself. I believe he fell in love with her voice when she read to him. Do you think that possible, Mr Gascarth?'

'If the voice were Molly's, yes.'

'He doesn't confide much in others. It's all part of what he'd think of as being self-reliant, I'm sure. But I know he didn't want to burden her, so he never told her how he felt. He wanted her to live her life. Joan, you see, is another matter. He can support her, and her little girl. That means a lot to him. So I think he will be content. Perhaps not half-mad with happiness, but yes, content.'

'She makes *me* half-mad with happiness. As for being content, well, I wouldn't be without her.'

'But a man like you – I mean, the way you speak, a man with a house of his own – in his family for years, from what you've said. You're as different from her as you could be. You know what they did in Barrow, sir, with the babes born in the workhouse? They put an address on the birth certificate. One Rampside Road. Even if there's no father to put down, at the least the poor child hasn't the other disadvantage of that paper saying they were born in the Union. It's not a lie, either, it's the correct address. But would a man like yourself really want to marry a workhouse child?'

'It's Molly I wish to marry. Where or to whom she was born is immaterial. I will probably burden her too in my own way, but evidently I lack Mr Fagan's scruples.'

'When she was brought here, Mr Gascarth, I was told she couldn't speak. That was wrong. It was only that no one had bothered to listen to her, so they hadn't. The other thing I distinctly remember was that, small as she was, she had learned to fear men. Not mankind, men in particular. I wouldn't want her to be feart of one now.'

'Those marks on her back, you mean?'

Annie stiffened.

'I'm sorry. I didn't mean to say that.'

'Perhaps you had better marry her then, and quickly,' said Annie quietly.

'You'll think I'm a cad, a bounder, Mrs McClure.'

'I'm sure I don't know, sir,' she said stiffly.

'I'd do anything for her.'

Annie studied him for a moment. 'Yes, you would. You've done so much already,' she said eventually.

'We would like to wed swiftly and quietly and we would like you and your husband to be our witnesses.'

'I'd be honoured, Mr Gascarth, and I'm sure Mr McClure would be too, though he'd probably been hoping he'd be the one to give her away.'

'When I said a quiet wedding, I meant Forrester's the solicitors. But I am sure Molly would be delighted if Mr McClure brought her in as his daughter. We have a reason for acting fast – not the obvious one, either. You see, someone called for Molly the day before we came back from London. A Mr Ashworth. Mrs McClure . . . you have gone quite pale.'

'It says Ashworth on her birth certificate. She knows that. She's seen it. Mr Gascarth – forgive me. I've feart a day like this one. You'll mebbe not want her now. Sorry, I . . .' Annie fumbled for a handkerchief.

'I hate to distress you. Though I can reassure you I most definitely do want her.'

'Wait till you hear what I've to tell you,' said Annie miserably. 'I don't know who your visitor was, though. I thought she had no one left.'

'He says he's her half-brother. Some newspaper is paying him, I think.'

Annie wailed her distress. 'Oh, Molly, my poor wee Molly!'

'Mrs McClure—'

'I don't know for sure who made them marks on her back or how, Mr Gascarth, but I think it musta been her father.'

'Where is he now?'

'Dead.'

'And her mother?'

'Dead also.' Annie covered her eyes with the handkerchief, her shoulders heaving.

'How?' he said softly.

Annie lifted her head and looked him steadily in the eyes. 'He was murdered by Molly's mother. They hanged her.'

CHAPTER TWENTY-SEVEN

Therapy

'I'm a precise sort of man, Mrs McClure. I make decisions very carefully so I tend not to go back on them. I am certainly not going to go back on marrying Molly because of what you told me. But as you are the nearest Molly has to a mother, I think you should know what *she* would be taking on.' He paused, looking at Mrs McClure's folded hands.

'I am going to tell you something no one else knows save a few medical men. I didn't know it until I was in Edinburgh – in the hospital. Neurasthenic, they called me. Others would say coward. There was a doctor there I disliked. I expect the feeling was mutual. His approach with us was to make us confront our greatest fears – as if we didn't do so anyway, night after night, the moment the lights were out. He made us do things we didn't want. There was a decent library in that place. There were men who revealed themselves to be poets. They, and I, were not allowed near those books once that doctor took over. I am no writer myself, Mrs McClure, but I can and do read.' He nodded towards the little bookcase. 'When I first met Molly, I was impressed when she told me that she read to Mr Fagan. I have since persuaded her to do the same thing for me, though there is nothing wrong with my sight. She has a beautiful speaking voice.'

'She has a Barrow voice.'

'Precisely. Just as you have a Belfast one, if I am not mistaken, stronger when I blunder and agitate you.'

'Not quite Belfast, but near enough.'

'It is restful for a man who still has nightmares to hear Molly's clear vowels. I have known women who are "refaihned", Mrs McClure, and want nothing more to do with them. They consider it the height of distinction to never say what they mean, to never betray either sorrow or joy. Anyway, I was telling you about that doctor – the one who deprived me and anyone else who loved books, of their company. He actually thought they were bad for us, made us too introspective, so he forced us instead out onto the sports field, no matter what the weather – and in Edinburgh it can be bitter – to play inane games or to run pointlessly round and round, churning up mud, until we were exhausted. I rebelled against games at school and I did not see the point of them as a grown man who had seen hell first-hand and still lived it in my dreams. In a way, though, I should be grateful to him. I collapsed one afternoon in the midst of this apparently healthful activity, for I have a weak heart, along-side all the damage done to me in the trenches, Mrs McClure, so I may not live long.' He paused and spread out his hands as if appealing to her. 'But for as long as I do live, I want to *live*. If Molly does marry me, she may well find herself bringing up a child of mine alone. Now, some men might baulk at what you've told me, might argue that murderous intent is hereditary. I don't believe that. War taught me that *any* man is capable of killing if he has enough reason. Perhaps any woman too. I intend to find out what compelled Molly's mother to do what she did, before this Ashworth fellow or his newshounds come back and tell her themselves. All I want to know now is if there is anything in Molly's history, Mrs McClure, that indicates that a child of hers – my child with her – might not be healthy. I would not want her to have that burden. If she were to find herself with a Freda on her hands, for instance—'

'Freda is a loving and loved little girl, Mr Gascarth.'

'I don't doubt it. She lives here with you. Not in the County Asylum.'

Annie flinched, for she had a constant fear of what would happen to Freda once she was too old for the Cottage Home and she crumpled the cloth of her skirt in her fists. 'Sometimes babies are born healthy but they die anyway, Mr Gascarth. Molly had all the usual childhood illnesses and there were times we worried for her, of course there were. Anything else I wouldn't know. And she doesn't know about them marks on her back. They look as if someone put cigarettes out on the poor mite's skin.'

CHAPTER TWENTY-EIGHT

Copping a Blighty

'You'll be marrying only one kidney come Saturday, Molly. And an incurable neurasthenic to go with it.'

Molly turned in the bed to face him.

'Then I'd best take good care of the one you have left. And the rest of you.'

He stroked her face.

'I ought not to be alive.'

'But you are.'

'You can be alive and not alive, in a way. But with you I live. For a long time I thought I didn't deserve to.'

'Because so many didn't?'

'Because Munday didn't.'

Molly waited.

'I don't think anyone can be cured of what I saw, Molly, though the doctors in Edinburgh said that talking about it would help. So I told them over and over. Yet I still get those screaming fits.'

'Not for a while, though.'

'You see? You're good for me. But I ought to let you know what you're letting yourself in for.'

She saw his eyes slide away from her to stare into the distance. In that moment she wondered what the last thing was that Mark saw, before he was deprived of his sight for ever. She could see that whatever Anthony Gascarth saw, it was not the familiar room in that ancient house, not the hangings of the bed, the dressing gown thrown over the armchair with its comfortably worn upholstery. It wasn't her, yet he was so close that she could feel a hectic warmth radiate from him.

'It was one of those bloody stupid offensives. We had orders to advance the line, straighten it out, if you please, so that whoever drew the maps far behind the lines could please himself with something as neat as the borders the British have drawn through Africa. I wonder if one day someone in Whitehall will make some dry calculation of how many feet cost how many men. Anyway, ours not to reason why. Fritz, of course, didn't want to renounce an inch – he had his orders too, so can't blame him. That day I stepped up and replaced a poor sod on the firing step. It was one of my jobs later to write to his mother and tell her he'd died bravely, and instantly. For once it was true – the sniper got him through the eye.

'I came round in the dressing station, not knowing how I'd come to be there. It took me a long time to remember what happened. It was the farrier who got me away who filled in some of the detail and then, of course, it all came flooding back and hasn't left me alone since . . . I realised, eventually, I couldn't be dead – the dressing station was in a church, you see, so there was a moment when I thought I'd actually got to heaven, until I realised that in heaven the stained glass is probably in one piece and they don't have sandbags. And besides, I was hurting like hell by then. To start with, I hadn't realised how badly hit I was.

'Anyway, to go back ... there I was kneeling on the poor corpse with the bullet through his eye, when it went quiet over on the other side. I didn't trust that silence, of course, and waved at the others to keep low. I was pretty sure Fritz was only waiting for me to pop my head up and he'd take a potshot at me. It went on, a queer sort of waiting silence, then some rustling. I knew what was expected of me then, and so did the men. They were looking at me – a callow schoolboy, but the right school, you see. I peeped, of course. Impatience often gets the better of caution, you know. It was dusk, the kind of dusk that you can see a tree move and think it's a man, only by then the trees had been blasted out of existence. I watched the line where our opponents were, or rather, I thought they were. There are signs, you see. Someone gets fed up and rolls himself a cigarette. There's the *sense* of a movement – it's a bit like when someone stares at you and you turn round, though they've not made a sound. But there was nothing. Not even a rat stirred. We could take that miserable patch of churned earth and make it England, it seemed. So I gave the order and over we went. They *had* retreated, but not so far that they couldn't shell us.'

Molly ran her hand up his lower arm, coming to rest at his elbow.

'Do you remember that walk we took on the Embankment?' he said.

'Of course. We went up for tea on the Strand afterwards.'

'Do you remember the shrapnel marks on the Needle?'

'Yes . . . yes I do.'

'Think of that strafe in the body of a man.'

Molly began to weep.

'I would have died out there had it not been for Munday, but the fellow in the black cloak took his tithe all the same. I don't know where all the stretchers were – probably they were so busy in the dressing station that they hadn't enough cots for the wounded, so the bearers just put them down and went back to gather up the others as best they could. Munday got hold of a door from somewhere. The state of it, it must have been doing duty as a duckboard in a wider trench. Anyway, he came up, him and a farrier, a fellow from Remounts they'd got doing service as a stretcher bearer. I was yelling at them to take cover, to get back in the trench. I was gushing blood like the village pig, but somehow they bundled me onto that muddy door and began to scuttle off. There was this whine, a deafening crack, and then Munday wasn't there anymore.' Gascarth's voice rose, on the edge of a scream. 'Or rather, he rained down on me. I was covered in great charred, bleeding gouts of him. *That's* my nightmare, Molly. The one that never changes.

'But the other man . . . I have never seen such courage. His tunic was soaked with what had been my batman. He couldn't carry the door, of course. I was about to slide off into the mud, but that man scooped me up and slung me over his shoulder. I was wounded in the back – as you've seen – I was crouching and running, you see, when the shell burst. I was quite sure that whenever my tunic came off I should come away with it, but at least when they laid me out I might make a decent-looking corpse. Not like some I'd seen. Not like Munday. I can remember the farrier's bony shoulder still, my face bouncing against his spine. A lanky fellow, but strong. He took no notice of me telling him to leave me there and save himself.

'But he got me back behind the lines. And I lived. Some men got God out there, Molly. By all that's romantic, I should have as well. God and I had only had a nodding acquaintance before the war, if I'm honest, though I expect a vicar would beg to disagree. Instead I mislaid religion altogether. I got into a bit of an argument with a padre in the field hospital before I was sent back to Blighty. He preached that I should see my recovery as God's plan for me. "What about God's plan for Munday?" I said. I told you he was a twin, I think. His brother fell at Verdun and that put the poor mother in Littlemore Asylum. Whenever we had leave, Munday used to come to London with me, as the doctors wouldn't let him go and see her in case she thought she was seeing a ghost or thought that Munday's twin was alive after all. She was out, though, before her other son died.

'I insisted they brought the corporal from Remounts to see me. To my shame, I can't even remember his name properly. I remember it as Lovage, like the plant, but it wasn't that.'

'Loveridge.'

'How did you know that?'

'You said it. That night you were yelling.'

'Ah! So I hadn't forgotten. I'm glad of that. The man was an illiterate Gypsy who couldn't have spelled what he was called anyway. I wanted to recommend him for a medal – as an officer

I was entitled to do that, but he'd have none of it. Told me he'd been in prison as a conchie, not so much because of political principles but because, as he said, "I didn't think it had anything to do with me." He'd been released to be a farrier because he couldn't stand being cooped up any longer and he did know a lot about horses. They'd never have given a man like that a medal if he *had* wanted one, but I told him he certainly deserved one. I told him I would come and find him in peacetime, and he just smiled and said that it was nigh on impossible to find a man who kept moving.'

CHAPTER TWENTY-NINE

Furness Abbey Hotel

It was odd for Molly not to cross the entrance hall and take her position at the little piano in the alcove. It was odder still to be waited on by a beaming Herbert and an officious Mr Slaney, and to feel the weight of her new ring and the gleam of its partner on the hand of the man who sat opposite.

'The champagne is on the house, Mrs Gascarth,' said the hotel manager as Herbert expertly eased out the cork with no more than a tiny *phut*. Four flutes were arranged on the tray, but Robert McClure leaned forward and drew one apart.

'Not for me, thank you,' he said.

'Very good, sir,' said Slaney. 'We have our home-made lemonade, if you would prefer?'

'Thank you, yes.'

'Just a small one for me, please,' said Annie to Herbert.

Out of the corner of her eye Molly saw her new husband ease the normally taciturn Robert McClure into conversation, then felt Annie's hand cover her own.

'How does it feel, our Molly?'

'Being married? I hardly believe it yet. Everything was arranged so quickly, with the special licence and all, and then it all happened so fast too. I can't hardly remember what I signed up to, but I do remember Mr Forrester telling us it was a solemn legal undertaking and having to swear there was no impediment. Then he gave us each a pen and showed us where to sign. I'd stopped shaking by then. If I hadn't had Mr McClure's arm to hold onto going in I don't know where I'd've got the courage from.'

'Thank you for letting him walk you in, Molly. It meant as much to him as when he gave away our Kathleen.'

'It was the first thing I thought of.'

Annie glanced at the two men opposite. 'You're not sorry that it wasn't—'

'A church wedding? No, not at all. Anthony wouldn't have wanted that. He doesn't believe, you see, and I wasn't going to ask him to do anything that'd make him feel uncomfortable. We're going on honeymoon, though.'

'Oh?'

'Just up to Grasmere for a fortnight. The Ravenswood Hotel. He says it's a quieter place than the Prince of Wales. When we come back, though, he says he has to go away a couple of days on business, and he wanted to know would I be able to come and stay with you.'

'I thought you were his secretary,' said Annie.

'I was – I am, I mean. But he said it was only a couple of days he'd be away and it would be tiresome for me. He's going to Rochdale, he says.'

Annie could see from Molly's face that she wasn't entirely convinced by the argument that a two-day trip within the same county would be tiresome, but chose not to say anything.

'He doesn't want me to stay at the Hall just with Mrs Jepson. He's afraid of that Mr Ashworth coming – the one who said he was my brother. Do *you* know anything about him, Mother Annie?'

Annie squeezed the fingers of one hand in those of the other, to stop them trembling. 'No, Molly, only what Mr Gascarth told me. Nobody mentioned a brother when you were sent to us.'

Then, to Annie's immense relief, Herbert came up to the table and whisked away the champagne in its bucket, the ice cubes rattling in protest.

'If the wedding party would like to follow me, your table is ready for you.'

CHAPTER THIRTY

Rochdale

Spotland Road reminded Anthony Gascarth of streets in Barrow, but the accents of the men drinking in the Albert were noticeably different. In either town he knew he stood out. He was taller than the other drinkers, his long-fingered hands unmarked by labour. He looked through the hatch and signalled to the barman.

'What will you have, Ellis?' he asked, turning back to his companion.

'Just a soda water, Your Honour. I don't touch alcohol now, not so much as a shandy. It's dangerous for a man in my position.'

'But you'd given up the job, I thought,' said Anthony.

'Oh, I've done that all right. But it's not given me up, you see,' said Ellis, touching a broad middle finger to his forehead.

'I *do* see.'

Ellis raised his eyebrows.

'After the Somme, I mean. The memories not giving you up,' said Anthony. 'I was sent to Dottyville. Had I been a Tommy no doubt they'd have shot me for cowardice.' He picked up the drinks and they headed towards the far corner of the snug.

'You never forget, do you, sir?' said Ellis, settling himself so that he could view the rest of the room. 'But you had it worse than me. It was my job to kill others, but nobody was going to kill me in return. And you had to go and find 'em to kill, like a poacher. They was delivered up to me. All I had to do was pinion them and turn them off quick. I took a particular pride in that. And of course I knew all their names, what they'd done.'

'There's one in particular I want to ask you about. Mrs Ashworth.'

Ellis shivered as though he'd touched a live wire.

'I was wondering why you'd come down to Rochdale.' A flicker of suspicion crossed his face. 'Not one of them reporters, are you? The last one come a few months ago, asking about that selfsame lady. I sent him packing.'

'No. I'm a gentleman. An antiquarian in a small way.' Gascarth could see that the older man didn't know what that meant, but that he was too proud to say so.

'You said you'd a family connection with the lady. You don't look the type that'd know anyone like Mary Ashworth, if I may say so.'

'Someone very dear to me was close to her, Ellis.'

'Hmm. Well, she's the one I see in my dreams, Mr Gascarth. Little Mrs Ashworth . . . I joined the abolitionists because of her, more than for all the others.' He sipped his drink. 'You see, I'd thought in that job I'd be doing a public service. For the common good, and all that. The final cog in the wheel of justice. Stopping bad people do more bad things to good people. But I was never asked to come and have breakfast with the governor, the way the chaplain was, after the flag had gone up and they was all cheering or praying outside the prison gates according to what side they was on. Well, they'd not be asking a trades-man to join them, would they? And besides, I allus had to stick around with the prison doctor for the hour the regulations said, and then bring up the deceased. Not for Mrs Ashworth, though. I were that upset my assistants said they'd do it for me and to go and get a cup of hot sweet tea instead. I'm sorry I didn't stay, though. I'd've liked to see the lady's face after, just to know was she at peace, you know.'

Gascarth thought of the dead faces he'd seen in France. What had that little poet chap in Edinburgh said about them? *Like a devil's sick of sin.*

'Back here it's worse, in a way,' went on the hangman. 'There are men would want to buy me a pint and be disappointed if I didn't tell them all the gory details. Men who come into my barber's shop who don't need a haircut; I'd give up that job too only I must eat. Ghouls, all of them. I'm glad it was me did the hanging, not them. There are others avoid me like the plague even now, or use me to frighten their children and I've moved house.' He shook his head. 'The wife has put up with a lot. If I hadn't stopped when I did, she'd've left me. So I've to thank Mrs Ashworth for that too.' Ellis rubbed his eyes with the fingers of both hands. 'I don't know how much you want me to tell you, Mr Gascarth.'

'As much as you're willing.'

'I was pernickety, Mr Gascarth. I used to check and double-check my measurements: weight, height. It decides the length of the rope, you see. If it's too long the drop can pull a head right off. If it's too short and the condemned don't weigh much, they strangle. If there's so much of a quiver on the rope once they've gone through the trap, you know death weren't instant. After I'd done my training I used to set myself calculations to do at the kitchen table until Doreen yelled at me for it. So I'd go to the Reading Rooms instead. I expect the other men there took me for someone working out the odds on the nags. Are you a religious man, Your Honour?'

'I'm not. Had it burned out of me in France.'

'I was brought up on Bible study. Only it depends which bit you read. "Eye for an eye, tooth for a tooth", it says there in Leviticus or wherever it is. But that doesn't make sense, does it? Take a life, lose a life sounds fair, only it don't bring the person back and you can't know what anyone would have done with their lives if they'd been left to get on with them in peace. But Mrs Ashworth was hanged, I think, because they said she wasn't a faithful wife, more'n because of what she'd done. Think of all the people who killed her, Your Honour. It wasn't just me. Nobody will remember me, anymore than they remember the names of the men that drove the nails into Our Lord – put them through his wrists and his feet; it had to be his wrists, you know, or they'd've torn straight through the palms once they'd got him upright. It's just logic. Take it from me who knows how important the weight of the human body is, sir. They won't know the names of the people up there in Dundee or whatever juteworks they go to, for to get the rope they hanged her with, but some clerk in their offices made out an invoice to His Majesty's Government and *he* knew what it was for. Somebody delivered the parcel, some harmless little fellow driving a van who likes his pint on a weekend. I reckon a man'd do his job differently if he knew it was hanging hemp he was making instead of something wanted by a ship's chandler. Somebody went to a builder's merchants and got the sand to fill the weight. I always used a weight, Mr Gascarth. I'd fix it to the rope the night before so's the fibres would be proper stretched. Precise, I am. Everything makes a difference. You look proper peaky, Mr Gascarth. You might do well to have a glass of stout next, not another bitter.'

'It's nothing. Do go on.'

'I get lots of letters, even now. But I never had one like yours. Most of 'em don't put their names to them. Or they'll write things like "ex-soldier" and it's all in capital letters in case their handwriting would give them away. Yours was different. Polite, like. And when you said you wanted to ask me about a family member – "in strictest confidence" you said – well, I thought it wouldn't be right to turn you down. A family member, though . . .' Ellis peered at Gascarth, reading his face like a map from forehead to chin. 'No, you're a bit older, so it can't be . . . and anyroad, it were a little girl she had, that Mrs Ashworth.'

'Yes, a little girl.'

'I never wanted to hang women anyroad, right from the start. It disappointed me, in a way, that a woman would do something bad enough to fall into my hands. I did turn off a baby farmer once. The chaplain remarked that she died bravely but I don't think bravery had owt to do with it. The woman was that hard it didn't matter to her whether she lived or died. You'd have to have no human feelings surely, to do what she'd done. Poor little mites, and their poor desperate mothers giving her money to care for them, not suffocate them.'

'Was Mrs Ashworth brave?'

Ellis's face twisted as though he was in pain. 'No. Not at all. I got into the condemned cell the night before dressed up as a warder. If she'd seen me in my normal togs she'd've known who I was. I needed a look at her neck, Mr Gascarth.'

Anthony flinched.

'You can tell a lot from a neck. The weight and strength of a person. She was like a scared little rabbit, half-paralysed she looked. The two wardresses with her weren't in a much better state. After I'd seen her I went back to the gallows and got them to put planks across – in case she weren't able to stand unsupported on the trap, poor thing, and needed somebody either side of her. I said to the medical officer would he make sure that she had a strong shot of brandy five minutes before – it does put heart into them – but he said he'd thought of that only she'd said no. Her husband was a drunk and so she never touched a drop, she'd told him. Said someone had to be sober for the little girl.'

Gascarth groaned.

'I'm sure you've heard enough, sir.'

'No. Go on. Otherwise I'm ignoring what she suffered.'

'Yes,' said Ellis, slowly. 'It is something like that, in't it?' He took a sip of his drink. 'I went to her cell, three minutes to nine. She was standing there ready, in a neat little blouse and skirt, the wardresses either side of her, both of 'em crying, poor things. I went behind her, took her left wrist, then her right, got her pinioned. I told her that when we got there she was to put her feet where the chalk mark was and just to look at me. She nodded her head, like a well-brought up child. Then I walked ahead – Strangeways is a good place, there's no distance in it, but I could hear they were just about dragging her behind me. I was glad of the planks, then, for I could see we were going to need them, and that I'd allowed a longer length of rope. If they have to be supported, you see, the drop ain't as sharp.'

Gascarth twitched in his chair as if pricked with a needle. 'Don't stop, Ellis.'

'Are you sure?'

'*Yes!*'

'Very good, sir. With a man, you've to tie his ankles together on the trap. I won't do that with a woman, for it's not decent to be scuffling around her stockings. I always insisted on a belt to go round where her skirts end. I make all this sound a long process, Mr Gascarth, but it's longer in the telling than it ever is in the doing, I swear. While my assistants were doing that, I had the white hood over her head and the noose after. She was making this sound all the way through, somewhere between a gasp and a sob. That's what I hear, Mr Gascarth, when I turn out the light, what I hear if I wake in the night. I resolved it'd be quick for her, and it was. The reverend was droning away but she can't have heard any of it. But it wasn't a sob, not really. I heard her clearly enough standing next to her. "My little girl . . ." Those were the last words she spoke; I could hear her through the cloth

– it sucked in at her mouth. But the moment the hood was on I pulled the lever.' Ellis pressed his hands on the scarred table.

'There's not a day I don't think of her, Mr Gascarth. That woman died to save her baby. And there's not a day goes by I don't wonder what happened to that poor child. The Board of Guardians took her, I expect.'

Anthony reached into an inside pocket and took out a photograph. Wordlessly he laid it on the table between them. The former hangman bent his head to look and went utterly still.

'That's her!' he whispered. 'That's Mrs Ashworth.' He lifted a pale face to Anthony. 'How did you get this?'

'It's her child, Ellis. I married her three weeks ago.'

Ellis studied the photograph again. Watching him, Anthony felt as though all the sound had been sucked out of the pub, as though they sat there alone. At last the man lifted his head.

'What are you going to tell her?' he asked quietly.

CHAPTER THIRTY-ONE

The Chapter House

'Would you come for a walk with me, Molly?'

'Of course. Though it's not a very nice day – not that I mind. Galoshes and a brolly and we'll be fine.'

Something of the glowering sky had depressed her mood, Molly told herself, but she knew it wasn't that. Anthony had been withdrawn ever since he'd come back from Rochdale four days earlier. She had asked gently several times what troubled him, but he'd merely looked up from what he was doing with a distracted air, and answered, 'how could I be troubled so long as I have you?' But she knew something was wrong. A little doubting voice nagged at her: *He's regretting what he's done and is working out how to tell you.* She wondered who else knew of their marriage, outside the Hall and Roose Road, but then who would he tell? A solitary man since returning from Edinburgh, by all accounts, he'd not kept up with the men he'd known when they were boys, nor those he'd served with – he'd said as much. Molly had never pressed the point, afraid he would tell her that the friends he'd really cared about were dead or damaged.

Yet 'Mr Anthony is a happier man when he's around you, lass,' was Mrs Jepson's blessing. Waking in the hotel in Grasmere and opening her eyes to see her husband's face, awake or sleeping, had been deliriously joyful – as had being woken by him during the night. Then there'd been that mysterious journey to Rochdale, a place he'd never mentioned before, and his face had been shadowed ever since.

'I thought we'd go down to the abbey,' he said.

*

By the time they got down there it had started to rain, a fine drizzle pattering on Anthony's gamp. Out of sight of the house he had pulled her arm under his and kept it there, so that both were more or less dry, though the going was muddy. But he didn't speak until they were within the abbey grounds, when he said, 'Thank heavens nobody's about but the custodian. We can shelter in the entrance to the chapter house.'

The rain was falling steadily on the far side of the Norman arch, but under the vault, without the incessant spattering on the umbrella, the world seemed oddly silent.

'Anthony, please tell me what's wrong,' said Molly, unable to keep the anguish out of her voice. 'You've been keeping something from me ever since you came home.'

'I want you to know that I love you, Molly.'

'But?'

'There is no but, Molly. I love you unreservedly.'

'Have I done something wrong?'

'No. How could you? And nor did she, poor woman.'

'*She?* Oh no, no ... We're not married at all, are we? You already have a wife.'

'No, Molly. Don't doubt me. The only wife I've ever had, or ever will have, is you.'

'Anthony, is this anything to do with what you were doing in Rochdale?'

'It has everything to do with that.'

'And that man who said he was my brother? For the love of God, do I have to drag this out of you?' She began to beat his chest with her fists. Gascarth tried to put his arms around her but though she stopped pummelling him, her elbows held him at a distance.

'Listen, Molly. There is no easy way to say this.'

'My mother and father aren't dead, are they? They didn't want me. But nobody had the heart to tell me. I'm a bastard, after all.'

'You know that's not true. You've seen your birth certificate. Oh, they're dead, Molly, they're dead. What Mrs McClure told you is true.'

'So what *is* it, then?'

'Your mother – probably in self-defence, and almost certainly to defend you from him – stabbed your father to death.'

Molly went so white he thought she was about to faint; he tightened his grip on her.

'So she's alive? In prison?' Her voice was barely above a whisper; he strained to hear her above the driving rain.

Miserably, he shook his head. 'No, Molly. The jury asked for clemency ... there was a petition got up to save her.'

'*No!*' Then, to his relief, she began to cry. He held her, stroking her hair, her head tucked beneath his chin. Eventually, between the sobs, he heard her cry 'I can't even visit her grave, then. I've daydreamed about that for years. That I'd find out where they were, and I'd plant flowers over them. But she'll be in the prison, won't she? They'd not let her out, not even dead.' She lifted her head, and he cradled her face in his hands.

'I'm sorry, Molly . . .'

'Mother Annie knew it all, did she? And she never told me? I trusted her!'

'You did right to trust her. Molly, don't blame her. How could she have told a little girl?' He brushed a strand of hair from her forehead. 'She wept when she told me. She's carried the knowledge with her all these years – her and Mr McClure.'

'No one else knows? Mark?'

'No. But that's why you were given another name and sent to Barrow instead of to a Manchester home. It was Mr McClure told her to say nothing then, but to be prepared to tell you one day. I offered to take that burden from her and I am honoured that she let me.'

'Them marks you found on me. The ones you said was chickenpox. They weren't, were they? Then it was him made them – my own father.'

'It could only have been him.' Anthony hesitated, remembering what Annie had told him of the newspaper reports, remembering the hangman's testimony of the prayers and protests outside the prison, those people who had never known her doing what they could to keep her alive, and when they failed, to ensure Mary Ashworth did not die alone. *Not today. She's had enough for now.* 'Your mother died because she wanted to protect you from worse.'

'But I'm a monster's child.'

'If we were to let this change us, then he'd have won, wouldn't he? It makes no difference, Molly. You're your mother's child, the child of a courageous woman who would do anything for her little girl, right up to sacrificing her own life. Her last words were of you.'

'How do you know that? The papers might've made that up.'

'It wasn't in the papers. The man I went to see in Rochdale was the executioner.'

'*Ohhh!*'

'You look like her. He thought I'd shown him a photograph of your mother.'

'Better that,' said Molly, pale-lipped. 'At least I don't look like him.'

*

'Oh Mark!' cried Molly. 'It's so good to see you.' She sped along the path through the hollyhocks to greet the man Fallowfield was helping down from his cart.

'When shall I come back, Mrs Gascarth?' asked the carter.

'Oh . . . Mark, are you in a hurry? Will you eat with us?'

'I'd be glad to. My next job is this evening.'

'About two then, mebbe?' asked Fallowfield.

'Thank you. If it's not putting you out.'

'Or if you're not in a hurry, I could walk you down to the station instead,' said Molly.

'Why not?'

'I'll get yem, then. Good afternoon to you both,' said Fallowfield. He made a sound the horse recognised, the cart moved off.

As before, Mark laid his hand on Molly's shoulder and followed her along the winding path to the door.

'Last time I came you were Mr Gascarth's servant. Now you're his wife.'

'I'm still getting used to it,' she said, turning her head.

'It suits you, married life. You've a different way of talking now.'

'I'm still the same,' she said, disconcerted once more at his perceptiveness, wishing she could see his expression.

'I always thought you should make something of yourself. And you have.'

Molly didn't quite know how to respond to this. The idea of 'making something of herself' through an advantageous marriage didn't seem to be quite what those suffragist women had tied themselves to railings for or gone on hunger strike. But she couldn't see his face to know for sure that's what he meant.

'I'll take you through to the piano, will I? Then I'll go and see Mrs Jepson about our dinner.'

'I'm glad you said dinner, our kid,' said Mark, and she could hear the smile in his voice. 'Tonight's job is in Dane Avenue, with a lady who always tells me what she had for "luncheon".'

*

To Molly's relief, her change in status had not altered Anthony's easy manner with Mark, nor his with his host. The blind man's congratulations, so far as she could see, were heartfelt.

'We'll be able to wish you every happiness too before long, won't we? You and Joan,' she said. 'We look forward to meeting her.'

'Ah!' said Mark, laying down his fork but not letting go of it. 'There's been a bit of a change of plan. Joan released me.'

'Oh, I'm so sorry,' said Molly, glancing at Anthony, who was frowning slightly.

'Don't be. I think it took a bit of courage on her part, if I'm honest. It all seemed to work out so neatly, didn't it? Her work with the League, her little girl wanting a dad. I'll be honest. That was the hardest part. We said I'd still be her uncle but that wasn't enough for the poor kid.'

'How did you tell her?' asked Anthony.

Mark paused. 'Her mam told her that she missed her dad too much. That she was right fond of me, but that nobody should wed unless they are absolutely sure that the person they're marrying is "the one". And that we weren't, not for each other. It's easier between us now, if I'm honest. Joan and Edie still come round twice a week for tea. We're friends. We mighta wrecked all that.'

*

Mark's hand went back on her shoulder as they walked down to the abbey and his train.

'I *am* sorry,' said Molly. 'I wanted you to be happy.' The tears that came to her eyes surprised her. *Why does it matter so much – now?*

'It's a relief, Molly. It wouldn't have worked.'

'When did it happen?'

'Three months ago. Just after you wed.'

There was a small silence then. 'If she hadn't released you, would you have released her?' said Molly eventually.

'I wouldn't, though I wanted to.'

'Oh, Mark . . .'

'I'm pretty set in my ways, to be honest. Living there in Hardwick Street, for instance. It's where I grew up. I don't remember anything really of Cleator Moor, apart from the bad things – my father hitting my mother when he was drunk, the smell of the spirits on his breath. It's odd that I don't have images. I remember life there as I know life now. Sounds and smells. And I certainly don't remember anything of Manchester. I was born there, that's all.'

'So was I. And I don't remember anything either.'

'That man, Molly. The one that said he was your brother. Did he ever come back?'

Molly shivered. 'He did. I wasn't there at the time – I'd gone to see Mother Annie. Anthony threatened him with trespass. It was Mrs Jepson told me he'd come; I wonder even if Anthony would have said anything otherwise. Then there was a seedy-looking man with a notebook came, wanted to see inside the Hall. Mrs Jepson was there that time and told him it was a private house. The man said he meant no harm, that he'd just walked up from the abbey and liked old places. Only when Mrs Jepson asked him to tell her what he'd seen in the ruins, he didn't really know how to answer. It turned out the man had been in the hotel, though, asking questions about us. Herbert called Mr Slaney and he was asked to leave.'

'Do you still play there?'

'Sometimes. Not as much as before, but Anthony does encourage me. Only I like the time we have together in the evenings too much.'

'And the rest of the time?'

Molly laughed. 'That too!'

'I hope you're not disturbed again, though.'

Molly hesitated. 'Well, I am too, only . . .'

'Only?'

'I want to know more about my mother – and at the same time I don't, if that makes sense?'

'I think so. You want to know she was a good person.'

'She was. I'm sure of it. Anthony went to meet the man who hanged her—'

'Good God!'

Quietly she told him of what Anthony Gascarth had said, sheltering from the rain. 'Everybody knew before me, Mark. In the first place Mother Annie, though I don't blame her for keeping quiet, even if I was angry at first. I've wondered what I'd have done in the same situation and I've had to admit I wouldn't have said anything either. She didn't know what the hangman was able to tell Anthony, only what was in the newspapers they got for her in the public library, and that wasn't good. All sensation.'

'When it was a tragedy.'

'Exactly. The other thing is how Anthony was when he came back from Rochdale – where he saw the hangman. He looked as if he'd met Death himself. He's had enough to put up with. His weakened heart and then everything that happened in the war, you know.'

'I do know.'

'I don't want him taking any risks. We have a quiet life here, and we're always together. Even in London we have our own little rhythm. We eat in the same restaurant. A theatre treat. A museum. It's enough.'

'I can understand that. And you, Molly, are enough for any man.'

'Oh, Mark. Did you notice what I left out, though? What Anthony doesn't do?'

'Earn a living? God, sorry, Molly, I shouldn't have said that. I take it back.'

'You're right, though. We live on rent other people pay. Living in homes I've never seen.'

Mark whistled.

'He does good things, though. Sends money to the Limbless – and now to St Dunstan's.'

'Charity – though I know they do good work.' He stopped. Molly felt his hand slip from her shoulder, and so stopped too.

'What do you mean "now"?'

'I mean . . . he asked his agent's advice.'

'Your husband doesn't need to do anything on my account,' said Mark, his voice hard. 'He pays me when I tune his piano. That's all that's needed – work for men like myself. Not alms.'

'He wasn't thinking of alms,' said Molly, close to tears. 'They have workshops to train the men. That's what he liked.'

Mark scuffed the ground. 'Don't cry, our kid,' he said quietly.

'I don't want to fight with you, Mark. I couldn't bear it.'

'Me neither. And I like Mr Gascarth. I really do.'

'He likes you too. He's always asking if I've seen you, when I go to Mother Annie's.'

'Hmm.'

'Only you're never there. But I do always ask about you.'

'She said. I should invite you back to Hardwick Street, shouldn't I? You and Mr Gascarth? Only you've to get away from all that.'

'What's wrong with Hardwick Street, Mark? Mother Annie always said how happy she was there.'

'It *was* happy,' said Mark, relaxing before her eyes. 'She and Robert were living downstairs, Mam and my real dad – I call Thomas Maguire my real dad because he's the one brought me and my brother up, the way Robert McClure is *your* real dad because he was there for you – we were upstairs where I live now. I've not changed a thing since Mam and Dad died. I know the place like my own finger ends. I could tell you everything about a pair of miniature china cats on the overmantel because I remember what they looked like. I lift down the brass candlesticks once a week, and give 'em a good polish and put them back exactly where they were. I measure the distance between them and the cats with the breadth of my hand. I can tell from my fingertips when I've got them gleaming, and then I give them another wipe over so's I don't leave prints. There's a picture of the Holy Family hanging over the range. I liked it when I was a little lad. They're under a rose bower, but St Joseph's carpenter's bench is there too. I didn't know they had rose bowers in the Holy Land but perhaps they do. The rose of Sharon is in the Bible, isn't it? I only turn up the gaslight when I've visitors. Joan still has the key, same as a couple of the neighbours; I'm well looked-after. I always recognise Joan's footsteps, same as I'd always know yours, and if she's been in cleaning or whatever when I'm out, I always know because of this Lily of the Valley she wears – and the smell of beeswax and Vim, of course.'

'That's good, isn't it?'

'It is. It's proper friendship, that is. But I know we shouldn't have tried to make it anything else.'

'I'm sorry.'

'I told you, don't be.'

'But companionship?'

'I've got that, and not just with Joan. I can always tell if it's evening because downstairs is a greengrocer's now, and I hear him locking up, same as I hear him in the morning. There's a sort of smell in the air at different times of day, depending on what time of year it is too, but mainly I know what's going on because of mothers calling in the kiddies for their supper. I smell tobacco in the evenings too: the men taking a turn outside and talking to each other about whether Ray Bennion will ever score any goals. Or about their pigeons. I go down and pass the time with them some evenings. People are kind. It's a quiet life I have.'

CHAPTER THIRTY-TWO

Love in the afternoon

Molly walked home slowly, thinking of Mark on his train home. He had his stick with him, the one he held clear of the ground when he was with her, preferring instead that she guide him, as she had done whenever they'd met for so many years. She imagined him arriving at Barrow, wondering who would help him. She saw him climbing onto the bus, the conductor leading him to a seat and making sure he got down at the right stop. She saw him rattling his keys in the lock and going up to that little flat that hadn't altered since he saw it for the last time, a boy in khaki.

I could have been living with him there. He's as good as said it. Only he never said it in time.

Molly wiped her eyes and blew her nose. She'd reached the Hall. Anthony Gascarth was standing in the doorway, exactly as when she had seen him for the very first time.

'My love?' he said. Without saying anything, she walked into his arms.

'You saw him onto the train?' he murmured, kissing the crown of her head.

Molly nodded.

'I'm not surprised at his news. Are you?'

'A bit.'

'You ought not to be, Molly. That poor woman must have known she was only ever going to play second fiddle.'

'Don't . . . please don't.'

'I don't know that the best man won, Molly. But I am glad it was me all the same. Look at me, dear girl . . . Those are tears, aren't they?'

'It's only silliness. Honestly.'

'I'll let that go by, Molly.' He bent and kissed her, and she gave herself up to his kiss. Then, 'Molly,' he murmured, 'can I tell you what I was thinking about when you were out?'

'Yes . . .'

'I was thinking that this evening we could bring the hip bath up to my bedroom – our bedroom, I should say – instead of bathing downstairs. I should like to undress you – bit by bit – and lower you into the water – and soap you. Afterwards, I'd lift you out and dry you and then carry you over to the bed. You'd be all warm and pink and still a little bit damp.'

Molly's face was flaming, but a part of her mind was thinking about the time it would take to heat the water and the labour of bringing up pail after pail. She'd be flushed and sweaty and ready for a bath then. Mark's barb about her husband not working for a living had stuck in her skin; for all his good intentions Anthony would never understand how hard others toiled.

'Never mind this evening, Molly,' he was whispering. 'Would you come upstairs now?'

*

Anthony slipped quietly into sleep as their lovemaking finished, his head on her breast, his body melded to her side. *I'd wanted to talk to you,* thought Molly, stroking his silky hair. *I wanted to tell you I love you and not to worry about Mark for I can see that you do.* She pulled the sheet over them both, because as she'd held him she'd noticed the sheen of cold sweat on his skin, on every part of him she could touch. There was something about that slipperiness she hadn't liked, that cool leaking from every pore. Yet everything else – yes, everything else – had been normal, if something so deliriously pleasurable could be described as normal.

Watching the light fade beyond the curtains wasn't normal, though. *Working people can't lie abed in the afternoons, can they? Only when work is short, but if a baby comes then how can it be cared for on the dole?* She thought of all the men working in the sparking crash of the shipyard, longing for the hooter to release them, the greasy-handed women streaming out of the jute works in Abbey Road, but not to go home and rest. Life in the Cottage Home had also been regulated by mealtime bells and lists of chores that had to be done on specific days. School had imposed its own rhythm. Then, working as Gascarth's maidservant, fires had to be laid at a certain time, vegetables chopped, laundry pummelled in the dolly-tub. And the Master's books, of course. He'd been very exacting about how and when they had to be dusted, as he was about nothing else. Molly smiled into the dusk. That was still her task. Everything else, though, had a formlessness these days. *So when did I last have my monthlies?*

*

Annie McClure put her arms around Molly.

'I knew it!' she cried. 'I knew as soon as I saw you.'

'How?' said Molly, astonished.

'Your face – it's so rosy, so happy. Softer, somehow, though you've always been lovely. How do you feel?'

'A little tight, just under here,' said Molly, the side of her hand pressing just below her breasts. 'A funny metallic taste in my mouth sometimes. But I feel well, very well.'

'What does your husband say?' said Annie, smiling.

Molly hesitated.

'What is it, dearest?'

'I haven't told him yet. It's not that I think he would be unhappy. Far from it. It's just that he doesn't seem quite himself at the moment. Not in the best of health. He's thinner, tires more easily. When he's asleep – he'll often fall asleep in a chair, with a book in his hand – I look at him. He has dark shadows below his eyes. His fingernails are a funny colour – bluish.'

'How long gone are you, Molly?'

'About two months, I think.'

'Perhaps wait until three, then. To make sure that Baby has taken. Don't look so worried – you look so well I'm sure everything will be fine and you've all that fresh country air. But you might have a word with Mrs Jepson about getting you a bit of liver on the side.'

Molly pulled a face.

'A bit of iron, that's all. Or you could take a tonic instead. We could walk down to the chemist if you're able for it and get some of Dr Williams' Pink Pills.'

'I'm able,' said Molly, cheering up. 'I'm not waddling yet.'

'But your husband needs to see a doctor, and soon.'

'I've never known him do so. All he's ever said is that he saw plenty when he was wounded.'

'Men are odd, that way, believing they have to soldier on. It's possible he has seen someone and doesn't want to say. But wait another month before telling him about Baby. If anything did go wrong – not that I think it will – the shock of it would be no good for him.'

Molly nodded. 'You know, Mother Annie, this baby changes everything.'

'That's the way of babies.'

'I meant, between you and me. I was so angry with you about my mother and you knowing and not saying anything.'

'I'm sorry, Molly. I didn't know what to do . . .'

'But I'm not now. I don't know how big this baby is yet. Maybe no bigger than a pea. But I'd do anything to protect him – or her. I see now that all you were doing was trying to protect *me*.'

'Oh, Molly, my dear little Molly.'

Annie was holding Molly when both women heard a halting footstep in the hall, and the door opened. They separated as Robert McClure came in. He took one look at Molly's face and smiled. 'You're going to have a wean, aren't you?'

Molly looked from one to the other and said, 'How will my husband not guess if you two have?'

'Because it's not guesswork, so it isn't,' said Robert, smiling. 'We've been there, after all.'

1000

'Perhaps he *has* guessed, Molly, and is just waiting for you to say,' said Annie. 'He might have noticed, you know, that the curse hadn't come.'

Molly pondered this. 'I might wait another month anyway. Not tempt fate, and that.'

*

Annie never forgave herself for that advice, though Molly quickly forgave her.

Ten days later Molly was leaning over the bed she and Anthony shared, stripping off the sheets for laundering. She had a hand to her back and was straightening up when she heard a loud knock at the main door of the house. The bedroom door was open, the casement also, for it was a fine day. She heard Mrs Jepson's voice first, uncharacteristically short. 'What dosta want again, you?'

Molly's skin prickled, but she couldn't make anything of the murmured reply, other than to say it was a man's voice. Her immediate thought was that Norman Ashworth had returned. That wasn't the way the cook spoke to the Gypsies who called occasionally, selling pegs, or to the gentlemen of the road asking for a glass of water and a hunk of bread, for Mrs Jepson knew as well as anyone that times were increasingly hard.

Molly was standing in the bedroom doorway when she heard Mrs Jepson shout, 'Get out of it!' and then more clearly, for her face was evidently turned into the house, 'Master!'

There was a rumble downstairs; Molly recognised the sound of the library door opening and Anthony's reluctant tread, followed by a roar of rage and what sounded like a scuffle. The sounds were moving off, so Molly went to the window and looked down into the garden. Gascarth had his back to her; he was pushing at a smaller man in a scruffy raincoat. Molly gasped, for she had never seen her husband handle anyone roughly. The stranger staggered a little but didn't give way.

'Just asking for your side of the story, guv'nor! You'd do well to give it!'

'There is no story! I've told you to go!'

'Oh, there's a story all right! Your man in London was very pleased to give it. And the name of the lady you've the breach of promise with.'

'Breach of promise?'

'Lots to tell us. Quite overcome she was, when she heard who you'd married, guv'nor. "A murderess's daughter!" she cried. I'd to be quick with the *sal volatile,* I can tell you.'

'You *cur!*'

What followed looked to Molly to take place in helpless slow motion, including her own reaction. She watched her husband sink to his knees, his hands flailing forwards to grasp ineffectually at the reporter's legs, as if imploring him to go. Molly felt as though her own feet had turned to wood and had become one with the dark floorboards, as the kneeling Anthony Gascarth swayed sideways and fell. She saw his hair gently lift on impact, remembering he'd said he needed to get it cut.

'Lumme!' shouted the visitor and pulled back as if from flames. He turned and ran, leaving Gascarth slumped on the path. His sudden movement threw a charge through Molly, who tore down the stairs without touching the banister and out into the garden.

Anthony Gascarth's lips were blue. His eyelids fluttered and his mouth moved. It looked to Molly as if he was trying to speak. She would always remember that moment, hoping that he was saying her name, that somehow that was the last word he meant to speak, not that enraged 'you cur!' Instinct said that the only thing she could do was to hold him, his limp shoulders and head, and sob that she loved him, but by the time she said 'I'm expecting, husband,' she could see that the light had gone out of his eyes.

Molly was conscious of Mrs Jepson beside her, her fingers unbuttoning Anthony's shirt, feeling the side of his neck, then his wrists, then the words, 'Our little Ant, our little Ant,' turning her tear-tracked face to Molly. 'He's gone, poppet. Oh, God help him, he's gone!'

*

It was some while before Molly could be persuaded to let go of Gascarth's body. She remembered a succession of mainly trousered legs around her, soft murmurs, hands on her shoulders giving up and withdrawing. Fallowfield came first, then a doctor, who knelt beside Molly and told her gently, 'Your husband knew. But he refused to tell you though I told him he should. It was only going to be a matter of time, but he said that was time he'd spend with you, not going uselessly to get other opinions.'

White-faced, Molly nodded, knowing that she had urged him to see someone only to be told 'don't worry, dear girl,' except he already knew he was doomed. A police sergeant came from Barrow. Molly heard him taking a statement from Mrs Jepson, and her determined assertion that 'the poor lady won't be able to tell you owt and in't in a state to speak anyroad.' The policeman muttered something about it being 'a bad business' and 'folk should leave well alone' but he did undertake to bring Annie McClure to the Hall himself. Molly looked down at her husband's dead face and tried to remember who had closed his eyes.

'You did, dear,' said Mrs Jepson two days later, when asked. Only when the policeman mentioned the coroner had Molly looked up, with the cry, 'No, he's been cut up enough!' The doctor had intervened then and said he would sign the death certificate as heart failure 'hastened by childhood rheumatic fever and injury sustained in the service of his country'.

Annie came, carrying an old grip, not with the sergeant but with the undertaker's men. It was only then, with the shadows lengthening, that Molly could be persuaded to let go of her husband's body, to be led indoors. Mrs Jepson tactfully asked her where she wanted to sleep.

'Not our old room! Oh, I never finished changing the sheets!'

'Never mind that,' said the cook. 'What about the little guest bedroom?'

That is where Molly woke during the night, not knowing how it was she had fallen asleep, but feeling she had failed Gascarth by doing so. She sat up with a cry and a rustling in the darkness told her she wasn't alone.

'Molly?' said Annie. 'I'm here, on the truckle bed.' There was a creak, then a movement of Molly's bed as Annie sat down and took her hand.

'Take care of your baby, Molly.'

'I must. Apart from memories, it's all I have left of him.'

'Bring up his child in the house he loved, Molly.'

CHAPTER THIRTY-THREE

Joan

Molly stood at the graveside and watched her husband's coffin lowered. She heard the clergyman's words as if they came from a distance, but she picked up a clump of reddish earth when nudged to do so and heard the thud as it struck oak. One by one the others around the grave followed her, Mrs Jepson being the first of them. The McClures stood at her shoulder while Agnes sniffled, Daniel patting her arm. As Molly embraced the girl who had rejoiced so much at what she'd thought of as a romantic novel come to life, she thought there could be no plot where the bridegroom died in the heroine's arms after a mere three months. Sergeant Burch gave her a professional handshake but she read the compassion in his eyes. The usually gruff Fallowfield wiped away a tear. Mr Slaney and Herbert had come from the hotel, though they left promptly, to make sure that everything was ready for the little funeral party; Herbert looked to Molly genuinely shaken out of his usual sunny self.

'Hello, our kid,' said a familiar voice. 'I'm so sorry.'

'Oh, Mark. I'm glad you came.'

'I couldn't not. He was a good man, your husband, and you made him happy, Molly. You must always remember that.'

'But it's my fault he's dead, Mark. If it hadn't been for me, there'd never have been that set-to with the reporter and he might still be here.'

'Don't. Don't ever think like that. It's not what the doctor said, is it?'

'No, but . . .' Molly noticed the woman standing two paces behind Mark. As if he had sensed the direction of her gaze, Mark turned and said, 'Molly, this is my friend Joan Caulfield. I asked her if she'd bring me today.'

'I'm glad you did, Mark,' said Molly, looking into Joan's face. 'Thank you for coming, Joan. You'll join us at the hotel, I hope?'

'If I'm not in the way.'

'No friend of Mark's could be in the way.' *She looks kind,* thought Molly. *She'd have tried to make him happy, if he'd let her.*

*

Joan approached Molly where she stood looking down at the closed fall of the hotel's piano. Most of the little funeral party had left.

'Mrs Gascarth?'

'Molly. It's silly, isn't it, but what I'm remembering now is playing "The Grasshopper's Dance" for him. It went down well here too.'

'Nothing's silly that reminds you of him.'

'I don't suppose I'll play it ever again.'

'You will. You'll do it to keep him close.'

'Do you get over it, Joan?'

'No. But you manage. You become different, I suppose. Having my little girl helped. My husband never knew her, so I talk to her about him.'

It was on the tip of Molly's tongue to tell Joan she was expecting, but she held back. *Perhaps she's guessed, the way Mother Annie did. But I held back from telling Anthony, so I'm going to hold back from telling everyone else for a little bit longer.*

'Mark said you went to the Technical School for the typing,' Joan was saying.

'That's right. And for shorthand. My husband made me into his assistant, after I was his servant. Before we got married, I mean. He wanted me to have a skill.' Molly stopped as the realisation hit her. 'He knew, didn't he, Joan? Even then. He wanted me to have something to fall back on.'

Joan cleared her throat. 'It's to his credit that he did and I've a suggestion to make, Molly. You mightn't need it, as you're bound to inherit, being his widow, but if you wanted some work I could put it your way. I've a job in the Town Clerk's office. Sometimes we've too much to do, especially for the big committees, and we've to farm it out. I'm presuming, I expect. Always wanting to organise things . . .'

'I'm glad you asked me.'

'You'll have an awful lot to think about just now, I know.'

'If I don't keep it going, it'll be as if he got that training for me for nothing.' Molly looked down at her hands, flexing her fingers and then pattering out words against the air. 'I worked up to a good speed.' She looked at Joan directly. 'How will I find you?'

'I'll give you my address. And you can always get a message to me by Mark.'

*

'I'll have to go to London, Mother Annie.'

'Whatever for?'

'I have to see that man Sanderson, see what he said to that reporter.'

'You don't really believe that about the breach of promise, do you?'

'No. I never did. Mrs Jepson had already told me that the woman had left Anthony, not liking what she saw when he got back from the war. That's not what troubles me. It's that he trusted Sanderson and Sanderson broke that trust. I want to know why.'

'It'll be because every man has his price, Molly.' Annie reached across the tea table and took hold of both her hands. 'You look marvellous. Blooming. But don't go alone. And don't do anything that'll harm your baby.'

'I won't. Only if I do nothing I'll fret. The problem will still be there. And who would go with me?'

'If she can get the time off, I think I know just the person.'

*

Molly ran from room to room of the London flat, looking for something she knew she wouldn't find.

'Molly, stop! Show me first where I'd get the makings of that cup of tea we talked about,' said Joan, holding up the half-pint of milk she had picked up from the grocer on the corner. 'Then I want you to take me round and tell me whatever you want to about what it was like being here.'

'Sorry, Joan. I didn't mean to . . .' said Molly, sinking into a chair. Joan came and stood behind her, resting her hands gently on the younger woman's shoulders, before pulling up a chair for herself.

'When the telegram came,' Joan said, 'I don't know what I would have done without the kindness of neighbours. But there wasn't a one of them I thought I could ask to come with me to all the places we'd been when we were courting. All the little special places that didn't mean anything to anyone else. I went round myself – you know, Walney Island, or where I'd wait for him when we were going to the pictures, or where we stood to feed the ducks in Barrow Park. It was all I could do not to talk to him, only I wouldn't have been the first to have been taken off to Moor Hospital for such a thing. Everyone takes grief differently, Molly. There'll be days when you think you're doing all right, considering. And other days when you just don't want to live.'

'I'm sorry.'

'Stop saying that. What for?'

'Making you come all this way.'

'It's a treat. I'm glad Annie McClure thought of me and you agreed. But would you have asked me if Annie hadn't said anything?'

'I was afraid you might have thought it a cheek of me.'

'Molly, I know we spent the whole journey down *not* talking about Mark Fagan, but I want you to know I've had no regrets about turning him down. And I'm quite sure he has none about being turned down. He's an obstinate beggar, that one. I know he'd have stuck with our engagement if I hadn't spoken up, because he's honourable. But it would have been a disaster for both of us. I know how he feels about you. No – hear me out. You'll do, Molly Gascarth. I watched how you were on the way here, leading the way out to the taxi stand, telling the man where you wanted to go and then cool as a cucumber through all that traffic.'

'I thought the first time a bus would've tipped over onto us.'

'Just what I was thinking!' Both women laughed.

'But here it's different,' said Molly, her smile evaporating. 'The last time I was here was with him. The *first* time I was here, I heard him in that room over there.' Molly glanced over her shoulder. 'He was on the floor, screaming. I don't know what happens when we die, Joan, but if it's anything like life, then who will comfort him? Who'll keep watch in a chair in case the terrors come back?'

'He died in the comfort of your love, Molly,' said Joan.

'I sometimes feel as though none of it happened. As if I'm going to wake up because someone's ringing a bell and I have to go and see to some rich lady who can't or won't do a thing for herself – or that Miss Tweed back from China to tell me my place. That's what my life was supposed to be. As if even the Hall was a dream. Other days I think he's still alive. He could move like a cat, Joan. I'd look up and he'd be there looking at me.' Molly couldn't stop herself looking round. 'You see? But I've just been into that room – where he was screaming – it was ours, later.' Molly glanced at Joan from under her lashes, and could see from her face that the older woman knew all that must have happened behind that door. 'Someone has been in and changed the bed. It must be Mrs Bonelli who comes in for the laundry – I've never even met her. Everything is tucked in more tightly than I ever manage. Nobody's slept on them pillows. It's as if we were never here.'

'That can't have been deliberate.'

'I'm sure it wasn't. I'm sure the poor lady came in and did exactly as she always did, after we'd gone. She wasn't to know . . . that I'd . . .' Molly leaned forward, her face in her hands.

Joan squeezed Molly's knee and said gently, 'You'd wanted to see if there was anything left of him, didn't you? A dent, a hair?'

Molly nodded behind her hands, her shoulders shaking.

'Give yourself time, Molly. But you will find ways to cope.'

*

Later, the two women stood in the doorway of the room that had briefly been Molly's and before that Munday's. Speaking quietly, as though there was someone in there she didn't want to disturb, Molly said, 'It looks as if Mr Munday has got it back. As if I was never there at all.'

'I'm to sleep here though, aren't I?'

'Yes. If you don't mind.'

'Molly, I think it's all right to speak to ghosts, whether you believe in them or not. If they're there they'll appreciate it. What would you say to Mr Munday if you thought he could hear you?'

Molly paused, then said into the empty room, 'Look after him, won't you? Wherever you both are.'

CHAPTER THIRTY-FOUR

Overture and beginners

Molly did sleep, though she hadn't expected to. Worst was waking up, turning to the pillow next to hers and finding it empty. There'd been that fleeting moment between sleeping and becoming fully conscious which had been not happy as such – just normal. And then her loss engulfed her, like a musty blanket coming over her head and shutting out the sun.

Molly could hear Joan moving about in the kitchen and felt a surge of relief that the woman who had become her friend was there, not least because in a few hours Sanderson would call.

'I know I should have looked at the files last night,' Molly said to Joan over the breakfast things.

'There was enough to deal with then without that too,' said Joan. 'We'll divide them up and I'll go through them with you. But what are you expecting to find?'

'I don't know if I *am* expecting to find anything, at least not about what Sanderson said to the reporter,' said Molly. 'I just feel I ought to be prepared, in every aspect. He's such a horrible man.' She screwed up her face. 'Why's someone like that alive and not our husbands?'

'Don't. Keep the emotion out. Think of it as just business that has to be got through.'

Ten minutes later Molly had the box files out on the table and felt more confident. She knew her own work had been done properly, and she had organised the older files properly too. Now she and Joan just had to look at what their contents had to say.

*

'Good afternoon, Mr Sanderson,' said Molly. She wondered if she was supposed to shake hands with the man on the doorstep, or if that was just something men did. Sanderson's arms stayed firmly by his sides.

'Good afternoon, Miss Dubber – or should I say, Mrs Gascarth?'

'Mrs Gascarth,' she said coolly. *You know perfectly well that he married me.* 'Do come in.'

Molly felt the man's eyes on her as he followed her. She tried hard to relax her shoulders, sure that her efforts only made her look more awkward and tense.

'This is my colleague Mrs Caulfield,' said Molly, leading him into the room.

'I see,' said Sanderson. 'I didn't think there'd be company.'

Joan's eyes and Molly's met, and Molly read the message in her friend's face. *One up to you already, Molly Gascarth.*

Sanderson's eyes flickered over the box files she had left heaped on the table. Although she had waved an arm in the direction of a chair, he remained standing.

'I will send a messenger for them later,' he said.

'I beg your pardon?'

'I shall arrange it forthwith. I appreciate your gathering them together for me.'

'Would you sit down, please?'

'I don't require any refreshment, thank you. I am a busy man. I expect you want me to find a tenant for this flat. It happens that I have an ideal person in mind.'

Molly stood up then, pressing her hands together to stop them trembling.

'As you won't sit down, Mr Sanderson, I think we can conclude our business quickly. Your ideal tenant, I'm sure, can find somewhere else to live. Mrs Caulfield and I were expecting you to come here and give me a summary of my husband's affairs, just as you did when . . . when he was alive—'

Sanderson's loud laughter drowned her out. Eventually he recovered himself, after theatrically pulling out a large white handkerchief and dabbing at the corner of his eyes, where Molly could see no moisture.

'You cannot be serious, Mrs Gascarth! I have offered to give your late husband's affairs space in my own busy office – though to be honest, my expert advice would be to divest yourself of at least some of the properties. I know buyers who would give you a fair price and my own percentage for brokering the sales would, of course, be low – out of respect to Mr Gascarth's memory. I came here today merely as a favour to your husband, in acknowledgement of our long history. My other clients come to *me*. Nor am I in the business of explaining myself to young girls, whoever their husbands may have been. With respect, you could hardly make sense of the complexity of Anthony Gascarth's affairs. You would be well-advised to leave such matters to myself – on existing terms, of course.'

'There will be no terms, Mr Sanderson,' Molly heard herself say. 'I have brought out the files because Mrs Caulfield and I have questions for you. Specifically about the railwaymen's cottages in Stewarts Lane.'

Molly saw Sanderson's bravado congeal and a cold rage take its place.

'You don't know what you are talking about!'

Molly blinked. 'If I don't, then perhaps you ought to explain.'

'One could hardly expect you to understand.'

'No? My husband trusted you, Mr Sanderson. Even before I opened the files I know you abused that trust, talking to a newspaperman about his private affairs. I saw my husband die, Mr Sanderson. Confronted by that shabby little man you felt so free to talk to about matters that don't concern you, he collapsed—'

'Young lady, are you insinuating—'

'I am not insinuating anything!'

'I'd have you know you are making libellous accusations. Your husband was a very sick man, Mrs Gascarth—'

'One you took advantage of. I do understand figures, Mr Sanderson, as does Mrs Caulfield, who works in the Town Clerk's office in Barrow.'

'Where?' sneered Sanderson.

'So neither of us see an explanation for why repairs to simple railwaymen's cottages always cost much more, for what they are, than maintaining the bigger houses around here. Not only that, but the repairs are repeated again and again, always by the same contractor. I know, for instance, that in Barrow—'

'*Barrow* again? It's hardly London.'

'It isn't. But whenever there was anything to be done at the Cottage Homes, the Board of Guardians always got three tradesmen round to price the work. I remember them calling.'

Molly immediately realised her blunder.

'Brought up by the Board of Guardians, were you, Miss Dubber?'

'Mrs Gascarth!'

'You weren't my client's secretary at all, were you? You were his skivvy. I smelled a rat when I saw you that first time, and I wasn't wrong. I've an instinct, see? Makes me good at my job. Did well for yourself, I'll say that for you. Not bad for a murderess's child.'

Molly's hand went to her mouth and Joan gasped, 'How dare you!' but Sanderson went on as if she hadn't spoken.

'Of course, Mr Gascarth was never himself again after what he went through in the war. Impaired his judgement, you might say.'

'Leave now, Mr Sanderson,' said Molly.

'I beg your pardon?'

'The door, Mr Sanderson. It's behind you.'

The man's eyes darted to the table. 'The Nine Elms properties. You said you'd questions. I'll get the file and show you.' He reached for the files, but Joan pulled them out of his reach. He glared at her, muttering under his breath. 'Maligning a man of my integrity . . .'

'Stop it, Mr Sanderson,' said Molly. 'The file isn't there.'

'You little—'

That was the moment that Molly remembered a blowy April afternoon in the back garden of number four, Roose Road. Five little girls, Myrtle and herself included, had decided to have a screaming competition. The winner was not going to be the one who could scream the loudest, but the longest. The most effective way not to use up air was to get to a single high note and hold it there. On a signal from Myrtle, each child took the deepest breath possible and then in unison let loose an eldritch screech. Children in the other gardens rushed to the fence to see what was going on, but Mother Annie, as she had to do, hurried out of the house to tell them off.

'What's this caterwauling?' she called above the din. 'Stop it now!' The five little girls were marched inside and given brass polishing to do as a punishment. But Molly learned later that their house mother wasn't so much cross with them but mortified at the thought there might be complaints to the Guardians. Robert McClure was told about the incident at the dinner table.

'At least I know with lungs like theirs that none of 'em will be going to Oubas House,' said his wife, naming the children's annexe to High Carley Sanatorium. Three of Molly's school companions who had been sent there had not come back.

The adult Molly's lungs were still strong and the effect of that sustained scream in an enclosed space had the shattering effect she had intended. Sanderson gazed at her with a stunned expression, whilst Joan's was full of admiration. When Molly opened her mouth wider still Sanderson fled, pushing his hat onto his head as if he intended to punish it. She held the note until she heard the flat door opening and a babble of voices. Then she stopped dead, panting and holding onto the back of a chair for support. *I'm not as good at that as I used to be,* she thought. Then Joan's arms were around her.

'You were magnificent, Molly!'

The two women were clinging to each other when they were brought back to the present by an orotund voice.

'Mesdames?'

Molly looked up to see a middle-aged man she didn't know standing in the doorway. With a flourish, the figure bowed, taking off an imaginary hat. For a moment she thought the intruder was wearing a cape, but it turned out to be an ordinary coat draped across the man's shoulders as though it was one.

'I believe it was you who sent out that cry of distress, dear lady.'

'It was,' croaked Molly.

'We failed in our attempts to detain the interloper, I am afraid. Wretched man, Sanderson; we are made poorer by his acquaintance.'

Molly gaped at him, lost for words. *He talks like somebody out of a book.*

'Sweet ladies, forgive me. I think I know what is in order. Hot sweet tea, if I am not much mistaken. The estimable Mrs Bonelli is, at this moment, in my apartments. Let me summon her – or better still, perhaps you would like to depart the field of battle – on which you have clearly triumphed, given the hasty retreat of the vanquished Sanderson.'

'I beg your pardon?'

'No, 'tis I should plead *your* forgiveness. Harold Symonds, thespian, at your collective service. If you would do me the honour of accompanying me to my modest abode, then I think we can prevail on La Signora Bonelli to provide all four of us with a restorative cup. That excellent lady is Italian, of course, but by dint of patient instruction she has at last learned to make "a noice cuppa char".' The man's sudden switch to broad Cockney in his last four words startled Molly almost as much as his entrance had. He was looking at them expectantly.

'That'd be very kind of you, sir,' said Joan, 'and of Mrs Bonelli.'

'What names shall I give? Mrs Bonelli will want to know.'

'This is my friend Joan Caulfield,' said Molly. 'I am Molly Gascarth.'

Symonds was momentarily lost for words.

'Forgive me. I had no idea. You must be . . . ?'

'His wife. Widow, I mean. We were only married a matter of months.' Molly reached for Joan's arm.

'Ah! It was *you* that nasty little ferret came asking questions about? Of course I couldn't say anything, not having ever had the honour of your acquaintance. Nor would I have done if I had – I closed the door in his pustular face. Of course, back then Mrs Bonelli and I signed the petition that was got up to save your poor mother. The least one could do. Dear ladies, it would be an honour if you were to accompany me . . .'

CHAPTER THIRTY-FIVE

Schwartz

Harold Symonds's apartment was so different from the austere space that had been Anthony Gascarth's that if she hadn't crossed the landing to his door, Molly would have thought herself in another building entirely. The walls were papered with some dark Victorian pattern of acanthus leaves, which from wainscoting to just above a tall man's head height were crammed with photographs of Symonds himself in various guises and at all ages. A tiny trembly dog with bulging eyes and legs like twigs emerged from amongst the many pot plants that filled the room and tried to sniff the visitors.

'Benson!' boomed the actor. 'You anticipate your cue, sir!' The dog retreated back amongst the plants. The air was heavy with the rubbery hothouse scent of their foliage, mixed with the eau de cologne worn by their owner.

'Since a boy,' Symonds said proudly, waving an elegant hand at the photographs. 'Born to the profession. Here I am in my debut in the Scottish Play,' he said, pointing to a tinted photograph of a little boy wrapped in plaid, posed against a rugged painted landscape of mountains – Molly guessed this was a theatrical backdrop.

'I was ten when I played MacDuff's doomed child; already fascinated by makeup and dressing up, you see. Father was Banquo and Mother sat in the prompter's box. I remember my lines to this day: "He has kill'd me, mother",' Symonds added in a voice so like a child's as to make Molly shiver. In another image, the actor was made up as an Egyptian. In the frame next to it, he wore a powdered wig, a tricorn hat and a large beauty spot. Molly wondered about asking Mr Symonds if he had ever acted in *Love in a Village* but found she didn't yet want to share with anyone else the memories of that enchanted evening in the Lyric, Hammersmith, not even with someone who probably knew the play and would have appreciated her opinion.

'Here I am as Polonius,' he said, gesturing at a photograph of a portly figure in Elizabethan dress standing before a tapestry. 'That wasn't my stomach, of course. Strapped on padding. But it's the closest I ever came to playing the Prince of Denmark. Now too old, too old, my maidens.' He paused, his head on one side as he regarded his visitors.

'Would I be right in thinking that you sweet damsels hail from the provinces?'

'We're from Barrow,' said Joan.

'Ah, Barrow, Barrow!' exclaimed the actor, as though he spoke of somewhere impossibly exotic. 'My salad days! *Dick's Penny Plays* and blood-tubs.'

'Pardon?' said Molly.

'My years in repertory,' he said. 'No need to pay royalties for the penny plays. Writers all corpses, you see. Fortunately, one of them was Shakespeare.'

'Blood-tubs?' asked Joan nervously.

'Melodramas, dear lady. Worth paying the scribblers for because you knew you'd get a full house. Barrow, Morecambe, Lytham St Anne's . . . those motherly landladies and their cakes.'

Molly was astonished to see tears in Symonds's eyes. Or was he simply being an actor, unable to resist playing to his tiny audience? He was in the act of turning back to the wall to point out other triumphs, when a little bright-eyed lady dressed all in black appeared from the kitchen with a tea tray.

'Take no notice of 'eem, pretty girlies,' she said affectionately. ''E's never off the stage.' Arold! You 'aven't even let 'em sit down.' Mrs Bonelli put the tea tray on a low table and swept some books off a cracked leather sofa. ''Ere, *bella*,' she said to Molly. 'Sugar an' milk?'

'Just milk, thank you.'

'My lady?'

'Both, please,' said Joan.

For a minute there was near silence in the crowded room; Molly could hear the snuffling of the little dog. She drank down her tea and looked at her companions.

'I don't know what to do,' she said.

'Then do nothing,' began Symonds. 'I have always found that the best course of action. After a while someone else has to make the decisions, and then they can be blamed.'

'*Stai zitto*, 'arold,' said Mrs Bonelli, flapping her free hand at him. 'Let the lady speak.'

'That's exactly the problem,' said Molly. 'Mr Sanderson wanted to go on making the decisions. He as good as told me

I wouldn't be capable. Only, Joan and I have found something odd in the accounts and so I have dismissed him.'

'Oh, you splendid girl!' said Symonds, striking his knees. 'Mrs Bonelli, I think this calls for the Tokay.'

'Oh ... please, not for me. Or perhaps later. I'm not very used to drink, and certainly not in the daytime,' said Molly.

'Later then, but celebrate we must.'

'But where am I to find a replacement for Sanderson? I have no idea where to start.'

Symonds and Mrs Bonelli exchanged glances.

'Schwartz,' they said in unison.

*

Molly's first surprise on meeting the theatre accountant was that the expected Mr Schwartz was in fact Mrs Schwartz, a stout middle-aged lady with adult children and spectacles, also a widow. 'Schwartz was a good man, but he lacked staying power,' was all she said about him. 'But one gets by, with the help of family and neighbours – and as long as income exceeds outgoings, even if by not much of a margin.'

Betty Schwartz listened carefully to what Molly and Joan had found in the accounts, before saying, 'Sanderson appears to have been defrauding your husband for some time. Until you came, nobody was checking on him. There's no attempt even to cover his tracks.'

'My husband was too trusting, Mrs Schwartz.'

'Do you think you should trust me?'

'I do, Mrs Schwartz. By instinct.'

'I shall insist nevertheless on being utterly transparent with you. I will do nothing without your knowledge or consent.'

*

'I never thought they meant a woman,' said Molly, leaning back in her seat as the northbound train gathered speed.

'I thought Betty was pretty scary to start with. The way she looked at us over those glasses. But she never talked down to us. And she complimented you on how well you'd kept the books,' said Joan.

'I didn't even know you could have lady accountants,' said Molly.

'She did say she was the only one in her year. And that if her father hadn't supported her things could have been very different.'

'She's had an interesting life, hasn't she?' said Molly. 'Keeping the theatre's accounts . . . dealing with people like Harold Symonds.'

'I expect theatre managers are a bit more hard-nosed than the actors, otherwise they'd never make any money. But she talked about the theatre as if it was a family, how everybody has to rely on everyone else. Not just the actors knowing when to come in on cue, but the scene painters, the costumiers, the front of house. All that so that the lights can be dimmed and you and me sit in our seats and are taken to a different world for just a couple of hours.'

'We're lucky, aren't we? In spite of everything. Not like that poor family we went to see in Nine Elms.'

'We are, Molly. But at least things'll be better for them now that Mrs Schwartz has everything in hand.'

'Anthony should have gone down there, Joan. He should never have assumed everything was all right. Damp walls – that poor little coughing boy! His mother at her wits' end, never getting ahead of the dirt no matter what she did.'

'How could she? Having to cook in the same room they slept in.'

'It makes me realise how lucky I was to be in the Cottage Home, Joan.'

'Try not to blame your husband, Molly. From what you said about him, he'd been brought up to not know about places like Nine Elms.'

'Nor Egerton Buildings back home,' said Molly, naming the tenements put up for the shipyard workers.

'They're better than what we saw in Stewarts Lane, believe me. I grew up in Sloop Street.'

'I didn't mean to talk out of turn. I'm sorry.'

'You didn't. But people would do anything for you back there. Same as we saw in Stewarts Lane. They might be longing to be rehoused but there's some there will worry about not being with their old neighbours anymore. And even if your husband was brought up in a softer way than us, Molly, he saw *you*, didn't he? Not just a servant.'

Molly looked out the window, lifting her chin and trying to blink away the tears.

'Nobody expected I'd last. The other girls were frightened off – or wouldn't do.'

'But you did last. You'll never be sent away from the Hall now, Mrs Gascarth.'

'I don't know. I've to see what the solicitor says.'

*

The two women parted at the station at Barrow.

'Are you sure you don't want me to come up with you, Molly?'

'No, I'll be fine. I've kept you from Edie long enough.'

'They know you're coming?'

'Not to the hour. I was going to leave my luggage at the hotel and if it stays fine, walk up and send for it later. You've done so much for me, Joan.'

'Molly . . . Molly, don't cry. I've enjoyed myself – in a manner of speaking. I'll be happier still if Mrs Schwartz manages to get Sanderson arrested for fraud.'

'Would you come with me to London again, Joan? Bring Edie with you?'

'Oh, I would.'

'I think Mr Symonds meant it when he said he'd get us matinee tickets next time.'

'As long as it's not for a blood-tub!'

*

Molly riffled through the few letters that had arrived in her absence. Two envelopes wrung her heart, for they were addressed to Anthony Gascarth. 'Tomorrow will do,' she murmured, wondering who she had missed out in going through his address book and writing to give his correspondents the news that they would never hear from her husband again. That activity had given an oddly businesslike shape to the days following his death. Setting down the commonplace formulae 'regret to have to inform you' and 'sudden passing' on page after page of the fine writing paper in the bureau had given her a target; a certain place in the alphabet had to be reached before she would allow herself a break. Just once she had put down her pen in anger at destiny, remembering that it would have been her task as a wife to go through that same address book to write Christmas cards. Yet they'd not been granted even one December as Mr and Mrs Gascarth.

She felt the two stray letters addressed to Anthony mocked her. The catastrophe of his death felt so huge to her, looking at them, that it seemed impossible that not everyone should know about it.

There was one letter addressed to her as Mrs Anthony Gascarth, that she recognised as having come from Mr Forrester, the solicitor. Molly frowned. She was due to meet him in three days' time. Surely he wasn't writing to postpone? Molly picked up the paperknife and slid it under the flap.

Your late husband left further instructions that I have now had time to look at. Some of them regard insurance arrangements; he has been admirably thorough so I can assure you that you will be more than adequately provided for. There is one specific request that I had not anticipated, as his instruction was in an envelope your husband left with

*me with express instructions that it should only be opened
in the event of his death and that under certain conditions.
I am therefore writing to you to ask that you be accompanied to our imminent meeting by Mr Mark Fagan, whom I
understand to be a piano tuner.*

Molly sat some time staring at Mr Forrester's words, trying to
make sense of them. *Mr Forrester mentions the insurance first,
so that must be the most important thing. Maybe there's something I have to sign and Anthony's named Mark as a witness, or
as someone he knows would act in my best interests.* She caught
herself up. *No, would he really be asking a man as can't see to be
a witness?* Molly tried to remember if she had ever seen Mark
sign anything. *I'm sure he could; his hand would remember.
But what must that be like for him? Wondering if the letters he
puts down still look like they did when he could see what he was
doing?* She frowned. Molly didn't think she could tell herself
what things really looked like even ten years ago – too much
interference with whatever had happened since. *But Mark'll still
see the world, in a manner of speaking, even if it's only the world
as it used to be.*

She took out a fresh sheet of writing paper and one of the
black-edged envelopes and wrote a message to Joan to pass on.

The solicitor's request was a puzzling surprise. But the best
Molly could say about the one she got the following day was
that it was soon over.

CHAPTER THIRTY-SIX

The Hon Mrs Fanshawe

Because she knew she would have to sooner or later, Molly walked down to the abbey the following morning to retrace the steps she had taken with Anthony, pausing under the arch where he had shared the revelation that Annie and Robert McClure had known the full story of her parentage. *I forgive you, Mother Annie, but there was nothing to forgive.* The spectre of Norman Ashworth was always at her shoulder. Her own half-brother, a man she must have been too young to remember, if indeed she had ever met him at all, had not reappeared. Nor had the reporter whose appearance at the Hall on that dreadful day had robbed her of Anthony forever. *Even if the police said the blame would not stick to that man in spite of the rights and wrongs of it, maybe his paper is worried about that just the same.*

A light drizzle began to fall as Molly made her lonely way around the ruins. As she was wearing the beautiful coat Anthony had bought her in London, less serviceable than her old one, she decided to go to the hotel for a cup of tea. This too was a bridge that had to be crossed, for the last time she had been there was after Anthony had been buried. Herbert was solicitous and kind, and would not accept payment for the tea nor the small cake she chose from the stand.

'With Mr Slaney's compliments,' he said. 'He's gone to Carlisle today and will be sorry not to have seen you, but I know that's what he'd want.'

Molly sipped her tea, conscious that it, as other things also, had a different taste now that Anthony's child grew stealthily within her. *I suppose this is what ladies do,* she thought, looking round at the familiar furniture, the aspidistra in its pot, the piano she thought of as her own. *Well, once Baby is here I won't be able to do any of it anymore.* She bent her head, hiding a secret smile, and stroked the gentle slope of her stomach. Mark came into her head then. A note in Joan's handwriting had come back confirming that he would meet her at Forrester's office.

Molly didn't hurry home. Though she hadn't needed to let out her clothes yet, the fashions being still quite loose, she felt she was slower and occasionally stiff in her back. But as she spied the Hall through the trees she saw that a visitor had called. A Bentley 8 Litre stood outside the house, a hatted chauffeur inside it with his newspaper spread over the wheel. Molly was certain she'd never seen the man before. *Perhaps it's just somebody who has come up from Furness Abbey,* she thought, although it was unusual for anyone to risk such a grand car on the gravelly lane. The man didn't lift his head as she walked past and along the path through the flowers, the path where Anthony had collapsed. She sniffed as she put her hand on the latch and the old door creaked open. It was an unfamiliar smell in that setting but one she had noticed pregnancy made her very susceptible too. She felt a bubble of nausea rise up. *Who's been smoking?*

Mrs Jepson pounced the moment Molly entered.

'You look as if you've been waiting behind the door for me!'

'I have. You've a visitor. Wouldn't be turned away, she wouldn't. Jepson did try.'

'*Oh, do cut out that rot!*'

Molly looked over the cook's shoulder to see the speaker lolling in one of Gascarth's grandfather's magnificently carved chairs. The visitor looked to her as exotic as an image in a magazine, the kind that Agnes treated herself to once a month, and as out of place. Even in her smart coat, Molly felt immediately dowdy. This woman was glossy, from the chestnut gleam of her single-buttoned shoes, the shimmer of what had to be silk stockings, up to the shingled hair that glistened as though it was varnished. The stranger's coat with its deep fur collar hung carelessly open; beneath it Molly spied the soft drape of lilac wool crepe. The wearer's face was not immediately visible, concealed behind a cloud of white smoke emanating from a long, fine cigarette mounted on a holder. A pursed Cupid-bow mouth, painted a vivid red, blew the cloud away, and Molly stared into eyes that were so dark a blue they were almost violet. This vision looked as out of place in Lindal Hall as it was possible to be; the dark furniture, the craquelured paintings, the Turkey carpet on which cigarette ash was scattered, presented themselves to Molly's eyes for the first time as though they belonged in a museum, not in a twentieth-century that had experienced a world-changing war.

'Mrs Gascarth, I presume? Can't say I can see what the fuss is about,' drawled the woman.

'I don't think I've had the pleas—' began Molly, but she was interrupted by a laugh.

'Been taught to ape your betters? Oh dearie me. You're parroting the words but, oh lord, that accent! Don't like that fag ash on your mangy old rug, do you? I can see you're itching to get your dustpan and brush and sweep it up.'

Molly coloured, for this was exactly what she'd been thinking. The only course of action was to ignore the provocation. She was convinced that if she rose to the bait and kneeled before her that the woman would either drop more ash on her head or even rest her well-heeled foot there.

'I'll tell you who that is, our Molly,' said Mrs Jepson.

Molly started. She'd forgotten the cook was there.

'Nobody asked *you,* Jepps!'

'She promised the Master, that one. Just as well they hadn't wed, as "in sickness and in health" wouldn't have mattered a tinker's cuss to her.'

The visitor rolled her eyes. 'God, how *dull* you people are!'

'Broke his heart, she did. Up there in Scotland, he was, shut away with them other poor souls—'

'In an *asylum,* Jepson.' The woman smiled. 'Poor little Anthony's nerves just couldn't take the strain.'

Molly gasped. She clenched her fists, longing to slap the stranger's face.

'What is it you want, Miss . . . ?'

'The Hon Mrs Colin Fanshawe, if you please!'

'Poor Fanshawe,' muttered Jepson. Rage crossed Mrs Fanshawe's beautiful face, quickly replaced with her customary look of smooth disdain.

'Why've you come here?' persisted Molly.

A smirk, then, 'We girls should stick together, shouldn't we? That's what we're always being told, isn't it? Now that we can all vote, even skivvies like yourself.' Mrs Fanshawe waved her cigarette holder, scattering ash in an arc. 'Well, it wasn't to see this place, anyway. Couldn't understand why Anthony wanted to bury himself in this hole. *I* would never have done it. Not when he has that comfortable little lair in London.' The violet eyes held Molly's. 'Don't suppose he told you I'd been there, did he? Nor to that wretched little Boche eating place he was unaccountably fond of. I wonder what else the dear departed didn't tell you.'

Molly felt as if she was struggling to breathe. Had the woman stood up and placed a smooth, manicured hand around her throat and squeezed she was pretty sure she couldn't have felt worse.

'Didn't you ever wonder where he was when he wasn't here?'

'Buying books,' Molly croaked.

This met with a peal of laughter. 'Oh, sweet innocent! Anyway, must dash. A house party in the Lakes with some friends, don't you know? Can't wait to tell them I've met the grieving widow.'

The woman stood up then, nudging her coat onto her shoulders.

'That's of course if you're married properly, dear. It's not as if it was announced in *The Times,* was it? No, silly me! "Miss Molly Whatshername, daughter of the notorious Mary Ashworth?" Wouldn't be quite the ticket, would it?'

*

304

Molly passed the next two hours with Mrs Jepson in the kitchen, but no work was done.

'Take no notice of that one,' said the cook for the third time, pushing another steaming mug of tea across the table. 'She wasn't good for him then, and she only wants to do him harm now he can't defend himself. Being a man, it took a war for him to see the error of his ways. And being an honourable one, he waited for her to give him the push. Fanshawe, is it she calls herself? No doubt one of those chinless wonders she went dancing with in America whilst he was over in Flanders. It's true, Mr Anthony *weren't* the same man when he came back. How could he be? From the stories I've heard, you'd have to be made of stone not to come back different from that. But I'll tell you, Molly, for all he suffered, he came back a better one.'

'Why did she come here then?' said Molly, in a fresh wave of weeping.

'To make trouble,' said Mrs Jepson promptly. 'Always did. Edith Peveril is one of them ladies brought up to think the world's there to do her bidding. Wouldn't know how to boil a kettle or brush her own hair, I shouldn't think. One of them girls that was paraded in front of Queen Mary – a what d'ye mecallit?'

'Debutante,' said Molly. Agnes had shown her pictures of these ethereal beings in one of her magazines.

'That's it. Debbytont. Said she was the most beautiful girl of her year, she did. Can't think why, personally. Always looked like a piece of porcelain. The kind you've to handle carefully or you'll crack it and that you'd not want to eat off for fear you scratched it with your irons. And for Jepson. a nice smile never goes amiss.'

'But my husband loved her.'

Mrs Jepson paused. 'I don't know as I'd rightly call it love, Molly. It were more of what you might call an obsession. And as I said, he was a different man then. He'd got money, and she liked that well enough, knew well enough how to reel him in when she wanted. She was part of his "set", I think they call it. Like a gang, only for grown-ups as don't have enough to do with their time and too much money to do nothing with. I'll be honest with you, Molly. It's not good for a man not to frame himself, in my view. He was always a bright lad, could have been good at the college and all. He went off to study after he came back from Scotland only he got himself another sort of break-down there, to go with the one he was trying to fix himself of when he was took to that hospital in Scotland. Perhaps he stud-ied too hard, with nobody there to put a damp flannel on his forehead and tell him it was time he should lay down. Never did things by halves, did the Master. A few of his college friends came here to see how he was doing, but they made a bit of a mess of the house. Somebody got drunk in the library and was sick on the carpet. He threw 'em all out, went for a walk down by the abbey and next thing was he was going off to London or France or somewhere and Jepson was to look after the place and turn away visitors.'

'You said you were his aunt, first time I came here. I thought—'

'It were just a manner of speaking? Like you'd call an older party "Auntie" if you liked them?'

'Yes. A bit like the way I call Mrs McClure Mother Annie.'

'I'm his flesh and blood, Molly. I'm his father's sister but me and old Mr Gascarth – he was twenty years older'n me – don't have the same mother. I'm merry-begotten as the country folk have it. Mr Anthony's grandfather got a servant into trouble, Molly, and you're looking at the trouble. Eccentric old fellow he was – well, it's him did them carvings so you know that. Other men would've sent away maid and babby to the workhouse and nobody would have said he'd done wrong by it either. More likely they'd have blamed the maid for being in his way, for such is the world. Instead he got her a little cottage to live in and put it in writing that whenever I wanted there'd be a job here where Mother had worked. So here I am. To begin with I were that angry with Mr Gascarth when he took up with you.'

'You never said.'

'Jepson's a good servant, Molly. What you see you don't say owt about. But I was angry with him on your account. It took me a bit to see he weren't taking advantage of you. And then he wed you. For me that was right and proper. It was like drawing a circle and the ends meeting, that was.'

CHAPTER THIRTY-SEVEN

Forrester's

Molly's heart swelled as she walked along Duke Street to the solicitor's office. A neat black armband was the only thing that marked her out as still in mourning, only months after she had walked this same pavement on the arm of Robert McClure, clutching a bridal bouquet. To her relief, Mark was waiting for her in front of the solicitor's plate glass windows. He wouldn't be able to see her tears but he'd know they were there. She called his name.

The blind man's face swivelled in her direction.

'Molly!' he said. 'Let me just pay this little perisher for bringing me here.'

A small grimy-kneed boy in a man's cap emerged from behind Mark. Some coins were pressed into the child's hands.

'Thank you, Mister. Good morning, lady.' Then the boy bolted like a rabbit.

'You'd think he was afraid you'd take the money off him again,' said Molly, watching the child disappear into the crowds.

'I'm relying on you seeing me home after,' said Mark, smiling. 'Otherwise his fee for waiting for me might have been a bit steep. Well, shall we go in? See what this mysterious summons is all about?'

*

'Mr Fagan?' said the solicitor, holding out his hand. Sensing the movement, the tiny rustle of the man's jacket sleeve straightening, Mark put out his own hand and Forrester's met his.

'Mark Fagan, sir. Your humble servant.'

'Please, do sit, both of you.' Molly guided Mark's hand to a chair back, and both of them settled expectantly in front of the solicitor's desk.

'Might I say how terribly sorry I am for your loss, Mrs Gascarth? I never imagined when I had the honour of marrying you that I would be seeing you so soon as a widow.'

Molly bowed her head.

'Your husband's will has left you well-provided for. Normally, as his closest and only next of kin, you would inherit everything. He has, however, made a condition regarding the future of Lindal Hall. If you wished to dispute this, then we can examine ways in which this might be done.'

'I wouldn't want to go against his wishes in anything, Mr Forrester. Not when he was alive, and certainly not now.'

'Understandable. Let me acquaint you with the detail first, though. There is another document. Its existence is peculiarly illustrative of your husband's character.'

Molly nodded, for the solicitor's expression suggested he was looking for her permission to continue.

'Your husband's will was put together with my help just a month after your marriage. I hadn't acted for him before, except in my role as registrar and it took a while for me to retrieve the deeds and so forth relating to his property. His father's solicitor is deceased, and I had to deal with the partner he had turned all his work over to, but who knew nothing material about the Gascarth estate. I have also heard from an accountant in London, a certain E. M. Schwartz. I'll confess I wrote back to this person as "Dear Mr Schwartz" only for the lady to correct me for my presumption. Perhaps, when you next have any dealings with Mrs Schwartz, you would repeat my apologies to her. You do, of course, inherit all the London properties without let or hindrance. Anthony Gascarth had very clear ideas about his estate. Those ideas also struck me as just, so I did not attempt to deter him in any way. Indeed, I wasn't entirely able – or willing, to be honest – to reduce his words to the customary dry legal language, not least because he told me he was dying.'

There was silence in the little office, but the street sounds continued: the rumble of a cart, the rattle of an omnibus. Mr Forrester cleared his throat.

'He had made earlier wills, the first before he went to Flanders. His concern then was always for the house, his books. He wanted nothing to change. He was searching, always, for someone who understood Lindal Hall – those were his exact words to me. He believed that he had found that person in you, Mrs Gascarth. I am convinced that this gave him great comfort.' The solicitor smoothed out the paper that lay between them.

'I have here the notes Mr Gascarth made for the preparation of the will. As a result, he has made over the life interest in the Hall to you. He told me that that was his intention, even if you had refused his offer of marriage.'

'Th-thank you . . . I don't know what you mean by life interest, though.'

'It meant that even had you and Mr Gascarth not married, you could have lived in the Hall for the length of your natural life. You would have benefited from the rent of the Home Farm, but would not have been able to raise a mortgage on it. Nor were you to change anything about the house, though here Mr Gascarth said he was sure you would not have wished to. That meant that if you'd wanted to replace a worn-out curtain you would have had to consult me first and the replacement would have had to have been as close to the original as possible. I'm afraid he would have denied you one of those modern kitchens. Mr Gascarth further stipulated that not so much as a tree was to be cut down, unless that tree were rotten or dangerous, in which case you would again have had to consult me first. You *did* marry, but all those conditions still apply.'

'He was right,' said Molly. Tears came into her eyes as she remembered that first glimpse of the Hall, the hollyhocks and Canterbury bells.

'Unsurprisingly, Mr Gascarth specifically mentions his library. If you will permit me . . .' Forrester smoothed down the page again and read: '"My wife is the only person whom I truly believe will respect my books, including those which we are told should not be put in a servant's way. A library is more than a mere collection of individual volumes. It is in their entirety that their character emerges. I will lie quiet knowing that they are safe in her care. I rather hope that before too long Mrs Gascarth will remarry . . . "'

Molly gasped, but not so loudly that she could not hear Mark's sharp intake of breath.

'You see, he thought of everything. "I would be glad if the Hall could be filled with childish voices again, something which has not been its experience for many years, and that the forms of the village school be occupied again by pupils from the Hall. I would wish only that any children she and her husband might have should grow up to respect both building and contents as they are. They will not be permitted to inherit; I say this in their best interests, for in my opinion every child should make his or her own way, just as the former Miss Dubber, now Mrs Gascarth, was obliged to do. On Mrs Gascarth's death, whether she dies as a married woman, or as a widow, whether mine or another man's, the Hall should revert to the National Trust.'

'I haven't even thought about marrying again,' said Molly, bewildered. 'Though I'd want to respect my husband's wishes, whatever they were.'

'There is a little more, Mrs Gascarth,' said Forrester, glancing at Mark. 'I explained to my client that this suggestion – I cannot call it a stipulation, for it wasn't his to make – had no part in a will. I persuaded him to put it in a letter instead. Anthony Gascarth had ideas as to whom you should marry, Mrs Gascarth. I don't think he thought better of them in wedding you himself, because he knew even then you and he would not enjoy a long life together. One learns in this profession to read between the lines, Mrs Gascarth, not just what is legally signed and sealed. I understood that, if he had not expected to die early, then he might not have asked you to marry him at all.'

Molly stared down at the envelope and the words there in black ink. 'To be opened by Mrs Molly Gascarth in the event of my death. Anthony Charles Gascarth of Lindal Hall, Lancashire.'

Mr Forrester silently proffered a paper knife.

*

My dearest Molly, she read silently to herself,

I am a precise man, as you know. It is my habit not to act until I have thought things through thoroughly, to consider every eventuality. Yet this letter follows six others that I have consigned to the fire as not expressing my intent.

When I first thought of writing this, we were lovers. I was, in my old-fashioned way, aware that I had already availed myself of the privileges only a husband is entitled to. I am sure your redoubtable friend Agnes would express what we knew of each other far more directly. However, I intended to make good – to ask you to be my wife. You accepted, and so now you are reading this as my widow.

You love me more than I deserve, you courageous young woman. Courageous at taking on a man who has been irreparably damaged in a war that should never have been fought. I do not have your grit. I don't have the words to tell you that I am dying, that you will live most of your life without me.

I would urge you, though, not to live it alone. We recognise each other, we men who have gone through Hell and come out the other end, scorched and maimed in mind if not in body. There is another who loves you but who has never spoken. I have seen the unguarded tenderness of his expression when you speak, the way he turns his sightless eyes to you. I believe you love him too, and always have. I know I have taken advantage of his silence, of his belief that he could never be worthy of you because he will never, this side of heaven, be able to see your face. My own passion for you got the better of me. If I had not known I was dying, I would have stood aside, encouraged him, even. Instead I persuaded you to love me because I wanted that happiness before my end. It was my last chance.

You may consign this letter to the fire too and ignore its contents if you wish. All I really want to say is that if Mark Fagan ever tells you how he feels, then you can reject him or accept him as you please. You are a free agent. Do not feel that you cannot love another man – a worthier one, I am sure – out of misplaced loyalty to my memory. On the contrary. I want you to be happy and I would be happy if you had the comfort of Mark's arms around you. I rather hope that you will share the contents of this letter with him.

I love you,
Anthony.

*

Wet-eyed, Molly looked first at Mark, sitting in patient silence, then up at the solicitor.

'If you will both excuse me for a moment,' said Forrester, 'I ought to have a word with my secretary.'

*

'Here, Molly,' said Mark, handing her a pressed handkerchief. 'I can tell from your breathing you need it.'

'Oh, Mark, I've something to tell you.'

'It's your letter. You don't have to.'

'This isn't in the letter. Anthony never knew. I wasn't sure . . . I thought it better to wait, and then it was too late.'

'You're going to be a mother.' Though Mark was smiling, Molly read sadness in the sightless face.

'You don't look happy for me, Mark.'

'I am. It's that the child will not know his father, that's all.' He put his hand over hers. 'I wonder why Mr Forrester wanted me here, though. Perhaps it was just for moral support.'

Molly was speechless. *Will you not speak, Mark? Even without knowing what is in the letter, isn't it clear to you?*

All he said was, 'Would you take me back to Hardwick Street?'

'Of course. I said I would.'

CHAPTER THIRTY-EIGHT

Hardwick Street

Molly watched Mark move around the rooms above the green-grocer's with the confidence of a sighted man. There was no hesitation in the way he prepared the tea things. She was wondering how long it might take him to walk with the same fluency around the spaces of the Hall, when it occurred to her that the fact that nothing was ever to be changed there, by Anthony's express wish, meant that yes, he could learn.

Remember you're a widow, Molly, by only a few weeks. And you're going to have a baby. Try to be decent, can't you? Even though she knew Mark couldn't see her flushing, she looked down at her lap, her hands twisting together. *It's the wrong time for that hope, no matter what Anthony said.* She looked up, to see Mark's face turned to her, waiting.

'I was going to marry Joan so's little Edie would have a father,' he said. 'And to stop the chattering about her and me.'

'*Was* there chattering? It was nobody's business, surely?'

'Doesn't stop them, as you well know. Annie told me about the reporters that came bothering you.'

'They've left me alone. Perhaps they've consciences after all – given what happened.'

'They'll come back, Molly. Once it gets out you've inherited. Because it will. Some of the big estates get posted in the newspapers. That man who says he's your half-brother? You'll hear from him sure enough.'

'Oh, I hope not!' cried Molly. 'There was a woman who turned up as well – said she'd been engaged to Anthony and made all kinds of snide comments. The reporter said Anthony might have been got for breach of promise – but she's married to someone else now.'

Mark gave a small, unhappy laugh. 'Anthony Gascarth didn't breach promises, from what I've seen. To no one.'

Molly didn't know what to say to this. Eventually she said, her heart thumping, 'Why didn't you marry Joan? She'd have been good for you.'

'She would, Molly.' He drank off his tea. 'There are plenty women want to marry us. Us meaning men who are missing bits. It's not just that there aren't enough trouser-wearers to go round, though that's got something to do with it. And it's not that there isn't fondness there quite a lot of the time. Only with some of 'em, you can see – in a manner of speaking – that it's not really the man himself they're after. It's that in marrying him the world will think well of them – noble and self-sacrificing heroines binding themselves to poor, maimed wretches who'll always be dependent on them.'

'Not Joan, surely?' cried Molly, appalled at the bitterness of his tone.

'No, not Joan. I suppose I just wanted you to know that there'd been other opportunities, not just her. You're right, Joan would have been good for me. Only it's me that wouldn't have been any good for her.'

'Why not?' whispered Molly.

'I cared about Joan – still do – but I don't love her. If you've known what love is, really known it, then settling for second best just won't do. You've not told me what's in that letter, Molly, but I can guess. Your husband wanted me to marry you, didn't he?'

Molly nodded.

'Say it. I know you're moving your head, but not if you mean yes or no.'

'Yes.'

'I can't, Molly.'

She wanted to say, 'let me read it to you at least,' but was afraid she wouldn't get the words out. Instead she said, 'I'd best go, then,' and got to her feet. 'I want to see Mother Annie.'

'The fact he's left you everything makes it more difficult, not easier,' he said, but Molly didn't answer. He heard her hurried movements, the opening and closing of the door at the top of the stairs. He put his head into his hands and groaned.

*

Annie McClure folded the letter. 'Have you read this to Mark?'

'No. He guessed what was in it, asked me, and said at once he couldn't marry me. The inheritance gets in the way as well,

I think. As if he's afraid folk would think he wanted me for Anthony's money.'

'Oh dear. You know, Molly, there are plenty other men would hate the idea of a widow finding another man. Your husband hated the idea that you were going to be left alone, even if he didn't know about the babby. You won't be, not really, not so long as Robert and I are alive, but it's not as if you'd want to be living here again. But you and Mark . . . sometimes I've wished I could knock your two heads together.'

'Anthony is barely cold, Mother Annie! I loved him. I *miss* him. I keep expecting him to appear at my shoulder, keep thinking I hear his voice. I'm heartsore that he didn't tell me how ill he was.' Molly paused, avoiding Annie's eyes. 'I've never told anyone but I'll tell you this: I agreed to marry him when I thought I'd lost Mark for always.'

'I thought that,' said Annie quietly. 'But I did think Mr Gascarth would make you happy.'

'He did. Oh, he did.' Molly started to cry. 'I'm ashamed of what I did. I'm sure he knew too but he wanted me all the same. But I never regretted marrying him and I would do anything to have him back. *Anything.*'

Annie handed Molly a folded handkerchief and moving her chair closer, put her arm around her.

'It's not decent to be thinking of such things now. With Anthony barely cold,' said Molly.

'Except Anthony is as clear as he could be about what he wants you to do. Not that you have to do it.'

'Oh, Mother Annie, I'd have taken Mark years ago, if he'd wanted me.'

319

'Years ago?' said Annie, smiling. 'You're barely twenty.'

'Well, it feels like all my life. I've always loved Mark. I . . . I loved Anthony too, but I couldn't have if I'd ever thought Mark wanted me.'

'I do not know if you aren't blinder than he is, Molly. Or if the pair of ye are just stubborn.'

'I forget that he's blind sometimes. It's him has to remind me – and he does. But I'd best stop this nonsense. I've the baby to think of. Anthony's baby.'

'Babies need fathers, Molly, in my thinking. Same as they need mothers.'

CHAPTER THIRTY-NINE

Risedale Maternity

Christmas came and then the new year, with muted celebrations at the Hall, although Molly dutifully went out to gather winter greenery despite Mrs Jepson's warnings not to overexert herself.

'But Jepson'll not have you hanging them up, she won't. You're not to be messing about with ladders with that belly on you.'

Molly obediently got out of the way, disappearing to the library to work on typing up the committee papers Joan forwarded to her. She sometimes felt guilty for doing the work. *It's not as if I need the money and perhaps somebody else does. But I do need to be useful.* At seven months, though, she knew she could not keep going for much longer. Her back ached and the swell of her pregnancy nudged the rim of the desk. Yet she'd noticed that when the baby was restive, the clack of the keys seemed to soothe him – or her. They soothed her too. In the first three months of widowhood, Molly had found herself straining her ears to hear the creak of a door, or Anthony's soft step. When she found herself doing this she would glance first at her wedding ring, then at the black armband she had resolved to wear for a year and finally she would stroke her stomach. In that way she chased away the illusion that her quiet life at the Hall was pretty much what it had been like before Anthony Gascarth had declared his love, with the Master disappearing at whim and returning just as unexpectedly. The rhythm of the keys striking the unfurling paper, the lines of typescript marching down the page, and above all the noise, suffocated her irrational thoughts. And of course there was the satisfaction of chunking all the papers together at the end of the day and sealing them in their envelopes, before walking down to the hotel to post them.

Molly enjoyed her pregnancy but not the loneliness of it, the not being able to share the changes in her body with the man who had brought them about. It was Joan who understood this more than anyone, encouraging her friend to tell her how she had passed the night, how many pints of milk she was drinking to douse the heartburn, what times of day the baby lay quiet in her womb and when the kicks were at their most lively. Joan, Molly knew, had held the telegram telling her the father of her child had 'died of his wounds' and, as she'd put it, 'I felt as though I was going to have to struggle up a hill in a storm without a guide, without maps.'

Annie McClure made the journey to the Hall when she could, sometimes with Robert, but Molly knew the near impossibility of entrusting a house full of little girls to someone else. She longed to see the woman she thought of as a mother more often, but making the journey into Barrow was becoming increasingly difficult. She felt like a bird that didn't want to leave her nest, and told Joan so.

'You'll need to think about where you want to have your baby,' her friend reminded her. 'What's the doctor advising?'

'He says I'm healthy but as it's my first he thinks Risedale Maternity.'

'That's where I went for Edie. I'm glad I did.'

This choice was contested by Mrs Jepson on the grounds that, 'You might come back with the wrong babby.'

'I'll know my child. Anthony's child,' said Molly.

What she shared with no one, but thought about in the dead of night when the baby's restlessness brought her up to the surface, was the woman lying in quicklime in Strangeways Gaol. 'Mother,' whispered Molly into the darkness. 'What was it like having me? What did you think when you saw my face for the first time?' And it was a question she asked again silently when weeks later a kind nurse helped her to sit up, the bloodied sheets were pulled away, and a cool, damp flannel was put to her forehead.

'Baby will be back soon as soon as Doctor's checked him over. He's a bonny little fellow with a good pair of lungs by the sound of him.'

'I can hear him,' said Molly faintly, astonished to find that her nipples itched.

'What'll you call Baby Gascarth?'

'Anthony Robert,' said Molly as the door opened and another nurse appeared, carrying over a bundle swathed in a cobweb blanket. She handed her burden over to Molly with a smile.

Molly looked down at her son. A crumpled, angry little face looked up at her and a tiny hand unfurled.

'He has his eyes,' whispered Molly. 'And that's my husband's hand, only in miniature. But he's too impossibly small.'

'I sometimes think that as soon as they're born is the best time to see who they look like,' said the first nurse. 'Folks say newborns just look like each other, but I know different. It's when they put on weight and their little wrists get them creases as if you could unscrew their hands like a dolly's that you don't see so easily what you just seen.'

The two nurses remade the bed as best they could around Molly. Straightening up, the one who had brought the baby in said, 'We'll need to take him away again soon so's you can rest a bit.'

'But I'm not remotely tired. I could get up and run a race if I was let to.'

The nurse looked at her with an 'I know better' expression, but all she said was, 'Make the most of rest when you can, Mrs Gascarth. There'll be precious few chances to relax for at least three years.'

Molly remembered those words often over the coming months, though she was encouraged by Joan's reassurance that, 'It does get easier. Either that or you stop bothering your head about whether you've done it right, let alone what you look like.'

After three months Molly put away the letters of congratulation in a folder in the back of the filing cabinet Anthony Gascarth had bought. There was just one she reread before putting it away. Apart from the uncertain signature, the letter was in Annie McClure's hand, but the words were Mark's. *I am sure you will be the best of mothers. Your baby's father would have been proud of you, and him.*

'I wish you would come, Mark. I know you can't see my baby, but I wish I could tell you what he looks like. And I'd like to see him in a man's arms,' whispered Molly, her lips against her baby's silky hair – and the very next day a letter of a very different kind arrived.

*

14 Leigh Street
Bloomsbury, W.C.1

Dearest lady
My grovelling apologies for the tardiness of this missive. Mrs Schwartz and Mrs Bonelli, excellent females both, have upbraided me for this failing. Being the correct and organised person that she is, I am sure our accountant has already put pen to paper to congratulate you. We had the news from Mrs Caulfield, whom I am honoured to have as a regular correspondent. Mrs Bonelli, I know, is mortified that she has not written to you yet, but claims to be embarrassed at her lack of proficiency in the language of Shakespeare (how she manages with that of Dante is not a matter of record) and has badgered me to write myself that she may at least add her name at the foot of this missive.

*

Molly smiled. Mrs Schwartz had indeed written soon after the baby's birth. *And how like dear Joan to remember to let them know without making a fuss about it*, she thought. Mrs Schwartz had also informed her that the family in Nine Elms were now rehoused 'in a nice dry flat where there's a proper sink, a bathtub and no cockroaches'. Of Mr Sanderson there had been no word.

*

He has abandoned his business, leaving his partner to tidy up the mess. That gentleman either does not know where he has gone or chooses not to say. I suspect the former, as my contacts tell me that the poor fellow has discovered that he too has been cheated.

*

The remainder of Harold Symonds's letter was in similar oracular style, but it was the closing paragraph that made Molly sit up with excitement, jigging little Anthony on her lap. 'We're going to have visitors, Anty! From London!'

*

Mrs Bonelli says I am an insensitive boor, wanting to break in on your sylvan solitude. She says it is obvious I have never been a father if I intend bothering you so early in your maternity.

Well, all I can say in my defence is that I was a lad of twelve I believe when I realised that fatherhood and I would never encounter one another. But I digress. There is no intention of imposing on your hospitality. I have already telegraphed my old landlady, Mrs Tickell, and that dear soul replied, I fancy with tears in her eyes, that it would do her good to see me again. I shall travel with my colleague Mr Boxall, even though he says I have quite wearied him with my recollections of my days in Rep – he comes to please me, dear young fellow. Benson, of course, will be of the party. Mrs Bonelli will not join us; she cannot be parted from whatever fulfils the role of the dolly-tub in these unashamedly modern times.

CHAPTER FORTY

The play's the thing

'My dear lady,' said Harold Symonds, gesturing widely as though he wanted to scoop up the entire entrance to the Hall and hold it in his arms, 'this is exquisite. Do you not agree, Mr Boxall?'

His companion, a young man of meek expression and unruly hair, said, 'The feast scene in the Scottish Play, sir – what could be better than that table? Blood-boltered Banquo from Stage Left.'

'We don't want any blood bolts in here, young man,' said Mrs Jepson, 'whatever they might be.'

'Not a drop, Mistress, not a drop,' said Symonds. 'I rather think more cheerful fare for our Mrs Gascarth and that dear little chap of hers. "With mirth and laughter let old wrinkles come" – although perhaps not just yet,' he added, seeing Mrs Jepson's disapproving expression. 'The play is the thing – when was it not? But not here. I rather fancy the abbey.'

'It'll rain,' said Mrs Jepson ominously. Molly put a hand on her arm.

'There's the infirmary chapel,' said Molly. 'I mean the monk's infirmary – not High Carley Sanatorium,' she added, seeing their puzzled faces. 'It's roofed.'

'Then I shall inspect it this afternoon. And speak to the custodian, though I am quite sure that we will have no difficulties given that this is to be a private party for the inhabitants of the Hall, Boxall and I the only players – but Boxall is a most versatile young man, most versatile. You shall pick the audience, Mrs Gascarth, though we would be honoured if Mrs Jepson would be of the party.' He bowed low. 'Your friend Agnes and her swain, of course. Mrs Schwartz, naturally.'

'Mrs Schwartz is here?' said Molly, astonished.

'Staying at the hotel by the abbey. I rather think she is in her bath at the moment, though that establishment is a little short of modern plumbing. No theatrical digs for Mrs Schwartz, oh no. She keeps our accounts but does not wish to live with us. For Mr Boxall and myself, staying with dear Mrs Tickell in our old rooms in Albert Street is just like old times.'

'*Your* old times, Mr Symonds. I don't think I was alive then.'

'Cedric – don't bring that up again. One will require a fit-up, of course.'

'A fit-up?' said Mrs Jepson. 'I don't know that I like the sound of that.'

*

The fit-up turned out to be a complete portable proscenium and stage, with drop curtain and frame for all limelights and footlights. Some of this had to be discarded, as even Mr Symonds's enthusiasm could not provide power to that corner of the abbey where no power lines lay.

'The bard had no need of such things,' he declared to Molly. 'We will have candlelight if we need it, and do our best not to set fire to ourselves nor to this charming backdrop. I fancy, though, that we may be able to do without anything remotely at risk of pyrotechnics, as we are fast approaching the longest day of the year, and I note that at this distance from London the light endures rather longer.'

Mr Fallowfield, Herbert Lowther, Agnes's Daniel, Mr Slaney and the hotel carpenter had presented themselves as stage-hands and the entire fit-up had been brought by cart. To Molly, watching the unloading, it looked like a pile of lumber: pieces of wormy wood, dusty pieces of canvas and moth-eaten curtains. Yet when it was assembled she exclaimed at its prettiness. The backdrop that had been unrolled was a rustic scene of thatched, half-timbered cottages, nothing like the sturdy, high-shouldered houses of the towns of North Lancashire. She wondered what state the other canvases were in. They were rolled up against the back frame of the stage, but looked tatty and uneven, bunched like a row of swifts' nests under eaves.

'It's a little the worse for wear,' said Mr Symonds. 'Belonged to a retired theatre manager, a neighbour of my temporary land-lady. She said he was famous for not throwing anything away, and my goodness, that was apparent from the state of his house! Fortunately for us, he'd always insisted that, no matter how many cinemas opened in Barrow, there would still be a place, somewhere in the future, for the return of the travelling show. I fear that the appearance of a London actor-manager on his doorstep asking for the loan of this fit-up has rather reinforced that delusion. In one thing, he is right, of course. There is no replacement for the live, spoken word, as we shall prove.'

During the days leading up to the performance, even the suspicious Mrs Jepson had mellowed. In large part this was down to young Mr Boxall's praise of her 'butter pie', a tasty concoction of potatoes and onions in shortcrust. 'One of the Master's favourites,' she'd proudly informed him.

'He looks like our Stan Laurel,' she'd confided in Molly, the 'our' because the risen star of Hollywood comedy had been born in a terraced house about ten miles up the road. 'Only he's prettier.'

Molly wrote the invitations to 'a Shakespeare Solstice' believing that all of this had been done at too short notice, yet by some happy accident almost everyone had replied saying that they would be glad to come. The exception was Myrtle, too near her confinement. The McClures wrote back immediately, explaining that the 'Mother' in one of the other Cottage Homes would cover for them, in exchange for an evening when they would repay the favour, allowing her and her husband a rare night out at the pictures. To Joan, Molly wrote that Harold Symonds had expressed the hope of seeing her again, and, if both were able, would Mark like to come with her? Standing by the pillar box, Molly separated that envelope from the others, which she posted at one go. She looked at it for a full minute before sending it to join the rest.

On the afternoon before the performance, a procession of servants carried a collection of folding chairs from the hotel to the abbey. Standing with Mrs Schwartz, her hands resting on the handle of the baby carriage and watching those neat young men advancing across the grass, for the first time Molly wondered at the oddness of this occasion. Mr Symonds was eccentric – that was evident – but this?

'Why this, Mrs Schwartz? I would have thought Mr Symonds would have wanted an engagement at one of the Barrow theatres. To go to all this trouble just for a little group of people – my household, my friends . . . Why?'

Mrs Schwartz didn't reply immediately. Molly could see she was considering her words.

'I've known Symonds for years. In some ways he is very old-fashioned. Chivalrous, you might say. He also believes, to his marrow, in the power of the spoken word, on the stage.'

'So why isn't he at His Majesty's before fifteen hundred people, instead of in a ruined abbey in front of twenty?'

'Ever read *Hamlet*, Mrs Gascarth?'

'Read it, but not seen it. There's a complete Shakespeare in my husband's library. We're not getting *Hamlet* this evening, are we? How would Mr Symonds and Mr Boxall manage all the parts?'

'We won't. There are just the two of them. I understand that this evening's programme will be rather more cheerful than that family feud in Denmark.'

'So . . . ?'

'Remember that bit in Act II where Hamlet conspires with those travelling players?'

'Where he gets them to put on a play about a man being murdered by his brother, and then he watches his wicked uncle's guilty reaction?'

'Precisely.'

'I still don't understand. I've not murdered anyone.' A horrible thought gripped her. 'This hasn't anything to do with . . . ?' Molly couldn't get out the rest of her words. She longed to lift Anty out of his pram and hold him tight and kiss him, *but leave him, Molly, the poor little mite is fast asleep.*

'Your poor wronged mother?' said Mrs Schwartz gently. 'No, not at all.' She patted Molly's hand where it gripped the handle. 'You'll see. And not just you, I think.'

*

At five o'clock, the two actors heaved a grip onto the stage, climbed up themselves and pulled the curtain closed with them behind it. Molly sat at the back of the chapel, sheltered by Mrs Jepson, and quietly fed Anty in the lull between the afternoon's bustle of activity and the start of the performance. As the day had been fine, there had been quite a few visitors getting down at the station to wander around the abbey, and to stop and wonder at all the activity inside the Infirmary Chapel. But closing time had come and they'd been ushered out.

From behind the curtain the actors' voices carried.

'Your hose, Mr Symonds.'

'Your farthingale, Mr Boxall.'

'Would you help me tie it on?'

Some grunts and rustlings followed.

'Not too tight, Mr Symonds!' squeaked Boxall.

The scuffling sounds from the stage eventually subsided into a concentrated silence. Then: 'Stay still!' hissed Symonds, 'Or this'll end up all over your wig.'

Molly and Mrs Jepson exchanged glances, but before they could say anything the mutterings behind the curtain were drowned out by the roar of the evening train approaching Furness Abbey station.

'I wonder if everyone will come?' she said.

'What was that?' said Mrs Jepson.

'Would you watch Anty a moment?' said Molly as the sound of the train died down to a hiss of steam.

'Of course. Go and make sure they know where to come to.'

Behaving as if you're at school, Molly reproved herself, *trying to catch sight of a lad and the pretending you're there by accident. Only you never did do that back then, did you? That's when you were serious – when you knew that you'd never get on if you didn't knuckle down to it yourself.* Tears stung her eyes as she remembered how Anthony Gascarth too had been keen that she should 'get on', organising everything for her: buying her the typewriter, encouraging her to play the little Broadwood, sending her to the Technical School. *You thought of everything, didn't you? Even to who I'd marry next. Only things don't always go according to plan, do they?*

She hurried along the side of the long wall of what had been the infirmary. She could see Mrs Schwartz in a natty little panama hat with a deep red ribbon, worn at a fetching angle; she was directing the little gaggle of people. The McClures were at the front, Robert throwing his bad leg wide as he stumped towards her, holding his wife's arm. *I was so lucky to have been sent to them.* There was Herbert, his freshly pomaded hair gleaming in the late afternoon sun, and Mr Slaney in a three-piece suit that looked too warm for mild June. Agnes followed, clinging to the arm of a bemused Daniel.

And finally there was Joan, with Mark's hand on her shoulder, Mark's stick swinging back and forth in a practised arc. A moment later, Molly's hand was in his and Joan was saying, 'I'm just going to catch up with Mrs Schwartz.'

'I'm sorry I've not been much of a friend,' said Mark, his face inclined towards her. He was frowning slightly.

'I didn't think that,' said Molly softly.

'So you're a mother, now?'

'I'm blessed, yes.'

'Look like his father?'

'Oh yes! Even the shape of his feet … I think he'll have Anthony's long legs. His hair is darker, more like mine, but soft like his father's. I'm being silly, aren't I? He's got baby hair – of course it's soft. Come and meet him.'

Inside the chapel, the little party were taking their seats. Herbert, in his waiter's uniform, needed to do nothing to transform into a front-of-house manager. After a last muttered consultation behind the curtain, he stepped forward holding a small handbell. Two brief shakes and the murmured conversation died into expectant silence. Molly sat at the back with Anty in her arms, so that she could leave quickly if he started crying. Mark sat beside her, his legs crossed, his body leaning slightly away from hers. Joan had not come back; she was sitting the other side of the aisle with Betty Schwartz.

'Ladies and gentlemen, may we present a Shakespeare Solstice,' said Herbert, and moving to the side of the stage, he pulled a rope; the curtains flowed back revealing the two actors. A cloud of dust billowed with them, motes floating in the light that streamed through the blank window arches. Molly gasped, and sensed Mark turn towards her.

CHAPTER FORTY-ONE

All the world's a stage

Harold Symonds was resplendent in what Molly knew from illustrations in the Roose Road *Children's Encyclopaedia* was called a doublet and hose. The costume looked as stiff as a carapace, from the starched ruff downwards, though the actor's hose-clad legs, emerging from the voluminous breeches that covered his thighs, appeared sprightly and muscular. It occurred to Molly afterwards that there was something odd about the way men's legs were expected to disappear from sight, except in the privacy of a bedroom, once little boys left off short trousers.

But it was Symonds's companion that left the audience open-mouthed. Where was Mr Boxall? The delicate figure whose hand was held aloft by the older actor, as though they were about to start a courtly dance, looked like a pretty porcelain doll of an Elizabethan lady. The whited oval face was almost indistinguishable from the ruff framing it, the tinted lips curved in a timid smile, the head in its curled russet wig tilted coquettishly to one side. Molly was sure the stiffness of that dress, with its rigid stomacher and the farthingale that held out the skirts, would keep any unwanted suitors at a distance as much as a suit of armour. Yet the doll was able to dip effortlessly into an elegant curtsey, her free hand held out to the side.

'Ladies and gentlemen,' began Mr Symonds, letting go of his companion's hand and walking to the front of the little stage, 'I see from your questioning faces that an explanation is in order. Mr Boxall in his wig and padding is following a great Shakespearean tradition. In the Bard's day no woman was permitted to tread the boards, just as, not even two decades ago, no woman in this country was permitted to vote for the gentleman – or lady – who might represent her in what we are pleased to call the mother of parliaments. Extraordinary, don't you think, that even the great Miss Ellen Terry would, in Shakespeare's day, have been prevented from speaking the words that in her mouth seem to have been written for her?

'But to our programme. Our theme is a perennial one – that of love – in all its forms.'

Behind him, Mr Boxall simpered, and dipped another curtsey.

'We offer you not an entire play, but excerpts, such as will serve our purpose. Think of these as little vignettes, pretty coloured illustrations in a book which make you want to read the whole story. We will give you the merest outline of what the characters mean to each other – and what they do that makes the course of love not run smooth. For as you will see, it is not just circumstances that conspire against lovers, but the lovers themselves. But first, I think, a sonnet.'

Holding his skirts, Mr Boxall pattered forward. Symonds turned to him, and took both his colleague's hands in his own. Molly was aware of a fidgeting in the audience, a silence that wasn't so much expectant as awkward, the only sounds the twittering of the birds on the other side of the empty window arches. For here was an older man, looking down into the painted face of a younger one with an expression of adoration, and doing so publicly. Then Symonds spoke.

*

'Let me not to the marriage of true minds
Admit impediments. Love is not love
Which alters when it alteration finds,
Or bends with the remover to remove.
O no! It is an ever-fixed mark
That looks on tempests and is never shaken:

*

Molly felt the tension ease in her hands and shoulders. Symonds had delivered his lines without flourish or declamation. The old Symonds, who reminded her of nothing so much as the actors in the silent films who had to exaggerate every gesture because they were incapable of sound, had been emptied out and filled only with the beauty of those three-hundred-year-old words. Up there, on the ramshackle fit-up stage, he was also a younger man, with a younger man's glance and a younger man's hope in his eyes. And for his part, Cedric Boxall was not merely a man painted up like a Salzburg puppet. He had become a shy young woman with downcast eyes, learning that she was adored.

Watching Boxall, Molly thought of herself, hearing Anthony Gascarth tell her for the first time that he loved her. By the time Symonds spoke the closing words, '*If this be error and upon me prov'd, I never writ, nor no man ever lov'd,*' Molly could see that there was no one looking up at the stage who wished they were elsewhere.

Some scenes Symonds spoke alone.

'Surely everyone here,' he told his audience, 'with the possible exception of the faithful Benson,' – here the dog raised his head on cue to general laughter – 'and the exception only for the time being of Master Anthony Gascarth,' – here everyone turned to smile indulgently at Molly with the baby in her arms – 'has passed many minutes alone thinking of the loved one, without the courage to declare those thoughts. In our next scene, from *Love's Labour's Lost,* I want you to imagine four young men who tempt fate, resolving to put aside all thoughts of women for three years in favour of study and fasting – only to have their vow put to the test when they encounter four young ladies who have made *no* such vow.

'Ladies and gentlemen, how many young men were brought to this very infirmary in which we now sit, pondering in their illness whether their choice of tonsure and habit was the right one?' he asked impressively. 'How many of us *now* ponder on the choices we have made?'

There was some shifting on the seats at this rhetorical question. In the character of Lord Berowne, the actor launched into his first speech. Molly let Symonds's beautifully modulated diction wash over her as she remembered how long it had taken Anthony Gascarth to declare his love – so many times he had drawn back, usually by disappearing altogether. She mourned him afresh, sitting there holding the dead man's sleeping child. *We could have had more time together.* Then she thought of the man sitting silently next to her. *He came this evening, so he didn't ignore my invitation. But does he ever think now about what poor Anthony wanted him to do?* Then Shakespeare's words broke through her thoughts.

*

'A lover's eyes will gaze an eagle blind.
A lover's ear will hear the lowest sound . . .'

*

But I never heard poor Anthony. He'd just appear without me knowing he was there. He had to scream in his sleep for me to know how bad he felt.

In the following scene it was Mr Boxall who took centre stage, standing forward of the dust as Herbert unrolled another back-drop, this time of a sylvan scene. There were a couple of rents in the canvas, but even this had been planned for and Herbert and Agnes's Daniel obligingly mounted the stage carrying branches almost as tall as themselves, which they waved gently as young Mr Boxall spoke the part of lovelorn Helena in *A Midsummer Night's Dream*. To Molly's relief the actor did not attempt a pantomime falsetto; the softness of his delivery was feminine enough. *Is it my imagination, though, or is he looking directly at me? I thought they weren't meant to do that.*

'*Love looks not with the eyes,*' said Mr Boxall, '*but with the mind. And therefore is winged Cupid painted blind.*'

Molly heard the chair next to her creak and glanced at Mark. She could see he was listening intently. *That's the second speech in a row where they've said blind. But they say that 'Love is blind', don't they? Everybody says that.*

During the next scene, from *As You Like it,* she felt herself relaxing. Anty snuffled on her lap, opened his eyes momentarily and subsided back into sleep. She sensed, too, that some of the tension had gone out of Mark. In the Forest of Arden Silvius reflected on the nature of love, to the background accompaniment of Herbert and Daniel's rustling leaves.

*

'If thou remembrest not the slightest folly
That ever love did make thee run into.
Thou has not loved.'

*

Molly thought about the people in the audience with her. Had all of them loved and been guilty of folly? She saw Mrs Schwartz, sitting near the front, listening intently. She'd not said much about the deceased Mr Schwartz, only that he had died early. Molly found it difficult to believe that Mrs Schwartz had ever done or thought anything remotely close to folly; that lady seemed too capable, intimidating even. Mr Symonds had said in his letter that he'd realised long ago that 'fatherhood and I would never encounter one another', which she'd read as a conscious decision to avoid love. *He must've meant giving his all to the stage instead, mustn't he?* Then Molly looked in the direction of the two people who had taken her in on behalf of the Board of Guardians. She remembered from Roose Road Sundays that Mother Annie would accompany the little girls to the Church of England service in St Mark's with Mr McClure, even though she had always already gone to Vigil Mass in the Catholic church on the previous evening. Only at school, amongst the children of the Irish workers in the shipyard, the wireworks and the jute mill, had she learned that in *their* world a mixed union like the McClures was a rare event, and not looked that kindly upon by either side. Their love must have looked like folly, then. She wondered about Herbert, up on the stage solemnly waving his branch; he'd always been attentive to her but without a hint of wooing. *Who does he dream about?*

At the close of that scene, Herbert and Daniel abandoned their tree branches down the side of the stage. Molly saw Benson amble off to investigate them, only to be stopped by Betty Schwartz when he showed signs of cocking a leg over them. Herbert unfurled a plain, dark curtain, somewhat faded on the folds. Then he and Daniel took up positions stage left and right, a blue and grey strip of cloth stretched out between them. They crouched down and began to shake it up and down vigorously, as Symonds came forward to introduce the audience to the tryst of Ferdinand and Miranda on Prospero's island in *The Tempest,* culminating in a tremulous Miranda putting her hand in her suitor's and telling him, *'I would not wish any companion in the world but you . . . I am your wife, if you will marry me.'* Molly again marvelled at the look of love that passed between Harold Symonds and Cedric Boxall, thinking them very good actors indeed.

Then finally, the performance drew to a close.

Symonds bowed to his audience, drawing off an imaginary hat, just has he had done the first time Molly had met him.

'We players have strutted and fretted our hour upon the stage, ladies and gentlemen, but we cannot leave until we give you just two scenes from perhaps the greatest and most tragical love story ever written – *Romeo and Juliet.'*

Symonds played the first scene alone, Romeo as a fretful adolescent, addressing his absent friend Benvolio. With a sharp intake of breath, Molly heard the words, *'Alas that love, whose view is muffled still, should without eyes see pathways to his will.'* Despite herself, she looked at Mark, for there it was again, that reference to blindness. His face was turned to hers, his lips slightly open. She saw him mouth something. It looked like her name, but she couldn't be sure and she did not know if he even knew she was looking at him.

A flurry of soft-soled activity took place as the scene came to an end. Daniel and Herbert were manoeuvring an old stepladder into place at stage left. Up this Cedric Boxall climbed, hitching up his skirts with one hand, revealing a very male pair of shoes and socks. Daniel hurriedly propped a piece of stage set against the stepladder, painted to resemble an old stone wall with a balustrade atop. Settled at the top of this, Mr Boxall looked like an exotic bird perched on a nest. But as Mr Symonds began his lines, the illusion was complete. He was no longer a middle-aged actor but an ardent boy, and his Juliet a tremulous maiden prepared to defy anything and anyone for the man she loved. Molly saw the usually lugubrious Mr Slaney dab his eyes with a dazzlingly white handkerchief. Mrs Schwartz was doing the same. Molly could make out the gleam of tears on Joan's face. She heard Mark sigh and realised she was crying herself. Juliet looked down at her lover and said with almost unbearable gentleness:

*

'My bounty is as boundless as the sea,
My love as deep; the more I give to thee,
The more I have, for both are infinite.'

*

She felt Mark's hand cover her own, his fingers curling around hers. 'Molly?' she heard him whisper urgently against fervent applause. The two actors were taking their final bow.

'I'm here, Mark,' she said, looking up at him.

Right at that moment Anty stretched, took a deep breath, and howled.

CHAPTER FORTY-TWO

Kensington Gore

Mrs Schwartz said her goodbyes at the station on the day after the performance.

'Double-entry bookkeeping,' she said to Molly. 'It calls to me just as the footlights call these two gentlemen.'

'"Go, girl, seek happy nights to happy days",' quoted Symonds.

'I'll remind you I'm no girl,' said Mrs Schwartz, 'and that I'm travelling London Midland Scottish. You'll see me again at the end of the week in any case.'

'"Journeys end in lovers meeting",' said Symonds.

'Incorrigible man! I'm far too busy for any of that.' She turned to Molly. 'The play *was* the thing, wasn't it?' she said. With that, she made a last adjustment to the tilt of her panama in her reflection in the window of the carriage and hopped on board.

*

Two days after Mr Symonds's triumph in the abbey infirmary chapel, he, Mr Boxall, Mark and Joan were assembled in the library of the Hall to drink a solemn toast to the memory of

Anthony Gascarth. Confronted with his dead landlord's books, however, Symonds was uncharacteristically subdued.

'I knew your husband to be a perceptive man, Mrs Gascarth. I valued his opinion on my productions – those plays I directed in particular. I had not realised quite how cultivated a man he was until now, looking at his shelves. He was always anxious about how his books should be cared for; he said as much. I remember his relief when he told me about you – that he had found a treasure. A treasure greater than he realised at first. I know you will love and esteem him always, but I pray you do not immolate yourself alive in his memory in some emotional version of suttee.'

'There is my baby.'

'There is, but I was thinking of you, not only of him.' He patted her hand. 'Boxall and I should make our farewells, but in the hope that you and Mrs Caulfield will come to visit us again soon in the Smoke. Mrs Bonelli depends on it. The best box in our theatre will, of course, be set aside for our visitors, if you can bear to pass an evening in the company of the poor players. Ah – that reminds me. There will soon be a vacancy for a waiter at that fine establishment at which Mrs Schwartz put up. We have lured Herbert Lowther away and he will join us as a stagehand as soon as he has worked his notice. I rather wanted him for my dresser, only the man I have has given no cause for complaint . . .' Symonds's voice lowered confidentially. 'And Mr Boxall was violently averse to the idea. One cannot imagine why. Did you say our coats were upstairs? Needs must and Bradshaw is inflexible.'

'I'll get them.'

'No, no, Boxall and I will retrieve them. I rather think Mr Fagan would like a word.'

He did, though it was simply about tuning the Broadwood. He and Joan were staying on to supper, with the plan that he and Molly might play duets afterwards. But it was just after the two actors had gone upstairs that a thundering knock was heard; Mrs Jepson went to answer.

Symonds and Boxall missing their train was the least consequence of what happened next.

'Get out of it, you!' yelled Mrs Jepson. 'In't you done enough harm?'

Molly paled. 'Must be that reporter back,' she said to Joan. 'You'd think—'

What Molly thought was drowned in Mrs Jepson's enraged shriek and the shouts that followed.

'Molly Ashworth! Come out Molly Ashworth, or whatever you call yourself!'

Norman Ashworth pushed past Mrs Jepson. He fixed pale, watery eyes on Molly where she stood in the doorway of the library, clutching Joan's arm. He swayed, taking an uncertain step forward. It was immediately apparent to Molly that their visitor was much the worse for drink. She heard the swish of Mark's stick behind her, finding his way towards the noise, and wished he would stay back. *How can he defend himself against a drunk?*

'Come and greet your long-lost brother, then! *Half*-brother, I should say. *My* sainted mother never went round murdering folk!' Fumes of alcohol came off him in nauseating gusts. He peered at Joan, then again at Molly.

'You, in't it? That other one is too plain to be any kin of mine.'

Before Molly could answer this, an enraged Mrs Jepson had run up behind Norman Ashworth and whacked him across the shoulders with a warming pan. He spun round.

'You'll be sorry for that, you old hag!'

'Already am!' yelled Mrs Jepson. 'I was going for your head, I was.'

Ashworth gave the cook a great shove, sending her sprawling as the warming pan clattered on the flagstones. He turned back to Molly and Joan. 'Aw right? It's money I want, and I know you're not short of it. Call it blood money if you like, but it's mine. Up in the bedrooms is where folk usually have it. Oh – who's this?'

'Let me pass,' said Mark, behind Molly's shoulder.

'Best you can do?' jeered Ashworth. 'A moudiwarp? Fine job *he'll* do picking me out of an identity parade. Anyway, I'm a busy man, so keep well out of my way all of you if you know what's good for you.' That was when Ashworth produced his knife. Molly and Joan shrank back as the intruder went for the stairs.

'Where's Mr Symonds?' whispered Molly.

*

What happened next took Sergeant Burch some time to disentangle. There was what Mrs Jepson had to say, though her evidence could not be got at straightaway owing to the mild concussion she had suffered from striking her head on the floor. Molly told the policeman how she had pleaded with Mark to stay back, warning him that the intruder had a knife. But he was determined to follow Ashworth.

'I'll strike it out of his hand with my stick,' he'd said, groping his way to the banister rail.

What everyone was in agreement with was the origin and effect of the bloodcurdling laughter that met Ashworth when he reached the first floor.

'What the bloody hell was that?' The drunk man spun round as Mark began his steady ascent, his stick swishing *flick – flack* on the ancient oak treads. The laughter was repeated, followed by what appeared to be a distressed female voice, albeit somewhat alto in pitch.

'You have wounded me, sir!'

The maniacal laughter was louder this time. From below Molly saw Ashworth's eyes bulge like a frightened horse's. He was transfixed by something she couldn't see – something at his feet. His lips quivering in terror, he backed his way further up the staircase.

Molly found her voice. 'Don't go up there, Mr Ashworth! Don't!'

'Fiends, all of you!' shrieked Ashworth, his voice high with fear.

'Turn around, Mr Ashworth!'

'And be stabbed in the back by bloody Lon Chaney?'

Mark was to say afterwards that if he hadn't had hold of the banister rail as it doglegged on the landing then he would surely have slipped in the dark liquid that oozed across the boards.

Years of negotiating his way around in darkness had taught him caution. He slithered, losing his stick, but held tight to the ancient oak under his left hand. He paused, for the first time regretting his obstinacy in trying to take on a man he couldn't see but whose laboured breathing he could hear a couple of feet above where he stood. He knew the stick was somewhere close by, yet it hadn't clattered when it fell from his hand. It had made an odd, viscous, sucking sound. Mark wondered what on earth that liquid was he was standing in.

*

As Mark told Sergeant Burch afterwards, sitting at the great table, the only thing he could think to do was to continue.

'You get a sense for the size of a man, you know, from his voice, even if you can't see him. I'd taken him for a bit of a runt, if I'm honest, though a drunk runt can be another matter altogether. I knew about the knife, right enough, but I reckoned there wasn't much Ashworth could do to me that I hadn't faced in the trenches.'

'He'd been inside for grievous bodily harm,' the policeman said. 'Missed the other fellow's lung by an inch. So you kept going, you said. What were the others doing, so far as you could tell?'

'From her voice I'd say Mrs Gascarth was still at the foot of the stairs, yelling at Ashworth to not go any further. I couldn't hear Mrs Caulfield by then. I think she must have gone to help Mrs Jepson. I heard later he'd knocked the poor lady over.

Or perhaps she'd gone to the baby. He was in his pram in the entrance hall – he somehow managed to sleep through everything, until the doctor turned up. I heard Mr Symonds come out onto the landing. He said something like "Oh dearie me! Do duck your nut, sir," or words to that effect. But Ashworth swore at him, told him to keep back. That laugh Mr Symonds made, that had rattled him – it rattled all of us. And then I heard that awful crack – and the tumble after. Ashworth came to rest by my feet, but there was no sound out of him after that. If he'd rolled any further, he'd have tipped me downstairs.'

'Thank you, Mr Fagan. I'll give you a lift back to Hardwick Street when I've finished here – it was Hardwick Street you said, wasn't it?' said Burch, flicking back through his notebook.

'That's right, sir.'

'I expect it's a coincidence, but I wasn't long in the force when I was called to a disturbance there, involving a man called Fagan. One of our regular customers, you might say. Chap turned out to be a sheikh and got two years for it.'

'A sheikh?'

'Our way of speaking in the station. A bigamist.'

'Fagan is a common enough name,' said Mark, stiffly. 'There's nobody I know of with a story like that in Hardwick Street now.'

'I should think not,' said Burch. 'Word was that he went back on the boat after he was let out. So he's either dead by now or he's the Royal Ulster Constabulary's problem. But as I say, a coincidence.'

*

'I realise this is distressing for you, Mrs Gascarth – for it to happen in your own home, and all,' said the sergeant. 'But tell me again, did anyone at any time lay a finger on Mr Ashworth?'

'Only Mrs Jepson with the warming pan. All that red stuff on his clothes was just the pretend blood they use for the melodramas. I really don't know why Mr Symonds had got it with him. I mean, there wasn't any blood needed for the performance in the abbey.'

'Hmm. The pathologist will establish soon enough that it's not real blood. So you said Ashworth kept going up even though you were telling him to come down?'

'It was a strange thing to do, wasn't it? Put in a staircase that runs up into a ceiling?'

'It's a rum house you've got anyway, Mrs Gascarth, but that's the rummest thing about it. I'll not put it in my notes, but to my mind it's as if the house wanted to defend you.'

'Or revenge my poor husband,' said Molly slowly. 'But I wish it hadn't happened. I know it doesn't make sense, but when I could see what was coming it's as if everything was in slow motion.'

'Go on.'

'I mean, I could see what was going to happen but I couldn't get the words out. Then there was that terrible crack. Just to think of it puts my teeth on edge. Mr Ashworth never cried out, or groaned, or anything like that. He just tumbled. He sounded exactly like when the coalman called to Roose Road, and emptied his sack down the chute. He rolled onto Mr Fagan's feet. If he hadn't still been holding onto the banister, I think he'd have gone crashing down the stairs. Ashworth just lay there, looking like a heap of old clothes, completely still. It was horribly quiet then, after all that shouting and carrying-on. Mr Boxall knelt beside him in the middle of all that redness and put his fingers to the side of his neck. I came up the stairs then, holding onto Joan. I saw a trickle of blood had come from Mr Ashworth's ear, but it had stopped flowing by then. I think that must have been blood – not the theatrical stuff, I mean – for what else could it be, given where it was?'

'Where was Mrs Jepson all this time?'

'Downstairs still. Joan had put her in a chair and given her some water, only Mrs J had asked her for brandy instead, so she'd been to get it. So Joan didn't see all that happened. But I saw Mr Boxall close the poor man's eyes. Then he asked me where a doctor was to be found. He was as white as a sheet – Mr Boxall, I mean – but he insisted on going down to the hotel to get help, and to call the police.'

Sergeant Burch screwed the top back on his fountain pen and, taking a rectangle of blotting paper from the back of his notebook, carefully pressed it on his fresh handwriting.

'There'll be an inquest, Mrs Gascarth. Has to be. But they'll find for misadventure, or I'll eat my stripes. You can't be found guilty of laughing a man to death and you can't blame the house. No, you won't be made to take the staircase out, if that's what you're thinking. The man was warned often enough not to keep going.'

'But if he was trying to get away from Mark? Mr Fagan, I mean.'

'A blind man with only that thin stick of his? Ashworth had a knife, remember, and he was up above Mr Fagan. It looks to me that all Mr Fagan was wanting to do was to protect yourself. Perhaps if them actor chaps had come out of that room and overpowered Ashworth instead of cooking up the "Masque of the Red Death" things mighta gone differently, only neither of 'em look as if overpowering is much in their line. But I do have to warn you, Mrs Gascarth: Ashworth can't bother you anymore but the rags'll have a field day. They've the right to send report-ers to the inquest – can't stop them doing that and wouldn't want to. But if you think you've had trouble with them trying to rake up whatever tattle they could over your poor mother, it'll be nothing on what'll happen now. You might want to think about where you could go with the little fellow. Shut this place up for a month or so.'

Burch paused. From the staircase came murmured voices and the slow and deliberate steps of men descending with a heavy burden.

'What's through that door, Mrs Gascarth?' asked the sergeant.

'The kitchen.'

'Let's go in there a minute then, shall we?'

CHAPTER FORTY-THREE

14 Leigh Street
Bloomsbury, W.C.1

Dear Mrs Gascarth

Cedric and I were most distressed at being forced to leave you and Mr Fagan in the clutches of those burly officers of the law, without even the opportunity to say goodbye. I stood my ground as long as I could. Your correspondent is the very man who faced down the hostility of the pit at the Grand Theatre, Walsall, in July 1910 (though I shudder at the recollection even now, I spoke my lines to the end; I recall that the following act, a troupe of smallish persons known as the Horvath Midgets, met with a far kinder reception). I digress — what I mean is that though we were urged to 'get along now' once we had given our evidence, we refused to budge until we were reassured that you were not to be arrested.

I swear on my life, dear lady, that our intention had been only to frighten Mr Ashworth off the premises. I had not expected Lindal Hall to exert itself in quite that manner. I'm sorry to say that it was not the first time that my propensity to show off has caused unforeseen consequences.

I can only begin to imagine how it must feel to sleep under a roof where such an event has taken place – so soon, too, after the demise of your dear husband, a man I thought of more as my friend than as my landlord. I wonder where you and your dear little boy rest your heads at present? Perhaps good Mr Slaney has found you room at the inn.

My reason for writing, apart from to apologise for the manner of our departure – after, I might add, an idyllic few days which have directly resulted in Mr Boxall completely revising his opinion of the theatrical opportunities presented by the towns of North Lancashire – my reason, I say, is to warn you not to come here for the foreseeable future. I hear the squeak of those rodents from Fleet Street from the windows of this apartment. I durst not show myself at the casement for I have an aversion to being photographed without the veneer of greasepaint – I do not wish to appear in the newspapers as myself, in other words. Mrs Bonelli favours practical resistance to the besiegers; buckets of cold water are the demonstration of her resolve (with, I might add, edifying results).

Mrs Schwartz, who also wishes to be remembered to you, asks me to let you know that she will write if there is anything that merits your attention and thanks you for the trust that you repose in her – so all you need do is inform her of what address you wish her to use. The reptile Sanderson has still not been traced. We rather incline to the view that the vast continent of the Americas has swallowed him up – like the disappearance of Mr Bierce in Mexico, only without his talent. I mull over adapting some of that gentleman's work for the stage . . .

*

Molly read this letter, forwarded by Mrs Jepson, standing by a Belfast sink in Mark's little flat above the greengrocer's. She looked down on a yard where Anty's nappy squares fluttered on a washing line. The yard contained a bicycle with a large straw basket mounted above the smaller front wheel, and a panel advertising the greengrocer's name and the fact he did deliveries (though in practise, these were very few). Flimsy plywood fruit boxes in varying states of dilapidation were heaped against a wall; Molly had been told that she was free to help herself to them for kindling. She tried not to; she knew that the grocer also gave them to needy families.

Mark was out, tuning a piano in a big house in Thorncliffe Road, led there by a scrawny youth hopeful of earning not just his fee from Mark but of getting some boot-blacking at the back door. Molly had caught her breath when Mark had suggested Hardwick Street as a refuge, his face turned not to her but towards Sergeant Burch.

'I think that's a splendid idea,' the policeman had said. 'Last place they'll think to look – or by the time they do tumble to it they'll mebbe be slavering after some other story instead. But only if the lady agrees, of course.'

Mark had turned to her and said, 'I'd put the truckle bed up in the parlour-kitchen. You and Anty would go in the bedroom.' When Molly didn't respond, he added, 'And I can't see you, remember.'

Molly still hesitated, though her heart sang.

'They like me in Hardwick Street,' he went on. 'I'd just be helping out a friend. There's plenty there do that – take in the latest arrivals from Ireland, for instance, give them time to get themselves sorted. If you want to tell them a story, you could always say that you had to leave the place you were in because your husband died. It'd be partly true, in a way.'

'And also not true at all. Anthony wanted me to stay in Lindal Hall.'

The two faced each other without speaking, the contents of Gascarth's last letter in both their minds. Eventually Burch broke the silence.

'We'd be able to get a man round quick, an' all. If there was any trouble. No guarantee of that out here.'

'That'd be very kind of you, Mark,' Molly heard herself say. 'If it's not putting you out – or making life difficult for you in any way. And with Anty nearly walking, it'll be good there are other families around. He'd be like an only child here.'

*

And there she was. The perambulator that stood by the foot of the stairs to the street door was not, though, the one Molly used at Lindal Hall. This one had been passed on by the greengrocer and Molly was grateful for the dents in the metal work and the faded rustiness of the canvas of the once black hood. This meant it was not conspicuous in the eyes of the people of Hardwick Street. Indeed, a number of them had used it themselves. For the same reason, the beautiful clothes Anthony Gascarth had bought for Molly, at a time and place that felt so impossibly distant now that sometimes she wondered if she'd only dreamed them, had stayed behind in the now almost silent Hall, hung in a camphor-scented wardrobe in the bedroom she had shared with him.

Molly could see that Mrs Jepson had opened Symonds's envelope but didn't think she had read the contents. The cook had simply put in a note of her own, as sparse and to the point as the actor's letter was garrulous.

Four reporters com. But only one this week. Fallowfield has a shotgun. His mare cast a shoe. Made marmalade so sorspans is all clean. Have not touched them books. My best to you and little Mester. You are missed. Jepson.

*

Annie McClure had voiced some caution about Molly moving into Hardwick Street, though she could see the need for her to be out of the way of the journalists. Molly could see in the older woman's face that a real anxiety lay behind the words, 'Won't people talk about Mark having a woman living with him?' Molly nearly told her about an elderly woman she'd never seen before, who had come up to her as she pushed Anty in the direction of the baker's. The woman had admired the baby, then looked up at Molly to say, 'I'm right glad Mark Fagan has himself a lass at last. He'd make a right good father for that handsome ba'rn o' yours, too.'

Mr Long the greengrocer and his assistant had come up to move one of the narrow beds out of the only bedroom; it now stood in the main room against the wall opposite the range.

After the two men had drunk a cup of tea and gone downstairs, Mark had said to her, 'If anyone says anything they shouldn't about you being here, Long'll put them right.' Molly muttered something again about being sorry for the upheaval, feeling the heat rising to her face.

'There is none,' Mark told her. 'This place was a safe haven for me and my brother when we were little lads. It's right it should be the same for you.'

But it had wrenched her heart to see how Mark, with questing hands, had to negotiate the presence of the bed in a room where it didn't belong as everything else had had to be shifted to accommodate it. She wished she'd just encouraged him to sleep in the same room, without all the trouble of moving furniture about. After all, as he'd pointed out, he wouldn't be able to see her. Molly wouldn't allow herself to think about what it might have been like to have looked across from her bed to where he slept. But of course there was Anty, still waking hungry in the darkest hours. If Mark's sleep in the adjoining room was also broken at feeding times, he gave no sign of it. He was always up and dressed before her, painstakingly shaved, whether he had a job to go to that day or not.

When he wasn't out piano-tuning, for, as he said, 'There's only so many pianos a place like Barrow will take,' she saw him, on fine days, sitting out in the yard amongst the fruit boxes, capless, intently weaving baskets. He kept his materials in the little shed by the gate into the lane. 'Too messy to do upstairs,' he'd said as she'd admired the speed and sureness of his flickering fingers.

Molly cleaned when he wasn't there, but soon discovered she wasn't expected to. Mark invariably washed whatever crockery he had used the moment he'd finished with it. Once a week one of the older neighbour women would come in. The second of these, Mrs Tregaron, turned out to be the one who had stopped to admire Anty. The woman had glanced at Mark's bed, neatly made as it always was. She'd said nothing, but Molly was sure she saw disappointment flit across the woman's face.

'I'm just here till I'm sorted out.'

'Pity it's not longer,' said Mrs Tregaron, and proceeded to dust the ornaments on the overmantel.

Sometimes, when Molly lay awake at night after Anty had finished his feed, she found she was straining her ears to hear any sound from the next room. But Mark Fagan was silent. Molly wondered at how deep he'd had to bury the horrors he had endured, if they did not even surface in his sleep.

*

Then came the date of the coroner's inquest and the inevitable newspaper reports that followed, for their authors were up in the gallery. Sergeant Burch gave evidence first. Molly kept her eyes down when the policeman told the court of the Manchester murder but listened intently when he revealed Norman Ashworth's sorry, shabby life, looking for clues to an existence that might have been hers, had her mother not done what she had. Ashworth had avoided conscription because he'd been in prison for a burglary in which he had wounded the householder. There'd been other, shorter stretches, from when he had been seventeen years old. The knife he had produced at the Hall was exhibited. Molly shivered at the risk Mark had run to protect her.

The pathologist then spoke in a professionally detached way. Molly noted that he did not even refer to Norman Ashworth by name. He was 'the deceased'. Apart from minor bruising in the area of the shoulder blades, caused by Mrs Jepson with the warming pan, the only other injury was the one that had caused the fatal bleed to the brain: 'Consistent with the deceased hitting his head hard on a ceiling he had not believed to be there.'

The little party that had met to say goodbye to Mr Symonds and Mr Boxall were subdued – even Symonds, who gave his evidence in a measured, succinct way, much as he had spoken his lines in the Infirmary Chapel. Not for the first time Molly wondered which was the real man. He held his audience just as he had then; Molly remembered Anthony's comment about one of the actors in *Love in the Village;* he'd said something about the man having 'stage presence'. She could see that for Symonds, the witness box was a stage he made his own.

Mr Boxall, by contrast, turned out to have a stutter under pressure. Molly watched the faces of the jury as he stumbled out his account of how he'd leaked the Kensington Gore under the door: 'That was m-m-m my idea, s-s-sir.' Yet to her relief she saw the jurors warm to him. The resemblance to Mr Laurel no doubt helped; Molly was quite sure that if Symonds and Boxall did decide to attempt a northern tour, then their appearance that day could do no harm.

Mrs Jepson's tendency to refer to herself in the third person led to a perplexed query from the coroner himself.

'Is this another Jepson you are referring to?'

'I'm the only one I know, I'm sure.'

Joan gave her account in a way Molly thought unassuming, clear, respectful – *and respectable*. Then her heart thumped. *What if they realise I'm living under Mark's roof?* Her palms sweated until it was her turn on the stand, and with relief she confirmed that she was 'Mrs Molly Gascarth of Lindal Hall.'

Molly gave evidence wearing an old-fashioned hat Annie McClure had found for her, heavily veiled, but even so she was relieved that cameras had been banned from the courtroom, and an instruction had been given for 'no sketching' and Sergeant Burch had arranged for her to enter by a staff door.

Though the policeman had reassured her that, in his view, no one would be found to blame for Ashworth's death but himself, it was Mark's evidence and the manner in which he delivered it that clinched the verdict to come. As the court officer helped him to the stand, a low, voiceless murmur swept through the chamber, encompassing, so far as Molly could see through her veil, the jurors' bench as well as the public gallery. Mark was asked which version of the Bible he wished to swear on. 'Douai,' he said, the only witness that day to do so. When questioned as to why he had persisted in following Ashworth up the stairs, even though he'd been told the man had a knife, he said, 'Because I wanted to defend Mrs Gascarth. The man had no right to enter her home like that. And if the knife went into me it was less likely to go into her; I'd have had a chance to hold onto it. I suffered worse in the war.'

'How would you describe your relationship to Mrs Gascarth?' asked the coroner.

For the first time Mark hesitated. To Molly his pause felt like an age, though Joan reassured her afterwards that it could only have lasted through two ticks of the second hand on the clock hanging on the wall opposite Barrow's coat-of-arms.

'I have known Mrs Gascarth since she was a child of three. Her house mother at the Cottage Home in Roose Road is the daughter of my own mother's second husband, by his first marriage.'

Molly could see that this tie of family resonated with the jury. They would know that the second marriages Mark spoke of were not the stuff of gossip, the fodder of the scandal sheets, but a common experience in the streets of Hindpool or any other working-class district of the town, where widows and widowers with children to support and care for would throw their lot in together in practical companionship.

It was another family that Molly thought of as the jury retired to consider their verdict. In giving his evidence, Sergeant Burch had said Ashworth had been married, but his wife had returned to her mother, taking the baby with her. *So I've a nephew – or a niece – I must ask the sergeant which – and Anty has a cousin.* Mark had been brought off the witness stand to sit next to her, in the space that had been Joan's, but Joan was suddenly, mysteriously, somewhere else. He sat close enough for her to feel his warmth. Neither spoke, though a drone of conversation continued up in the public gallery. In an odd way it felt to Molly as though they were at a funeral. It occurred to her then that there must have been one, somewhere. Had Norman Ashworth been buried 'on the parish' here in Barrow, or had he gone from the hospital morgue to join his father in Manchester? *I had a brother, but not the one anyone would have wanted.*

She looked up as the jury trooped back into their places. Mark's hand touched hers briefly, as if to reassure.

The foreman cleared his throat as all present turned in his direction.

'Death by misadventure.'

Molly sighed her relief. She heard the coroner thanking the jury and the court was dismissed.

'All right, Molly?' whispered Mark.

'I think so. I'm grieving, though. For what might have been.'

'I understand that. I was only a little boy when my father left. None of us wanted him back – not Mother, nor me or my brother Joe. I couldn't understand why he couldn't have been like other fathers. But I grieved too, in my little boy way, for the father he might have been if he'd tried.'

'What happened to him?' Molly asked, conscious that this was the most intimate conversation she could remember having with him.

Mark's head came closer, as though he didn't want others to hear.

'He'd married Mother without telling her he'd a wife already and served time for it. Annie McClure's father was my real dad. He loved me and made a home for me.'

'Anty needs—' Molly began, only to be interrupted by a man standing in front of her with a notebook.

'Mrs Gascarth? I wonder if we could have your thoughts on today's verdict?'

Mark got to his feet, both hands clenched on his stick, his face swivelling towards the journalist.

'Leave Mrs Gascarth alone,' he said with quiet menace.

'Quite the hero of the hour you were, Mr Fagan. Our readers warm to a plucky ex-soldier, you know.'

Molly saw the man's eyebrows go up in surprise as a meaty hand landed on his shoulder.

'Court's cleared, sir. Time you went too,' said Sergeant Burch.

'I was just—'

'Hoppit, in other words.'

The man opened his mouth as though to protest, but looking at the policeman thought better of it.

'We'll take you out the back way,' said Burch to Molly and Mark. 'The others are waiting for you.'

They stood up. Mark's hand found Molly's shoulder.

'You could tell your own story, Molly,' he said. 'Instead of leaving it to the reporters to make things up.'

CHAPTER FORTY-FOUR

Hardwick Street

'Thank you,' said Molly, stretching her hand across the tea table to cover Mark's. She held Anty in the crook of her other arm.

'What for?'

'For everything. For today. For defending me.'

'I couldn't not, Molly.'

'I should go back soon, though. To the Hall.'

'Once all the talk dies down. Don't rush it, Molly.'

'I've caused you enough bother. I don't just mean you nearly getting knifed by my— No, I can't call him my brother ... by Norman Ashworth. I mean here too, turning your life topsy-turvy.'

'I've liked your company, Molly. I'll miss you when you go. And Anty.' He turned the hand that was below hers upwards, and wrapped her fingers in his. 'I thought I was used to living alone. Now it'll take a bit of getting used to again.'

'I was wondering – seeing as I won't be here much longer, I mean. I was wondering should we not put your bed back where it was? You've never complained, but I've seen how you've had to work your way around things not being where they were. It wouldn't be indecent. As you said, you cannot see me.'

Mark was silent for a moment, his dark opaque eyes flickering as she'd noticed they did whenever he was thinking carefully. Molly thought his face beautiful, perfect in that moment.

'All right, then. That's if you don't mind seeing me in vest and long johns.' He smiled gently. 'Only, do you think we could manage it ourselves? Without getting Mr Long involved? He'd oblige, I know, except it's only really our business, isn't it?'

'Of course,' she said, though she knew the moment either of those two neighbours turned up to clean that the game would be up. She rather hoped it would be Mrs Tregaron who'd come first, because the woman would be pleased her advice had apparently been taken.

They moved the furniture back to where it used to be that very evening, after Mr Long had shut up his shop and gone home. Molly found giving Mark instructions awkward at first, until he'd said gently, 'Think of yourself as being my eyes. Tell me to move left or right as though I can see but you're the one looking through them. Remember. I know these rooms. I know every squeak on the lino, every creaky board, so I can tell where I am.'

*

Afterwards he said, 'Can you manage Anty's cot back in? You could give him to me to hold.'

Molly managed to manoeuvre the wooden cot quickly without its occupant, who had barely stirred when he was picked up. The baby lay with his forehead resting against Mark's neck. The blind man held him firmly but gently, a hand supporting the little head. Looking at the two of them, she had to admit, not for the first time, the truth of Mrs Tregaron's assertion: 'He'd make a right good father for that handsome ba'rn o' yours, too.' She felt a surge of bitter regret too. Anthony Gascarth had never been able to hold his son.

When the cot was in place between the two beds, Molly eased Anty away from Mark and laid him down on his back. Anty sighed once, raised his fists either side of his face, and slept on. Then Molly watched Mark's hands trace the dimensions of the cot, measuring the spaces between it and the two beds either side.

'That's all good. All's as it should be,' he said.

Molly's stomach gave a queer fillip. *He's right.*

*

Each left the room in turn to prepare for bed, for Molly couldn't bring herself to undress in front of Mark. She felt it would be an insult to his keen sense of hearing.

'I'll turn out the gas, will I?' she said, when all was ready.

Mark turned in his bed and smiled. 'It's all the same to me, Molly.'

'Oh. Yes of course, I'd forgotten.'

'I like that you have. It makes me like other men.'

'You aren't like other men,' she said in a rush. 'You're a far better one.'

'I doubt it,' he said as she turned down the light.

After she'd settled into bed, he asked into the gloom, 'Do you mind me saying my prayers?'

'Of course not.' Molly lay there a little shamefaced. She'd not retained the Cottage Home ritual of prayers long into her time at Miss Cavendish's, abandoning it in reaction to Miss Tweed's ostentatious piety. That part of her life had afterwards been forgotten about entirely in the delirious joy of her time in Anthony Gascarth's arms. Yet all this time belief had been a quiet part of Mark Fagan's life though she had never known it of him. Now she listened as he quietly spoke the words of the Hail Mary, asking to be prayed for 'now and at the hour of our death'. A small litany of people followed, both dead and living: his mother, her husband Thomas Maguire, some names she didn't recognise but guessed were men he had served with. Then she heard him say 'Anthony Gascarth' but so naturally that Molly knew that this inclusion was not for her benefit, but was established habit. Amongst the living her own name and Anty's were quietly spoken, along with Mother Annie, Robert and Mark's brother Joe. Her eyes filled.

*

Mark woke at the first fretful murmur from Anty in his cot, but he kept his eyes closed so Molly would think he slept on. He heard her rustling, the soft thud of her bare feet landing in the rag rug, the rock of the cot as Anty was lifted out and the creak of the bed as mother and child lay down for the night feed. He fell asleep again to the tiny intimate snuffles of the child at the breast, but woke again, he didn't know how much later, aware that Molly was very close by. Feeling her fingers skim his hair, he concentrated on breathing regularly, so that she wouldn't realise he was awake. There was a rustle of cotton, and the scent of Ivory Flakes with which she washed her clothes was very close indeed. A touch of lips on his brow as soft as the brushing of a moth followed. It was all he could do not to respond, but he did nothing, wanting to know if she would think better of the little visit, or if she would come again the next night.

She did.

Afterwards Mark lay a long time awake, reliving all the moments he had spent with her once he realised that he loved her, and all the times when he had deliberately avoided her. There was the day she left the Cottage Home, when he had come so close to saying something only to be interrupted by the kindness of a cup of tea. Afterwards he'd told himself not to be a fool, that he had spared this beautiful, vibrant girl – for Mark had never doubted that Molly was beautiful – from being saddled with a maimed husband. He remembered his first meeting with Gascarth, and his sense in the way that intelligent, eccentric man spoke of Molly, that she, all without intention, had captured his heart. He'd liked Gascarth, and felt that his own sacrifice was not in vain if it delivered Molly to a man like him. He thought of dear, kind Joan whom he'd turned to, believing he'd succeeded in convincing Molly he was not the man she should love, only for Joan to have had the clear-eyed good judgement to jilt him. He thought of Annie McClure's gentle pleadings to 'have sense', for all she could see were two people who evidently did love each other but who were weighed down by baggage they created for themselves. Then Gascarth had died, leaving behind that extraordinary letter, in which the Master of Lindal Hall had tried to engineer things in his favour, but which he had obstinately rejected. Joan – for it must have been Joan, the only person besides Molly to have met Harold Symonds in London – had then given the actor the chance of the performance of a lifetime, in that unforgettable evening in the abbey ruins, in which the words of the long-dead Shakespeare seemed to have been written for him and Molly alone.

And finally, the malevolent Norman Ashworth had broken in on the quiet life Molly had hoped to follow in Lindal Hall. *I would have died for her that night and been glad to. But I didn't, just as I didn't that terrible day when all my pals lost their lives but I lost only my eyes. Mark Fagan, ask yourself why you were spared?*

He was tired, fretful and impatient all the following day. There were no pianos to be tuned, but the weather was dry, so he passed it in the yard weaving baskets and waiting for nightfall.

When Molly's lips touched his forehead again that night he opened his arms to her and, in the darkness that made them equal, his mouth searched for hers at last.

Holding her so close he could feel her heart beating against his, he whispered, 'Not more than this, Molly. I love you and I want to do things the right way.' He stroked her nose, running his finger down to her upcurved mouth. 'Besides, Anty might wake up. Will you marry me, Molly Gascarth?'

'I always wanted you to ask me, Mark. Yes.'

CHAPTER FORTY-FIVE

Manchester

'I couldn't have made this journey on my own, Mark,' Molly said as the train pulled into Manchester London Road.

'And shouldn't either. You might find something or nothing, or folk that aren't kind. No woman should face what you're facing on her own.'

Walking to the tram stop, Molly registered the idle stares they attracted, the blind man with his hand on her shoulder and his stick casting from side to side. She knew that Mark sensed them too. 'Folk go still and silent,' he'd told her once. 'Then I can feel their eyes on me.'

The tram itself had caused some anxious moments, with Molly craning her neck to read street signs as they flashed past, trying to match them with her map. Eventually she plucked up enough courage to ask an elderly lady if she knew the Ancoats stop. The woman beamed with pleasure, as though she'd been waiting for the question. 'Sure, isn't that where I'm going myself?' Her voice reassured Molly, her accent so close to Annie McClure's.

'What's the address you'd be looking for?'

'Rokeby Street,' said Molly, on tenterhooks for the woman's reaction.

'Two along from mine,' said the woman, and Molly's tension eased.

*

Number 17 Rokeby Street looked much the same as all its companions, much like the ribbons of houses facing each other near the shipyard in Barrow. Molly looked up and down the terraced row. The road was full of small children, from twelve-year-olds down to babies perched in perambulators, and she thought of Anty, doubtless being made a great fuss of at that moment, back in Roose Road. She thought of the difference in their start in life, Anthony Gascarth's son and these jostling children, and vowed that Anty would never be sent away to school. The small inhabitants of Rokeby Street brought up each other. Only at teatime, with the promise of bread and jam, would this junior parliament break up and the children be reabsorbed into the little parlours that opened directly onto the street.

'Do you remember anything?' asked Mark softly.

She shook her head. 'Maybe if we can go indoors there'll be something. Or even next door. I mean, the houses will be built all the same inside, won't they?'

'Are you sure about this?'

'I've the gentleman's letter here, haven't I? He was kind to write back so quickly. I was afraid he wouldn't know me from Adam, but he remembered everything. Said he'd never forget the trial, nor the evidence he had to give. I'm just lucky – if you can call it that – he's still living here. I can't back out now.'

Molly stopped in front of no. 17, willing memories into existence, but none came. The house looked like all the others, with its whitened step, the spruce net curtains. But she didn't knock. She didn't even know if the inhabitants knew a murder had been committed in their home, and had no intention of telling them. Instead she moved a few paces along, to no. 21. The knocker was in the form of a Kilkenny cat, its back arched. Molly pushed to the back of her mind the thought that whoever lived there might fight like the cats in that fable, until only their tails were left, and put her hand on the brass.

The door was opened so quickly that Molly realised Mr Matheson must have been standing right behind it.

'Oh Molly – little Molly! Come away in. And your friend . . .?'

'This is Mr Fagan.'

'Of course. You said in your letter. Only I hadn't realised . . . come in, Mr Fagan.'

The little front parlour was suddenly full. Molly and Mark subsided onto a velour settee, liberally provided with antimacassars. It was a fussy, feminine room. A woman appeared in the doorway, younger than Matheson, a little hesitant.

'This is Etta.' Matheson made the introductions and Molly gazed at the woman's kind, slightly faded prettiness, trying to remember her too.

'You won't have met Etta before,' said Matheson as though apologising. 'My wife died three years after . . . after what happened. Etta took me on a couple of years after that.'

'I'll make tea, will I?' said Etta.

'Thank you, I'd love that,' said Molly.

'And you, sir?'

'Thank you, yes.' The woman disappeared out the back, leaving the doors open, so Molly could catch snatches of contented humming as tea things were loaded onto a tray. She couldn't help but feel some relief that this was not the woman the newspaper reports had accused her mother of having wronged.

In the grate some coals simmered. 'There's a bit of a nip in the day,' said Matheson, and bent to the little coal scuttle to shovel on more fuel. Something clicked silently into place for Molly as he did so.

'"Cutty Sark",' she said, leaning forward.

Matheson glanced at the little shovel in his hand, and then at the fire irons stand where the brush and poker hung. Each one of them had as its handle the motif of the sailing ship.

'Yes. It was me told you that's what it was called,' he said quietly.

'They're brighter than I remember.'

'That's Etta for you. Always polishing. My queen of gleam. She's made this place nice, an't she?' he added, and Molly knew who had made the antimacassars, the runner on the sideboard embroidered with crinolined ladies, who had chosen the ornaments.

Etta herself came in with the tea tray, placing it on the table. 'I'll leave you to talk. You'll have a lot to catch up on.' Before Molly could say anything, the woman had flitted into the rear of the house, closing doors as she went. A moment later a dull thud indicated she had gone out the back.

'She's discreet, that way, is Etta,' said Matheson. 'Well, do you remember me, love?'

Molly hesitated. 'I remembered nothing before today, until the fire irons. I thought the house might remind me, the door knocker, even.'

'You were only a little dot, and anyway, you always came in the back way. We left a box outside the door so's you could get up on it and tap on the window to be let in. Maybe if we go out there later something'll come back.' He took a deep breath and smiled. 'You're looking very well, Molly. So where've you been all these years?'

'In a cottage home of the Barrow Guardians. My friend here, he's the brother of my House Mother. I call her my House Mother but she's been a mother to me in all ways. I'm a widow with a little boy. I do a bit of work for the Town Hall.'

'You've been through a lot for someone so young. I'm sorry for your loss. Does your little lad look like his father?'

'He does,' said Molly, smiling for the first time that day.

'He'll be a comfort to you, even if he doesn't know how much yet. And you, sir, how do you live?'

Mark caught the undertone of pity in Matheson's words. 'I'm a piano tuner,' he said. 'Before this –' he waved a hand across his eyes, 'it was the shipyard. The pianos are a lot cleaner.'

'Miss Molly here – Mrs Gascarth I should say – is a beautiful lass.'

'I know it, sir. Even if I can't see her, I know it.'

'We're to be married, Mr Matheson,' said Molly.

'God be praised! We should be drinking something stronger than this tea, then, only maybe not with what you've come to ask me about.'

There was a short silence, then Molly asked quietly, 'Am I like *her,* though?'

Matheson breathed in sharply, then beat his hands on his knees. 'Are you like her? Well, if I hadn't known you were coming, and I'd opened the door and seen you, I'd 'a' thought it was her back from the grave.'

Molly flinched. Her mother had a grave, yes, but no one could lay flowers on it. She was buried in quicklime inside the impenetrable walls of Strangeways Gaol.

'Only you're more confident, like. The way you carry yourself, the way you speak. Your voice is the same but not the way you use it. That'll be the Barrow way of speaking.' He paused and looked straight at her. 'I know what they said in the papers, what them lawyers cooked up, but I want you to know the truth of it. There was never anything untoward between me and your mother, never. I helped her whatever way I could. I went with her to the coppers at Goulden Street more than once when he'd battered her, but they said it was a domestic matter and nothing to do with them. There was an ambulance station alongside, though, and so she'd get a bit of patching up from them so it weren't a wasted journey.

'Them walls are thin, so I'm glad you weren't living next door but two along. Old Pewty was through there – he's been dead ten year or more – but he was that deaf it couldn't have bothered him. It happened when your father was in drink, mainly. She put up with it, poor martyred soul, until he started on you. His first wife drank too, they say. Fell down the stairs and broke her neck, though there've been times I've wondered about that.'

There was absolute silence in the room. Molly could hear the shouts of the children playing outside, the distant clang of a tram, but it was as if they were muffled, as though they were a memory of sounds more than the sounds themselves.

'I don't know what you'd done to upset him. What could a tiny tot do? You'd come round often enough asking me to "stop Daddy hitting Ma" and sometimes I went, just on the excuse to borrow sugar or something, to see if I could interrupt him. My wife told me not to interfere, of course. Between that and what they made out at the trial, things were never quite the same between us afterwards, but I shan't speak ill of the dead. Only, this time when you came you were crying and screaming, and your arm was all funny at the elbow.' He shivered. 'I remember it still. Your mother was out when it happened – he'd sent her to buy beer for him. So it was me carried you round to the ambulancemen and they took you to Mill Street. Your mother came to see you there, and between your plastered arm and the marks on your back—'

Molly closed her eyes momentarily.

'Mrs Gascarth?'

'P-please don't stop, Mr Matheson.'

'You were writhing about when I carried you to the ambulance men. I had no idea – I thought it were the pain of the break – I mean, that would be enough. But no, he'd burned you with a cigarette. Well, your mother saw all that. I walked her back here but she wouldn't speak and after a bit I stopped trying to get her to say anything, for I could see she was thinking. I offered to go in with her, and she said no, adamant she was – I can see her face still – that she'd have to put a stop to it once and for all. I thought she meant to flit, though I don't know where she'd 'a' gone. I think somehow she thought with you in that hospital, it all being clean with those nice starchy nurses, that they'd keep you in a place like that. Somewhere safe. He was drunk on the floor with his feet on the fender, if the reports are true. She took the kitchen knife to him.'

Mark reached for Molly's hand, held it.

'She did it for me,' said Molly.

'She was a good mother. She loved you. She'd 'a' done anything for you. Oh, child, your tears will open paradise for her.'

Molly wept openly, leaning into Mark's shoulder, with a child's desperation that nothing will ever come right. Later, she thought, *I haven't cried that way since Anthony died.*

'I never thought she'd hang,' said Matheson. 'Only they made out it was premeditated. She'd had that walk home to think about it so they said it wasn't as if she'd been defending herself; she'd gone in and killed him when he was unconscious. I'd always been brought up to be truthful, so I told them everything I knew, everything I remembered, but of course the thing they made the most of was when she said that bit about having to put a stop to it once and for all.' He wiped his eyes. 'Your mother was a good woman. You were the world to her, everything.'

*

In the little parlour at Lindal Hall, Mark stood up and began packing away his tuning hammers. Molly watched him, marvelling at the accuracy and speed of his fingers as he threaded each instrument through the loops inside the pouch. The collection looked to her like a cross between a surgeon's tools and a very large manicure set.

'There,' said Mark, stroking the fall of the little Broadwood. 'She should play better now.' He turned round. Anty was standing up, somewhat unsteadily, in the wooden playpen Robert had made for him. He banged a toy car against the bars.

'Mar, Mar,' said Anty.

Mark smiled. 'I don't know if that's "Ma" or "Mark".'

'It's Mark. He's looking at you.'

'How is he on his legs?'

'Getting there. I'm glad of the playpen.'

'We'll need something across the staircase, won't we?'

'We will.' Molly paused, realising that she was thinking about the dark oak stairs of Lindal Hall differently now. The terrifying image of the doomed Norman Ashworth, backing upwards and waving his knife, was fading. Instead she saw her son in the months ahead, showing her he could climb, one chubby leg following the other onto the same step before he summoned all his child's strength for the next one. He'd turn back to make sure she was watching him: 'Look, Mummy!'

'Shall we play for him?' said Mark. 'A duet, I mean. Something cheerful.'

'A waltz.'

'I'll budge up,' he said, settling onto the piano stool. 'As long as you place my hands at home.'

Molly sat next to him, their thighs touching, and gently took Mark's right hand, her fingers over his. Once she had placed it, he laid his left himself.

'Ready? I'll count us in.' He said the numbers under his breath and the waltz burst into life. Mark couldn't see the dark panelling of the Hall, the wavering candles of the winter afternoon. He was in a glittering ballroom, an orchestra striking up at the far end. He offered his arm to the most beautiful girl in the room – his Molly in a tulle gown – and led her into the fray. His arm went around her waist, she looked up at him, smiling—

But something interrupted the vision in his mind's eye. A gurgling sound, a joyful sound that grew and rippled around the room. Their hands flickered, the waltz surged and died. Molly turned round. 'Hark at him!' she said. 'Laughing like a drain!'

The child's merriment infected them both. Mark heard the rattling of the slats of the playpen as the little boy clutched and swayed. He could hear laughter in Molly's voice as she said, 'He loved that. We must do it again, Mark.'

'I'd like that,' he said. 'I'd like that always. Tell me the date you want, Molly.' He put his arm around her waist and dipped his head to meet the lips that waited for his.

HISTORICAL BACKGROUND

Anyone who has visited Townend, the eccentric National Trust property at Troutbeck, near Ambleside, will have recognised immediately the original of Lindal Hall, with its profusion of carvings, its library (including some titles which exist nowhere else in the world) and the oddest thing of all, a staircase that runs into a dead end – the ceiling. That staircase was brought to Townend from another house and the owner wanted to preserve it in its entirety. A number of the books in the Townend library are somewhat scurrilous in nature; I hope readers are not disappointed that I didn't weave them into my story (though I did consider it). I didn't do so because there was already a social imbalance between Anthony Gascarth and his new servant, along with an age difference. If he'd shown her rude books that would just have made him creepy as well.

I moved Townend to near Furness Abbey, the vast Cistercian house (second in importance only to Fountains Abbey) on the outskirts of Barrow-in-Furness. At one time, the abbey was served by its own railway station (the line is still in use) and adjacent to the station was the Furness Abbey Hotel, where Herbert Lowther works in the book. Mrs Schwartz was lucky to find a free bath after her journey north with Mr Symonds and Mr Boxall – though the hotel had thirty-six bedrooms it only had three bathrooms. Both the station and the hotel were damaged during the bombing of Barrow in 1941 and the hotel was demolished in 1953. All that remains of the complex is the Abbey Tavern (closed at time of writing) which occupies what used to be the station booking office and refreshment room. This excellent video by Gary Cunliffe reconstructs the story of the hotel and railway station: https://vimeo.com/141898896

Molly grew up in one of the Cottage Homes in Roose Road in Barrow, under the care of house parents Robert and Annie McClure (their courtship is told in my earlier book, *Annie of Ainsworth's Mill*). The cottage home model of caring for destitute children originated on the continent. The principle was to bring children up in a village-like atmosphere, with smaller groups of them living in houses, each under the supervision of a House Mother, as an alternative to the grimmer institutional setting of the workhouse. The Barrow Board of Guardians built their cottage homes on Roose Road in around 1905, being two pairs of semi-detached houses and an administrative building, accommodating seventy or so children of three and over. As soon as they were old enough, the Cottage Home children were expected to work as servants to maintain the homes they lived in. In *The Maid of Lindal Hall* Annie McClure refers to her bosses as 'the Guardians' out of habit, although from 1930, with impending reform of the poor relief system, their role was taken over by the Borough Council.

Incidentally, to avoid the stigma of a workhouse birth, from 1904 children born in Barrow Workhouse had the neutral address '1 Rampside Road' on their birth certificates.

Barrow Cottage Homes functioned in some form as a children's home at least up until 1948 (the year the Children's Act was passed), as my aunt was friends with a little girl who lived there. The buildings survive and are now all private housing.

I'm indebted to Peter Higginbotham's *Childrens' Homes: A History of Institutional Care for Britain's Young* (Pen and Sword, 2017) and to his related websites http://www.childrenshomes. org.uk/BarrowInFurnessBC/ and https://www.workhouses.org. uk/BarrowInFurness/

My father grew up in Barrow-in-Furness a bit later than the time my book is set, as he was born in 1933. He remembers, though, that the town had seven cinemas, with programmes that changed weekly, meaning that he could see a different film every day. Barrow was once well provided with live theatre too, in the Royalty Theatre and Opera House, His Majesty's, The Palace and The Coliseum (most of these changed their names at different times in their history and doubled up as cinemas). Opposite His Majesty's, in Albert Road, lived Fred and Mary Tickell. Fred was a crane driver at Vickers and Mary worked at Thompson's Bottling Works, but their home was also a lodging house for theatricals and their younger daughter Vera was called Bill by her father, who'd wanted a boy. A then well-known actor who regularly performed in Barrow was the aptly (and genuinely) named Norman Carter Slaughter, known as Tod Slaughter, whose speciality was 'blood-tub' melodramas like *Sweeney Todd* and *Murder in the Red Barn*. Travelling theatricals worked to a punishing schedule, performing one play whilst rehearsing for the one they would perform the following week and reading for the one beyond that. A good introduction to British touring theatre of the period, including the importance of theatrical landladies, can be found in the early chapters of Ben Iden Payne's memoir, *A Life in a Wooden O* (1977). The naming of Harold Symonds's little dog is a tribute to one of the great Edwardian actor-managers, Frank Benson.

Mark Fagan is active in the National League of the Blind, possibly the oldest disabled persons organisation in the world, founded in 1893 and registered as a trade union in 1899. The League campaigned for rights rather than charity. League members organised marches to London in 1920 and 1936, an approach that inspired the better-known Jarrow March and which contributed to the passing of legislation (the Blind Persons Acts, 1920 and 1938). The union changed its name to the National League of the Blind and Disabled in 1968 and survives now as part of the Community Trade Union.

LESMA, founded in the aftermath of World War One, is the forerunner of BLESMA, the British Limbless Ex-Servicemen Association. Like the League of the Blind, the Association was founded by the men it represented. St Dunstan's (now Blind Veterans UK) was established in 1915. At the time of this novel, they were based in St Dunstan's Lodge, Regent's Park.

John Ellis (1874–1932) was a British executioner, active in the role from 1901 to 1924. He was particularly shaken by the hanging of Edith Thompson in 1923 and though he conducted further executions, this appears to have contributed to his resignation the following year. Ellis attempted suicide after his resignation and was arrested (suicide was then a criminal offence); he succeeded at another attempt in 1932. Neither the Home Office nor the Prison Commissioners were represented at his funeral. Ellis's account of Mary Ashworth's execution is based on accounts in his autobiography, but his character is a combination of Ellis's and that of an earlier hangman, James Berry (1852–1913), who also wrote a memoir. Berry too contemplated suicide but was saved by religious conversion and subsequently campaigned for the abolition of the death penalty.

ACKNOWLEDGEMENTS

I'd like to thank my wonderful agent Annette Green for her continued, unwavering support, followed by my stellar editors, Claire Johnson-Creek and Katie Meegan and the rest of the team at Bonnier Zaffre: Kati Nicholl for copy-editing and Linda Joyce for proofreading and Jenny Richards for her beautiful cover design.

Particular thanks are due to fellow author – and expert guide to Furness Abbey – Gill Jepson. Barrow-in-Furness has changed significantly since I visited it as a child, not least in terms of declining employment in the shipyard, so her books *Barrow-in-Furness Through Time*, *Barrow-in-Furness at Work* and *Barrow-in-Furness in 50 Buildings* (all published by Amberley) were invaluable resources in recalling the Barrow that has vanished. Gill always responded promptly to my very diverse queries about Barrow history; any inaccuracies that may remain in the text will have nothing to do with her. Calling the cook at Lindal Hall Mrs Jepson is a small tribute but she is not a portrait of Gill – I don't even know if Gill likes cooking.

Thank you to my aunt, Meg Rowlandson, now of Ulverston, for her recollections of the Tickells (and for much else, going back a long way).

I made Miss Cavendish's cook a member of the McGovern family of Belcoo, a border village in County Fermanagh, in acknowledgement of the memoirist Ronan McGovern, once known as 'Little Retser', and our dear fellow writers on the Northern Soul Roadshow writing course (Irish Writers Centre), superbly facilitated by Fiona O'Rourke. They didn't know this at the time, but the gentle discipline imposed by the eXpress Writing Community, also run by Fiona O'Rourke, and the Writers' Hour run by the London Writers' Salon gave me the final crucial push to complete this book; I'll be back for more.

Dear Readers,

Thank you for reading *The Maid of Lindal Hall*. Readers of my last book, *Annie of Ainsworth's Mill*, will recognise the married couple who are now House Parents in the Cottage Home in Barrow-in-Furness where frightened little Molly Dubber is sent. Because Robert in particular had a difficult childhood, I wanted to give him and Annie a mission in life to try to make other children's lives happier.

As with all of my Memory Lane books, inspiration has come in some way from my family history. So-called 'ordinary' people have experiences that really are anything but ordinary. I have known Barrow-in-Furness since I was a child, for my grandfather spent most of his life after his apprenticeship in the Belfast shipyard Workman and Clark working for Vickers-Armstrongs across the Irish Sea, though with some to-ing and fro-ing in the 'hungry '30s' between England and the Belfast yards, depending on where there was work. A particular treat when going to see my grandparents in Barrow was the soft drink Marsh's Sass, sadly no longer made in the town.

My father also told me lots of stories about growing up in Barrow at a time when children, rightly or wrongly, seemed to have a lot more freedom than they do now. The town once had seven cinemas, with a programme that changed weekly, and entrance was cheap, so in theory you could go to the pictures every night. Dad saw probably all the Johnny Weissmüller Tarzan films in Barrow. The town also had a number of theatres, served by 'rep' companies, with melodramas, or 'blood-tubs' as Harold Symonds in the book calls them, being very popular. Mr Symonds and Cedric Boxall lodge with the Tickells, a real family who ran a boarding-house for actors.

Jokes made about Barrow being at the end of the longest cul-de-sac in England, the A590, are unfair; anyone who doesn't make that journey misses out on the friendly people you find there and no shortage of things to do. Like many other places, Barrow's industrial heyday in shipbuilding, steelworking and jute is over but is remembered in the Dock Museum. Much older than any of those industries, are the ruins of Furness Abbey, in a leafy setting on the edge of the town. This impressive Cistercian house was second only to Fountains Abbey in Yorkshire and I think we must have visited it every time we came to Barrow. And then there's the boat across to Piel Island, to see a castle built by a fourteenth-century abbot, and to drink in the Ship Inn where every new landlord is ceremoniously 'crowned' king – by having alcohol poured over his head.

Townend, the house at Troutbeck which I used as the model for Lindal Hall, was an accidental discovery made some years ago when we were travelling around youth-hostelling with our two young sons. We hadn't planned to

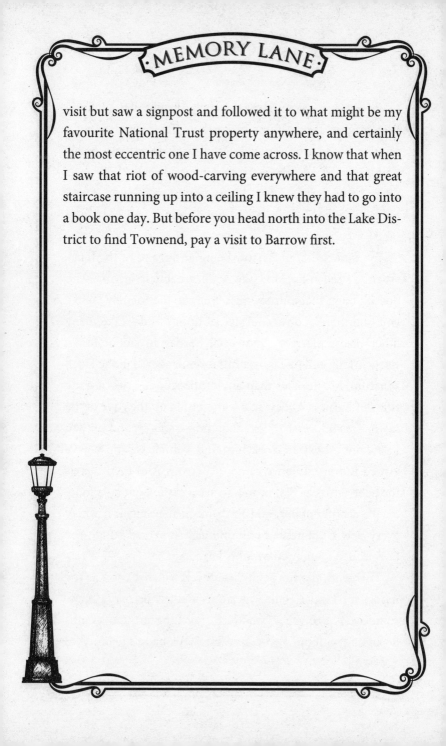

visit but saw a signpost and followed it to what might be my favourite National Trust property anywhere, and certainly the most eccentric one I have come across. I know that when I saw that riot of wood-carving everywhere and that great staircase running up into a ceiling I knew they had to go into a book one day. But before you head north into the Lake District to find Townend, pay a visit to Barrow first.

Butter Pie

Here is how to make Mrs Jepson's Butter Pie, that so delighted Mr Symonds. This is a recipe of the late chef Philippa James and is reproduced here by kind permission of the editor of *Lancashire Life*.

*

Butter Pie is also known as Catholic pie or Friday pie, and is an age-old dish, from around the Chorley and Preston area or, for the non-Lancastrians, a potato pie.

Serves four.

Ingredients:

For the pastry
225g/8oz Plain flour
50g/2oz Butter, salted or unsalted; you can adjust seasoning to taste at the table
50g2oz Lard, vegetable fat, or dripping
A pinch of salt, if used, and white pepper
Ice-cold water

For the filling
3 Large potatoes – a King Edward/Maris Piper type
1 Large onion
50g/2oz Butter, plus 100g/4oz for softening the onions

Method

1. Sift the flour and salt into a bowl and stir in the butter and lard (I tried with all butter and found this micro-waved really well, about 30 seconds to a minute, depending on the wattage, for each quarter of a pie). Using your fingertips, or a fork, incorporate the butter until it resembles fine crumbs, then drizzle in just enough cold water to make the pastry form a ball, pop into a plastic bag, press out the air, and leave in the fridge to rest for 30 minutes.

2. Meanwhile, peel the three large potatoes and the onion, cut the potato into thick slices, a little thicker than a pound coin, and the onion in to half rings. Parboil the potatoes until they are just soft but still holding their shape, about 8–10 minutes. Sauté the onions in the butter, over a low heat, until soft, but not browned, as this will spoil the end flavour.

3. Roll out about two-thirds of the pastry, to line a pie dish, and trim the edges.

4. Drain the potatoes, let the steam leave the pan, then, in the lined pie dish, layer the potatoes, onions and butter flakes, season with salt and white pepper and top off with the rolled remains of the pastry; 'stab' the top to make air vents.

5. Bake at 180°C/160°fan/gas 4 for about 30 minutes until golden. Serve immediately, with pickled red cabbage.

· MEMORY LANE ·

If you enjoyed *The Maid of Lindal Hall*,
you'll love these other books
by Katie Hutton . . .

·MEMORY LANE·

1897

Young Annie Maguire is leaving the only home she has ever known, the family farm in County Down, Ireland. Driven away by poverty and the death of Annie's mother, she and her beloved father are looking for a place to start again and settle in Cleator Moor, Cumberland.

Robert McClure also grew up in County Down. The illegitimate son of a land agent and the cook from the big house, he spent his childhood being moved from pillar to post, never sure who he was or where he belonged. That is until he found himself in Cleator Moor and invited to join the Orange Order, a Protestant Society.

On the 12th of July, day of the Orange March, Annie and Robert meet. Sparks instantly fly, but Annie has been brought up Catholic and is devoted to her community and religion. Brought together by chance, but with backgrounds worlds apart, Annie and Robert will have to fight to be together. But can their love really survive when the weight of the community is against them?

The Gypsy Bride

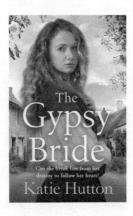

Oxfordshire, 1917

The granddaughter of a Methodist preacher, Ellen has her life mapped out for her. Engaged to the respectable Charlie, she is heartbroken when her fiance is killed in the trenches.

But then she meets Sam Loveridge. Mysterious and unruly, Sam is from a local Gypsy community, and unlike anyone Ellen has ever met before. She is swept off her feet and shown a world of passion, excitement – and true love.

But the conservative world that Ellen is from can't possibly approve of their relationship, and Ellen and Sam are torn apart.

Is their love strong enough to overcome their cultural differences, or will the hostility and prejudice they face destroy their chance of happiness?

The Gypsy's Daughter

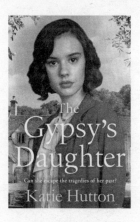

Kent, 1950s

Harmony 'Harry' Loveridge is growing up on a farm in post-war Kent. With a Gypsy for a father, she has had a somewhat unconventional, yet happy life.

But Harry has always hoped for more. And with ambitions to go to university, and a scholarship in sight, it looks as though she is about to get what she wants. That is until one fateful night, during the yearly hopping, when something happens to Harry.

Refusing to give up on her dreams Harry must draw on all her strength and courage as she embarks on her new life in Nottingham.

Will she be able to escape the tragedies of her past, or is history doomed to repeat itself?

Annie of Ainsworth's Mill

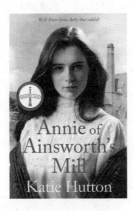

1897

Young Annie Maguire is leaving the only home she has ever known, the family farm in County Down, Ireland. Driven away by poverty and the death of Annie's mother, she and her beloved father are looking for a place to start again and settle in Cleator Moor, Cumberland.

Robert McClure also grew up in County Down. The illegitimate son of a land agent and the cook from the big house, he spent his childhood being moved from pillar to post, never sure who he was or where he belonged. That is until he found himself in Cleator Moor and invited to join the Orange Order, a Protestant Society.

On the 12th of July, day of the Orange March, Annie and Robert meet. Sparks instantly fly, but Annie has been brought up Catholic and is devoted to her community and religion.

Brought together by chance, but with backgrounds worlds apart, Annie and Robert will have to fight to be together.

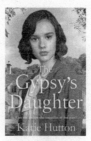

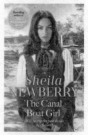

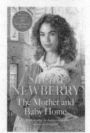

· MEMORY LANE ·

Introducing the place for story lovers – a welcoming home for all readers who love heartwarming tales of wartime, family and romance. Sign up to our mailing list for book recommendations, giveaways, deals and behind-the-scenes writing moments from your favourite authors. Join the Memory Lane Book Group on Facebook to chat about the books you love with other saga readers.

· MEMORY LANE ·

www.MemoryLane.Club

www.facebook.com/groups/memorylanebookgroup